AUG - - 2011
Fic LEE
Lucifer's lottery /
Lee, Edward, 1957-
33341005249262
H

"The living legend of literary mayhem. Read him if you dare!"

—Richard Laymon, Author of *Funland*

"Edward Lee's writing is fast and mean as a chain saw revved to full-tilt boogie."

—Jack Ketchum, Author of *Joyride*

"He demonstrates a perverse genius for showing us a Hell the likes of which few readers have ever seen."

—Horror Reader

"Edward Lee continues to push the boundaries of sex, violence and depravity in modern genre lit."

—*Rue Morgue*

"One of the genre's true originals."

—*The Horror Fiction Review*

"The hardest of the hardcore horror writers."

—*Cemetery Dance*

"Lee excels with his creativity and almost trademark depictions of violence and gruesomeness."

—Horror World

"A master of hardcore horror. His ability to make readers cringe is legendary."

—*Hellnotes*

TO SEE THE DEPTHS OF HELL

"You'll have exactly six minutes to listen to the Trustee, ask any questions you have, and then accept or reject the offer. And even if you accept, which I pray you'll do, you're under no obligation. Nothing becomes binding unless you say yes upon completion of the tour."

The tour . . . Those words bothered him more, perhaps, than anything else tonight. There was something potent about them. Even when he *thought* the words, they seemed to echo as if they were called down from a mountain precipice.

But then more thoughts dripped. "This is a pact with the Devil, you mean."

"Not a pact. A gift. One thing to keep in mind. The Devil doesn't *need* to offer contracts for souls very often these days. Think about that . . ."

Hudson's eyes narrowed. "But I'm about to go to the *seminary*. To be a *priest*!"

Her voice drifted in delight. "Perhaps what you see will dissuade you. Your reward will be beyond imagination. . . ."

Other *Leisure* books by Edward Lee:

THE BLACK TRAIN
THE GOLEM
BRIDES OF THE IMPALER
TRIAGE (Anthology)
HOUSE INFERNAL
SLITHER
THE BACKWOODS
FLESH GOTHIC
MESSENGER
INFERNAL ANGEL
MONSTROSITY
CITY INFERNAL

EDWARD LEE

LUCIFER'S LOTTERY

WITHDRAWN

ALAMEDA FREE LIBRARY
1550 Oak Street
Alameda, CA 94501

Dorchester
Publishing

For Rex Miller—Rest in peace.

DORCHESTER PUBLISHING

July 2011

Published by

Dorchester Publishing Co., Inc.
200 Madison Avenue
New York, NY 10016

Copyright © 2010 by Edward Lee

All rights reserved. No part of this book may be reproduced or transmitted in any form or by any electronic or mechanical means, without the written permission of the publisher, except where permitted by law. The scanning, uploading, and distribution of this book via the Internet or via any other means without the permission of the publisher is illegal and punishable by law. Please purchase only authorized electronic editions, and do not participate in or encourage electronic piracy of copyrighted materials. Your support of the author's rights is appreciated.

This is a work of fiction. Names, characters, places, and incidents are either the product of the author's imagination or are used fictitiously. Any resemblance to actual persons, living or dead, events, or locales is entirely coincidental.

ISBN 13: 978-1-4285-1126-2
E-ISBN: 978-1-4285-0941-2

The "DP" logo is the property of Dorchester Publishing Co., Inc.

Printed in the United States of America.

If you purchased this book without a cover you should be aware that this book is stolen property. It was reported as "unsold and destroyed" to the publisher and neither the author nor the publisher has received any payment for this "stripped book."

Visit us online at www.dorchesterpub.com.

ACKNOWLEDGMENTS

This project is a novelization of my previously published small-press novella *The Senary*. I liked the concept so much that my Muse demanded I transform it into a full-fledged novel for my mass-market readers. Ultimately, I must thank you, the reader, for buying it! I hope you like reading the book as much as I liked writing it. More thank-yous to: Don D'Auria, Wendy Brewer, Dave Barnett, Tim McGinnis, GAK, Bob Strauss, Larry Roberts, Jason Byars, William Patrick, Thomas Deja, and Christine Morgan. William at the Tyrone Barnes & Noble; *Shroud Magazine*; my friends at Wild Willy's in Largo, Florida, the coolest bar in the world: Nick, Rhonda, Johnny, Bob Monday, Sheri, Roz, Stacy, Mitch, Randi, English Richard, James, Royce, Doug, and the rest. Krist at Diabolical Radio; Tracy Lee Hunt and Temple Arnold Corson IV. Also to the following fans and readers: Paul Legerski; Sandy Griffin and Tony Brock; Jonah Martin, Rob Johns, James L. Harris, Jordan Krall, splatterhead4ever, harleymack, Amy M. Pimental, mrliteral, Horror Freek, Lilith666, Bateman, Lazy Old Fart, vantro, TravisD, JameyWebb, reelsplatter, boysnightout, Nephrenka, carthoss, Amano Jyaku, Insalubrious, VT Horrorfan, bgeorge, Tod Clark, John Copeland, dathar, godawful, Ken Arneson, Bob & Jaime Taylor, Killa Klep, darvis, antitheism, Onemorejustincase, S. Howard, S. Eliot-O'Leary, FrederickHamilton, niogeoverlord, horrormike, Serra, swix, vladcain, Kerri, lazy2006, bellamorte, GNFNR, mpd1958, sassydog, IrekB, jesus was a robot, dk78, FeedMeaStrayCat, sunnyvale22, goregirl, Zombified420, Becki, Patricia Maier, Cyberkitty, squeakytherat, sikahtik, Craig Cook, Queequeg. Plus, special thanks to Monica O'Rourke and Wrath James White for pulling off a dynamite Killer Con in Vegas.

LUCIFER'S LOTTERY

Prologue

Six minutes after he officially died, Slydes found himself standing agog on a street corner like none he'd ever seen. He stood as he had in life: broad-shouldered, tall, dark dirty hair and a bushy black beard. Blue jeans and work boots, and his favorite T-shirt stretched tight over his beer belly; it read ST. PETE BEACH – A QUIET LITTLE DRINKING TOWN WITH A FISHING PROBLEM. Slydes was a redneck, tried and true, a shitkicker. A *bad ass.* He'd seen a lot of outrageous things in his day, but now . . . Now . . .

This?

The wind screamed. Winged mites swarmed in the humid air and splotched red when he swatted them against his brawny forearms. *What kind of city is this?* he thought as his gaze was dragged upward. Dim, drear-windowed skyscrapers seemed a mile high and leaned this way and that at such extreme angles, he thought they might topple at any moment. Twisted faces that couldn't possibly be human peered out of many of the narrow panes, while other panes were either broken out or spattered with blood. The sky visible between the buildings appeared to be red, and there was a black sickle moon hanging between two of them. Slydes blinked.

A dream, it had to be. It was this notion that he first entertained. His Condemnation only minutes old, he couldn't remember much. He couldn't remember where he was born, for instance, he couldn't remember his age, nor could he remember his last name. Indeed, Slydes couldn't even remember dying.

But die he had, and for a lifetime of wincingly outrageous sins and wickedness, he'd been Damned to Hell.

So here he was.

A nightmare, that's all, he convinced himself. A red sky? Office buildings leaning over at sixty-degree angles? And—

SWOOSH

A black bat with a six-foot wingspan and a vaguely human face glided by just over his head. Slydes felt a stinking gust, then recoiled when the impossible animal shat on his head.

"Fucker!" Slydes yelled.

The bat—actually a Hexegenically created Crossbreed of one of several genera known as *Revoltus Chiropterus*—looked over its leathery shoulder and smiled.

"Welcome to Hell," it croaked.

Slydes stared after the words more than the creature itself. *Hell,* he thought quite obliquely. *I'm not really in—*

WELCOME TO ST. PUTRADA CIRCLE, HELL'S NEWEST FISTULATION & TRANSVERSION PREFECT, the sign said.

Slydes could only stare at the sign as the splat of monstrous guano ran down the sides of his face.

Hell's newest . . . WHAT?

At the corner another sign blinked DON'T WALK, and then a rush of pedestrians crossed the street. Slydes just kept staring . . .

He didn't know *what* they were at first: People? Monsters? Combinations of both? A slim couple held hands as they strode by, flesh rotting from their limbs and faces. Several impish children wove through the crowd, with fangs like a dog's and eyes as big and as red as apples. A werewolf in a business suit and briefcase passed next, and after that a fat clown with a hatchet in its face. To Slydes, the clown bid, "Hi, how are ya?"

Slydes could not respond.

If anything, the street was worse. Cars that looked more like small steam engines chugged by on spoked wheels, a smokestack up front gusted black-yellow soot and vapor. Carriages and buggies rolled by as well, hauled along not by horses but by things *like* horses, whose flesh hung in dripping tatters. One carriage was occupied by a woman with skin green as pond scum who wore a tiara of gallstones and a dress made from tendons meticulously woven together. She fanned herself with a webbed, severed hand. In another carriage rode a creature that could've been a pile of snot somehow shaped into human form. Then came a haulage wagon of some sort, powered by six harnessed beasts with festering carnation-pink skin pocked with white blisters; Slydes thought hideously of skinned sheep when they bleated and spat foamy sputum. A man perched behind them cracked a long, barbed whip—or . . . perhaps *man* wasn't quite right. He wore a wool cloak and banded leggings like a shepherd of the old days, yet atop his anvil-shaped head grew a brow of horns. The whip cracked and cracked, and the bleating rose to a mad clamor. Slydes looked one more time and noticed that, like the bat, these bald "sheep" had faces grimly tainted by human features.

"Oh my God, I am in some shit," Slydes stammered. Things were starting to click in his head, and with each click came more and more fear. Did a tear actually form in his eye? "I-I-I," he blubbered. "I don't think this is a dream . . ."

"It's not," sounded a voice that was somehow raspy and feminine simultaneously. The woman who approached him was nude, and yet—he thought at first—checkerboarded. Slydes squinted at her impressive physique and recalled women with similar physiques whom he'd raped and sometimes even murdered without vacillation. But *this* woman?

Every square inch of her skin was crisply darkened by

black tattoos of upside-down crosses. Even her face, around which shimmered long platinum blonde hair.

"Slydes, right?" she asked. "My name's Andeen, and I'm your Orientation Directress. You may not even realize this yet, but you're what's known as an Entrant."

"Entrant," Slydes murmured.

"And, no, this isn't a dream. You should be so lucky. This is all real. Over time your memory will re-form."

Before Slydes could mutter a question, his gaze snapped to another passerby: another impressively figured nude woman. Her arms, legs, abdomen, and face were but one colossal psoriatic outbreak. Only the breasts and pubis were without blemish.

"Rash lines," remarked Andeen. "In the Living World you have tan lines, here we have rash lines."

Slydes's gaze snapped back to the tattooed woman. "Here . . . as in . . ."

"As in Hell. You're dead, and for your worldly sins, you've been Condemned." Her slender shoulders shrugged. "Forever."

Slydes began to grow faint.

She grabbed his hand and tugged. "Come on, Slydes. We gotta get you out of this Prefect. Believe me, you *don't* want to be here." Then she tugged him down the street and ducked into an alley. "We'll lay low a while, and try to get you someplace where your ass won't be grass."

"I-I," Slydes blubbered. "I don't understand."

"Listen, there's no good place in Hell, but there are places that are worse than others. Like this place, St. Putrada Circle. You must've been a real scumbag to be Rematerialized *here*. Yes, sir, a real humdinger of a shitty person."

"I don't understand!" Slydes now sobbed outright.

"A Prefect is like a small District. And this one happens to be a Fistulation and Surgical Transversion Prefect. I'll keep an eye out for Abduction Squads. They'll Transvert anybody here, Humans and Hellborn alike, but Humans are the desired target. The Surgery Centers pay the most for Humans."

Slydes looked cross-eyed at her.

"The short version. Every Prefect, District, or Town has to have an active mode of punishment, while there are some areas, known as Punitaries, that exist *solely* for punishment. But anyway, this Prefect uses Fistulatic Surgery to conform to the Punishment Ordinances. Fistula is Latin; it means 'communication between,' and Transversion is, like, rerouting things. That's what they do here—they reroute your insides."

Even though Slydes didn't have a *clue* what she was talking about, he stammered, "Whuh-whuh-*why?*"

Andeen smirked. "Because it's perverse and disgusting, the way it's *supposed* to be. This isn't *Romper Room*, Slydes. This is Hell, and Hell is hard-core. Eternal torment, suffering, and abhorrence is the name of the game. It pleases Lucifer, therefore, it's Public Law." She smirked more sharply this time. "Look, go over to that public washbasin and wash the bat crap out of your hair. It's grossing me out."

Dazed, Slydes noted the elevated stone basin only feet from the alley mouth. He dunked his head in the water, agitated the rank guano out of his hair, then seized up and jerked his head out when he realized what he was washing in.

"That's not water! That's piss!"

"Get used to it," Andeen said. "Unless you're a Grand Duke or an Archlock, you'll never get *near* fresh water. Only other way is to distill it yourself out of the blood of what you kill."

Revolted, Slydes flapped the urine off his face, then noticed lower basins erected intermittently along the smoky street. "What are those things? They look like–"

"Oh, the commodes. It's another Public Law. In this

Prefect, it's mandatory that everyone urinate, defecate, and give birth in public."

Slydes's bearded jaw dropped.

"And there"—Andeen pointed—"across the street. There're the various Surgery Suites."

Slydes scanned the signs over each transom . . .

RECTO-URINARY TRANSVERSION

URETHRAL-ESOPHAGEAL REVERSAL

UTERO-RECTAL FISTULA

And many, many more.

Slydes could not conceive of any of this.

When he glanced inadvertently between two more spiring buildings, he could've shrieked. Far off in the distance, some monumentlike *thing* stood impossibly high, but it was a *figure.* He remembered seeing the Statue of Liberty once a long time ago, on a drug run between Florida and New York—that's what this reminded him of . . . sort of. *A giant statue,* he thought. *But . . .*

Andeen caught him staring. "Oh, the Demonculus. It hasn't been up long. Pretty awesome, huh?"

Slydes peered at her, incredulous, then peered back up at the statue. "A Deeeee—"

"Demonculus. It's farther away than it looks—that's actually the Pol Pot District over there. The Demonculus is 666 feet high. Looks like a statue, right?"

Slydes dumbly nodded, noting the pointed crown about the form's head, akin to the Statue of Liberty. But . . . was it a crown, or horns?

Andeen inspected her black fingernails with tiny white upside-down crosses. "Well, it's not a statue, it's a living thing—just another one of the Boss's obsessions."

The impact of her words finally registered. Slydes looked pleadingly at her. "Living . . . *thing?*"

"Um-hmmm. Once it's activated, it will tear the shit out of whole Districts to root out insurgents." She smiled at his trauma. "For the rest of eternity, Slydes, you're gonna be seeing some really wild and really awful stuff."

Her evilly tattooed hand pulled him back into the alley. "And look, there's an Abduction Squad. The clay men are called Golems. They're like state employees, public works, police, security, stuff like that . . ."

Slydes watched with a cheek to the edge of the alley wall as a troop of gray-brown things shaped like men thudded down the sidewalk, each shoving along a handcuffed Human, Demon, or Hybrid. The Golems were nine feet tall and walked in formation. Then they all stopped at the same time, and marched their prisoners into various Surgery Suites.

"And like I said, the state pays more money for Humans, so that's why we gotta get you out of the Prefect."

Slydes whipped his face back around, and repeated, helplessly now, "I don't understand . . ."

"Once you've seen what goes on here . . . you will. Oh, and check out this chick."

Slydes watched as a morose-faced nude woman who appeared to be half Human and half Troll staggered toward one of the street commodes. She leaned over, parted her buttocks, and began to urinate out of her anus.

"See?" Andeen asked. "Oh, wow, and check this out! Here comes a Uteral-Oral Fistulation . . ."

A woman in a bloody smock labored down the street. She was covered with red-rimmed white scales . . . and was obviously quite pregnant. She held a scaled hand to her bloated belly, and when she could walk no longer she stopped, leaned over, and—

SPLAT!

—out gushed a slew of amniotic water from her mouth. She maintained the uncomfortable position, and as her belly began to tremor, her jaw came unhinged. Her throat began to impossibly swell, and as her stomach shrunk in size, a squalling, demonic fetus slid hugely out of her mouth and flapped to the pavement.

"How's that for the spectacle of childbirth?" Andeen jested. "Pregnancy is a big deal in Hell, Slydes. If Lucifer had his way, every single female life form here would be pregnant at all times. You see, the more babies, the more food, fuel, and fodder for Lucifer's whimsy."

Slydes leaned against the wall, moaning, "No, no, no . . ."

"Yes, yes, yes, my friend. And if you think *that* was bad, get a load of this guy. Remember what I said about pregnancy?"

Slydes's gaze involuntarily veered back to the street. This time, a Human man stumbled along. He wore a wife-beater T-shirt and stained boxer shorts dotted with Boston Red Sox insignias. If anything, though, his stomach looked even more bloated than the woman who'd just delivered a devilish baby through her mouth.

Slydes stammered further, in utter dread, "He's not—he's not—he's not—"

"Pregnant?" Andeen smiled darkly. "Male pregnancy is a fairly new breakthrough here, Slydes. And you can bet it tickles Lucifer pink. Teratologic Surgeons can actually transplant Hybrid wombs into *male* Humans and Demons. It's a trip. Watch."

Slydes watched.

Grimacing, the bloated man stepped out of his boxers and squatted. Amid boisterous grunts and wails, his rectum slowly dilated, then—

He shrieked.

—out poured a gush of what looked like squirming hairless puppies, with tiny webbed paws and little horns in their heads.

"Ah," Andeen observed, "a brood of Ghor-Hounds. Pretty rowdy, huh?"

"Rowdy!" Slydes bellowed. "This is FUCKED UP! That guy just pumped a litter of PUPPIES out his ASS!"

"Yeah. And watch what he does now . . ."

Gravid stomach gone now, the exhausted man abandoned his litter on the sidewalk and trudged over to one of the street commodes. *What, he's gonna take a piss?* Slydes wondered when the man poised an understandably shriveled penis over the commode.

The answer to his question, however, would be a most resolute *No*.

Now the man's cheeks billowed. He began to grunt.

And his penis . . . began to swell.

"Ahhhh," he eventually moaned as the penis, next, began to disgorge firm stools. Quite a number of them squeezed out and dropped into the commode. When he was finished, he pulled his boxers back on, and at the same time caught Slydes staring agape at him.

"What's the matter, buddy? You act like you never saw a guy take a shit through his dick before."

"In case you're wondering," his hostess said, "the procedure that guy underwent is called a Recto-Urethral Fistulation . . ."

Slydes reeled. When he could regain some modicum of sense, he glared back at Andeen, and howled, "This is impossible! Women can't have *babies* out their mouths! Their mouths aren't *big* enough! And men can't shit *turds* through their cocks! Their *peeholes* aren't *wide* enough! It's IMPOSSIBLE!"

Andeen seemed amused. "You'll learn soon enough that in Hell . . . *anything* is possible. Now come on."

Dizzied, aghast, Slydes trudged after her. She walked fast, her high breasts bouncing, her flawless rump jiggling with each stride. "Once I get you out of this Prefect and on one of the Interways, you'll be a lot safer. Believe me, you don't want to hang out here." She grinned over her shoulder. "You're damn lucky I'm an *honest* Orientation Directress, Slydes."

"Huh?"

"There are a lot of dishonest ones. They'd tip off an Abduction Squad and turn you in—for money, of course."

"Huh?"

"Just come on. I know, you're confused right now, and you can't remember much. Eventually it'll all sink in, and you'll be all right."

Slydes sorely doubted that he would ever be all right, not in Hell. But he did feel some gratitude toward Andeen for endeavoring to get him out of the abominable Prefect. *Anywhere, anywhere,* his thoughts pleaded. *Take me anywhere because no matter how bad the next place is, it can't be as bad as this . . .*

"Here's the shortcut out, and don't worry about the gate." She lifted something from beneath her tongue. "I have the key."

Thank God . . . Slydes followed the lithe woman down another reeking alley whose end terminated in a chain-link gate closed by an antiquated lock. When Andeen finnicked with the key, rust sifted from the keyhole.

That thing better open, Slydes fretted.

"I guess the hardest thing to get used to for a Human in Hell is, well, the insignificance. Know what I mean?"

"Huh?" Slydes said.

"No matter what we were in the Living World, no matter how strong, how beautiful, how rich, how *important* . . . in Hell we're nothing. In fact, we're less than nothing." She giggled, still jiggling the key. "Do you follow me, Slydes?"

Slydes was getting pissed. "I don't know what'cher talkin' about! Just open that fuckin' lock so we can get out of here!"

She giggled but then frowned. "Damn. This bugger's tough. Check the alley entrance, will you—"

"All riiiiiiii—" But when Slydes looked behind him he shrieked. Proceeding slowly down the alley was a congregation of the short, dog-faced, implike things he'd seen previously on the street. They grinned as they moved forward, fangs glinting.

Slydes tugged Andeen's arm like a child tugging its mother's. "Luh-luh-look!"

Andeen's tattooed brow rose when she glanced down the alley. "Shit. Broodren. They're demonic kids and they're *all* homicidal. The little fuckers have gangs everywhere—"

"Open the lock!"

She played with the key most vigorously, nervous herself now. "They'll haul our guts out to sell to a Diviner; then they'll screw and eat what's left . . ."

"Hurry!" Slydes wailed.

Suddenly the pack of Broodren broke all at once into a sprint, cackling.

When they were just yards away—

CLACK!

—the lock opened. Slydes peed his jeans as Andeen dragged him to the other side. She managed to relock the gate just as several Broodren pounced on it, their dirty, taloned fingers and toes hooked over the chain links.

"Jesus! We barely made it!"

Andeen sighed, wiped her brow with her forearm. "Tell me about it, man."

"What now?" Slydes looked down a stained brick corridor that seemed to dogleg to the left. "How do we get out?"

"Around the corner," Andeen said.

They trotted on, turned the corner, and—

"Holy motherfuckin' SHIT!" Slydes yelled when two stout gray-brown forearms wrapped about his barrel chest and hoisted him in the air.

Tall shadows circled round in total silence.

Slydes screamed till his throat turned raw.

"One thing you need to know about Hell," Andeen chuckled, "is that *trust* does not exist."

Five blank-faced Golems stood round Slydes now, and it was in the arms of a sixth that he was now captive.

One of them handed Andeen a stack of bills. "Thanks, buddy. This guy's a *real* piece of work. He deserves what he's getting." Then she winked at Slydes and pointed up to another transom. It read: DIGESTIVE TRACT REVERSAL SUITE.

"For the rest of eternity, Slydes," she intoned through a sultry grin. "You'll be eating through your ass and shitting out your mouth."

"Nooooooooooooo!" Slydes shrieked.

The Golems trooped toward the door, Slydes kicking and screaming, all to no avail.

"Welcome to Hell," were Andeen's parting words.

Slydes's screams silenced when the suite door slammed shut, and Andeen traipsed off, greedily counting the stack of crisp bills. Each bill had the number one hundred in each corner, but it was not the portrait of Benjamin Franklin that graced each one, it was the face of Adolf Hitler.

Part One

The Senary

Chapter One

(I)

Six words drifted across his mind when he entered the bar:

A whore is a deep ditch . . .

It was a line from Proverbs, one of many that warned men of the power of lust. Hudson had studied the Bible with great zeal—and he still did—but what would seem strange about that? He'd graduated from Catholic U. with a master's in theology, and within a month would be entering the seminary. No, what might seem strange, instead, was *his* presence in this bar, a place known to be a *whore* bar, or at least that's what he'd heard.

His first name was the same as his last—Hudson—something he'd never understood of his parents, who'd both seemed distant or distracted since the time his memories commenced. He didn't get it. They were dead now. *They'll never get to see me ordained, and I'll never get to ask them why they named me Hudson.*

Six tiny cracks could be seen in the long bar mirror, but why would Hudson count them? *Obsessive-compulsive?* he wondered. How could he really ever know? His contemplations itched at him. He *knew* why he was here, and was slightly discomfited by the patrons. The bar was simply called LOUNGE; that's what the tacky neon said outside, and aside from its notoriety as an establishment that condoned prostitution, his friend Randal had warned that the place catered essentially to "white trash."

So . . . what does that make me?

His reflection in the mirror looked like that of a bus bum. Unkempt, hair in need of cutting, eyes open wider than they should be as if used to looking for something that wasn't there.

When he glanced down the long, dark room, he counted only six customers—three men, three women—then he noticed they were all smoking. Tendrils of smoke hung motionless in the establishment's open space, like slivers of ghosts. Hudson didn't smoke. He'd never even tried because he recalled a childhood sermon: "Your body is a gift from God, and any gift from God is a temple of God. When we inhale cigarette smoke into our bodies, it's the same as throwing rocks through the stained-glass windows of this very church. Desecration . . ."

Hence, Hudson never lit up. He did drink a little, however, and not once did he consider that the same minister who'd given the smoking sermon had never added alcohol to his list of substances that desecrated one's God-given body, nor that said minister had died years later of cirrhosis.

"I ain't kiddin' ya," one redneck with a Fu Manchu affirmed to another redneck with a bald head. "I know it was the same ho' who ripped me off a year or so ago. But she was so fucked up on Beans the bitch didn't even remember me!"

"What'chew do?" asked the bald one.

"Jacked her out's what I did—"

"Bullshit."

"Think so?" Fu Manchu pulled out a blackjack, jiggled it, then put it back in his pocket. "Jacked her out right in the car, gave her a poke, and took her cash but ya know what? All the bitch had on her was *six bucks* . . ."

The bald one looked suspicious over his Black Velvet and Coke. "You didn't jack no one out, man."

"Buy me a drink if I prove it?"

The bald one laughed. "Sure, but you *can't* prove it."

Fu Manchu flipped open his cell phone. "I love these camera phones, man." He showed the tiny screen to the bald one. "What? Ya think all that red stuff's ketchup?"

The bald one slumped and ordered the guy a drink.

A real highbrow crew tonight, Hudson thought.

One of the women—a middle-aged blonde—had drifted over to the cigarette machine. Very tan, in a clinging maroon T-shirt and cutoff jeans. She'd knotted the T-shirt to reveal an abdomen whose most obvious trait was an accordion of stretch marks. Lots of eye shadow. Veiny hands. *Too weathered,* Hudson judged.

"Hi, honey," she said in a Marlboro-rough voice and as she headed back to her stool, her hand slid along Hudson's back. "Come on over, if ya want. I mean, you know what this place is all about, right?" But before Hudson could even dream up an answer she was already back in her seat.

Indeed, Hudson did know what the place was all about—that's why he was here. Prostitution that was not quite the bottom of the barrel. He could afford little more. His conscience squirmed amid his blooming sin. Obviously she'd struck out with the other men in the bar.

Yeah, but the weathered ones know what to do . . .

"Another beer?" asked the barkeep. He was a ramshackle rube with a circular patch on his gas station shirt that read BARNEY.

"Yes, please."

The keep leaned over, as if to relay a confidence. He had shaggy hair, and a pock on his cheek that looked like a bullet scar, and he was probably sixty. "Don't worry, it's all cool. I know you ain't a cop."

"What?" Hudson questioned, dismayed.

"I can tell at a glance, you ain't got the look." The keep grinned. " 'N'fact, ya look more like a *priest*."

Terrific, Hudson thought.

"And you been sittin' here a while, right?"

"Yeah, an hour, hour and a half, I guess."

"I figure you must know what the Lounge is all about—" He jerked his eyes down toward the old blonde. "Like she done said."

Hudson's chest felt tight. "I-uh-" One of several TVs showed a baseball game. "I'm just in to watch the game."

"Sure, sure," the keep chuckled. He pulled out another bottle of beer and set it down next to five empties. Hudson paid for each beer one at a time, for in establishments such as this, tabs were never run.

"I kinda look the other way, got no problem with what a gal feels she has to do for money—" Then the keep winked. "As long as there's a cut for me. You wanna get some action in the bathroom, that's cool. Just make sure you slide me a ten first, ya hear?"

"Uh, uh-sure," Hudson blabbered.

"Ya been here a while now so I thought maybe ya didn't know the deal." The keep winked again. "But now ya do."

"Um, thanks for filling me in . . ."

The keep leaned in closer to Hudson. "But as for Thelma over there—"

"Who?"

"The blonde."

Hudson glanced over, and suddenly found that the woman's burgeoning bosom possibly nullified her beat looks. "What about her?"

"She's been around the block more times than the mailman, get it? Just some neighborly advice. She fucks like a champ but if you make any deals with *her* . . . wrap it—if ya catch my drift."

Hudson flinched when a toothy grin floated just to the right side of his face. It was Fu Manchu. "Wrap it? Shit, man. Thelma's cooch is *toxic*. She's got stuff up there that can melt a triple-Trojan like one'a them Listerine breath strips." He elbowed Hudson. "You do *her?* Put a scuba foot on your pecker." He and the barkeep broke out in laughter.

Hudson couldn't have been more uncomfortable. "Thanks, uh, thanks for the pointers, guys."

Hudson gazed up at the TV. Tampa Bay led New York six to nothing, but the sound was down. He glanced aside, pretending to be looking for someone. Two more women—younger but nearly as weathered as Thelma—sat apart at the far end, one brunette with a ludicrous mullet and a shirt that read DO ME TILL I PUKE. The other, a rusty redhead, wore a T-shirt that claimed NO GAG REFLEX. *Well, there they are,* Hudson thought. *So what am I doing? When am I going to make a move?*

But Hudson hadn't noticed the other man—he must've just come in. Young but somehow despondent, a false smile that looked on the verge of shattering. He was in a wheelchair. *Those two prostitutes must know him,* Hudson figured, for they both stood stooped, talking to the young man. Their grins could be described as vulturine. The man shook his head; then Hudson overheard him say, "I can't anymore." Then the redhead said, "Pay us twenty each to try. We'll give ya lots of time." But the man in the chair shook his head and wheeled away.

"Fuckin' cripple," the redhead whispered to her cohort.

Oh, what a bounty of goodwill in the world, Hudson thought, and then that's when it occurred to him: he'd seen the man before, in church.

Another TV hung just above the brunette's head, also silent: a dashing evangelist in a huge stadium. Hudson could read the closed-caption blocks as the revivalist's mouth moved.

WHEN YOU STRIVE TO NOT SIN, WHEN YOU MAKE THAT *EFFORT*, GOD HOLDS YOU IN SPECIAL *FAVOR*. GOD PUTS HIS SHIELD OF PROTECTION OVER YOU. SO TO *STAY* IN GOD'S FAVOR, WE MUST *ALWAYS* STRIVE NOT TO SIN. WE MUST DO EVERYTHING WE POSSIBLY CAN TO RESIST THE TEMPTATIONS THAT LUCIFER THROWS BEFORE US . . .

Hudson's eyes lowered—in shame. *No shield of protection for me today,* he thought to his beer.

Sin was everywhere. And he needed to know it before he could absolve it, just like Monsignor Halford had said . . .

I know I shouldn't be here but I'm staying anyway, he realized. *I'm here to pick up a hooker . . . and that's what I'm going to do because I'm not strong enough to walk out . . .*

He did good deeds. He felt he had true compassion. He gave to charities, he gave to the homeless—even though he was poor himself. Above all, he believed in God, and he could only pray that God's mercy was as everlasting as the Bible claimed.

AND MANY OF YOU MIGHT BE THINKING RIGHT THIS SECOND, "BUT PASTOR JOHNNY, I'M A GOOD PERSON, I GO TO CHURCH, AND I TRULY DO STRIVE NOT TO SIN . . . AND I'M TRULY SORRY WHEN I *DO* SIN . . . LIKE LAST WEEK WHEN I WENT TO THAT PORNO STORE, OR THE WEEK BEFORE THAT TEEN-SEX WEB SITE, OR THE WEEK BEFORE THAT WHEN I PICKED UP THAT PROSTITUTE . . .

Hudson stared.

IT'S NOT SUPPOSED TO BE EASY, MY FRIENDS, AND LET ME TELL YOU SOMETHING. IT WASN'T EASY FOR JESUS EITHER.

Hudson's soul felt stained black. *He's talking about me.*

Maybe Halford was wrong, but if I believe THAT, then how can I believe in the infallibility of the church?

AND SOMETIMES WE WANT TO *CHALLENGE* GOD, WE WANT TO SAY TO HIM, "GOD, YOU'VE GIVEN ME THESE DESIRES BUT TELL ME IT'S A SIN TO ACT ON THEM. WHY? IT'S NOT FAIR!" The evangelist seemed to look directly at Hudson. BUT HERE'S WHY IT *IS* FAIR, AND PLEASE, MY DEAR FRIENDS, *LISTEN* TO ME. IT'S FAIR BECAUSE GOD SO LOVED THE WORLD THAT HE GAVE HIS ONLY BEGOTTEN SON . . .

Hudson felt sick. Were his palms sweating? He couldn't keep his eyes off NO GAG REFLEX. *All I have to do is slip the keep a ten and go over there . . .* The other one, with the mullet, looked not half bad as well (except for the mullet). Had she tweaked her nipples? They stuck out against the DO ME shirt like bullet casings.

She looked right at Hudson—in the same way the evangelist had—and mouthed, *Blow job?*

MOST OF THE TIME, FRIENDS, BEING A GOOD PERSON ISN'T GOOD ENOUGH. WE SIN AND THEN DO GOOD WORKS BECAUSE WE THINK ONE GOOD THING CANCELS OUT THE BAD, BUT DON'T BE DECEIVED BY THIS. DON'T BE A *CRUMMY PERSON* BY PURSUING YOUR TEMPTATIONS. DON'T LIVE A CHUMP-CHANGE LIFE. WE TEND TO SIN IN SECRET, BECAUSE NOBODY CAN SEE. HUSBANDS, YOU THINK THAT NOBODY SEES YOU WHEN YOU WALK INTO THAT PORNO STORE, OR SLIP INTO THAT MASSAGE PARLOR. YOUR WIFE CAN'T *SEE* YOU WHEN YOU'RE DRIVING DOWN THAT DARK ROAD AFTER WORK TO LOOK FOR A STREETWALKER. AND WIVES? YOU THINK THAT NOBODY SEES YOU WHEN YOU

SNEAK INTO THE BATHROOM TO DO THAT LINE OF COCAINE. NOBODY SEES YOU WHEN YOU CHEAT ON YOUR HUSBAND WITH YOUR OFFICE MANAGER. BUT HEAR ME, FRIENDS. GOD *DOES* SEE YOU . . .

Hudson felt percolating now, half aroused just from the contemplation, even as the evangelist's silent words haunted him. Now DO ME was standing next to GAG REFLEX, whispering. Every image of carnality steamed in Hudson's mind.

GOD LOVES US *ALL*, HE WANTS *ALL OF US* TO JOIN HIM SOMEDAY IN THE FIRMAMENT OF HEAVEN, BUT THE TRUTH, MY FRIENDS, IS THAT MOST OF US WON'T GET THERE BECAUSE MOST OF US DON'T TRY *HARD ENOUGH* TO RESIST THE DESIRE TO SIN. AND SOME OF YOU MIGHT WANT TO SAY TO ME, "PASTOR JOHNNY? IF GOD REALLY LOVES ME, THEN HOW CAN HE SLAM HEAVEN'S DOOR IN MY FACE FOR ACTING ON THE DESIRES THAT HE GAVE ME?" BUT I SAY TO YOU, *JESUS* WAS SUBJECTED TO THE *SAME* TEMPTATIONS THAT WE ARE BUT HE *NEVER* SINNED, SO IN THE LIGHT OF THAT TRUTH, WHEN YOU DON'T TRY HARD ENOUGH TO TURN YOUR BACK ON THOSE TEMPTATIONS, IT'S NOT GOD WHO'S SLAMMING THE DOOR IN YOUR FACE. IT'S YOU.

Hudson tore his eyes off the TV, then groaned to himself. DO ME and GAG REFLEX were gone—

Damn it, he thought. *They must've left—*

He almost yelped as several hands played across his back. DO ME pressed in on one side, GAG the other. Cheap perfume and shampoo suddenly intoxicated him.

"Hey, there," GAG said. She began to rub his back where he sat, her breasts pressing. "My name's Sylvia."

"My name's Jeanie," said the other. "What's yours?"

Hudson couldn't resist. "How about . . . John?"

The two women looked at each other, stalled, then laughed aloud.

"I like this guy!" said GAG. "And we were wondering . . ."

"Yeah," said DO ME. Her hand rubbed his chest, and when the keep disappeared in back, she smoothly rubbed his crotch. "Ever had a doubleheader?"

Hudson was taken aback. "Uh, well—"

GAG's breath smelled like Juicy Fruit. "Ask anyone. Me'n Jeanie do the best doubleheaders. We know all the right stuff guys like—"

Hudson opened his mouth . . .

They both flashed their bare breasts right in Hudson's face. Four pink, plucked nipples looked back at him. Hudson got drunk just from the sight. A side-glance showed him Fu Manchu and the bald guy both grinning at him, and nodding approval.

The T-shirts came back down when the keep returned. GAG's lips touched his ear when she whispered, "And it's only fifty bucks each, plus ya gotta give the—"

"Ten to the bartender." Hudson finally said something coherent. "Yes." He felt flushed, prickly. *Here goes. Monsignor Halford better be right . . .* He looked in his wallet. "I only have sixty dollars on me. Is there—"

"An ATM?" DO ME finished his question. "At the bank—"

"—right across the street," the other hot, wet whisper brushed his ear. "You could be back in five minutes."

Hudson felt disconnected from himself when he stood up. "I'll be right back . . ."

GAG gave his buttocks a squeeze when Hudson rushed out. He crossed the parking lot with a drone in his head. Darkness had arrived like an oil spill; the old sodium lights painted glowing yellow lines across the cracked asphalt. His anticipation revved his heart. *I'm going to be in the seminary soon, but in about five minutes I'm going to be standing in a dump bar's bathroom with my pants down in front of two hookers. Oh, God . . .*

He quickstepped past a dollar store, then crossed the street to the bank. Six people stood in line before him at the ATM, mostly half-broken rednecks or old people. *Come on, come on,* he thought, tapping his foot. When he glanced across the street, he saw GAG and DO ME watching him through the glass door. *With my luck someone else'll pick them up while I'm waiting in this line!*

Finally Hudson got his turn and withdrew five twenties. He grimaced at the receipt where it read AVAILABLE BALANCE: $6.00.

"Damn it," he sputtered, and then he stood there for a time, spacing out. *Put the money back in the bank and go home!* his alter ego yelled at him. *You don't need to do this! Look at yourself! You're a scumbag! You're a whoremonger!*

But he could, couldn't he? He looked at the cash. He could redeposit it right now, save it for the things he needed rather than wasting it on this experiment in lust. But—

Instead he put it in his pocket and left the machine.

On his way back his mind was clogged with the lewdest images. Even as the block letters flashed behind his eyes—DON'T BE A *CRUMMY PERSON* BY PURSUING YOUR TEMPTATIONS. DON'T LIVE A CHUMP-CHANGE LIFE—Hudson couldn't see them.

The drone dragged him on. He had no awareness of making the mental decision to stop, but when he realized he had, he found himself several yards from the dollar store where a skinny woman in a dirty sundress and lanky hair was having a conniption at the front door. A pair of scrawny little kids with dead eyes stood next to her. "Fuckin' bullshit! I can't fuckin' believe it!" she was yelling at herself. "It's not supposed to be this fuckin' hard!"

Hudson wanted to move on, to the tacky delights that awaited. Instead, he said, "Is something wrong?"

"Yeah! *Everything's* wrong! I got two fuckin' kids to feed so I go in there to buy food"—she held up a plastic card with an American flag on it—"and the machine says my food credits are all used up. My fuckin' husband maxed out the card out before he split yesterday. Instead of paying the power bill, he spent the money on crack; then he maxes out the card and leaves town! Fucker leaves me with two kids and no food, and even if I *had* food, I can't cook it 'cos I got no power, so I gotta buy Pop-Tarts and canned spaghetti, but I can't even buy *that* 'cos my fuckin' piece of shit husband MAXED OUT MY CARD!"

The woman looked close to a psychotic break. Meanwhile, her two children looked up at Hudson, stared a moment, then looked away.

The woman's eyes were red now. "Mister, could you give me five or ten bucks? Please? This shit's fuckin' killin' me."

"I—" Hudson began but didn't finish.

"My fuckin' food card doesn't renew till the sixth—that's over a week from now. I'll have to feed my kids garbage till then."

"I—" But Hudson thought, *I could give her twenty bucks and still have plenty for the whores . . .*

"Aw, fuck it!" she wailed. "You guys are all the same! Don't wanna help anybody. Ya think I'm gonna buy *drugs* with the money. Shit! Does it look like I'm tryin' to buy drugs!"

"I—"

The woman shoved both of the kids. "Come on, we're going home . . ."

"Wait," Hudson said. She turned and glared at him. Hudson took everything out of his wallet and gave it to her. "This should help," he said.

She looked cockeyed at the $160. "Aw, fuck, man! Thanks!

You saved our asses!" She yelled at the kids. "Come on, you little crumb-snatchers! In the store! They close in ten minutes!"

Hudson watched blankly as she pushed her kids back into the store. The woman fully entered, but then stuck her shabby head back out.

"Hey, man." She smiled. "God bless you."

I hope so, Hudson thought. "Good night."

He turned and headed down the sidewalk. Behind him, from the bar, DO ME and GAG screamed at him.

"What did you *do?*"

"You *ASSHOLE!*"

"Scumbag motherfucker!"

Hudson looked at them in the doorway and shrugged. He cut across the sodium-lit bank parking lot, then headed through the alley toward his cheap cinder block efficiency. *I guess this is hopscotch of the new age,* he thought, taking awkward steps around the used condoms and discarded hypodermics that littered the asphalt. Behind him, in the distance, he would still hear GAG and DO ME cursing. Then he laughed when it fully sunk in:

I almost picked up two prostitutes a week before I enter the seminary and take initial vows of celibacy . . .

A minute later he was home, not really knowing if he felt good or awful.

(II)

Smoke the color of spoiled milk gusted from the intermittent censers as far as the eye—be it demonic or Human—could see. *What an interesting color,* Favius mused, mystified. He stood on the southernmost ramparts, proud to know that a large part of this security sector was under his command: sixty-six meters of a multiple-square-mile construction reservation recently dubbed the Vandermast Reservoir.

Its depth? Sixty-six feet.

The reason that Favius marveled at the hue of the censer smoke was simply because of the *contrast:* out here, in the black-sand expanse of Hell's Great Emptiness Quarter, everything, like the sand, was black. The walls of the Reservoir itself were black, as were the sub-inlets and enormous inflow pipes. The causewalks, too, were black—constructed of basalt bricks—and even the barracks were black. Very little of the scarlet sky could be viewed just then, due to the blankets of black clouds. Favius noted only a single rift in said cloud cover, which revealed a sickle moon.

A sickle moon, yes, that was black.

Hence the sickish-white smoke rising from the curtilage of untold censers amazed this steadfast servitor of Satan. The churning wisps of contrast broke the endless visual monotony of what he'd been looking at for longer than he could remember.

Bronze-helmed and breast-plated, Favius had long ago earned the rank of Conscript First Class. This rank he'd earned faster than most due to his predilection for logic, efficiency, and unhesitant brutality. In life he'd served the in the Third Augustan Legion, circa AD 200, slaughtering women and children in a village called Anchester during Rome's occupation of Angle-Land. Now, in death and damnation, he was a loyal member of Grand Duke Cyamal's Exalted Security Brigade. Since time was not measurable in Hell, Favius had no way of calculating how long he'd actually been serving this post, but it had to have been the Living World equivalent to hundreds of years.

The notorious Exalted Security Brigade were sworn on their damned lives to guard by all means necessary the six-billion-gallon facility. Directly under his command were a hundred foot soldiers and countless Golems, all who coalesced to form a living and not-so-living security shield. This far out in the Quarter, infiltration and/or vandalism against the Reservoir was unlikely, but no chances could be taken.

If this project were not very important, Favius knew, *my expertise would not be needed here, and nor would the Brigade's . . .*

Sword always in hand, Favius turned and gazed out at the bleak and awesome sight: the Reservoir's empty pit. He remembered when the Emaciation Squads had first broken ground with mere shovels, digging out and carting away the sinking black sand and corrupt soil. Surely millions of these workers had toiled themselves, literally, to nothingness, and when their labors had reduced them to sunken-faced twigs, they were buried alive *beneath* the unholy Reservoir's soil, where they would twitch and mutter and think—forever.

All in the service of their detestable Lord.

I am so honored, the Conscript's voice creaked through his mind. Only the most loyal, the most trusted, and the most heinous of Lucifer's soldiers were granted such esteemed duty.

A noxious breeze trailed across the Conscript's helmed face, and at once he smiled. The breeze carried the rich, organic stench of the Mephistopolis, the place he dreamed of returning to once his duties here were done. He longed to rape, to maim, to slaughter: his natural instincts. And just then he dared to wonder, *How much longer?*

Such thoughts, he knew, could be deemed treasonous in the event any Archlocks were about—Archlocks, Bio-Wizards, or other servitors skilled in the reading of minds. Favius indulged himself, raising from about his muscled neck the pair of Abyss-Glasses—Hell's version of binoculars. Instead of lenses, the powerful viewing device was fitted with a pair of eyeballs plucked from the sockets of a

Dentata-Vulture, an infernal creature possessed of superlative vision. Favius's tar black heart fluttered when he scanned the farthest fringe of the Reservoir, admiring the fencelike barrier of Golems forever watching outward for signs of assault or trespass. Within this impenetrable wall of manufactured monsters patrolled Conscripts of Favius's class who were overseen only by one of sixty-six Grand Sergeants. Favius hoped that one day he might rise to such a hallowed rank . . .

He snapped to attention at the sudden, encroaching sound: footsteps and the clatter of plate-mail. He held his legionnaire sword in the present-arms position. *Grand Sergeant Buyoux,* he realized.

"Stand at ease, friend Favius," came his superior's voice. The Grand Sergeant wore a full smock of plate-mail armor, from knees to the top of his head. Only his poxed face showed through an oval in the hood. He carried a flintlock sulphur pistol, and emblazoned on his chest was the seal of Grand Duke Cyamal—a trine of sixes fashioned via intricately engraved skulls.

"State the status of your post, Conscript."

"All clear, Grand Sergeant!" Favius barked.

"As always, a good thing." The corrupt face in the oval smiled thinly. "And now? State the status of your disposition."

"My heart sings in the unblessed opportunity afforded me, the opportunity to serve our abyssal Lord! I *exist*, Grand Sergeant, for no other purpose than to be of use to Lucifer!"

"Yes, you do, don't you?" Buyoux's voice receded as he looked distractedly back and forth over endless causewalks and the great black gulf of the empty Reservoir. "Loyalty is so rare these days. I heard that a full dozen of the Somosan Guard defected to the Contumacy recently, *after* destroying several Hell-Flux Generators and Agonicity Stations in the Industrial Zone."

"Blasphemy, Grand Sergeant!"

"Um-hmm." Then suddenly the Grand Sergeant seemed to stare off, not into the as-yet-unfilled Reservoir, but more into his own reflections. Favius *wished* he might read the Grand Sergeant's mind.

"Have you ever wondered, Conscript?"

"I do not wonder, sir!" Favius snapped. "For to wonder is treason without proper license!"

"Yes, and you may consider *this* your license then, but have you ever wondered when our responsibilities at this ghastly reservation might be at an end?"

Favius shivered. He did not answer.

Buyoux's voice, now, could barely be heard. "We'd all be mad not to wonder about that, yes? In an eternity where time cannot be calculated? Where day and night do not exist and where the sky is always the same color of ox blood and where the moon never changes phase? Lucifer Almighty." But then the Grand Sergeant nodded. "No doubt, at least, you've heard rumors . . ."

"I've heard nothing, Grand Sergeant. I do *nothing* but stand my post and command my rampart, by your nefarious grace."

Buyoux paced back and forth, his Dark Ages armor rasping. "Things are going well, I can tell you that, and soon? I'll be able to tell you exactly *why* the Unholy Ministry of Engineering ordered the very construction of this Reservoir in the first place . . ."

Favius stood still as one of the Golems, his ears itching to know.

"Soon, just not now." Buyoux eyed the muscled Conscript. "For the love of every Anti-Pope, I've always wondered why they would build *this* in such a pestilent perimeter of wasteland."

"The more removed the Reservoir is from the City,

the safer it shall stand against infiltrators," Favius dared speculate.

Again, Buyoux nodded. His keen discolored eyes suddenly went flat. "And safe it had best remain . . . or we'll all be fed alive into a Pulping Station, of that you can rest assured."

Why, though? Favius did indeed wonder. *Why* had they built this strange place?

"And friend Favius, would your heart sing as well were I to tell you that after what must be centuries, we may be privileged enough to leave soon? To return to the Mephistopolis?"

Favius began to shake, his heart racing. But he did not reply.

"I can tell you this. The last of the Emaciation Squads have finished their toil."

Favius wanted to shout aloud but, of course, could not. Instead, his exuberance seemed to build up from within, threatening to blow him apart.

Next Buyoux pointed over the rampart, to the termination of the great endless Pipeway connected to the Main Sub-Inlet. "And did you know that the Pipeway is now complete?"

"I-I," Favius stammered, "I did not know, your wretched Grace."

"Well, it is, and you know what that means . . ."

Favius's eyes bloomed. "Soon, then, they'll begin to fill the Reservoir . . ."

"Indeed. With exactly what, I've not yet been apprized, but the sooner it is filled, the sooner its actual use will be realized, and, hence?"

"The sooner our duties here will have been discharged."

"Quite correct. So who says hope does not exist in Hell, hmm?" Buyoux studied Favius in his stance. "I'm feeling charitable today, Favius." He held up his own pair of Abyss-Glasses. "You're a loyal servant and inexhaustible soldier; therefore, you deserve a glimpse. Would you like a glimpse?"

Favius could've collapsed from the joy of the prospect, but he answered via protocol. "I am unworthy and undeserving, Grand Sergeant. I am but rags in your presence."

"No, you're not," Buyoux's word came, drained. "We're all the same, if you want to know the truth." He gave Favius the Abyss-Glasses. "Go ahead. You have my permission."

Favius's large hands trembled when he took the glasses. The model supplied to Grand Sergeants was hundreds of times more powerful than the pair Favius had been requisitioned.

Very slowly, the Conscript turned and raised the Abyss-Glasses to his jaded eyes . . .

The sights took his breath away: the blazing scarlet sky shimmering above the illimitable city. Here was Osiris Heights with its gleaming black monoliths and ceaseless pillars of smoke from the Diviners Stations. Next, the recently rebuilt Bastille of Otherwise Souls, the eternal black prison for Humans damned only for the sin of suicide. Bosch Gardens was a frenzy of giant beaked Demons pitchforking a pitiable Human horde into steaming crevices or feeding the children of Crossbreeds into the mouths of mammoth Gastrodiles. Gremlins prowled through subcorporeal footholds in the coal black clouds, while Gargoyles skulked the ledges and sills of leaning skyscrapers and pointed pinnacles rising to titan heights. Between the drab buildings of the Ghettoblocks stretched cables from which the Damned unwisely hanged themselves, only to learn that the death they longed for would never come, leaving them to hang by their necks, alive, for time immemorial. Gryphons and Wolf-Bats, some the size of airships, glided serenely through the soiled air. Favius zoomed in on a middle school's playground, where sinister and often-fanged teachers fired young students back and forth on catapults, punishment for earning superior grades. On a foul street corner—the Filth District?—several slug-colored Ushers torqued the arms and legs off a Hybrid man for evidently double-parking his steam-car; and on another corner, a pack of Broodren were raping a half-bred Succubus while simultaneously disemboweling her by a hook shoved down her throat.

"It's-it's . . . beautiful," Favius whispered in awe.

"Yes, it is," his superior replied in similar awe. "Look to the North Quadrant. There's something there you'll find very interesting . . ."

Favius followed the instruction, then paused, locked in a rigor of shock and wonderment.

"It's the Pol Pot District, and as you can see, fine Conscript, good things are all about."

Favius could barely maintain his train of thought. There, spiring from the middle of the smoke-hazed District known for beautification via staked heads and "cubing" the Human Damned in massive industrial compactors, was a great statue-like obscenity higher than any building in the vicinity. An enormous, horned *thing* standing perfectly still.

Parched, Favius uttered, "Antichrist Almighty . . . A Demonculus . . ."

"So it is. The myths are true. While we've been guarding this wasted post for centuries, the De Rais Academy has built *that.* I can scarcely believe they did it. We all thought it was impossible . . ."

"The sorcerial technologies must have multiplied by leaps and bounds," Favius, in his awe, postulated.

"And why not? It does in the Living World. Stands to reason the same should be true here." Buyoux's blemished lips turned to a sharper smile. "Who knows when they'll be able to bring it to life, but when they do? Our troubles with the Contumacy will be finished in short order."

"I pray Satan . . ."

The Grand Sergeant pointed down off the rampart. "Now, follow the Pipeway, and maximize your magnification . . ."

Favius did so, training the supernatural binoculars on the massive pipeline sixty-six yards in diameter.

"A hundred miles, a thousand," Buyoux uttered, "no one really knows. But pay heed. What is *your* interpretation, Conscript?"

Favius followed the perfectly straight line of the Pipeway from its connection here at the Reservoir all the way across the black, blasted plain of the Great Emptiness Quarter. It took minutes to follow the Pipeway's complete terminus at the Mephistopolis, and there, where it seemed to officially end, he noticed the features of the Sector District it disappeared into . . .

Gushing smokestacks pumping endless soot into the air, squat buildings stained black from said soot, and the workers *atop* those buildings stained as well. Yet this zone's most salient feature clearly existed in its *composition*. The outline of its high buildings, towers, and industrial structures appeared fuzzy, blurred, imprecise. *Spongy*, Favius thought. The mishmash of colors—all drab reds, greens, and yellows—offered the most bizarre contrast. Then, Favius knew . . .

"Rot-Port?" he asked rather than stated.

"I think so, almost assuredly," Buyoux said.

"The District where all within is composed of some type of rot. The walls of the skyscrapers and buildings, the streets and sidewalks, even the very bricks themselves are manufactured by using deliberately cultured strains of rot, waste, and mold."

"You know much, Favius." The Grand Sergeant seemed pleased. "You've performed duties there in the past?"

"No, Grand Sergeant, but I have heard of the place."

"Splendid. Then what else is Rot-Port known for other than its plaguey composition?"

"I believe, sir, that Rot-Port is the most active harbor in the Mephistopolis, and the largest guarded District along the Gulf of Cagliostro."

"You've learned well," Buyoux approved, "for that is quite true. It's the most elaborate Port District in the city." Now the Grand Sergeant eyed Favius narrowly. "Speculations?"

An excited hush caught in Favius's armored chest. "It must be the Bloodwater of the Gulf itself that the Engineers mean to fill this Reservoir with . . ."

Buyoux nodded, arms crossed as he looked out. "And it's no stretch to assume. Rot-Port is guarded nearly as well as Satan Park and the very domain of Lucifer's new manse. If any District is impervious to insurgent meddling, it is there. Therefore, we may well have the answer . . . or at least half of it."

Favius understood at once. "Yes, Grand Sergeant. The other half being this: what *purpose* could there be in tapping six billion gallons of the Gulf and pumping it *here?*"

Yes. All at once, like a bomb going off, it made perfect sense now, but that only left the even more bizarre question.

"Until *that* is answered, soldier, we can only tend to our tasks—to the death, if need be—and wait." Buyoux's voice ground lower. "At least we'll have something to ponder until the time comes when our Great Dark Lord deems that we should know."

Favius felt an ecstatic privilege having the conclusion shared with him. Joy was little felt here—save for the joy of serving Satan—but now he'd been blessed with a joy greater even than that of slaughtering the innocent.

"Our respite is finished now, good servant," Buyoux said and took back the Glasses.

"Thank you for bestowing me the honor, Grand Sergeant . . ."

"You deserve it." Again, Buyoux's voice declined in volume. "There are great wonders afoot, here, there, all about. And we are privileged to be a part of it."

"Yes, your Wretched Eminence!"

Buyoux seemed to pause, suddenly taken by the Conscript's adornments on his arms and face. "Tell me, just how many women and children did you kill in Angle-Land?"

Favius paused. "I . . . never kept count, sir. Hundreds, I'm sure."

"But what of the men?"

"They were hobbled and enslaved, then forced to build fortifications until they dropped."

"Then why not do the same to the women and children?"

"It was viewed as too great a risk, Grand Sergeant. Better to butcher the women so that their wombs may never bear future enemies, and better to butcher the children so that they may never grow to adulthood to raise a sword against Rome."

Buyoux's scabbed brow rose. "My. You are quite a killer . . ." He patted Favius's armored back. "And soon, by the grace of the Morning Star, you may be killing again."

Favius snapped to attention. "I live to serve Lucifer!"

Buyoux, hands behind his back, began to walk away. "And, Favius? Mind your tongue."

"I would halve myself with a halberd before I would betray a confidence, Grand Sergeant!"

Buyoux, still smiling, raised his left forearm. "Until we meet again, hail Satan . . ."

"Hail Satan!"

Favius brimmed in the news of his departing commander. *Yes! There IS hope . . .* What else might the Grand Sergeant have implied of the future? But as he turned to ponder this question he found himself staring down at the rampart's stone floor . . .

He stared.

The shining black surface of basalt shined like polished obsidian; and in that reflection he peered at the adornments of his Oath in the Brigade.

The prideful thought slipped into his head: *Praise to Lucifer. My adornments look so much better than the Grand Sergeant's . . .*

Indeed. Onto nearly every square inch of Favius's body had been grafted the severed face of a murder victim, the Human Damned, the face of a species of Demon, a Hybrid, a Troll or Imp—it didn't matter.

Favius liked his modifications, especially those most recent. Onto each cheek had been grafted the face of a butchered demonic newborn babe.

(III)

Gerold rolled out of the downtown library, into stifling heat.

Jesus . . . Between Florida's high temperatures and the outrageous humidity, he felt as though he'd just rolled into a pizza oven. He wilted even before he'd made it to the Fourth Street bus stop.

Gerold didn't walk, he rolled. In a Tracer EX2 wheelchair. The IED near Fallujah had penetrated the floor of his Hummer, just a week before the vehicle had been scheduled for up-armoring. Gerold had killed four insurgents that day with the caliber .50—his first enemy kills, he was pretty sure—and felt awful about it, even knowing that the four would've gladly killed him and *not* felt awful about it. On his way back to the firebase, the bomb had gone off, shattering his spine and shredding his kidneys. He'd never walk again, and would need dialysis for the rest of his life.

Still, he kept the faith, or at least he *had* until last night.

Shit. Last night. What was I doing? Then: "Shit!"

In a gust of exhaust-stoked heat, the bus roared by when Gerold was but five yards from the bus stop. The driver had pretended not to see him, and he knew why. *Because it's a pain in his ass to lower the wheelchair ramp . . .*

Sweat trickled down his forehead as he wheeled north.

Last night. He couldn't stop thinking about it. The last time he'd been in that bar was three years ago—on a thirty-day leave—and, yes, he'd solicited a prostitute, the very one he'd seen last night wearing the NO GAG REFLEX shirt. The sin made him feel tainted, but he wanted to be with a woman, if only for a few minutes, in case he got killed when he went back to his combat duty station. Last night, though? *Why? Why go in there knowing I can't do anything anymore! It doesn't make sense!* It was almost as if some cruel sliver of his psyche had forced him in there just to make him feel lousy. Impotent. Sterile.

That's when he had snapped, and determined to go to the library the following day . . .

Gerold had opted for a manual chair rather than a battery-powered one; at least if his legs no longer worked, he'd have strong arms. But . . .

Big deal, he thought now, huffing as he wheeled farther up. The heat was killing him. And though Florida possessed mind-boggling heat, it also possessed mind-bogglingly attractive women. They walked by this way and that, braless breasts bouncing beneath sheer tops, with sleek tan legs, silken hair, and beaming faces. However, this, too, had become an annoyance even worse than the heat because as the women passed they either averted their eyes or merely didn't see him at all, as though he were utterly invisible. Just more reminders of what he could never have.

Up the road he wheeled around to the Fourth Street Shrimp House, one of his favorite restaurants before he'd shipped out. He knew it was his subconscious that had brought him here—the same cruel mechanism that had sent him into that bar last night. As he stared at the specials sign, he realized that his ruined kidneys now precluded him from eating fried seafood because it would raise his creatinine levels and force him into an emergency dialysis session.

Fuck! he thought.

Today just wasn't Gerold's day.

"Hey, I remember you," said one of the cooks. The slim, straggly man stood outside the restaurant, smoking. "You used to eat here all the time, but then . . . Oh, you went into the army, right?"

Gerold remembered the guy, because the restaurant had an open kitchen. "Yeah. Got back a year ago . . . like this."

"Sorry to hear it, man, but, shit, my uncle was in a chair for thirty years and he always said 'walking or rolling, it's still a beautiful world.' "

Gerold couldn't reply.

"You guys are hard-core," the cook went on. "I hope you know that all of us peacetime candy-ass civilian punks honor your service."

"Thanks," Gerold said.

"Come on in. Your lunch is on me. All-you-can-eat clam strips, man, and they're hand-dipped. None of this pre-breaded frozen shit."

Gerold felt dizzy in despair. "Thanks but . . . I can't now. I don't even know why I came here. I'm on a restricted diet 'cos of my kidneys."

"Shit, that sucks. Those fuckers." The cook paused. "Did you . . . Well, never mind. None of my business."

"What?"

"Did you get any of them?"

Gerold didn't look at him when he said, "Four, I think. With a machine gun called an M2. It tore them apart."

"Fuck 'em."

"Half hour later . . . this happened."

The moment collapsed into cringing awkwardness. "I gotta go," Gerold said.

"Sure. See ya around."

I doubt it. Gerold wheeled away, back up into scorching sun. His throat felt swelled shut; he didn't want the cook to see the tears in his eyes. Eventually he made it to one of the covered bus shelters—*finally, some damn shade*—but when he wheeled in, a squalid face peered over very quickly. It was a woman, probably a lot younger than she looked. She wore dingy shorts and a baggy men's white T-shirt. "Hey," she said and smiled.

"Hi." Gerold knew at once what she was, from the smile. Her teeth were gray, from either meth or crack. *A street whore,* he knew. There seemed to be twice as many of them now, since the recession had bitten in.

"You know," she began, and now her bloodshot eyes were intent on him. She stood up. The sweat-damp T-shirt betrayed flat, dangling breasts. "We could go over by them trees." She pointed.

Gerold saw one of many stands of trees around the park. Gerold sighed. "I'm not looking for any action, if that's what you mean."

She walked over and without warning began to rub his crotch.

Gerold frowned.

Her desperate whisper told him, "Let's go over to them trees. Twenty-five bucks. I've done guys in chairs before; some of 'em get off."

"I don't get off!" he spat.

"Hmm? You sure?" She kept rubbing, her grin knife-sharp. "You feel *that,* don't you?"

"No," he grumbled. He was enraged and humiliated. "I'm paraplegic. You know what that means? It means *dead from the waist down.*"

"Come on, just let me play with it anyway. Twenty bucks. You'll like it."

"Get away from me!" he bellowed.

"Well fuck you, then!" she yelled back. "Fuckin' cripple."

"Yeah," he said, grimacing. He got out his wallet. There was his bus pass and a fifty-dollar bill. "Do you have a knife or a gun?"

"What?"

"I'll give you fifty bucks, my bus pass, and my bank card—"

"For what?"

"I want you to kill me."

The junkie face seemed to pucker like a pale slug sprinkled with salt. She left the shelter and jogged away.

Anyway, *that's* what had brought Gerold down here in the first place. *That's* why he'd been in the library: to use their computer, go online, and read about castor bean poison, which he'd found quite easily. Just as easily, however, he'd found that the extraction process was way too complicated, save for anyone but a chemist; and then when he'd looked up some other poisons, he'd caught the librarian eyeing his screen with a troubled frown on her face. He'd felt idiotic so he'd left in a rush.

SWOOOSH!

The next bus drove right by, its driver pretending not to see Gerold waiting in the shelter.

No. Today just wasn't Gerold's day.

(IV)

When Hudson finally fell asleep, he dreamed almost in flashback: the recent past. A year ago when he'd graduated from Catholic U., he'd taken a summer job for a Monsignor Halford, the chancellor of the Richmond Diocesan Pastoral Center. Hudson needed a letter of reference to get into a quality seminary, so here he was.

Halford had to have been ninety but seemed sharper and more energetic than most clerics half his age. He did not beat around the bush with regard to spiritual counsel. He said right off the bat, "The only reason you're working here is for a reference, but I won't give you any manner of reference or referral unless you do this: take a year or two off, go into the work force—not volunteer work or hospices—you'll do plenty of that during your internship." The pious old man chuckled. "Work a real job, live like real people, the *other* people. You have to *be* one of them before you can be one of us. Work in a restaurant, a store, do construction work or something like that. Earn money, pay bills, know what it's like to live like *they* do. Go to bars, get drunk, smoke cigarettes, and, above all . . . familiarize yourself with the company of women, like St. Augustine. There's nothing worse than a young seminarist going straight from college to seminary and taking all his idealism with him. Those are the ones who fold halfway through their pastorship."

Hudson sat agog. *St. Augustine was a whoremonger before he found faith* . . . "You don't mean . . ."

"I mean as I've said," the elder replied in a voice of granite. "Am I *ordering* you to engage in sexual congress outside of wedlock? No. But hear this, Hudson. A venal sin now is much more forgivable than a grievous sin later, later as in *after* your ordination."

Hudson couldn't believe such an implication.

"Are you receiving my meaning, son?"

"I'm . . . not sure, Monsignor."

"In the real world you'll be subject to the same temptations that Christ faced. We in the vocation *all* need to know that."

"But I'm perfectly happy with a vow of celibacy."

The monsignor smiled, and it was a *sardonic* smile. "Go out into the world first, and that includes the world of *women*. If you don't, you'll probably quit in ten or twenty years. It doesn't do God any good to have priests that quit when they start feeling that they've missed out. It's the same things with the nuns—good Lord. I've been around a while so I know what I'm talking about."

Before the notion to ask even occurred consciously, Hudson began, "Monsignor, did you ever . . ."

The old man lurched forward in his chair. "Did I ever break my vow of celibacy? Are you being audacious enough to ask me that? *Me?*"

"I-I-I," Hudson bumbled. "Not audacious, sir. But . . ."

"Fine. It's an honest answer. God needs priests with balls, too."

Hudson's brow shot up.

"No, I never broke my vow of celibacy, and I've been a priest for almost seventy years." The monsignor's gaze sharpened to pinpoints on Hudson. "But I'll tell you this. I *almost* did many times, but in the end, I resisted."

"That's . . . probably easier said than done."

"Nope. I asked God to take the burden of my temptations off of my shoulder and onto his. And he did. He *always* does"—very quickly, the Monsignor pointed—"*if* you have faith."

"I have faith, Monsignor."

"Of course you do, but you're also full of idealism—you're too young to know what you're talking about." The old smile leveled on Hudson. "I'll bet you don't even masturbate—"

Hudson didn't, but he blushed.

"I won't ask if you do or you don't, but know this, young man. There'll be none of that shit after you're a priest."

Hudson had to laugh.

"All I'm saying is it's reasonable in God's eyes to get all of that out of your system before you take your true vows. That's why I won't give you a referral until you've gone out into the world for a year or so. You see, if I recommend you to a seminary, what I'm really doing is recommending you to God. Don't make a monkey out of me in front of *God*."

This guy's a trip, Hudson thought. "I understand, sir."

"Good, so where are you going?"

Hudson drew on a long breath. "Florida, I think. I grew up in Maryland, where I learned to shuck oysters. I could get a job doing that."

"Good, a real-world job, like I've been saying."

"A friend of mine lives down there now. We were acolytes together."

The old priest's eyes widened. "Is he in the vocation?"

Hudson chuckled. "No, sir, I'm afraid not. He's, I guess, lost his faith, but—"

"Excellent. You can help him find it again while you're shucking oysters in Florida and experiencing real life. The real world, Hudson. You need to know it before you can be a priest."

"Yes, sir."

The monsignor looked at his watch. "I have a golf match now. Make sure you clean all the windows in the chancellery today. Then you can take off. Go to Florida, live amongst the other people. Then come back in a year or so and I'll get you into any seminary you want."

"Thank you, Monsignor." Hudson kissed the old man's ring as he reached for his golf bag . . .

That was the dream. Hudson awoke late, slightly hungover. He supposed a soon-to-be seminarist getting half drunk was easily more pardonable than soliciting hookers. He was proud of himself for resisting the temptation last night, but then . . .

Pride's a sin, too.

Had it really been resistance, had it really been *faith?* Had passing up the prostitutes to help a poor woman *really* been a good deed? *Or was it just guilt?*

He hoped it wasn't the latter.

He had very little money right now, especially after emptying his wallet to the poor mother last night. And he'd been let go at the Oyster House several days ago due to a recession-induced lull in local tourism. It didn't matter, though; he'd be leaving for the seminary in Jersey in less than a week, and he could always get a meal at the church where he helped out with lay duties. He had to go there today, as a matter of fact, to help Father Darren prep for the late service. *God will provide,* he thought, and believed it. But still . . .

It would be nice to have a little cash for his remaining days in town.

Hudson grimaced when a knock resounded at the door.

Oh, for pity's sake . . . It had to be somebody selling something. No one else *ever* knocked on Hudson's door. He pulled on his robe inside out.

"Look, whatever it is you're selling," he preempted when he opened the front door, "I'm flat broke—" But the rest was severed when he looked at his caller.

An attractive but blank-faced woman stood without. The cause of Hudson's jolt was her attire: a long black surplice and, of all things, a Roman collar. A *female minister?* he hazarded. *Must be asking for donations*—He could've laughed. *Lady, you picked the WRONG door to knock on today!*

Her blonde hair had been pulled back; her eyes were an odd dull blue. She was in her forties but striking: shapely, ample bosomed. A stout wooden cross hung about her neck.

"Are you Hudson Hudson?" the woman asked in the driest tone.

"Yes, and I'd love to give a donation but I'm afraid—"

"My name is Deaconess Wilson." She stared as she spoke, as if on tranquilizers.

"I'm sorry . . . Deaconess, but I don't have any money—"

"I'm here to tell you that you've won the Senary," she said.

Hudson stalled. "The *what?*"

She handed him a nine-by-six manila envelope. "May I . . . come in, Mr. Hudson?"

Hudson winced. "I'd rather you didn't, the place is a—" He looked at the envelope. "What is this?"

"It . . . would be easier if I told you inside . . ."

He stepped back. Obviously she was Protestant. "All right, but just for a minute. I'm very busy," he lied.

She entered slowly as if unsure of her footing. Hudson closed the door. "Now what's this? I've won the *what?*"

She turned and stood perfectly still. It occurred to Hudson now that whenever she spoke, she seemed to falter, as if either she didn't know what to say or she was resisting something.

"The Senary," she said in that low monotone. "It's like . . . a lottery."

"Well I never signed up for any *Senary*, and I never bought a ticket."

"You don't have to. All you have to . . . do is be born." She blinked. "I've been instructed to inform you that you're the twelfth person to win the Senary. Ever. In all of history."

"Oh, you're with one of those apocalyptic religious sects—"

"No, no." The deaconess ground her teeth. "I'm just . . . the messenger, so to speak." Then she flinched and shook her head. "I'm-I'm . . . not sure what I'm supposed to say . . ."

Crazy, Hudson thought, a little scared now. *Mental patient with some religious delusion. Probably just escaped from a hospital.*

She groaned. "You see, every . . . six hundred . . . and sixty-six . . . years, someone wins the Senary. This . . . time it's . . . you."

She reminded Hudson of a faulty robot, experiencing minor short circuits. Several times her hands rose up, then lowered. She'd shrug one shoulder for no reason, wince off to one side, flinch, raise a foot, then put it back down. And again he had the impression that some aspect of her volition was resisting an unbidden impulse when her hands struggled to rise again.

Shaking, they stopped at the top button of her surplice. Then, as if palsied, her fingers began to unfasten the buttons.

Her words faltered. "Sssssss-atan fell from Heaven in 5318 BC. The fffffffff-irst Senary was held in 4652 BC. It was wuh-wuh-won by a Cycladean coppersmith named Ahkazm."

Crazy. Pure-ass crazy, Hudson knew now. Yet, he didn't throw her out. Instead he just stood . . . and watched.

Watched her completely unbutton the surplice, skim it off along with the Roman collar and cross. She jittered a bit when she faced Hudson more resolutely, as if to display her total nakedness to him.

I don't BELIEVE this . . .

"Listen," he finally forced himself to say. "You're going to have to—"

The image of her body stunned him. Her torso was a perfect hourglass of flesh; high, full breasts; flat stomach and wide hips. Her skin shone in perfect, proverbial alabaster white.

Hudson's eyes inched lower, to her pubis, where his speechless gaze was hijacked by a plenteous triangle of bronze fur.

This deaconess had one full-tilt body . . .

"I-I-I," she faltered. The dull blue of her eyes seemed to

implore him. "I've been instructed . . . to tell you that you kuh-kuh-can sodomize me if you sssssso . . . desire, or-or-or I will give you . . . oral . . . ssssssex. It'sssss part of winning the Senary." She seemed to gag. "It'ssss what they said to say." Then she turned, quite robotically—showing an awesome rump—and foraged through some old cupboards.

"*They* said?" Hudson questioned. "Who's *they?*"

"A Class III Machinator and his Spotter," she told him, still rummaging. "They're Bio-Wizards. They work in a Channeling Fortress in the Emetic District. They're mmmmmm-achinating me. That's why . . . I'm acting errrrrrr-atically. They're manipulating my . . . will." Then she bent over, to search a lower cabinet.

Holy moly! As wrong as all this was—especially for a future seminarist—Hudson couldn't take his eyes off her physique. When she'd bent, the action only amplified the magnificence of her rump. "What are you looking for?" he finally asked.

"Ah. Here." She straightened, holding a bottle of Vigo olive oil. She stood awkwardly then, and began smoothing palmfuls of the oil over her body. Hudson stared, stupefied.

What am I going to do? he thought. *I've got a buck-naked deaconess with a body like Raquel Welch in* Fantastic Voyage *lubing herself up with my Vigo. This is insane. SHE'S insane.*

She sat up on the dowdy kitchen table and lay back, continuing to spread the oil. Her skin glimmered almost too intensely to focus on for long. "They t-t-told me you'd like thissssss."

"Uh, well . . ."

"I-I-I'm chaste, by the way—I have . . . to tell you that, too." Now her hands were reoiling her breasts and belly. "It's a prerequisite. Any Senarial Messenger mmmmm-ust be virginal, as well as a guh-guh-guh-godly person." She pulled her knees back, then splashed some oil between her spread legs. "You kuh-kuh-can put it right . . . here," she said, and touched her anus. "Would you like to?"

Hudson stared at the question as much as the gleaming spectacle. Simply *thinking* about doing it seemed more luxurious than anything he'd ever fathomed. But—

I am NOT going to have anal sex with a crazy deaconess!

"Or-or-or . . . here," she said, now pressing the perfect breasts together, to highlight the slippery valley. "Just nuh-nuh-not my vuh-vuh-vuh-vagina . . . I mmmmmust remain chaste."

The action of her hands, in tandem with the shining, perfect skin, nearly hypnotized Hudson. It seemed as though she were *wearing* a magnifying glass out in the sun; that's how brightly she gleamed. His arousal became uncomfortable in his pants. *This woman's off the deep end. I need to get her out of here.* Yet every time he resolved to tell her to leave, the image of her body grew more intense, silencing him, *commanding* him to watch.

Now her hands massaged the oil into the abundant triangle, which began to shine like spun gold.

This is too much . . . Hudson thought.

The woman simply lay still, waiting.

"You-you-you-you're allowed to," she droned.

Hudson reeled, staring.

"No," he blurted, cursing himself. *I want to, damn it, but . . .* "You're going to have to leave, miss. Are you on medication or something? Drugs? I could call a hotline through my church—"

"You're-you're-you're . . . not interested?"

"No."

"Oh," she responded. "Okay." Then she dully put her raiments back on, adjusting the white collar. She shambled to the sink to soap and wash her hands.

For land's sake. What is going ON?

Hudson watched, mute, as she ground her teeth a few more times, winced, then headed for the door.

"You're-you're under no obligation, by the way," she said, her back to him. "I'm-I'm-I'm ssssss-upposed to tell you that, and muh-muh-make it clear."

"What is this Senary stuff!" Hudson barked.

"But if you're . . . interested . . . Fuh-fuh-follow the instructions," she feebled, and then she walked out of the apartment, leaving Hudson dumbstruck, painfully aroused, and smelling olive oil.

Did any of that really happen? He stared at the closed door for five full minutes. Perhaps he'd dreamed it; perhaps he was sleeping. He pinched himself hard and frowned. *But if you're interested . . . follow the instructions.*

Only then did he realize he was still holding the envelope she'd initially given him.

He opened it and pulled out, first, a plain sheet of paper on which had been floridly handwritten:

> YOU HAVE WON THE SENARY. ALL WILL BE EXPLAINED IF YOU CHOOSE TO PROCEED. SHOULD YOU DECIDE THAT YOU ARE INTERESTED, CARRY ON TO THE FOLLOWING ADDRESS AFTER SUNDOWN WITHIN THE NEXT SIX DAYS.

An unfamiliar address—24651 Central—was written below, which he believed was somewhere in the downtown area. Hudson read what remained.

> YOU ARE UNDER NO OBLIGATION TO ACCEPT, AND WHETHER YOU DO OR NOT, YOU MAY KEEP THE REMUNERATION.

Remuner—

Hudson dug back into the envelope and discovered *another* envelope.

It felt fat.

He tore it open and found—

Holy SHIT . . .

—$6,000 in crisp and apparently brand-new one-hundred-dollar bills. The bills were oddly bundled, however, in paper-clipped divisions of six.

Chapter Two

(I)

"You gotta be shitting me!" Gerold muttered when he wheeled up to Worden's Hardware Store. He'd always liked the place because it reminded him of days past—days when recessions weren't strangling the economy and changing the way people shopped. Now everything was malls, Internet shopping, and Home Depots the size of naval vessels. *Whatever happened to mom-and-pop shops?* Modernity, that's what. There was no place for them these days, just as there was no place for small, family-owned hardware stores like Worden's where the people working there actually knew what they were talking about.

Hence, Gerold's displeasure, after wheeling three blocks in the sun from the bus stop. The sign was a sign of the times: SORRY, WORDEN'S IS NO LONGER IN BUSINESS. THANK YOU FOR FIFTY YEARS OF SUPPORT.

Gerold had specifically come here for something, but now he'd have to bus to Home Depot. *Shit.*

He'd come here to buy about twenty feet of decent gauge rope so that he could hang himself. "Not today," he mumbled and wheeled off. He wasn't up for the extra bus to Home Depot right now. *Looks like I'll have to go to work tomorrow after all . . . 'cos I won't be dead yet.*

He'd already figured how he would do it, but it would

have to be late. Gerold's apartment was on the third floor (the only inexpensive apartment building in town with an elevator). He'd wait till two, three in the morning, tie one end of the rope to the balcony rail, then fling himself off. If anybody even woke up in the apartment below, Gerold felt sure he'd be dead before they could do anything, and he didn't like those people anyway—a snitty retired couple who always ignored him and frowned when he was doing his laundry. He guessed they thought a paraplegic's dirty laundry was grosser than theirs.

Maybe when I hang myself, I'll do it naked, with my catheter bag hanging. When those assholes come out in the morning for their coffee—surprise! The idea made Gerold smile.

Months ago he printed a how-to sheet off the Internet: the precise way to make a hangman's noose.

The sun's heat drummed into him, but in the time it would take the next bus to come, he could be home anyway. Several rednecks in a dented hot rod grinned at him when the WALK light came on. "It says *walk*, not *roll!*" one of them laughed. Gerold said nothing; he was used to it. His rolling trek continued, down the main road. Eventually, though, he stopped, and he didn't know what caused him to do so. He sat there for several minutes, staring.

His eyes had fixated on a looming crucifix . . .

The church, he realized after several more moments. Why had he wheeled a block past his apartment? *Subconscious, probably.* The dying Catholic in him knew the never-changing rule: *If you kill yourself, you go to Hell. No matter what. No exceptions.*

It seemed like a ridiculous rule.

Shit, I don't even know if I believe in Heaven or Hell . . . Still, without much forethought, he wheeled toward the high-ceilinged church, the same church he attended every Sunday. *What am I doing? If I don't believe in Heaven or*

Hell, then that means I don't believe in God, and if I don't believe in God, why am I rolling this FUCKIN' chair toward the CHURCH?

A slim, dark-haired man in his midtwenties came out of the rectory/school building. He was toting a garbage bag. "How's it going? Is there anything I can help you with?"

Gerold felt silly. "Well, um . . ." That's when he recognized the guy—one of the church assistants. He wore black shoes, black slacks, black shirt, but no white collar. "I've seen you plenty of times."

"Yeah, my name's Hudson."

They shook hands. "I'm Gerold."

"I've seen you, too," Hudson said.

I'm easy to remember. The young guy in the FUCKIN' chair. "Oh, and you know, I think I saw you in the bar last night, the Lounge . . ." Gerold's eyes thinned. "Er, well, maybe it was someone else."

"I confess," Hudson said. "It was me. I was . . . having a few beers."

"Oh, yeah, and the baseball game." But now it all felt dismal. It reminded him of going there in the first place, and seeing those two hookers.

"You look like something's on your mind," Hudson said.

"Yeah, I guess there is." Then Gerold laughed. "I'm not even sure why I came here."

"There's a late service at 7:30, but you've still got a few hours to wait."

"I . . . have a question, I guess."

"Okay."

"But . . . you're not a priest, are you?"

"No, no, but I hope to be some day. I leave for the seminary next week. I just help out around here, Communion prep, Epistle readings"—he held up the big plastic bag—"taking out the garbage. If it's spiritual counsel you want, I can make an appointment for you with Father Darren."

The thought chilled Darren. "Oh, no, see, he knows me—"

Hudson laughed. "He's a *priest*, Gerold. He's sworn to confidentiality."

Gerold wasn't convinced. He didn't want to be embarrassed or look foolish. "I'd rather ask you 'cos you strike me as a regular guy."

Hudson chuckled. "Well, I am, I suppose. What's your question?"

"If," he began but at once, he didn't really know what to say. "If you're sorry for your sins, you're forgiven, right?"

"Sure. If you're really sorry."

"Well . . . is it possible to be sorry for a sin you haven't committed yet but know you will?"

Hudson paused, and something about his demeanor darkened. "I'm not liking the sound of this, Gerold. Are you talking about suicide?"

Gerold could've howled. *How the hell did he know!* "No, man. It's just a question. I'm curious."

Hudson's look indicated that he didn't believe it. "The answer to your question is *no*. Being truly sorry for a sin is fine, even a potential sin, but only along with an act of repentance. How can a person repent if they're dead?"

Gerold said nothing.

"Let's go into the office right now. I'll hook you up with one of the hotlines."

"No, no, you've got this all wrong," Gerold lied, sweating hard now. "I'm not going to kill myself—"

"Let me get Father Darren. He'd be happy to talk to you—"

"No, no, please, it's nothing—"

"Gerold. Swear that you won't kill yourself, or I'll call a hotline right now."

Gerold cringed in the chair. *Me and my big mouth!* "I swear I won't kill myself."

"Swear to *God*."

Gerold sighed. "All right, I swear to God I won't kill myself—"

"Swear to God on the *Bible*."

Gerold laughed. "What, you carry a Bible around in your back pocket?"

From his back pocket, Hudson produced a Bible.

"Come on, man," Gerold groaned.

"Swear on it."

Gerold put his hand on the Bible. "I swear to God on the *Bible* that I won't kill myself."

"Good." Hudson regained his ease. "If you break that, you'll be in a world of hurt. God's a nice guy but he's also been known for some big-time wrath in the past. Trust me, you don't want to incur it—"

"I'm not gonna kill myself, man . . ."

"You're coming to the service tonight?"

"No. Sunday."

"For sure?"

Jesus! "Yes. I always do."

"Good. I'll make an appointment for you to talk to Father Darren afterward, okay?"

Gerold slumped in place. "Okay."

Hudson grinned. "Now, if you don't show up, I'll find out where you live—it's in the church records—and I'll bring half the congregation to your apartment, and there'll be a big scene, and you'll really be embarrassed—"

Gerold laughed outright now.

"—so you'll be there, right?"

"Yes!" Gerold insisted. "I promise!"

"Good." Hudson winked. "I'll see you then."

"Yeah. Later." Gerold thought, *What a pain in the ass!* But at least he was laughing as he wheeled back down the block. His shadow followed him along the sidewalk. He didn't feel very good about lying so outright but what could he do? Hudson expected him in church Sunday, but he was certain he'd be dead by then.

(II)

The Electrocity Generators hummed as the main phalanx of Ushers marched in formation about the security perimeter. The brimstone wall completely encircled the construction site, each joist fitted with a chapel in which Mongrels and the Human Damned were mutilated and sacrificed on a regular basis. The constant torture and screams and death kept the Hell-Flux about the Demonculus *rich*.

In the tallest minaret, the Archlock Curwen—the Devil's Supreme Master Builder—watched from the eyelike observation port. He existed as Hell's most talented Organic Engineer.

He looked up, up, up . . .

This close, the 666-foot figure looked mountainous. Tens of thousands of forced laborers had been required to build it, most of the abomination's body being forged out of noxious slop by the bare hands of trained Trolls and Imps. The majority of the labor contingent, however, had been comprised of sundry other denizen slaves engaged in the task of hauling the immeasurable amounts of construction material from the Siddom Valley's famed *Basin Putrudus*, the Inferno's most immense corpse pit. Technically, the Demonculus was a Golem—the largest ever built—but unlike this lower variant, it was not made of corrupted clay; instead, the appalling wares of the Basin Putrudus were used: peatlike muck commingled with the putrefaction of unnumbered dead bodies—millions, no doubt. The material's very *vileness* gave the Demonculus its sheer power. *So gorgeous*, Curwen mused. Looking at the motionless creature now, he thought of a heinous version of the Colossus of Rhodes . . .

The Master Builder was pleased, as he knew Lucifer would soon be as well.

Curwen had died in 1771 when suspicious villagers had raided his subterranean chancel and caught him in an act of blasphemous coition with a conjured demonness. He was buried alive on Good Friday. Yet his unrepentant sorcery—including the untold murder of children, the consumption of virginal blood for ritualism and sport, and the overall pursuit of all things ungodly—left him in great favor upon his death and descent into Hell, such that the ultimate Benefactor here entrusted Curwen to this most unholy of endeavors. Indeed, Lucifer had told him outright in his impossible, shining voice, "My brother Curwanus, you are perhaps the only of the Human Damned I trust; hence, it is into your hands that I place this task, one of the greatest offenses against God ever devised. I have foreseen that you shan't disappoint me."

Indeed, I shan't, Curwen thought, still staring up at the beatific—and atrocious—thing. Soon, he knew, the lifeless horror that was the Demonculus's very body would thrum with life . . .

MY life. To forever serve the Lord of Lies . . .

In his lofty title of Master Builder, Curwen wore the brand of the Archlock on his forehead—the inverted cross blazing within the Sign of the Eye, proof of his Oath of Faith and completion of Metaphysical Conditioning—and a radiant warlock's surplice of spun lead. This rarest of garments shined much like Lucifer's voice, and proved still more of his Lord's trust in him. And being one of status, Curwen knew that the Demonculus was but one of many such new projects serving Satan's un-divine plan, projects of the most serious import. He'd heard rumors—which were rife in Hell—that something incalculable was brewing in the Great Emptiness Quarter. Though he hoped that all ungodly pursuits succeeded grandly, his pride made him hope that the Demonculus succeeded above all the others, for there was no true god but Lucifer, the Morning Star, once the Angel of Light but now the Prince of all Darkness.

The creature's sheer height—that of a seventy-story building—forbade the use of scaffolds, which turned impractical past 300 or so feet. Instead, crew pallets buoyed in the air by noble gas balloons—Balloon Skiffs—sufficed, each overseen by a Conscript and Air Operator. From the skiffs, Imps and Trolls leaned out to manipulate the Demonculus's flesh, with bare hands and styli administering the final touches to the thing's pestilent outer skin. Many such artisans fell—indeed, some jumped of their own will—but were replaced by the next cycle.

The Master Builder watched fascinated as the highest such balloon hovered at the Demonculus's face, a slab of horror with gashes for eyes and mouth. *Soon,* Curwen thought, *unholy life will shine behind those dead eyes, while* MY *heart beats in its infernal chest . . .*

Hundreds of feet below him, a clamor rose, as did Curwen's joy. Ushers and Constabularies were unloading prison wagons full of the next round of sacrifants, most of whom appeared to be women and children.

(III)

After sundown within the next six days, the words rolled around his head like dice. Hudson walked down the side road toward the glittering lights and hot-rod-and-motorcycle traffic of the main drag, his return trip from that evening's church duties. The money hadn't vanished yet, so by ten P.M. he had no choice but to believe that the entire incident with Deaconess Wilson was not the product of a dream.

That's a lot of money, he thought.

Walking along, he wondered briefly about the young guy he'd spoken with earlier—Gerold, in the wheelchair. Hudson had seen that look before during his volunteer duties in hospices and critical-care wards. *The look of death in someone still alive.* One could only do so much, he knew, but at least Hudson felt some relief in the nearly universal notion that true suicidals *never* raised the issue. He felt reasonably sure that Gerold would attend Sunday services and talk to Father Darren afterward.

He damn well better.

He walked into the Qwik-Mart, a ubiquitous 7-Eleven clone that was stuck between a pizza place and a Thai restaurant. It was here that Hudson's best friend from childhood worked night shifts—Randal—who'd now risen to manager. One could never see inside due to the literal wallpapering of the front glass with poster-size advertisements: mostly LatinoAmerica! phone cards and the state lottery. PLAY TO WIN! one poster assaulted him. *Doesn't everybody?* Hudson figured. *Does anybody play to LOSE?* But then he caught himself staring.

Lottery, he thought. *Senary.* Then: *It's like . . . a lottery,* he recalled the naked deaconess. *But how could I win when I never played? I never bought a ticket, never got my numbers.* Hudson didn't even believe in lotteries, which tended to bilk money out of the poor with false hopes. When he nudged the thought behind him and edged into the store, an irritating cowbell rang.

No customers occupied the disheveled and poorly stocked store. A rat looked up from the hot-dog rotisserie, then darted into the gap between the wall and counter. *I pity the rat that eats one of those hot dogs,* Hudson commiserated.

He frowned around the establishment. No customers, true, and no Randal.

A door clicked, then came the aggressive snap of flip-flops. Hudson's brow shot up when a skanky young woman in frayed cutoffs and a faded but overflowing bikini top snapped out of the rear hall. Her sloppy breasts were huge, swaying as though the top's cups were hammocks, and no doubt most of their distention could be attributed to the fact that their scroungy owner had to be eight-plus-months pregnant. The tanned, veiny belly stretched tight as an overblown balloon around a popped-out navel like someone's pinkie toe. *That's not a bun in the oven,* Hudson thought. *It's the whole bakery.* But he saw women such as this all too frequently. A prostitute even lower on the social rungs than the women he'd nearly solicited last night. These drug-addict urchins were the flotsam of the local streets.

"Is, uh, Randal around?"

She frowned back, neglecting to answer. She kept her lips tightly closed, and began looking around the store. Hudson immediately got the impression that she had a mouthful of something and was desperate to find a place to expectorate.

When she found no convenient wastebasket—

splap . . .

—she bowed her head by a carousel of potato chips and spat on the floor.

Then she winced at Hudson in his neat black attire. "What are you, a priest or somethin'?"

"I'm a . . . seminarist-to-be," Hudson replied.

She kept wincing.

"Is Randal around?"

"I don't know the asshole's name, buddy," she snapped. She yanked off several bags of chips, attacked a Mrs. Freshley's snack cake rack, paused, then darted behind the service counter and grabbed a carton of Marlboros. "The tightwad poo-putt motherfucker's in back." Then the cowbell clanged and she flip-flopped briskly out, milk-sodden breasts tossing as if they sought to rock their way out of the top.

The sidewall was hung with black velvet paintings of either Elvis, Jeff Gordon, or Christ. The Jesus paintings were cheapest. Randal appeared next, looking displeased. "Oh, hey, man."

"Hi, Randal. An . . . acquaintance of yours just made a speedy exit. Probably *not* on her way back to Yale."

"The dumb ho. Pain in the ass. Gives the worst bj's in town but at least I talked her down to fifteen." Randal shook his head—a shaggy head and an atrocious Taliban-like beard. "Guess I get what I pay for."

"You may have gotten a little *more* than you paid for." Hudson pointed to the floor where the woman had spat.

Randal's nostrils flared, like those of an indignant bull. "That *bitch!* She spat my load on the *floor?*"

"And then promptly relieved you of some chips, snack cakes, and one carton of Marlboros."

"That *bitch!* That thieving pregnant *bitch!*"

"'The wages of sin are death,'" Hudson recited. "It's God's way of saying 'what goes around, comes around.' Think about it."

"Oh, listen to Mr. Almost-A-Priest over here. Mr. *Celibacy*. I've seen you eyeball chicks before." Randal grinned wickedly. "Didn't Jesus say that if you look at a chick and think, 'Wow, I'd love to plug *her* slot,' that's the same as *really* doing her?"

"Well, not in language quite so refined," Hudson laughed, "but, yes, he did." He was going to further point out his lifelong celibacy but then declined. *Don't be a hypocrite. Crude as he may be, Randal's right. Last night I came very close to being a whoremonger.*

"So what is it, next month you're going to this seminary?"

"Next *week*," Hudson corrected.

"Fuck, man. Change your mind. You can still do good deeds and shit without becoming a *priest*."

"Well said, Randal, but, no, I'm not changing my mind. It's something I've been thinking about my whole life pretty much. You're my best friend, you should *want* me to pursue my dreams."

"If *never getting laid* is your *dream?* You're fucked up."

"Thanks."

"Besides, look what you're doing to me. You'll be leaving me stuck in this criminal armpit town of ours. I'll be all alone with junkies, bums, whores, psychos. How can you do that to me?"

"You'll manage. And since I won't be seeing you again for a while, why don't you go to church with me this Sunday? It'll be like old times, when we were kids."

Randal hesitated. "Naw, not my style. I haven't been to church in so long, I'd probably get repelled by the cross, like a fuckin' force field."

"Have some faith, Randal. You used to."

"Yeah, before I started working here." He clattered out a mop and bucket. "Here's my faith, man. This *mop*." He ground his teeth. "How do you like that dizzy, knocked-up ho? Walks in here with a bellyful of white trash and rips *me* off? Hocks my jizz on the floor?" He sloshed the mop over the spot. "Got to clean this up before some junkie, bum, ex-con, or all of the above walks in here, sees it, then slips on purpose. Then the redneck scum sues the store for ten million bucks and wins."

Wow, that's some heavyweight cynicism, Hudson thought. He watched Randal haphazardly mop up the expectorant, then roll the bucket back down the hall. "You know, you've got to be the only guy in town who *wants* to stay a virgin his whole life."

"There's plenty of Catholic clergy in this town, and everywhere, Randal. Sexual abstention is an utmost oblation to God. Christ was chaste, so when a mortal man strives to be chaste, he struggles to *imitate* Christ. God likes that."

Randal looked off, nebulous. "Speaking of celibacy, wasn't there some saint a long time ago who actually cut his own johnson off to prove his faith in God?"

Hudson sighed. "Actually *several* saints are rumored to have done that but no one knows for sure."

Now Randal looked focused. "Okay, so say a saint did it—he cut off his meat missile . . . Aren't saints supposed to be—shit, what's the word? *Pristine?* When they die, they don't rot?"

"There are dozens of cases of dead saints being exhumed and their bodies found in pristine condition, yes."

Randal stroked his chin, in deep thought. "Okay, so say some saint in the Middle Ages cut off his pud. Well?"

"Well *what?*"

"Well then his pud would be pristine, too, right? It would have to be. So when he dies, he never rots, but neither does his cut-off dick."

Hudson groaned.

"Serious. If it's true, then there's probably some box somewhere that's got some saint's dick in it, and it looks like it got cut off a minute ago."

Hudson shook his head at the whimsy. "Randal, if you used your powers of creative thinking for something practical, you'd be a genius."

"Yeah." Randal began to diddle with a clipboard, his ludicrous contemplations already faded. "Anyway, as you can see, my job's a pile of shit, so how's *yours* going? The oyster shucking business?"

"They were about to lay me off again so I just put in my notice and they let me go on the spot."

"Wow, that really *shucks*, man." Randal laughed. "Get it?"

Hudson groaned. "It's no big deal because I'm leaving next week anyway."

Randal poured two coffees, but the brew looked like squid ink. "That pregnant hooker really pisses me off. One of these days I'll find a *decent* one."

"Most of those girls are drug addicts," Hudson affirmed. "When you solicit them for sex, you're helping them remain in an environment of moral bankruptcy, degradation, and misery."

"For fuck's sake," Randal sputtered.

"If you give them money for drugs in exchange for action, it's the same as if *you're* buying the drugs yourself. It all goes to the same place, the same evil. Besides, hookers *and* johns offend God."

"Here we go with *this* shit again." Randal grabbed a broom and whisked it around the store, half assed. "If there was a God, then there'd *be* no drug addiction, so then there'd be no girls offering to do you for money."

Hudson frowned. "I think God is about free will, Randal. It's about the *choice*. Does one choose to do drugs or does one choose not to? Do they choose to consort with prostitutes or do they choose *not* to? God's really got nothing to do with it."

"Whatever . . ." Randal swept some dust beneath the counter. "So, what? You came in here tonight just to try to con me into going to *church?*"

"Well . . . I wanted to ask a favor."

"Fuck no, man. Get out of my store." Randal hooted. "Relax! I'm kidding." Then his eyes darted. "Damn, I forgot." He opened the glass door on the rotisserie, then spat on the hot dogs.

"What the hell!"

Randal smirked. "Those fuckin' things are a buck a pack

wholesale. But if you spit on 'em every hour, they last longer. Only people who buy 'em are the bums and illegals. Big deal. Besides, the heat kills the germs."

Hudson didn't know what to say.

"So what's this pain-in-the-ass favor?"

Hudson didn't like to lie but in this circumstance—*A nude deaconess?*—he could surmise no other option. "I found a hundred-dollar bill today in the street but, I don't know—it feels funny."

"Funny?" Randal questioned. "As in fake?"

"Well, yeah, I guess. It's, like, brand-new. But I've seen you check bills here with the funky pen . . ."

"Anything for a friend." Randal got it. "You want to make sure it's not funny money before you try to spend it."

"Exactly."

Behind the counter, Randal produced a fat black pen whose body read SMARTCASH—COUNTERFEIT DETECTION MARKER. Hudson gave him one of the ultracrisp bills.

"I get a 20 percent commission if it's real, right?" Randal posed, holding the uncapped marker.

Anything for a friend, my ass, Hudson realized. "Yeah, sure."

Randal rubbed the bill between his fingers. "Wow, that *is* new." He grinned up. "You sure you're not printing these up in your pad?"

"With what? My oyster board?"

Randal chuckled. "Or maybe in the church! That whacko Father Darren's probably printing his own funny money and getting you to pass it!"

"Hilarious."

Randal drew a quick notch on the bill, then gave the iodine-saturated ink time to dry.

It's fake, Hudson knew. *It's got to be fake. It's just some scam I haven't figured out yet.* Six grand landing in his lap out of the blue like this? *Too good to be true.*

Randal shrugged, deposited the bill in the register, and gave Hudson eighty dollars back. "It's real."

"You're kidding me . . ."

"It's as real as my coffee is bad."

"*That's* real."

"I'm gonna spend my end on another hooker tonight, but not that ratchet-job knocked-up cow that just left. What'cha gonna spend the rest on?"

Hudson wavered, suddenly hard-pressed to conceal his excitement. *But this is avarice, isn't it?* He'd been given a very mysterious $6,000 via a very mysterious scenario. Nevertheless, the money was real, and the arcane note she'd left indicated that he could keep it under no obligation. "I'll probably put it in the church plate."

Randal bristled. "Fuck that! Put it in *my* plate! That damn church gets all kinds of money!"

"Tell you what, I'll take us both out to dinner before I leave."

"Cool!"

Two roughneck construction workers came in and each purchased a hot dog. Hudson cringed as they left.

"I should've asked them how my spit tastes." Randal honked laughter.

"That's pretty revolting, man."

The bell rung. "You wanna talk about *revolting?* Check this homeless scumbag out," Randal said.

A malodorous man who surely weighed 400 pounds squeezed through the door. He mumbled to himself, his lips like mini bratwursts on the huge, greasy face. A rim of long gray-black hair (with flecks of garbage in it) half circumscribed the bald, dirt-smudged head. Stained orange sweatpants clung to elephantine legs, and for a shirt he wore a reeking yellow raincoat. He seemed to jabber something like, "I am by a vent with a bone," and, "Would somebody please cut off my head?"

Jesus, Hudson thought. *The poor bastard. Totally destitute and schizophrenic.* It seemed there were more and more of these lost souls popping up all the time since the recession hit.

Randal cut Hudson a snide grin. "So we're all children of God, huh? Well if so, then God's got a *shitload* of fucked-up kids."

"It doesn't involve God at all," Hudson answered, unfazed. "Humanity exists in error ever since Eve bit the apple. God gave us the brains and the wherewithal to help people like this guy, with medical technology and compassion. But we have to *choose* to have the grace to do it." Hudson reached in his pocket.

"Don't you *dare* give that walking garbage can money," Randal ordered. "The shit-smelling fucker rips me off all the time." He rapped a baseball bat against the counter, and yelled at the man, "Get out of here! I've got you on tape ripping off Wing Dings and Yoo-hoos three nights in a row!"

The man looked back, wobbling. His phlegmatic voice fluttered. "I wanna-wanna ha-ha-*hot* dog! It was Peter Lawford—Bobby watched the door . . ."

Randal CLACKED! the bat again. "Take your crazy ass *out* of here! Otherwise I call the cops *after* I joggle that piss sponge you've got for a brain!"

"Fucker," the voice rattled back; then he hitched and released a trumpet blast of colonic gas.

"Aw, Jesus! You're a fuckin' animal! How can somebody homeless weigh *that* much? You shoplift five thousand calories a day?"

Hudson's eyes teared from the sudden waft.

"You're a fucker!" the man warbled back.

Randal waved the bat. "I'm *killin'* ya if you don't GET OUT!"

The huge man shimmied in place, then leaned over, stuck his fingers down his throat, and—

"No! Don't!"

—burped up what had to be a gallon of vomit. It hit the floor like a bucket of barley and vegetable soup.

"Holy shit!" Randal came around the counter with the bat, but Hudson grabbed him.

"Just let him go, man. He's messed up, he can't help it."

Randal fumed, but by now the man had already wobbled out of the store. He looked at the splatter of vomit on the floor and nearly keeled over.

"Yeah, he can't help it—shit."

"It's called compassion, man," Hudson said, gagging at the smell. "You really have a lot of ill will inside, Randal. He can't help the way he is."

Randal wailed. "He just puked Niagara Falls on my floor!"

"Compassion, Randal. Compassion."

"Fine, smart guy. Ready to walk it like you talk it?"

"How's that?"

"Now you can have some compassion for *me*." Randal threw Hudson a mop. "And help me clean this up."

Hudson laughed and said, "Sure."

(IV)

That night Hudson was heckled by a stew of awful dreams. He heard a wind that sounded like screams. Words seemed to fly in the air as if abstract birds: "DON'T BE A CRUMMY PERSON!" and "I AM BY A VENT WITH A BONE," and "WALKS IN HERE WITH A BELLYFUL OF WHITE TRASH AND RIPS *ME* OFF?" and "I'M HERE TO TELL YOU THAT YOU'VE WON THE SENARY."

He dreamed, first, of being body-rubbed by GAG and DO ME, both naked, of course, but just as the duo prepared to fellate him, they began to cackle like witches. Hudson's eyes sprang open to see they now both had vampire fangs. Next, the dream showed him a Polanski-like tracking shot which soared about the nighted town amid an aural muttering that could only be described as *black*, and suddenly the point of view soared down onto a drab sidewalk and a fence and a trashily dressed woman climbing *over* that fence with a shovel in her hand, and as she did so she *spat!* in disgust, and now that Polanski dream-camera moves off; it's picking up speed as it absurdly changes tenses; it seems to swerve, then dive, and caroms off to a strange smoking street tinted in weird light, which then opens to a football stadium–sized clearing sitting in the middle of a city crammed with leaning decrepit buildings, and this clearing is surrounded by a wall of pale white bricks the size of houses, and within this wall stands a drab statue hundreds of feet high, the largest statue Hudson has ever seen, and then the "camera" zooms in on the statue's face, which looks like a great grimacing mask of mud, after which a squeaking noise is heard and visible however tinily along the top of the wall is a young man in a wheelchair and then—ZAP!—the point of view *explodes* to another grim and impossible place where hunched and vaguely *un*human workmen labor in silence as they build a house but very soon it becomes discernible that the workmen aren't using bricks to build the house, they're using human heads, and then, next, the camera shoots upward, rocketlike, and only plunges after an exceedingly long period until it fires through a stained-glass window and stops in the chancel of a church where six horned demons that look like skeletons covered with raw chicken skin cavort within a circle of brown ashes and stinking candles. A woman lies naked on the floor, her arms and legs lashed wide. One demon studies a scroll of yellowed paper while the other five amuse themselves by fondling the squirming woman. A lipless mouthful of pus sucks at the fur-rimmed flesh between the woman's legs, two more sloppily suckle her bosom. The first looks up from the scroll and orders, "The Benumbment Spell has taken effect. The Inscriptions must begin." But the entity's voice sounds echoic and like gravel being poured from a dump truck. On command, each of the remaining things dip long, jointy fingers into what looks like a mortar. The fingers come away brown. "Anoint her," speaks the primary demon. "Make her despoilment rich. It nourishes the Flux . . ." With their sullied fingertips, the demons begin to write on the woman's luxuriant, nude body, and in the midst of the dream, Hudson's psyche becomes active, and he wonders, *What was that stuff in the cup?* But the query is stifled when he sees exactly *what* the demons are inscribing: a multitude of sixes. "Good, good," the first demon approves. "The anointing is sufficient." The voice crackles and grinds. "We must discorporate shortly. Light the Subservience Ash." Then it begins to intone words in some unknown language. Before the dream veers away, the woman's face is finally revealed: Deaconess Wilson.

That's when Hudson woke up.

What a pile of crap for a dream! his thoughts squalled. The recollections disgusted him. He dragged himself up, showered, then nearly howled when he looked at the clock.

Six P.M.

I slept the whole day away!

He searched the cupboards for something to eat but found nothing—just a bottle of Vigo olive oil. *Great . . .* Then he stared at the kitchen table, noticing the envelope full of money and the handwritten notice that he'd won the "Senary." *At least that part wasn't a dream.*

But what would he do with the cash? Save it? Or: *I'll put*

half in the bank and give the rest to the church or a homeless shelter.

Would that make him a better person in God's eyes? He wondered. *Don't be a crummy person,* the evangelist's words kept sideswiping him. But when he looked at the envelope again . . .

Maybe it's time to see what this Senary business is all about . . .

Two winos shared the bus shelter with him, sleeping or passed out. A third man, who looked normal, must've been possessed by some syndrome like Tourette's. He peered right at Hudson and spouted, "Fuck luck suck druck muck cluck nuck tuck BLUCK!"

And a good day to you, too, Hudson thought. He dressed normally, in faded jeans and a T-shirt, sneakers. The shelter's plastic windows shuddered when the bus pulled up.

Hudson took the first seat, while the winos neglected to get on. *Maybe they're . . . dead,* he considered, looking out the window at them. They remained sidled over in the shelter, drooling. The Tourette's man went all the way to the back; then the bus jerked away.

The Senary, Hudson contemplated. *What the hell is it?* He looked at the announcement, with the address and instructions.

. . . CARRY ON TO THE FOLLOWING ADDRESS AFTER SUNDOWN WITHIN THE NEXT SIX DAYS . . .

It had only been one day, and a glance to the horizon showed him he still had several hours before sundown. A copy of the *Tampa Bay Times* sat on his seat; Hudson picked it up, began to thumb through. One article enthused over the governor's bid to build a "biomass" electric plant; the plant ran on natural gas derived from elephant grass and dog feces. Then Hudson spotted this:

FEMALE PASTOR DISAPPEARS

The article went on to disclose that Andrea Wilson, forty, a well-regarded deaconess at the Grace Unitarian Church of St. Petersburg, seemingly disappeared from her post several days ago. She gave no notice of resignation, nor notice of taking leave.

It's her, Hudson thought when he looked at the accompanying picture, the blonde hair conservatively pulled back, the strongly angled but attractive face, and the Roman collar.

"She's such a wonderful person," quoted a woman who regularly attended the church. "She's so inspiring, so full of faith. And she's simply not the type of person to leave and not tell anyone where she went."

I know where she went yesterday, came Hudson's dreadful thought. *My apartment, to tell me I've won a contest called the Senary, and then strip nude and rub herself down with my olive oil . . .*

He wondered if he should call the police and tell them that he'd seen the missing woman, but . . . *No. What on earth could I say?*

He squinted at the next, shorter article, which reported that a grave had been vandalized late last night at Carver Forest Memorial Cemetery, and the very instant Hudson read the information, he glanced out the window to discover that the bus was cruising by a long, overgrown cemetery. The sign at a fenced entrance read CARVER FOREST. *Uncanny*, he thought. The spotty article went on to reveal that the grave vandalized had been that of a four-month-old infant who'd been murdered last spring.

Lord. What a world . . .

Hudson closed the paper when he saw his stop nearing. Had he turned the page he would've seen a grimmer article about the discovery of a dead newborn baby found in a recycle bin last night. Hudson pulled the cord. "Thank you, driver," he said, and the driver, in turn, frowned. The

Tourette's man railed from the back of the bus just as Hudson stepped off: "Fuck suck schmuck gruck huck puck duck buck zuck wuck six." Then the doors flapped closed.

Hudson turned as the bus pulled away. *Did he say six?* He squinted after the disappearing vehicle and saw the Tourette's man give him the finger through the back window.

He walked down Central, shirking at loud cars and motorcycles. He'd already memorized the street address (24651) because he didn't want to be consulting his wallet in this neck of the woods. The area was mostly ghetto, small saltbox houses in various states of disrepair. *Maybe this isn't such a good idea,* he considered when he noticed stragglers obviously selling drugs only blocks deeper off the road. Burned-up yards fronted most of the little houses; piles of junk sat like tepees amid trashed cars. *So much for urban renewal . . .*

He sensed more than saw a figure behind him.

"Yo!" came a girl's voice.

Hudson turned, not quite at ease. A black girl in tight knee jeans and a zebra-striped tube top boldly approached him. Her dark skin gleamed over robust curves.

"How's, uh, how's it going?" Hudson bumbled.

"Why'n'cha lemme put some sizzle in your swizzle, man, like I'll lay some bigtown xtralicious super gobble game on you for, like, twenty-five bucks," she said.

"No, really, I—"

"Bullshit, man." She stood haughtily, hand on a cocked hip. "I knows a john when I see one, and *you* a john. Come on, pussy or mouth, I got both. You wanna fuck, I kin tell."

"No, really—"

"Yeah, you white guys're all cheap motherfuckers. Awright, twenty bucks for a blow."

Only now did Hudson fully realize how out of place he was. "I'm . . . not interested. I'm just trying to find an address."

The gleam of her white teeth matched that of her skin. "Shee-it. You lookin' for the Larken House, I know. Lotta folks always lookin' for it. 24651, right?"

Hudson was astonished. "Well, yes."

"Folks been walkin' by it since it happened."

"Since . . . *what* happened?"

"Don't'choo watch the news?" She adjusted her tube top. "Couple, three months ago, a brother named Larken, work construction, he cut off his ole lady's head when he found out the baby she had a couple months 'fore that were from a other dude. Cut her head off in the house, then walk right down this street and stick it on the antenna of the dude's car 'cos, see, he hadda old car that had one'a them old-fashioned antennas on it. Then Larken come back the house and cut the *baby's* head off, and he microwave it. Some say he fuck the headless wife on the kitchen table, too, but I dunno. Then he hang hisself. Said he had his cock out when he step off the chair." She looked at him. "Fucked-up house, man."

Hudson felt perplexed. "So that's why people walk by it? Because it's . . . infamous?"

"Yeah, man. 'Cos, sometime, they say, you kin see Larken in there, hangin' by his neck. Sometimes you hear the baby cryin'."

A HAUNTED house. Terrific, Hudson thought. "Most of these houses don't seem to have addresses, even the ones that are obviously lived in."

"Shee-it, sure. They take the numbers off so the pigs get confused," she said. "You gimme twenty dollars'n I show you where the house is."

"I'd be much obliged." Hudson slipped a twenty from his pocket and gave it to her.

She grinned, stuffing the bill into her top, and pointed to the small, boarded-up house right in front of him.

"That's it? For real?"

"Fo' real, man."

At first Hudson thought he was being taken but when he peered over the door, he noticed a black metal number six but also the ghosts of numbers that had fallen, or been taken off, a two and a four to the left, and a five and a one to the right.

"Thank you," he said but the girl was already walking away.

Hudson peered at the squat house. It looked in better repair than many of the others on the street, even with its windows boarded over. Clapboard siding, fairly faded, portico over gravel where a garage should be, one level save for an awned attic. Screen door with a ripped screen.

What should I do, now that I'm here? he quizzed himself. Was he really going to break into a house where murders had occurred? And what if there were homeless people inside, or addicts? *Am I REALLY going to do this?*

But then he thought: *The Senary . . .*

The instructions, however, mentioned after sundown. Hudson still had about an hour, he thought. *I'll get something to eat and think this over.*

He jaywalked to a Zappy's Chicken Shack. Six patrons stood in line, and five of them appeared to be African American prostitutes. When his turn came, a Hispanic woman with half of one ear missing asked if she could help him.

Hudson ordered the Number Six special: three wings, a biscuit, and a drink. *There's that number six again,* he reckoned. Just as he would sit down with his food, one of the prostitutes, a scarily thin woman with huge eyes and pigtails, slipped beside him and whispered, "Gimme a wing." Hudson did; then she whispered lower, "Why'n'cha lemme put some sizzle in your swizzle, man, like I'll lay some big-town xtralicious super gobble game on you for, like, twenty-five bucks."

What, is that the patented line around here? Hudson politely informed her that he had no interest in her proposal, and edged quickly out of the restaurant.

God, these are good! he thought, scarfing his remaining wings and biscuit as he walked down the street.

He still had time to kill, but he didn't want to get killed himself as sundown approached. He walked down Central a ways, trying to look inconspicuous and knowing he wasn't doing a very good job. Sirens rose and fell in the distance, and then he jumped a bit at either a faraway gunshot or backfire. *Hurry up, sundown,* he thought, and patted his wallet to make sure it was still there, then the other pocket where he'd slipped a slim flashlight. At the corner a dark hulk loomed, and then a shadow covered Hudson: the shadow of a cross cast by the sinking sun. *A church,* he noticed next of the drab, pilelike edifice. For no apparent reason he stopped to study it. The sign read: GRACE UNITARIAN CHURCH OF ST. PETERSBURG, but a smaller sign in magic marker added, CLOSED UNTIL FURTHER NOTICE.

This is the deaconess's church!

An old building of streaked gray stone. High, double-lancet windows framed mosaics of stained glass that looked black, and drought had killed most of the ivy that crawled up the walls. Hudson was surprised to find the large front door unlocked, and even more surprised by his lack of hesitancy in entering. Fading sun tinted the nave with reddish light; as he approached, his nostrils flared at a smell like urine and something more revolting. He passed empty pews, crossed the chancel. Several apsidal rooms arched behind the altar, two empty but on the floor of one he found, oddly, a coping saw. Hudson ran his fingers along the thin blade and found it tacky. Could it be blood? *No, no, that's ridiculous,* he felt sure. It was probably tar or something, resin, maybe. Nevertheless, the saw irked him and he stepped quickly out.

Tires crunching over gravel alerted him; he hustled to a rear window in the dressing room where, in fading light, he saw a black car pulling out.

What would I have done if it was pulling IN?

And who might be driving it?

Probably just smoochers, he resolved. Or, in this area? A drug deal.

A draped baptistery stood to his right. Did he hear something? Hudson put an eye to the gap in the scarlet drapes, and seized up.

"Yeah, yeah," a man with his pants down huffed. He was in his fifties, graying hair on the sides of a bald pate, and he wore a dress shirt and tie. His cheeks billowed at the obvious activity at his groin. He stood before another man who was on his knees—a fetid, homeless man. Hudson could swear he saw flies buzzing around the bum's horrifically sweat-stained ball cap. Six inches of dirty beard jutted from his chin as his head bobbed frenetically back and forth.

Hudson pulled the curtain back. "This is a church, for God's sake!"

The corpulent client's face turned sheet white. "Shit! Shit shit shit!" he shrieked. He yanked his overlarge slacks up and barreled out of the baptistery, stumbled down the nave, and banged through the front door.

The homeless man raged. "You fucker, man!" Spittle flew from his chapped lips. "That was my trick, man! He was gonna pay me twenty bucks! I ought to kill you, man!"

Hudson stepped back, not nearly as afraid as he'd expect himself to be. "Relax." He kept his cool. "I was just looking around. Here." He handed the bum a twenty-dollar bill.

The bum turned instantly joyous. "Cool, thanks. Gimme another twenty and I'll do you, too."

"No. No, thanks," Hudson said, realizing now that the

man's beard was one of the scariest things he'd ever seen. "Who *are* you?"

"Forbes," said the bum.

"*Forbes?* So . . . Forbes, this is where you . . . do . . . business? A church?"

When the bum scratched his beard, dandruff fell like salt from a shaker. "Aw, Deaconess Wilson, she's cool. Let's me sleep here at night as long as I'm out by five in the morning." Now he lifted the liner out of the baptismal font and drank the water in it. "I feel bad 'cos, see, she sleeps upstairs and sometimes I sneak up there and watch her take showers and shit. She's got the best boobs—"

I know, Hudson thought.

"—and this big, gorgeous fur-burger on her, man. *Blonde.* And I just can't help it. I see *that* all wet and shiny in the shower, I just *gotta* beat off. Shit." He grinned, showing rotten gums. "Guess I'll probably go to Hell, huh?"

"They say only God can judge," Hudson said lamely.

The bum scratched his ass. "She gives me canned food a lot, too, makes me feel even guiltier. I guess I'm just a shit. It sucks when ya have to eat your own nut just for the calories, ya know? You ever do that?"

Hudson paled. "Uh, no."

"Yeah, man, when you're homeless ya gotta do it 'cos there's, like, a couple hundred calories in it. Been times it's the only thing that kept me from starvin'."

Hudson felt staggered. "There's a soup kitchen on Fifteenth Street. Forbes, *please.* Go there instead."

"Really?" The bum beamed. "Didn't know. But what're *you* doin' here, man? You a friend of Deaconess Wilson?"

Finally a topic of conversation he could take part in. "Not really, but I did meet her once. Do you know where she is?"

The bum reached down into the front of his rotten

jeans and scratched. It sounded like sandpaper. "Disappeared, they say, but . . . I don't know about that." He pulled his hand out and sniffed it. "See, when I'm sleepin' in here at night, sometimes I think I hear her coming in. I can hear her car."

"A black car?"

"Yeah. Old black car."

Interesting. "I just saw a black car pulling out of the lot behind the church."

"Shit! Really?" The bum scampered past Hudson, leaving dizzying B.O. in his wake. "Ain't there now," he said, peering out the window.

"Maybe she'll be back," Hudson contemplated. "Or maybe it wasn't her." He eyed the bum. "Say, did she ever mention a strange word to you? The word *Senary?*"

Forbes was only half listening. "Naw, never heard no word like that." He picked his nose and nonchalantly ate what his finger brought out.

What am I DOING here? Hudson asked himself.

The window was turning dark, and at once the bum seemed edgy. "Shit, it's sundown—"

Sundown, Hudson repeated.

"—and I gotta get out."

"But I thought you said you slept here."

"Yeah but I ain't gonna do that no more," Forbes said, and shuffled back toward the chancel. "Every night since the deaconess been gone, I have me these really scary dreams."

Hudson didn't know what compelled him to ask, "What . . . dreams?"

The bum's eyes looked cloudy. "Aw, weird, sick shit, man, like in some city where the sky's red and there's smoke comin' out of the sewer grates on every street, and black things flyin' in the air and other things crawling up and down these buildings that are, like, a mile high, and people gettin' their guts hauled out their asses and these big gray *things* eatin' girls' faces off their heads and drownin' kids in barrels'a blood and playin' catch with babies on pitchforks'n shit, and then, then this giant statue with the scariest face—oh, yeah, and a house, man. A house made of heads . . ."

Hudson stared.

"—and, fuck, last week, right before Deaconess Wilson disappeared, I was sleepin' in the pews and dreamed that these *monsters* were fuckin' with her, and reading all this evil shit like Latin or something."

"Monsters?"

"Yeah, man. Like, just skin-covered bones and horns in their heads. Had teeth like nails made of glass. They hadda bunch of candles burnin' in a circle and layin' inside the circle was Deaconess Wilson with no clothes on, man." Now Forbes looked sickened in the recollection. "They started writin' on her, man. They're *writin'* on her, with *shit*, but it wasn't just any ole shit—it was *Satan's* shit. Somehow I knew that in the dream."

Hudson was getting unnerved. He didn't believe in shared delusions or shared nightmares. But . . .

Forbes started toward the front door, but kept talking. "And last night, shit. I dreamed I seen the deaconess walkin' around here buck naked with her big tits and bush stickin' out, but ya know what she was carryin'?"

"Whuh-what?" Hudson grated.

"A coffin, man." He kept walking, his voice echoic in the nave. "But it was a *little* coffin. Like a *baby's*. So, shit on that, ya know? I ain't sleepin' here no more 'cos this place gives me fucked-up dreams." Rotten sneakers scuffed as the bum pushed open the front door and left.

Jesus, Hudson thought in the fading light.

He had every intention of following the man out, but for some reason his steps took him not toward the door but to the left, along the sides of the pews. He shined his flashlight beneath one, caught a breath in his chest, then knelt.

A shovel had been stashed there. Hudson fingered the earth on the blade and found it—

Fresh . . .

There was also a pair of work gloves on the floor that appeared soiled but recently purchased.

What the hell is this?

Stashed under the last pew in the farthest corner was a coffin.

A *little* coffin. Like a baby's.

The sun had sunk quickly, like something trying to escape. Hudson looked up and down the street to find it oddly vacant. The drab housefront peered back at him as if with disdain. *The Larken House,* he thought. *A MURDER house.*

Of course, Hudson didn't believe that a *house* could influence people by the things that had happened in it. *A HOUSE can't have power . . .* But maybe *belief* was the power. Could a person's *conception* of terrible events create the influence?

Hudson wasn't sure why he would even consider such a thing. It simply occurred to him.

He traversed the weed-cracked front path, surprised by his boldness, and opened the screen door. *No way the door's unlocked,* he predicted. That would be senseless.

The oddest door knocker faced him. It had been mounted on the old door's center stile, an oval of tarnished bronze depicting a morose half-formed face. Just two eyes, no mouth, no other features. The notion made Hudson shiver:

I knock on the door and Larken answers . . .

"Here goes," he muttered, then thought a tiny prayer, *God, protect me.* He grabbed the knob and turned it.

The door opened.

An unqualified odor assailed him when he entered. Not

garbage or excrement or urine but just something faintly . . . *foul.* Hudson snapped on his flashlight, panned it around the empty living room. His stomach sunk when he discerned brown footprints tracked over the threadbare carpet. *Old blood,* he reasoned. *From the murder night.* The compulsion to leave couldn't have been more pronounced but, *I have to stay,* he ordered himself. *I have to find out what this is all about.* He followed the footprints to a begrimed kitchen and was sickened worse when he saw great brown shapes of more dried blood all over the linoleum floor. The footprints proceeded to the microwave. *Larken must've killed his wife and the baby in here.* He eyed the kitchen table and gulped. In the corner stood a chair directly under a water pipe. *And that's where he hanged himself . . .*

Then Hudson froze at a sound: a quick *snap!*

A cigarette lighter?

That's what it reminded him of. His heart hammered. This was crazy and he knew it. An abandoned house in *this* neighborhood? *Vagrants, addicts, or gang members . . .*

Yet he didn't leave.

He turned the flashlight off and walked down a shabby side-hall toward the sound. He paused and, sure enough, in a dark bedroom he detected what could only be the flicker of a cigarette lighter. In addition, he heard an accompanying sound, like someone inhaling with desperation.

I could be killed . . . so why don't I leave? Hudson had no answer to this logical question, save for, *God will protect me. He HAS to.* When he took a step forward, the floor creaked.

His heart nearly stopped when a woman's voice shot out of the dark. "Oh, good, you're back. I'm in here." Then the lighter flicked again but this time to light a candle.

In the bloom of light, Hudson couldn't believe his eyes.

A woman sat on a mattressless box spring, holding a crack pipe. A white woman, with dark lank hair, wearing a bikini top and cutoff shorts. The hostile face glared at him.

"Shit, you're not her," she complained. "Who the . . ." But then she squinted. "Wait a minute, I remember you . . ."

Indeed, and Hudson remembered her. It was the pregnant prostitute he'd seen in the Qwik-Mart last night. It didn't take him long to realize why she looked different.

She was no longer pregnant.

"Yes," Hudson droned. "At the store. And I see that you've had your baby."

She maintained her glare. The huge breasts hung satcheled in the faded top. Her exposed midriff below the top looked corrugated now, rowed. All she said was, "What the fuck are *you* doing here? Are you with that woman?"

That woman, Hudson's brain ticked. "Do you mean . . . a blonde woman in a black gown? A white collar?"

The prostitute idly fingered groovelike stretch marks on her belly. "Yeah, like what a fuckin' priest wears, but it's a chick, not a guy." Then she calmly lit the pipe, inhaled deeply, then collapsed against the wall. Her expression turned to a mask of oblivion.

"What is this woman to you? Deaconess Wilson?" Hudson actually raised his voice.

The prostitute slipped up the stuffed bikini top to cover a great half circle of nipple. "She paid me six fuckin' hundred bucks, that's what."

Hudson was dismayed. *And I got 6,000.* "So, you've won the Senary as well?"

"I don't know what the fuck you're talking about. All I know is what I'm supposed to do."

"And what was that? What *did* you do for the six hundred?"

She shrugged. "Dug up a grave. Think I give a shit?"

Hudson stared in the flickering light, thinking of the article. "Was it . . . a child's grave?"

"Yeah, man. A baby's. She said the baby was murdered in this house, had its head cut off. Said she needed the head."

Confusion circled round Hudson like a feisty crow. "But . . . what happened to *your* baby? You were pregnant last night."

"I popped the kid out behind the Qwik-Mart," she said, pressing another piece of crack into the pipe. "Fuckin' mess. I dropped it in one of those blue bins the recycling trucks pick up; then I split. Couple hours later, I met *her*."

"And she—"

"Paid me six hundred bucks to dig up the grave." She sucked off the pipe and chuckled. "Kind'a weird, you know? An hour after I dump my own baby, this chick pays me to dig up somebody *else's* baby. Ain't that a trip?"

"Yes," Hudson uttered. "A trip . . ."

"She waited for me in her car. Didn't even take as long as you'd think, and the coffin was tiny, barely weighed anything. They always say six feet under, right? But this was like two, three. So I put the coffin in the back of her car, and she drives me downtown . . . and gave me six hundred bucks. Said she'd give me another six hundred if I showed up tonight. Said she needed me, said she needed my milk."

"Your *milk?* What on earth for?"

She shrugged again, and reloaded the pipe. "Said 'cos I was lactating. You think I care?" She held up a baggie full of pieces of crack. "I mean, *look* at all this rock, man. And when she lays another six hundred on me tonight? I won't have to blow another guy for a month. Fuck, I hate it. Crack doesn't leave a woman with any choice. You have to suck ten dirty dicks a day at least, just to keep up your jones. Think about that, buddy. Ten dicks a day. It's like letting guys blow their nose in your mouth for money. Every time I see another dick in my face I wanna cut my throat but I know that if I do . . ." She jiggled the bag of crack. "I'll never be able to get high again."

Hudson frowned. "Deaconess Wilson told me I won a contest of some sort, and told me to meet her here. Where is she?"

"Right here," answered a silhouette in the doorway.

Hudson grimaced from the shock. "God *damn!* Don't sneak up on people like that!"

The female minister stepped forward into the candle-light. Her face appeared either blank or simply content and her blue eyes, which struck Hudson as dull yesterday, seemed narrow and keen now. She wore the same black surplice and white collar.

"How irregular for you to take God's name in vain," she said. "You of all people—one who yearns to be a priest."

He had, hadn't he? He *never* did that. "You scared the shit out of me," he objected. "Now what's all this about? And furthermore, what are *you* all about?"

She glanced at the prostitute, who was relighting her pipe.

"What I'm all about, Mr. Hudson," the deaconess began, "is failure. You, on the other hand, are about success. I envy you—" Her voice hushed. "And I honor you."

"That makes no sense. I should leave."

"That is your prerogative, it has been all along. Didn't I make it clear that you are under no obligation?"

"Yes, but—"

"And now you want answers. First, answers about me."

"You got that right. A homeless guy living in your church had the same dream as me. I read an article in the paper about a baby's grave dug up, and it turns out this girl over here is the one who did the digging. And a half hour ago I see the coffin stuck beneath the pews at *your* church."

"It's all part of the science—"

Hudson's anger roiled. "The *science?*"

"You'll understand more should you choose to proceed far enough to speak to the Trustee."

Hudson opened his mouth to object further, paused, then decided not to.

Her eyes appeared as cool blue embers. "Do you choose to proceed?"

"Yes," Hudson said.

"Then follow me." The deaconess touched the prostitute's shoulder. "Come along. You bring the candles." Then she raised a plastic bag from which depended an object inside about the size of a softball. "I'll bring the head."

Chapter Three

(I)

A hundred Pipe Fitters—mostly half-Demon, half-Human Hybrids—clustered down below about the Main Sub-Inlet. *What are they doing?* Favius wondered, looking down from his precipitous sentry post on the ramparts. This was the end of the stupendous Pipeway that, Favius knew now, started all the way across the Quarter in the harbor of Rot Port. The Conscript studied the end of the Pipeway's Inlet, a great circular maw sixty-six feet wide. He marveled at the sheer *volume* of fluid that the Pipeway would be able to transfer. But still he thought, *Why? Why?* And what were the Technologists *doing* down there now? Teams of the Hybrids began scaling the Inlet's outer rim via ladders made of cured intestines, while others remained in the basin as if in wait . . .

But in only minutes more prison wagons hauled by strange, mutant beasts crossed the basin itself and stopped.

Immediately, Favius thought, *Corpulites* . . .

From the bared wagons, dozens of unfortunate victims were extracted: naked Hybrids bred especially by the Hexegenic Factories. Naked, yes, and bald, blinded, and bulbously obese. The Corpulites were a particular Organic Materials invention—living beings whose deliberately corrupted gene mechanisms caused grievous obesity. Satchels of fat hung from the arms, legs, bellies, and backs of captives. Horned Scythers were quickly dispatched, wielding great flensing blades, which expertly carved slabs of fat from the shrieking contingent. The blades glimmered, each downward flashing arc dividing still more fat from the living bodies of the Corpulites.

Now Favius's question had been answered. The fat was then passed up to the Pipe Fitters scaling the Inlet and promptly used to grease the fitting seams.

An immense shadow crawled past the perimeter; Favius was not surprised to see Levitators moving in a huge Y-connector. *Magnificent,* he thought. The screams of the butchered Corpulites soared like a thick breeze as Scythers continued to slough off the necessary fat, and when the great seam had been sufficiently greased . . .

Incantations boomed from megaphones, retarding the Levitation Spell and hence lowering the Y-joint perfectly into place, after which the Pipe Fitters amassed to lock down the bolts with their spanners.

Favius understood now—the Y-joint split the direction of catastrophic inflow into dual directions, making dispersion more even and efficient.

When the Fitters were done, they disembarked from the site on Balloon Skiffs, onto their next assignment. The Corpulites, however, were not so lucky. Now bereft of all body fat, they were left to bellow and squirm on the Reservoir's gritty black floor, knowing that eventually they would become one with whatever manner of filth soon filled this place to the brim.

Another great wonder on another day in Hell, the Conscript thought. *And I am honored to be a tiny part of it, a tiny part in Lucifer's plan.*

What greater gift could anyone ask?

(II)

So this is it, Krilid thought, half-queasy as he gazed down. It was in the mouth of an illegally duplicated Nectoport that he stood, leaning slightly out. The technology amazed him, and it verified rumors he'd heard for years that certain anti-Luciferic sects had engaged their own White Sorcerers to psychically steal the secrets from Lucifer's own Bio-Wizards and copy them for their own use. A Nectoport could be thought of as an invisible tunnel that, snakelike, covered great distances in seconds because it existed in a different phase-shift and therefore inverted true space—the ultimate achievement in occult science. The "tunnel" was reportedly capable of extending indefinitely, and all that was ever visible of it was the forward Egress and Observation Port.

But even with the security tether, Krilid found little piece of mind; the tether itself could break (causing a fatal fall), while this very assignment, for all he knew, could be bogus. In Hell, information was like character. One never knew what to trust—indeed, if trust even *existed* in this infernal sprawl.

Approximately a mile above the very spot in which Conscript Favius stood on his rampart, Krilid hovered. The spotty black clouds hid him fairly well, yet he could take no chances of detection. The clouds were patrolled now by demonic troops in balloons, and there were always the heinous Gremlins who lived and hunted in these clouds, semi-weightless monsters with saw-teeth and mouths that opened vertically beneath globose, black-veined eyes; not to mention untold flying things and Levatopuses, which were like bedbugs only they lived off the sooty waste in the clouds rather than a sleeper's blood. Krilid's direct field commander—the Fallen Angel Ezoriel—had provided not only the Nectoport but also a Hand of Glory, whose flame-tipped fingertips imparted a skirt of invisibility, which prevented unwelcome observers from seeing the Port's floating green rim of light.

Down there, he thought, staring at the Reservoir's nearly endless basin. Empty now, true, but soon it would be filled with six billion gallons of . . . something . . .

Something, yes. But *what?*

Krilid was a Hellborn Troll, squat, heavily muscled, but with a smushed head that looked lengthened and lopsided. This anomaly was caused through punishment a long time ago: Krilid had been captured by Municipal Golems, while stealing a box of Ghoul Steaks from a delivery vehicle in Boniface Square. He'd spent the night in a Constabulary jail, and the next day a Torture Detachment had slowly yanked his genitals off with pulleys, and then he'd been treated to the "Head-Bender," a later-model torture device in which the convict's head was placed in a specially constricted pipe-vise. Krilid's skull was pulverized to bits and then remolded, whereupon a Re-Ossification Spell caused the crushed bone to adhere after the fact. The pain was incalculable, such that he prayed they'd kill him and be done with it—Trolls, unlike the Human Damned, were mortal—but the officers of the Constabulary would have none of that. It served Satan far better for the deformed to *live*, protracting their misery.

And miserable Krilid had been, but he'd also been *mad. Being born a Troll is bad enough*, he knew, *but having to walk the streets with a bent head is even worse.*

Krilid wanted revenge. He could kill himself, sure, and then this horrific existence would be behind him, but somehow, now, that wasn't good enough. And going back to a life of petty crime seemed boring and scary. *Those bastards bent my head, damn it, so I'm going to get them back.*

That's when Krilid had joined an anti-Luciferic terrorist cell.

Ezoriel himself had recruited him, and through some manner of clairvoyance had already known of the dismal Troll's angst, pain, and yearning for revenge. "Serve God, in this place *abandoned* by God," the Fallen Angel had told him in a voice that shimmered. His face shimmered, too, like sunlight on a rippling lake, such that its details could not be perceived. "Join the Contumacy and be a part of God's glory when we overthrow Lucifer and take over. After that, rest assured—we shall convert this canyon of sin, hatred, and blasphemy into a place of hope, a place full of the love of God."

Krilid didn't know from God, but Ezoriel's recruitment speech was just what he'd needed to hear. These people were *terrorists* who raided, bombed, harassed, and/or destroyed anything or anyone serving the Morning Star. The Troll's biggest beef was with the Torture Detachment; hence, Ezoriel had granted his first request: to drop Sulphur Bombs on the place from the Nectoport. He'd scored multiple direct hits.

Since then, he'd bombed several targets in the Industrial Zone, had kidnapped a Grand Duke, had taken out several demonic police chiefs with a matchlock muzzleloader, and had helped blow up the Central Research Grotto at the Klaus Barbie District's Hexegenic Virus Labyrinth. They used a separate Nectoport to pipe in millions of cubic yards of methane pilfered from the Waste Pits at the city's largest Pulping Station, then set it off with limelight bombs. Most of the Labyrinth's service passages had collapsed, while the Central Research Grotto had exploded with such force it had cause a Hellquake that split the District in half. Krilid had partied hard that night at Ezoriel's fortress, and had even been rewarded with a liter of distilled water.

Now, though?

The Troll wondered as he hovered. His sextant showed him the area that Ezoriel had called the "Target Extraction Point," and on *this* mission, the "target" wasn't a building, nor was it a living target to be assassinated. Instead it was a living target to be "extracted."

Alive.

If the intel was correct.

Krilid identified a landmark after adjusting the sextant's gauges to accommodate the coordinates: "Sixty-six cubits out from the Reservoir's southernmost corner, where you'll see the Main Sub-Inlet," Ezoriel had told him.

The landmark—hard as it was to see against the Wandermast Reservoir's unrelenting *black*—was a particular pile of bodies from an Emaciation Squad. They'd died on their feet digging out this immense quarry and, via protocol, their twitching, unnourished bodies would be left to shudder there until the Reservoir was filled. When this happened, the landmark would be submerged, he knew, but at least he now had a general idea where to look for the "target" to be "extracted."

I'm not liking this, Krilid thought.

Was he being set up? The thought occurred to him, but any logical reason didn't. Ezoriel is said to have never told a lie.

But bad information isn't a lie, is it?

Perhaps Ezoriel didn't know for sure. "Unimpeachable authority," the Fallen Angel had said of his information source. "It cannot be doubted."

Yeah? Krilid questioned.

Then why had he been sent on this mission totally *alone*, and in an expensive Nectoport? To attempt an "extraction" in what was certainly one of Hell's most guarded secret projects?

It almost sounded to Krilid that he'd been sent on a suicide mission but no one had seen fit to tell him that.

(III)

The echoes of the deaconess's words trailed behind her like a banner as they mounted the dark stairs. "The attic is the best place, for the power of its ambience. The cliché—do you understand? The sheer *weight* of the idea?"

"No, I *don't* understand," Hudson said, the whore just behind him.

"The same as the house itself, and what happened in the house. The house has become what's known as a Bleed-Point, while certain things from the *history* of the house serve as functional Totems. They're Power Relics."

Certain things, Hudson wondered. *She means the head . . .* "What did you mean when you called yourself a failure but I'm a success?"

He could see the woman nod ahead of him. "You're on one end of the Fulcrum, I'm on the other—the *bad* end, I'm afraid."

"The Fulcrum, huh?" Hudson said.

"I was solicited because I was solicitable. My ebbing faith made me ripe for the Machinators. But you? You're actually the opposite. It's the desire of the powers I now serve that you make the *choice*. My rewards are minuscule compared to the rewards you will receive should you accept this incalculable prize."

Great, Hudson thought.

The stairs raised them into a long, dusty attic. Even after dusk, it was stiflingly hot. The prostitute began lighting candles from a bag she'd carried up, and in the growing light, Hudson saw that the attic was essentially empty, save for a couple of lawn chairs and a couple of boxes. The deaconess went to the back wall, then paced off six steps toward the room's center. There, she placed one of the chairs.

"This is where you will sit."

From a darker corner, then, she pulled out—

Whoa! Hudson thought.

—a brand-new pickax.

"And this is how we will access the Trustee."

"What are you *talking* about?" Hudson whined.

The deaconess smiled. She removed her Roman collar and started to unbutton her surplice. "Remove your clothes, dear," she said to the prostitute. "We must show our God-given bodies unclothed, to curry favor from our lord."

The prostitute smirked. "I want my fuckin' money first. You said you'd give me another six hundred."

The bills were produced like a finger-snap, and handed over.

"Curry favor from your *lord?*" Hudson questioned. "Somehow I don't think you mean the Lord God."

"Our Lord Lucifer," the deaconess said. "Certainly, you've already guessed that."

"Yeah, sure. But the thing I want to know is how did those skinny demons manage to get a hold of your Lord Lucifer's *poop* to write sixes on your body?"

The deaconess popped out more buttons. "It's a process known as Object Transposition, a very new occult science. It's subdimensional. The Demons—and the excrement itself, by the way—were only corporeal for the duration of the rite. Six minutes. But six minutes were enough." Then she dropped the surplice to the floor, to stand splendidly nude in the candlelight.

Hudson tried not to gawp at the robust physique. "You seem different today. Yesterday you were all fidgety."

She went behind the prostitute to untie her faded bikini top. When the garment dropped, buoyant breasts came unloosed, with large, irregular nipples that looked like plops of chewed beef.

"That's because I've acclimated to the entails of the Machination Link. And I'm not resisting it anymore. I've accepted it, the beginning of my glorious demise. I'm being *machinated*, you see—by a trained Channeler and a high-echelon Archlock who operate out of a Telethesy Unit at the De Rais Academy." She smiled. "Think of it as puppeteering—from Hell. Only now my own soul has amalgamated with the process."

Hudson stared.

"Oh, and Mr. Hudson? You'll need to remove your clothes as well."

Hudson winced. "I'm not taking off my *clothes*, for God's sake."

"For Lucifer's, not God's. It's all part of the protocol, I'm afraid. You must be as naked as Adam when he stalked out of the garden."

What am I doing? came the thought as he began to strip. At least being nude would make the heat more tolerable. The deaconess and the whore were already shining with sweat.

Now the deaconess was inspecting the prostitute's heavy breasts, twilling the meaty nipples with her fingers. "Let's see here now," she murmured. Milk sprayed out at once. "Yes, good, so *full*." Then the deaconess tasted a wet fingertip. "Ah. Soiled. Perfect." Next her hand stroked up and down the recently deflated belly, whose stretch marks now looked like the gouges of a garden claw. An abundant sprawl of black pubic hair jutted nestlike from between the prostitute's pasty legs. The deaconess ran her fingers through it, fascinated. "So how many babies have come out of here, hmm?"

"Six, seven—fuck, I don't know," the prostitute said, disconcerted.

"And you left them *all* to die?"

"Yeah. Fuck it. The world's a bunch'a shit anyway. Who wants to bring kids up with all this shit goin' on? Besides, I make more money when I'm pregnant."

"Really? How interesting."

"Sure. Kink tricks, you know? Lotta guys out there go nuts for knocked-up streetwalkers. They pay more. So I pocket the cash, and when it's time, I pop the kid out in an alley somewhere and walk away."

"Perfect," whispered the deaconess.

Hudson felt sick.

WHAM! WHAM! WHAM!

Hudson *and* the prostitute jumped at the start. The sound of impact shook the house. When Hudson cleared his confusion, he noticed the deaconess–

WHAM!

—driving the pickax point with gusto into the wall. After a dozenish strikes, she'd managed to tear out a hole about the diameter of a dinner plate, roughly four feet from the floor.

Hudson peered out the hole, which showed the moonlit backyard. Then he refaced the deaconess.

"I ask you once more, Mr. Hudson. Do you wish to proceed?"

Hudson could feel the sweat pouring out of him. He wanted to say *no,* and he wanted to leave, but instead?

"Yes."

"I thought you would." And now she had the plastic bag again, and reached in. Hudson grimaced before she even extracted the contents: the rotten head of a baby.

The small face had dried to a rictus. But then Hudson noticed something even worse. The *top* of the head was missing.

The deaconess threw the head through the hole in the wall, where it landed, bouncing, in the scrub-laden backyard.

"But I thought—"

"That I needed it for a ritual of some sort?" the gleaming woman finished. The nipples on the high breasts stood out as if she were sexually frantic. "Not the head itself. This. The skullcap." And from the bag she produced just that: the top of the infant's skull, which had obviously been sawn off. At once Hudson recalled the smudged coping saw at the church.

She's really been busy.

"The brain had already putrefied." She showed him the inside of the empty dome. Then she raised her brow at the prostitute. "I'm afraid the newborn of our friend here wouldn't do. It hadn't lived long enough to be touched by Original Sin. It had to be *this* baby, from *this* house."

"And what did you *call* this house, earlier?" Hudson asked.

"A Bleed-Point," she said, her bare, flat stomach glistening. Droplets of sweat beaded in her pubic mound like clear little jewels. "Think of it as a sieve."

"A hole between here and Hell?" Hudson figured but couldn't believe what he'd said so convincingly and with such nonchalance.

"Yes, but only a semidimensional hole. A viewport, so to speak."

So if I look through this hole, I see Hell? But when he did it was still just the mangy backyard in view. He paused and narrowed his eyes, to glimpse a raccoon waddling away with what was left of the baby head.

Good Lord . . .

"Come on, I gotta crack it up," griped the prostitute, scratching at imaginary bugs on her stomach. "When can I go?"

"Be patient," the deaconess assured; then her eyes returned to Hudson's. "You're still under no obligation. You can still leave."

Hudson churned in place. *Haven't I seen enough?* Now

he was genuinely beginning to want to get away from all this.

"But why not continue? You can even say no *after* you've taken the tour."

The tour . . .

She smiled thinly over the exorbitant breasts. "And I can assure you, it's *quite* a tour."

"Let's continue," the words clicked in his throat.

"A venturous man, and a wise one . . ."

Really? Hudson wondered. *I'm standing naked in a ghetto house with a deaconess and a crack whore for some—some Satanic purpose.* What, though? A *tour?* What could that mean? Foremost, Hudson thought of himself as a Christian. He *believed* in the power of God, and in his own salvation. So why would he want to go on a tour of Hell?

Maybe . . . seeing Hell will make me a better priest . . . After all, Christ descended into Hell after his Crucifixion, only to reascend on the Third Day, the resurrected Son of God.

The house creaked. The veil of candlelight wavering on the attic walls seemed to darken . . .

"Over here now, my dear," the deaconess said, positioning the prostitute behind Hudson.

"What the fuck's this all about?" she protested.

The deaconess touched her shoulder. "It's about you earning your money, just as *Judas* earned his." And then onto Hudson's bare back she squirted a liberal amount of baby oil from a small bottle. "Rub your hands around, dear, his back, his buttocks, his legs, but in motions like this . . ." The deaconess then put a hand on Hudson's back, and through the oil made motions that were invariably like *sixes.*

"Like sixes," she said. "You do the back, I'll do the front."

The prostitute frowned, then proceeded.

More warm oil was applied to Hudson's chest, and then Deaconess Wilson's adroit hands began to massage it in.

She smiled, rubbing six after six after six over his gleaming skin.

Hudson stood petrified, arms and legs rigid at the luxuriant sensations that seemed to envelop him. Never in his life had he been touched so directly, so intimately by women. *This is the ultimate tease,* he thought, gritting his teeth. The prostitute's hands swept slowly about his clenched buttocks, while those of the deaconess smoothed over his nipples, then down across his stomach, then—painstakingly—around his groin and over his inner thighs. The sensations began to crush him, and when he looked down, his arousal was plain.

"He needs to be stimulated till he can't see straight." Now the deaconess's grin looked vulpine, her hands stoking him. "He needs to be *titillated* till he's fit to *burst.* He needs to be *bursting* with sperm."

Madness, Hudson thought. Each sixlike motion over his slick skin made Hudson feel as though he were standing on a high wire. Now the deaconess urged herself right up against him. He cringed in place as the large, slippery breasts slid over his skin. The confusion blankened his mind until all he could contemplate was lust even as he strained to resist it. She bowed his head down, placed a nipple in his mouth, and whispered, "Suck . . ."

Hudson did so, uncomprehending. The nipple swelled in his mouth to the size of a bonbon; meanwhile, her hand played over his stomach, then slid to his genitals, which caused him to lurch. Fingers teased him, not overtly, but only traceably.

All right, I can't let this go on anymore, he determined, but then the woman's fingers seemed to sense the thought, and began to fondle him more pointedly.

"Harder now," she told him, and switched nipples.

It seemed the harder he sucked the nipple, the more of his will drifted away. Suddenly, Hudson was lost, lost in unreckonable sensations, lost in this brazen sin of flesh. His erection throbbed against her hot belly as the fingers played further. He was sucking the nipple so obsessively that sometimes he forgot to breathe, which caused him to break, gasp, and then begin sucking again. One of her hands played with the back of his head, as a mother's might. Hudson had to wrap his arms around her to keep from falling.

The deaconess chuckled in his ear. "They were definitely right when they told me you'd like this."

They, Hudson thought, but kept sucking.

This went on for minutes and minutes; Hudson was cross-eyed when she pulled her breasts away and then actually looked at her watch.

"You're . . . *timing* this?" came the nearly delirious query.

"Oh, yes."

He managed a frown, even as the voracious sensations rose. "Let me guess. Sixty-six minutes?"

"Of course," she whispered. "Only thirty-four to go now. Try to enjoy every one of them. The more excited you are, and the more seed you produce, the more positive the conduction."

"The conduction," he groaned. His penis felt *strained*. It felt like a spring about to break.

The desire to climax was excruciating, and his desire for that to happen wiped his mind, even as his unheard thoughts stretched like rubber bands: *I can't-I can't-I can't let this happen . . .*

The deaconess had leaned briefly away, and returned.

Where did she—

She came back, but seemed intent on her watch. Hudson felt brainless now, his body nothing but an arrangement of frantic sexual nerves beginning to short-circuit. Then—

"Now, now," she snapped abruptly and took Hudson's erection into her mouth. Her lips stroked over it at a mad

ALAMEDA FREE LIBRARY

speed; Hudson was reeling—knowing the dreadful *sin* of it all, knowing that he *must* pull away and leave this evil place, but before he could—

His climax occurred like an ash can going off. The deaconess mewled as Hudson felt his ejaculation belt into her mouth, and when he was finally finished, he fell over.

The orgasm had beclouded him. The prostitute crawled to a corner, muttering, "Bunch'a nutty bullshit." When Hudson looked again, the deaconess was spitting his copious ejaculation into the baby's skullcap. It looked like a mouthful of thin yogurt.

"This really is some fucked-up shit," the prostitute remarked, but then the deaconess was briskly approaching her.

"Up, up! Quickly."

"Hey!" the prostitute squealed when the other woman's hand grabbed her hair and lifted.

"The seed must be covered without delay—"

The deaconess held the top of the baby's skull beneath one of the prostitute's sodden breasts, and with her fingers she began to urgently milk the nipple. The white fluid sprayed out at first, then began to dribble. "As much as possible. Help me."

The prostitute looked disgusted when she girded the breast with her hands and squeezed. The extra pressure trebled the volume of milk coming out. When the lactation began to peter out, the process was switched over to the other breast.

Hudson could only watch, head spinning.

"Good, good," the deaconess murmured, transfixed. By the time the second breast had been exhausted, the skullcap was over an inch deep with milk.

"Now . . ."

Hudson stared, and so did the prostitute. The deaconess stood firmly with her legs parted. She lowered the skullcap to her crotch.

What's she going to do?

The prostitute shrieked, and even Hudson yelled aloud in his stupefaction. A tiny glint showed him what the deaconess had produced: a razor blade, which she immediately slipped right up the middle of her clitoris.

Instead of screaming, herself, she moaned in what could only be ecstasy.

"Lady, you're fuckin' cracked!" spat the prostitute. Hudson looked away but something kept dragging his eyes back to the event. Two fingers were kneading the split clitoris, squeezing out blood. The blood ran right into the skullcap.

"There," she announced when she was done. Between the sperm, the milk, and the blood, now the skullcap was over half-full.

"Can I *go* now?" the prostitute asked.

"Bring me that box," the deaconess said, "and remove the stand, then, yes, you may be on your way." She held the skullcap ever so carefully, so not to spill its macabre contents, while the sickened whore dragged a cardboard box to the room's center, then removed a Sterno stand.

Hudson thought, *Why do I think we're NOT going to be cooking a Chinese pupu platter?*

"Set the stand immediately below the hole in the wall, please."

The prostitute's pallid breasts depended as she leaned to do so. She glared at the deaconess, half in derision and half in nausea. "Look, I know that I'm one of the most fucked-up people to ever be born but, shit, lady. This shit here? It's even more fucked up than me."

"Go with the blessing of the Morning Star," the deaconess said with a great pumpkin grin. "Take your money and your drugs and your hatred and despair, and give thanks as you revel in your curse. Spread your degradation in the glory of his name, sell your body to the lustful, and indulge yourself in reverence to him. Have *more* babies to leave to die in gutters, and spread *more* disease, and continue to let yourself be used as a reservoir of filth and an altar for every offense against God . . ."

The prostitute stared.

"One day, you will receive a wondrous reward . . ."

The prostitute raked up her clothes, then barged out of the room, and thunked down the stairs. A moment later, Hudson heard the front door slam.

The deaconess looked at Hudson. "Do you wish to continue?"

He wanted to say *no* with all his heart, yet something . . . Something made him say, "Yes."

"Good." She smiled over the skullcap. "Let's begin . . ."

Hudson sat mute in the chair as he watched her. It didn't surprise him when she placed the skullcap atop the Sterno stand, though he couldn't imagine why. From the box she also withdrew the strangest of objects: a foot-long cutting of ordinary garden hose.

A match flared as she bent to light the Sterno.

"Bubble-bubble, toil and trouble?" he misquoted *Macbeth*.

"These are powerful cabalistic components, Mr. Hudson." The bleeding between her legs had ceased, leaving her pubic hair matted crimson and the insides of her toned thighs streaked. "What you need to know is that in Hell, ideas are objects, notions are material, symbols are tangible *things* wielded as tools or burned as fuel, and the waste of lust is the Devil's *favorite* tool. Symbols of fecundity and creation when turned to waste become occult energy."

"Milk, sperm? Come on," Hudson challenged.

"Yes! What a great spoiler of God's intent. Mother's milk but from the teat of a mother who *murders* her babies. And sperm, sacred by God's gift of procreation, but sullied when spilled deliberately outside of the womb—a harrowing offense. And now . . . blood . . . The blood of the chaste, virginity upheld to honor the chastity of Christ, and then spoiled for this atrocious ministration to bid the glorious and unholy power of Lucifer."

Hudson looked perplexed at the skullcap sitting above the flame, and then he looked into the hole in the wall.

Just nighttime outside.

"Don't get it."

"You will, once you really *see*." Her naked body gleamed, not merely from the profuse sweating but from excitement. The candlelight crawled. "It's all science, or I should say sorcery, which serves as science in Lucifer's domain. What we're doing here is called an Ethereal Viewing. I told you, this house is a Bleed-Point; the horrors that occurred here have bruised the skin between the Living World and Hell. This rite will eventually *nick* that bruise enough that you'll actually be able to see the Trustee, and converse with him, too."

"The Trustee," Hudson muttered. "A demon?"

"Possibly. I'm not sure. But *I* won't be able to see him. Only you."

"Why?"

Two perfect drops of sweat dripped off the tips of her nipples. "Because *you're* the person who's won the Senary. There's not much more I need to say to prepare you." She stood behind him and errantly rubbed his shoulders. "Just sit and wait . . . and reflect on the fact that *very few* people ever receive an opportunity such as this."

Hudson jerked his head back. "But why? Why me? And *don't* say it's because I won the Senary!"

"Just be patient."

"So . . . what? When all that crap in the baby skull starts to boil, the hole in the wall becomes a window to Hell? I'm supposed to believe that?"

Her fingers glided hard over his sweat-slick shoulders, then slid forward to rub his pectorals. "That's as good a way of putting it as any. Upon boiling, the steam that rises off the Elixir will trigger the Conduction. You'll have exactly six minutes to listen to the Trustee, ask any questions you have, and then accept or reject the offer. And even if you accept, which I pray you'll do, you're under no obligation. Nothing becomes binding unless you say yes upon completion of the tour."

The tour . . . Those words bothered him more, perhaps, than anything else tonight. There was something potent about them. Even when he *thought* the words, they seemed to echo as if they were called down from a mountain precipice.

But then more thoughts dripped. "This is a pact with the Devil, you mean."

"Not a pact. A gift. One thing to keep in mind. The Devil doesn't *need* to offer contracts for souls very often these days. Think about that . . ."

Hudson's eyes narrowed. "But I'm a *Christian*. I'm a theologian and student of Christ. I'm about to go to the *seminary*. To be a *priest!*"

Her voice drifted in delight. "Perhaps what you see will dissuade you. Your reward will be beyond imagination."

Hudson gave her remark some thought, even in the "afterglow" of his sin. *So THAT'S it! They want to tempt me, they want to make me break.* Suddenly the madness and sheer impossibly of everything made wild sense.

What greater way could there be to prove his faith? To take this tour and realize these rewards, only to say no in the end? Christ had been tempted, hadn't he? Only to likewise say no.

Hudson resolved to do the same.

The prospect made him gleeful, but then he heard the faintest bubbling. The contents of the skullcap—the Elixir—was boiling.

"It's time," she whispered and stepped away. "Look at the hole in the wall . . . and prepare to meet the Trustee."

Hudson tensed in his seat, squinting. The teeming night was all that continued to look back at him from the hole. The steam wafting off the skullcap was nearly nonexistent. *How on earth can*—but after a single blink . . .

The hole changed.

In that blink the hole's ragged boundary of Sheetrock and shingles had metamorphosed into something like ragged flaps of what he would only think of as organ meat. Hudson leaned forward, focused.

My God . . .

What he looked at now was a room, or at least a room of sorts. *Is that . . . No, it couldn't be,* he thought, because the room's walls appeared to be composed of sheets of what looked like butcher's waste (intestines, sinew, bone chips, and fat), which had all somehow been frozen into configuration. Amid all this sat a splintery wooden table on which had been placed . . .

That's a typewriter! Hudson realized, and he could even read the manufacturer: Remington. Atop a shelf in the rear, more odd objects could be seen: a package of Williams shaving soap, a square tin of Mavis talcum powder, and an empty can of Heinz beans. Hudson meant to glance behind him, to question the deaconess, but her hands firmly pressed his temples.

"Don't take your eyes off the Egress," she said.

When Hudson refocused on the hole . . . a man stepped into view.

The Trustee . . .

It was a very gaunt, stoop-shouldered man who looked back at Hudson. "There you are, at last," he said in a squeaky accent that sounded like New England. He had close-cropped hair shiny with tonic and a vaguely receding hairline to show a vast forehead, which gave the man an instant air of learnedness. He wore a well-fitting but threadbare and very faded blue suit, a white dress shirt, and narrow tie with light and dark gray stripes. Small, round spectacles. His jaw seemed prominent as though he suffered from a malocclusion. The only thing about him that wasn't normal was the pallor of his face. It was as white and shiny as snow just beginning to melt but marbled ever so faintly with a bruised blue.

The man sat down at the rickety table. He paused momentarily to frown at the typewriter, then his eyes—which were bright in spite of the death pallor—looked directly at Hudson.

"I presume the Senarial Messenger has apprized you of the fact that we're subject to a considerable time constraint, the equivalent in your world of six minutes. So we must be concise and, above all, declarative," the man said. "My name is Howard, and I bear the curious title of this term's 'Trustee to the Office of the Senary,' and I'm speaking to you from a Scrivenry at the Seaton Hall of Automatic Writers. It's located in a quite malodorous Prefect dubiously known as the Offal District . . ." Abruptly, then, he smirked. "Are you able to hear me, sir?"

Hudson's mouth hung open for a time, but he eventually managed to say, "Yes . . ."

"Splendid. It's my infernal pleasure to tell you that you've won the Senary—"

"What's the Senary?" Hudson blurted.

"Denotatively? From the Latin *senarius:* anything of or relating to the number *six.* But here we're only concerned with its *con*notation. The Senary is a drawing, in a sense, but those eligible are not random. Aspects of your own . . . resolve present the most pertinent considerations. Let me reiterate, we must be expeditious, and as I have no way of discerning that constant unit of measure known as time, your colleague will alert you when one minute remains. Do you understand?"

"No."

"That is immaterial. You've been invited to partake in a—"

"A tour of Hell?" Hudson interrupted.

"Quite right. Only a smattering of persons, in all of Human history, have received this lauded opportunity. Indeed, you're one of a privileged lot. It is guaranteed that no harm will come to your physical body, nor your Auric Substance, should you choose to proceed. You will be returned, intact, to make your final decision. At the end, in other words, you'll be free to return to your normal life, should you so choose. But I can say to you, sir, that in 6,660 years . . . no Senary winner has ever elected to *not* accept the prize."

Hudson could think of nothing to say, save for, "I-I-I . . ."

This man, Howard, held up a warning finger. "We mustn't be frivolous with verbosity, sir—I can only presume that time is growing short, so without further delay, I must show you the Containment Orb." Then he reached beneath the table and brought something up—something on a stick.

"Huh?" Hudson uttered.

The object on the stick, about the size of a basketball, looked brown, mottled, and, somehow, organic. A twist at the top reminded Hudson of a pumpkin's clipped stem, and in the middle of the bizarre thing was a half-inch hole. Howard pointed to the hole. "The intake bung is here, as you can perceive—"

"But, what *is* that thing? It looks like a brown *pumpkin*."

"Hell's rendering, you might say—in specificity, the *Feotidemonis Vulgaris*, commonly referred to as a Snot-Gourd. It's been eviscerated completely, of course, and disenchanted by Archlocks, so to serve as your Auric Carrier. And—"

Howard swiveled the peculiar fruit on the stick, to reveal its other side—

"Holy shit!" Hudson profaned.

A semblance of a face existed on the other side of the *thing.* Two eyeballs had been sunk into the pulp; below that, a large, pointed snout as of some oversize rodent had been affixed. Also a pair of fleshy lips, and lastly, two ears, though the ears were maroon and pointed.

First he thought of a nightmare rendition of Mr. Potato Head, but then thought, *A jack-o'-lantern from Hell,* but just as he began his next question, the deaconess tapped him from behind. "Tell the Trustee there's only one minute left."

Hudson bumbled, "Uh, uh, I'm supposed to tell you—"

"So I've gathered," Howard said, still holding up the hideous brown fruit with a face. "By now, it's my hope that you can cogitate the entails of what awaits; hence, I ask you, sir . . . Do you choose to proceed?"

Hudson blinked. *No obligation,* his thoughts raced. *Guaranteed that no harm can come to me, that I'll be returned intact . . .*

And my opportunity to be the first in history to say no to their faces . . .

"I ask once more, sir. Do you choose to proceed?"

"Yes!" Hudson whispered.

Howard seemed to smile, however thinly. "A wise choice. I look forward to our coming discourse. Tell the Senarial Messenger I'm at the ready." Then Howard stood up and came round the table. He turned the Snot-Gourd back around and held the side with the hole in it up to the hole in the wall . . .

The deaconess looked longingly at Hudson. "Do you have . . . any idea how privileged you are?"

A tour . . . of Hell. He wiped his face off in his hands. "I don't even know how to answer that. Oh, and the guy says he's ready."

"Can you still see the Auric Carrier?"

Hudson looked back up. In the opening, the appalling fruit remained, showing the hole cut in it. "Yeah. It's a . . . messed-up pumpkin, and there's a hole in it. He called it a Snot-Gourd."

"Hmm, all right . . ."

"But he's blocking the hole in the wall with it. Don't I crawl through the hole?"

"Oh, no. Via this ritual, nothing solid can move from here to there, and vice versa."

"Then how—"

"Remember, nothing *solid*. Be careful; make sure the end of the hose doesn't actually *touch* the intake opening in the gourd. Try to keep it a few millimeters away—"

Hudson shot her a funky look. "What?"

"It's your *breath* that will be transferred from here to there," the deaconess explained. "On this side, it's just breath, but on *that* side . . ." And before Hudson could even plead for more information, the deaconess got him out of the seat and urged him closer to the wall. In her hand now she held the short length of garden hose, one end of which she moved toward his mouth.

His eyes flicked to the bubbling skullcap. "No way I'm drinking that crap!"

"Of course not. You *breathe* it—the fumes."

When Hudson's lips parted to object further, she placed the hose in his mouth.

"It's time, Mr. Hudson. I'll be waiting for you when you come back." She pressed his shoulders with her hand, to gesture him to lean over. She held the other end of the hose into the faint steam coming off the Elixir. "Now. Count to six, then inhale once very deeply and hold it . . ."

Hudson's lips tightened around the hose. *I can't believe I'm going to do this . . .* And then in his mind he counted to six and took a hard suck on the hose.

The warm air tasted meaty in his mouth. The fumes made his lungs feel glittery.

"Keep holding it," he was instructed; then the other end of the hose was placed in his hand. "Now, once you've lined the end up . . . exhale as hard as you can."

Hudson's cheeks bloated. Very carefully he manipulated the end of the hose to fit over the hole in the gourd—

—and exhaled.

Hudson's soul left his body, and he collapsed to the floor.

Part Two
Grand Tour

Chapter Four

(I)

Perfect, Gerold thought, and that's exactly how it looked. He'd tied the hangman's noose as though he were an expert, and when Gerold appraised it on the balcony of his second-story apartment—at three A.M.—he felt a comforting satisfaction. He secured the other end to his balcony rail.

Suddenly the moment was in his face.

How do I feel?

The warm night seemed to throb from without: insects issuing their endless chorus. The moon hovered, light like white icing.

I feel great.

In that instant, then, he realized that this was a great night to die, and Gerold was not only okay with that, he was ecstatic.

He'd bussed earlier to Home Depot for the rope after working his shift at the air-conditioning company where he processed calls and kept the books. "Can I have tomorrow off?" he'd asked the boss when his shift was done, only because he didn't want to leave them hanging.

He *himself* would be the one hanging.

"In *this* economy?" the boss laughed. "*Sure* you can have tomorrow off."

No more struggles, no more buses passing him by for the

inconvenience of lowering their wheelchair ramp, no more pretty girls passing him on the street as though he didn't exist.

His gaze stretched out into the moon-tinged darkness. *Yes! A great night to die!*

Someone in the morning, probably walking their dog, would see him hanging. Gerold knew he'd have a smile on his face.

He placed the noose about his neck and tightened it down. He felt no reservations. But when he put his hands on the rail, to haul himself up and fling himself off . . .

"Hey! You up there!"

Gerold was appalled when he looked down.

"Don't do it!"

"Aw, shit, man!" Gerold yelled. Just down below, some old guy with a splotch on his head like that guy from Russia was walking his Jack Russell. "Nobody walks their damn dog at three in the morning!"

The dog yelped up at him, tail stump wagging. The old man had his cell phone out. "I'm calling the cops—"

"No, please, man! Gimme a break!"

"Don't do it!"

In *seconds,* it seemed, he could hear sirens.

Quick! Now! Gerold grabbed the rail, his muscles flexing.

"What's going on up there?" said the old biddy from the balcony below. She looked up, curlers in her hair. Across the way, lights snapped on in various apartments. Figures appeared on balconies.

"That young man above you is trying to hang himself!"

Gerold had himself half propped up on the rail, when he heard pounding at his front door.

You've got to be shitting me . . . He knew he didn't have time now—the door exploded open and hard footfalls thunked toward him.

Disgusted, Gerold lowered himself back in the chair,

and took off the noose. *This is so FUCKIN' embarrassing! Why can't people mind their own business?* He unraveled the noose and untied the other end just as two police officers barged out onto the balcony and jerked the chair away from the rail.

"It's all right, buddy," one of them said. The other cop, a sergeant with a pitted face, grumbled, "So much for a quiet shift."

"Look, it's not what you think," Gerold bumbled. "I was just . . ."

"Come on. We'll get you taken care of."

Another siren approached, an ambulance, no doubt.

"Life ain't that bad, pal."

As Gerold was rolled backward into the apartment, he saw that a crowd of spectators had gathered down below. *Shit, shit, shit, shit!* he thought, and then they took him down and out.

His face turned red. Were fifty people in pajamas and nightgowns congregated outside? It looked it.

Can't even fucking kill yourself without other people butting in, he thought, humiliated. He'd probably be in the papers tomorrow. His *boss* would see it, his landlord, the neighbors. They'd all think he was nuts. As they put him in the ambulance, he could see the headlines: DISTURBED VET TRIES TO KILL SELF BUT POLICE INTERVENE.

In the back of the ambulance, two EMTs said nothing as he was driven away. They were eating doughnuts.

I guess I just can't do anything right, Gerold thought, feeling like the perfect ass.

They took him straight to the local hospital, where a silent intern took his vital signs; then another intern wheeled him to an elevator and took him up. The first thing he saw upstairs when the doors opened was a sign: PSYCHIATRIC UNIT. He felt like a putz as a drab-faced admittance nurse rolled him down stark halls. Eventually an abrupt turn took him past blue-painted metal doors with chicken wire windows. Faces appeared in some of them. Voices bled from others. "Abandon hope, ye who enter here," someone said, and another: "Where's my cake?"

A dark-haired woman in a white lab coat eyed him from behind a desk when he was wheeled into an office. She looked tired and displeased. *Probably on call,* Gerold figured.

"Well, well, well." Her eyes were bloodshot when they scanned a computer screen on her desk, no doubt his records sent over from VA. "Gerold, I'm Dr. Willet. My, what an inconvenience you are."

Gerold was outraged. "*Sorry* about the inconvenience."

"Suicide is the coward's way out. There are patients in the quadriplegic ward who would sell their souls to be you."

"I know that," Gerold said. He wanted to spit. "I'd trade places with any of them. The fact is, I'm sick of living. I feel I have the right to kill myself."

The woman scowled. "Oh, but you don't. Life is a gift, Gerold, and suicide is a crime. It's a form of homicide, and you can be prosecuted for it."

"Come on," he scoffed.

"Not in this day and age, of course. Everyone's a victim, hmm?" She had large, fake eyelashes that looked whorish. "You're sick of living? Tell that to the people in the Sao Paulo ghettos, or Paraguay, or Chad. You're young, capable, and have a lot to contribute in spite of your disability. But, no. You'd rather *kill yourself* because you can't hack a little hardship. Tell the people in Sao Paulo or Paraguay or Chad about your hardship. Tell the people in the quad wards how miserable your life is."

I can't believe this! "You really know how to make a guy feel good."

"You should feel *ridiculous*, Gerold. You're wasting tax dollars and wasting time, when you should be *contributing*."

Gerold winced. "What, is this some new kind of behaviorist psychiatry?"

"You don't need a psychiatrist, you need a kick in the ass."

Wow, Gerold thought. *I picked the WRONG NIGHT to try to off myself.*

"There's nothing wrong with you mentally—I could tell that the second you rolled in here." The frown on her face kept sharpening as she continued looking at his records on the screen. "There are better ways to get attention—"

"Listen, lady! I don't want attention! I want to be dead! I'm sick of this!" Gerold bellowed. "It's my business."

"Well then next time, do it right. We've got people here who need genuine care. We don't have the time or money to screw around with whiny pains in the ass like you."

Gerold was flabbergasted.

"I hope they bill you for the 911 call, the police time, the EMT time, the fuel—everything," she said. Disgusted, she tapped a bit on her keyboard. "Tomorrow morning you'll be transferred to the VA hospital. Nurse!"

The drab nurse returned, rubbing sleep from her eyes.

"Take this upstanding gentlemen and pillar of the community to the precaution wing and get him a bed."

"Yes, Doctor."

When Dr. Willet came out from around her desk, she didn't do it on her feet. She did it in a wheelchair.

Her body was gone from the waist down.

Oh, my God, Gerold thought.

"I'd be sick to my stomach if I had one. You're a disgrace, Gerold. You ought to be ashamed of yourself." For the first time, the doctor smiled. "Now get the hell out of my office."

Gerold wished he could shrink into nonexistence when the nurse wheeled him away.

(II)

Your name is Hudson Hudson and you've just won the Senary. Your soul has been turned into gas and squeezed into Hell through a hole in the wall.

And here you are . . .

Regaining consciousness reminds you of the time you got your wisdom teeth pulled at the dentist's. You're a balloon underwater that has just risen to break the surface. First, senses, then awareness, then memory. The only difference is, that time you awoke into your physical body, but now . . .

I don't have one, comes the oddly calm realization.

There's a faint noise, something reverberant like water dripping in a subterranean grotto. Your eyes open in increments but only register scarlet murk, just as another sensation registers: rocking back and forth and up and down as if in a car with too much suspension. Your vision struggles for detail as the dripping fades, to be replaced by a steady metallic clattering along with a *hiss.*

Then your vision snaps into perfect, even surreal, focus.

The macabre lips on the Snot-Gourd scream.

You're in a vehicle of some kind, which idles down a street whose surface is chunks of wet bone, split ankles and elbows, and other odds and ends of meaty gristle. "How's that for your first glimpse of the Offal District?" comes the familiar New England accent. "My own reaction was much the same, but of course, that's why they *call* it the Offal District. It's constructed primarily with surplus scraps from the Pulping Stations: less-edible organs, joints, bits of bone."

You look up and scream again when you realize exactly what you're looking at: a very black sickle moon hanging in a scarlet sky.

The attempt to move your arms and legs comes reflexively; then you remember, *My body's back in the house with the deaconess, but my consciousness . . . is in the pumpkin . . .*

Your cue ball–size eyes blink. *I'm in Hell . . .*

"The Senarial Sciences here are impressively successful," Howard tells you, sitting off to the left. He cranes around and looks into your eyes as if looking into a fishbowl. "I trust your senses are in proper working order?"

"I . . . think so," you reply through the brutish, demonic lips.

"Your Auric Carrier is quite the top of the line." Now Howard is cleaning his round spectacles with his shirttail. "You have the mouth of a Howler-Demon, the eyes of an Ocularus, the nose of a Blood-Mole, and the ears of a City Imp. Each represents a superlative. It is with only the greatest acuity that we wish you to perceive everything."

"But, but—"

"Just relax, sir—if that possibility exists—and give your psyche time to acclimatize to the new environs, as well as the new vessel for your soul. There's no rush—answers to all your questions will be furnished. Just relax . . . and behold."

You try to nod. *Relax? Good Lord . . .* First, you focus on your immediate surroundings. You appear to be sitting in the elevated rear seat of a long automobile—that is, not actually sitting since you no longer possess a rump; instead your Auric Carrier has been mounted on a stick in this queer backseat. The clattering vehicle reminds you of pictures you've seen of cars from the 1920s, spoke-wheeled and long-hooded monstrosities like Duesenbergs and Packards. Yet no hood actually forms the vehicle's front end; instead there's a long iron cylinder showing bolts at its seams, and a petite pipe where one would expect a hood ornament. It's from this valve that steam hisses out.

Howard talks as if he can detect your thoughts. "It's a steam-car, the latest design, an Archimedes Model 6. It burns sulphur, not coal—Hell never enjoyed a Carboniferous Period." The car rocks over more chunks of butcher's waste. "The sulphur heats the blood and other organic waste in the boiler; steam is produced and, hence, mobility. Nothing like the motors of my day, I'm afraid, though I never liked them. Awful, soot- and smoke-belching contraptions. But this suffices more than, say, a buggy drawn by an Emaciation Squad."

You don't understand how your head—the Snot-Gourd—can turn upon the command of your will—*I'm just a fruit on a stick!*—nevertheless, it does, and now that you're getting used to it you find the courage to look upon the more distant surroundings with greater scrutiny.

The street *stinks,* and then you spot a globed pole that names the street: GUT-CAN LANE. Mottled storefronts whose bricks contain swirls of innards pass on either side. You notice more signs:

SCYTHER'S

PAYCHECKS NOT CASHED

THYMUS GRINDER'S

TOE-CHEESE COLLECTOR

A chalkboard before a café boasts the day's specials: BROILED BOWEL WITH CHIVES and BEER-BATTERED SHIT-FISH.

When the steam-car clamorously turns through a red light—Abattoir Boulevard—you detect buildings that appear residential, like festering, squat town houses whose walls are impossibly raised as preformed sheets of innards.

"I don't believe this place," you finally say. "Everything's made of . . . guts."

"Construction techniques differ greatly here from the Living World; where you utilize chemistry, physics, electrical engineering, we utilize Alchemy, Sorcerial Technology, *Agonitical* Engineering."

"But how can they make guts and bone chunks . . . *hold together?*"

"Gorgonization, Mr. Hudson," Howard replies and points past the vehicle's rim. "*Your* masons pour cement into molds and allow it to dry, ours pour *slaughterhouse residuum* and Gorgonize it with Hex-Clones of the Medusa's head."

You see what you can only guess are demonic construction workers emptying hoppers of butcher's waste into various sheet and brick molds. After which several cloaked figures with purplish auras walk slowly past the molds bearing severed heads on stakes. Each severed head has living snakes for hair. The horned construction workers are careful to look away from the process. Hoods are then placed over the Gorgon heads; then the molds are lifted, revealing solid bricks and wallboards fully hardened.

Impossible, you think. *And everything here is made of it . . .*

"Fascinating, eh?" Howard remarks as the car rattles on. "At any rate, untold Districts exist in Hell, to compose an endless city called the Mephistopolis. Lucifer prefers diversity to uniformity; therefore each District, Prefect, or Zone features its own decorative motif. You'll see more as we venture on."

Beyond, though, you have the impression of losing your breath when you see what sits beneath the bloodred sky. It's a panorama of evil, leaning skyscrapers that stretch on as far as you can see.

"Hell is a city," Howard explains, "which I didn't find all that surprising myself. Why would it be? More and more the Living World is becoming metropolitan, so why shouldn't Hell follow suit? Progress is relative, and so is evolvement, I suppose. Lucifer has seen to it that Hell progresses in step with Human civilization. It's only the *direction* of the steps that are antithetical. It provides for a rich environment, and more so in this District than most others." And then Howard's nose crinkles at an awful smell that reminds you of the Dumpster at the restaurant where you used to shuck oysters. "It's just that the smell is *appalling*, not to mention the clamor—a babel of filth and noise, a breeding pot of cheapness and vulgarity. This horror-imbrued place reminds me of New York City in 1924. Ugh! I hope you've never had the misfortune of visiting there, Mr. Hudson."

You try to frown again but then think of something. "Hey. How do you know my name? I didn't tell it to you back when we were doing the hole-in-the-wall thing."

"An Osmotic Incantation apprised me of everything about you. *Every aspect.* It's necessary, and part of my duties in this little side job of mine as the Trustee for the Office of the Senary."

"Side job? But didn't you say something about being a writer? That you worked in the Hall of Writers?"

"The *Seaton* Hall of *Automatic* Writers," Howard corrects. "One of many, but my facility devotes itself entirely to the writing of fiction. This is my forte; my job, since my Damnation, is to produce copy—novels, novellas, stories—which a select group of Wizards known as Trance Channelers then communicate to fiction writers in the Living World via the process of Automatic Writing and Slate Chalking. It's Lucifer's way of influencing worldly art forms so, quite wisely, he picks the most qualified of the Human Damned for the task."

A *writer*, you think, *in Hell?* "So . . . before you came here, you were a writer, too?"

"Indeed I was, sir, a writer of weird tales, and it's been conveyed to me that my work has since risen to considerable acclaim. Just my luck, eh? *Posthumous* acclaim—now I know how Poe felt."

"When did you die?"

"March 15, 1937—the Ides. Fitting that I should expire on the celebration day of the Mother Goddess Cybele. I penned a tale concerning that once but—drat!—my memory fails me. Something about rats . . . The Rats in the . . . House? The Rats in the . . . Tower?" Howard shakes his pale head. "Such are the pitfalls of Damnation. You're not allowed to remember anything gratifying. But it was some ballyhoo called Bright's disease that killed me—shrunk my kidneys down to walnuts—oh, and cancer of the colon. Too much coffee and soda crackers, I can only presume. It's no wonder 'The Evil Clergyman' wasn't very good." As Howard straightens his tie, he appraises the orb of your head with something hopeful in his eyes. "Are you a reader, sir? Perhaps you've heard of me—my name is Howard Phillips Lovecraft."

You strain your memory, picturing a beaten paperback with a foamy green face and glass shards pushing through the head. "Oh, yeah! You're the guy who wrote 'The Shuttered Room!' Wow, I *loved* that story!"

Howard's bluish white pallor turns pink as he stares, vibrating in his spring-loaded seat. Then he hangs his head over the side of the open-topped vehicle and throws up.

"Are you, are you all right?" you ask.

Howard regains his composure, slumping. "Sir, I can tell you with incontrovertible authority that I most certainly did *not* write 'The Shuttered Room.'"

"Oh, sorry. You know, I could've sworn that your name was on it."

Questions upon questions still bubble up in your gourdhead, but they all stall with every glimpse you take of the nefarious street. *Panels* of guts raised like Sheetrock, *cinder blocks* of such butcher's waste formed walls, sidewalks, and even entire buildings. You turn away as you drive past.

"And in the event that you're wondering," Howard mentions, "you're able to traverse the Snot-Gourd by means of a Psychic-Servo motor. Your impulses engage the gears."

You hadn't thought about that, nor about how the steam-car itself is even being maneuvered. "Is it some kind of black magic that's driving the car?"

"Not at all, and my apologies for failing to introduce you to our driver." Howard leans forward and pulls back a webbed canopy before them, which reveals a hidden driver's compartment whose bow tie–shaped steering wheel is surrounded by knobbed levers. Seated just behind the wheel is—

Holy SMOKES! you think.

—a stunningly beautiful nude woman. Hourglass curves rise up to grapefruit-size breasts, which offer nipples distending like overlarge Hershey's Kisses. By any sexist standard, she's perfect in every way . . . save for one anomaly.

She's made of clay.

"She has no name," Howard explains. "She's a Golemess. Dis-Enchanted riverbed clay is what she's made of. Her male counterpart—Golems—are quite larger, while these female versions are manufactured more petitely, and to be sexually provocative."

The wet grayish clay shines—indeed—as if a centerfold has been airbrushed. Her hair, however—on her head as well as between her fabulously toned legs—bears sculptor's marks.

A Golemess, huh? you think. *That's a pretty attractive piece of clay . . .*

"Quite a comely monster," Howard says, "though my detractors could hardly conceive of me making such an observation, I suppose. They said I was homosexual, for goodness sake, in spite of my having *married* a woman! Regrettably, though, love is quite temporary, and I'll admit, her pocketbook was impressive to a poor artist such as myself. But, more dread luck—barely a year after we were wed, she was dismissed from her lucrative position! We had to move into an absolutely *pestilent* rooming house in Brooklyn; one could scarcely distinguish between the tenants and the rodents! And forty dollars a month the slum barons charged!"

You hardly hear Howard's odd aside of petulance, in favor of scrutinizing the Golemess's astonishing features. She was what Randal would probably call a "brick shithouse," and . . .

You could literally build one out of her.

"Pardon my digression," Howard says. "It's just that I have so much rancor now—a sin, of course: wrath—but still . . ." Howard seems dejected. "I can scarcely believe that Seabury Quinn was the name of the day while I foundered on considerably lower tiers. Gad! Have you ever read his work? Let's hope not. As for the Golemess, you may be wondering if it's sexually *functional,* which I can happily or unhappily asseverate. Quite a lot in Hell is, for reasons that need not be expounded upon. The common veils of empiricism are no less prevalent here than in the Living World. So, too, are the notions of invidiousness. I was an atheist but hardly a *bad* sort, yet here I am. The circumstances which led to my Damnation are barely even explicable. You, on the other hand, are in quite another circumstance, hmm?"

Your pumpkin-face frowns; at least you are getting the knack of it now. But you barely understand your fussy tour guide. "Because I'm going to the seminary, to become a priest?"

Howard grimaces over a bump and another waft of organic stench. "Miasmal! Ah, but to respond to your legitimate query, you, Mr. Hudson, are more than just a priest-to-be, you're one who is spiritually well-placed on the—how shall I phrase it?—the plus side of the Fulcrum . . ."

Your furry brow arches. *The Fulcrum* . . . The deaconess had said something similar, hadn't she?

The steam-car, at last, pulls off the chunky pavement as the Golemess turns the wheel. A sign floats past: TOLL BOOTH AHEAD. You can't keep your thoughts straight.

"I just don't get it. The Fulcrum?"

"Think of the apothecarist's triple-beam balance," Howard tells you, "where the weights on one side are godly acts, and on the other side, *un*godly acts. Very recently, I'm told, you have tipped the scale to *100 percent* Salvation."

"Howard, I don't know what you're talking about."

"In spite of your *capacity* for sin—which all men and women possess—you've managed to clear the balance, from 99 percent, to 100. It is that achievement which has enabled you to win the Senary. You've tried with much diligence to lead a life that acknowledges God in the utmost, and when you *do* sin, you're truly sorry and you make every effort to repent. It's your own volition, Mr. Hudson, your own—and I emphasize—your own free will. That notion alone—free will—provides the summation of it all."

The steam of your soul feels hot in confusion. "Free will? A triple-beam balance? Ninety-nine to 100 percent?"

"Your excursion several nights ago? The Scriptures state quite interestingly that 'a whore is a deep ditch.'"

The line rings a bell in your bizarre head. *Those two hookers at the Lounge the other night* . . . "You don't mean—"

"You had decided in your heart that you would partake in the delights of two ladies of the night? You even willingly ventured to procure the necessary funds, yet, at the last moment you decided to bestow those funds upon someone else, someone in grievous need . . ."

The redneck woman with the two kids at the Dollar General! you remember.

"And what you hitherto purveyed was what God perceived as the ultimate act of charity, so said St. Luke,

'Whosoever has two coats must share with one who has none . . .'"

Your jaw, however awkwardly, drops. "I gave the money to the poor woman instead of the two bar whores . . ."

"Indeed," Howard says, half smiling. "And that gesture suffices. Allow me to convey it this way: if you were to die right now, your soul would ascend to the Kingdom of Heaven in a most instantaneous manner, where you would live in the Glory of God, forever."

You feel a vast echo in your psyche.

When Howard taps the shapely clay shoulder of the Golemess, the steam-car stops, and he looks right at you, probably for effect.

"Lucifer wants that 100 percent, Mr. Hudson, and he's willing to pay *exorbitantly* for it . . ."

Your head seems to quiver. "I—"

"Of course, it's much to take in, and it's our good fortune that our previous time constraint no longer exists, so put your multitudinous questions aside for a bit, and enjoy the ride . . ."

You take the advice as the car clatters on, though you have to admit, there's not much to enjoy. You seem to be leaving the Offal District through an archway in a great fortresslike wall of hardened organic waste via blocks the size of minibuses. Next comes a road of crushed sulphur, which grinds grittily beneath the car's narrow tires. "Here a toll, there a toll, everywhere a toll," Howard complains as they idle up to a shack whose single occupant is a man with a face axed down the middle.

"Toll," the attendant somehow utters.

Howard hands him a canvas sack that contains something the size of a melon. The toll-taker peeks in, nods, then waves them on.

"What was in the bag?" you have to ask.

"The gonad of an immature Spermatagoyle. They sell

them to wealthy culinarists and executive chefs who carefully extract the seminiferous tubules. It's a favorite dish of Grand Dukes, Barons, and the higher Nobiliary, for it's the closest thing you'll ever get to spaghetti in Hell." Howard's brow raises. "But I suppose you're a bit of a culinarist yourself. It's my understanding that you are an oysterman, yes?"

"I used to shuck oysters in a tourist trap," you append.

"Ah, the fruits of the sea. I grew up in a veritable *nexus* of shellfish and crustaceans. Oysters as large as your open hand, and lobsters the size of infants." Then Howard's face seems to corrugate in aggravation. "And wouldn't you know it? My iodine allergy prevented me from being able to eat *any of it!*"

Poor guy, you think.

"And though you excelled in university," Howard states the dim truth, "you might be interested to know that it was understandably forecast that I would surely do the same at Brown University, but—curse Pegana—my shattered nerves—thanks to a mother off her rocker—foreclosed the possibility of my even graduating high school. Lo, I would never be a university man . . ."

This guy really gets off track, you think. "Where are we going?"

"The Humanus Viaduct, which runs from the Dermas District to Corpus Peak, crossing the Styx."

DERMABURG, reads a skin-toned sign that floats by.

Howard gestures the sign. "This District is made of—as you may have ascertained—skin." And as Howard speaks the words, your Ocularus eyes remain peeled on the new surroundings. Row houses and squat buildings line the fleshy street, all covered by variously colored cuttings of skin. Some seem papered with dermal sheets as impeccable as the skin of the deaconess, while other edifices suffer from acne and other outbreaks. The car, then, turns right at a perspiry intersection. You glimpse the sign: FASCIA BLVD.

"A whole town made of skin?"

"These days, the majority of it is Hexegenically Engineered, save for the loftier real estate here, south of town, where *natural* epidermis is procured. Oh, there's a City Flensing Crew now . . ."

You notice the activities on one corner, where a troop of beastly, slug-skinned things with horns, talons, and terrifying musculatures prepare themselves around a row of Humans pilloried nude. Cuts are made at the back of each victim's neck, taloned fingers slide in, and then the entire "body suit" of epidermis is sloughed off, leaving the victim skinless from the neck down.

You wince as the beasts go right down the line.

"The attendants are called Ushers, a longtime purebreed that serve as government workers and police," Howard explains. "Human skin is much more valuable."

"Ushers," you murmur. "So they . . . peel the skin off and then—"

"Stretch it over wall frames." Then Howard points again.

At the opposing corner, workmen congregate at a corner unit (more of the hunched, implike creatures) to evidently build an addition. But when two of them raise a wall frame, you see that long, banded-together bones comprise each strut rather than two-by-fours. After the frame has been erected, other workmen stretch skin over it.

As for the pilloried "victims," you see that they're actually willing participants; when released—skinless now—an Usher hands them some money, then sends them on their way.

"Lucifer prefers Hell's denizens to *choose* to sell their skin, rather than merely taking it," Howard says.

"They *sell* their own skin?"

"For narcotics. The Department of Addictions has devised delights that make de Quincey's opiates and Poe's liquor seem paltry. Few can rehabilitate themselves, but when they do, they're forced into a Retoxification Center."

You watch the skinless queues trudge to a nearby fleshy alley, where an overcoated Imp in sunglasses waits to sell them various bags of cryptic powders. When one Human woman—who'd been attractive before her flensing—failed to produce sufficient funds, the Imp said, "A blow job or an ovary. You know the prices, lady," and then he parts his overcoat to sport a large maroon penis covered with barnacles. "To hell with that," she says, then sits down, crosses her ankles behind her neck, and sticks a hand into her sex.

You don't watch the rest.

The Golemess turns onto another road called Scleraderma Street, where some of the structures have hair growing on their roofs; others have collapsed to ramshackle piles from some dermatological disease; one has broken out into shingles, another is covered with warts.

And on another corner, you glimpse another sign: SKINAPLEX.

"What's that?"

"The motion picture show? They're rather similar here as in the Living World. And perhaps you'll be satisfied to know that Fritz Lang and D. W. Griffith are *still* honing their art."

Now you can see the marquee, complete with blinking lights: TRIPLE FEATURE! THE SIX COMMANDMENTS—WITHERING HEIGHTS—ALL DOGS GO TO HELL.

"Can we get out of here?" you plead. "I've had enough of skin-town."

Howard chuckles. "Save for the revolting B.O., it's actually one of the more sedate Districts. You'll be happy to know, however, that we're merely passing through."

The last row of houses, you notice, are actually sweating. As you pass the District gates, more glaze-eyed denizens straggle in and head to the pillories.

Now the road rises through a yellow fog so thick, you can't make out the endless scarlet sky. "So now it's the . . ."

"The Humanus Viaduct. It begins at a lofty elevation and provides a spectacular view. Lucifer wants you to be fully aware of the *immensity* of the Mephistopolis . . ."

Lucifer wants me . . . Your thoughts stall.

"He hopes that you'll want to return."

Now your monstrous lips actually laugh. "Fat chance of that! So far I've seen a town made of *guts* and a town made of *skin!* What, he thinks I want to move in?"

"The *immensity*, Mr. Hudson, and in that immensity you'll consider the value to someone of your very *privileged* status."

"I still don't understand what you—"

Howard holds up a pale hand. "Later, Mr. Hudson. There's still much more for you to envisage . . ."

The car chugs ever upward, and in the fog, you can swear you catch glimpses of horrid, stretched faces showing fangs in vertical mouths.

"Gremlins," Howard specifies. "Wretched little things. They live in fog, swamp gas, and clouds, and even are said to have cities in the higher noctilucent formations."

You spy more fangs snapping in a split second. "But-but-but—"

"Nothing can do us harm, so you needn't fear, Mr. Hudson." Past the buxom driver's shoulder, Howard points to a trinket of some kind dangling from the rearview mirror: a small metal Kewpie of a robed man holding a staff in one hand and an upside-down baby in the other. The pewtery detail implies that the baby's throat has been slit, and its blood is trickling into a bucket. "We're protected by the St. Exsanguinatius Medallion. It's quite a potent Totem."

Great, you think.

The car lumbers on, and Howard slouches back and begins to idly hum a tune, which seems aggravatingly familiar. In time, the name comes to you: "Yes, We Have No Bananas."

Finally, the fog expels the steam-car onto a high, rough-hewn mountain pass. You yell out loud when you peer over the side and see less than an inch of the cliff-road's surface sticking out past the outer side of the tire. "There's no safety rails!" you shout.

Howard frowns. "That would hardly be logical in Hell, Mr. Hudson. Now, if you'll put your consternation aside, I'll welcome you to one of our attractions here: Corpus Peak. Corpus Peak is a man-made—er, pardon me—a Demon-made mountain. It is composed, in fact, of exactly one billion Demon corpses . . ."

When the words finally register, you grind your teeth and peer once again over the side, and in a few moments it's the image that begins to register, however grimly. The vast side of the "mountain" sweeps down hundreds of feet, and in it, you notice the rigor-mortis'd cadavers of Demons.

"A-a-a *mountain* of dead Demons?"

"That's correct. The first billion Hellborn, in fact, to die under Lucifer's initial scourge when he took over. All manner of demonic species: Imps, Trolls, Gargoyles, Griffins, Ghouls, Incubi, Succubi—everything. The Morning Star wanted his first monument to be symbolic. 'Serve me or die.' He liked it so much that he ordered the highest echelon Bio-Wizards to put a Pristinization Hex on the entire mountain. The corpses, in other words, will never decompose."

You keep staring at the twisted faces and limbs of the mountainside. *Kind of makes the Hoover Dam look like Tinkertoys.*

"And below," Howard adds, "the abyssal river Styx."

Only then do you let your vision span out, to a ghastly, twisting waterway of black ooze marbled with something red. "*What* is it called?"

"The Styx!" Howard exclaims. "It's the most renowned river in all of mythology! Surely you've read Homer!"

"Oh, yeah, that's right. I forgot about that one. But I was thinking of the rock band." You try to shrug. "Never got into them."

The noxious river is so distant you can't see details but you can make out tiny things like boats floating on the putrid surface as well as swarming, dark shapes beneath. Every so often, some colossal *thing* breaks the surface, swallows a boat in its pestiferous maw, then resubmerges.

You're grateful for the distraction of still another sign: THE DEPARTMENT OF PASSES AND BYWAYS UNWELCOMES YOU TO THE HUMANUS VIADUCT. You envisioned yourself gulping when you get a good look at this "bridge," which stretches miles from the top of the corpse-mountain, across the appalling river, to a polygonal black structure sitting atop another mountain (this one of pinkish rock). The sights are spectacular in their own horrific way, yet your thoughts can only dread what must be to come.

The bridge—this Humanus Viaduct—is scarcely ten feet wide and consists of objects like railroad ties lashed together, one after another—countless thousands of them—which all comprise the spans of the bridge. A meager rope-rail can be seen stretching on either side.

"We're not driving the car over that, are we!" you object.

"Why, of course, we are," Howard says. "The view is thrilling, and it's crucial that you be thrilled."

"No way, man! That bridge looks like something in a damn Tarzan movie! It'll never hold us!"

"Mr. Hudson, please, don't worry yourself. Naturally the Viaduct has been charged by various Levitation Spells."

You try to feel reassured. You can see the rickety bridge sway in a sudden hot gust, and as the car rises to the gatehouse, your vantage point rises as well. Now you can see the surface of the links.

And all at once, you don't need to be told why it's called the *Humanus* Viaduct.

Atop the links of railroad ties exist a virtual carpet of naked human beings, who have all been lashed together as well. All these people—like the ties, thousands upon thousands—form the actual driving surface of the bridge.

You can only stare when you rattle through the gatehouse and pull in. The Golemess robotically shifts the vehicle into a lower gear; then you lurch forward.

"We're driving on *people,* for God's sake!" In a panic you look down. "And they're still alive!"

"Indeed, they are. Hell exists, in general, as a domain of all conceivable horror, where every ideology functions as an offense against God. But in particular, it's a domain of punishment. Hence, the 'human asphalt' beneath us."

They chug onward, narrow tires rolling over bellies, throats, faces, and shins. You watch the faces grimace and wail. "How come they don't die?"

"They're the Human Damned—who *cannot* die. That is why they call it Damnation; it's eternal. Only Demons and Hybrids can die here, for they have no souls. But as for the Human Damned, their bodies are nearly as eternal as their spirits. When your soul is delivered to Hell, you receive what we call a Spirit Body that's identical to the body you lived in on Earth. Only total destruction can 'kill' a Spirit Body, in which case the soul is spirited into the Hellborn life form with the closest propinquity. It could slip into something as large as an Abhorasaur, something as commonplace as an Imp, or something as minuscule as a Pus-Aphid."

Men bellow, women shriek, as the steam-car rocks on. Rib cages crack and sink inward, bones snap.

Yet in spite of the horror you're witnessing, more questions spin in your mind. "Great, but I don't have a 'Spirit Body.' I have a *pumpkin*—"

"A Snot-Gourd."

"Okay, so what happens if this *Snot-Gourd* gets destroyed?"

"An astute question but immaterial. Should your Auric Carrier be subject to mishap, your Etheric Tether would simply drag your soul back to your physical body at the Larken House. But I say immaterial since you are not, as yet, one of the Human Damned."

As yet, you consider. *I'm not Damned . . . but they WANT me to be?*

The Viaduct sways back and forth as the car lumbers ahead. In the middle—with already several miles behind them—the bridge dips so severely that you feel certain it will break from the vehicle's weight. *Levitation Spell, my ass.* But soon enough, you begin to ascend again, that queer black shape drawing closer. You think of a pyramid with a flat top.

"So what's with the pyramid-looking thing? A rest stop, I hope."

"A pyramid? Really, Mr. Hudson, you must've studied your geometry with the same zeal you studied Homer. It's not a pyramid, it's a trisoctahedron: a quadrilateral polygon bearing no parallel sides, also referred to as a trapezohedron. Lucifer is very much enamored of polygons, because in Hell, geometry is thoroughly non-Euclidian. Planes and the angles at which they exist serve as a heady occult brew. I wrote of such stuff and wonder now from whence the ideas arrived." Howard seems to be trying to recollect something. "Gad, I do hope my Shining Trapezohedron in 'Haunter of the Dark' was born of my own creativity and not that of some sheepshank scrivener in Hell." Suddenly a look of utter dread comes to his marbled face. "What a cosmic outrage that would be."

You still don't know what he's talking about, but in an attempt to divert your attention from the staggering height, you offer, "Maybe it was Lucifer's idea, and *he's* the one who piped it into your head."

"Impossible," Howard quickly replies. "Fallen Angels, though essentially immortal, are completely estranged from creativity and imagination. Every idea, every occult equation and sorcerial theorem, every ghastly erection of architecture, and even every invention of social disorder—it all comes from a single source: the Human Damned."

This is getting too deep for me, you consider. Your pumpkin-head reels—or it would have, if it could. Now you think of ski lifts carrying skiers to the peaks, only there's no snow here, just craggy rock pink as the inside of a cheek. As you near the black polygon, you discern that it's about the size of Randal's Qwik-Mart. Just when it appears that the steam-car would drive directly into the polished black side of the thing, an opening forms: a lopsided triangle that stretches from the size of a Dorito to an aperture sizeable enough to admit the car.

Well, that was nifty . . . I guess. Relief washes over your psyche; the Humanus Viaduct is at last behind you. *But now what?*

"Welcome to the Cahooey Turnstile," Howard says, "a superior mode of entertaining your tour. The process saves us from driving for untold thousands of miles."

"What do you mean, turnstile?" you counter. "You mean like in a subway?"

"Think, instead, of an occult revolving door."

A revolving door . . . to where?

The aperture closes silently behind, leaving you to peer around the unevenly walled room of smooth black planes. It looks like something born of science fiction, save for the sputtering torches that light the chamber. Then—

Whoa!

A shadow moves. When the Golemess shuts down the steam-car, you see the hulking shape approach: a sinewy Demon with meat cleavers for hands and a helmet fashioned from the jaws of some outrageous beast. Below the forward rim of teeth like Indian arrowheads, two tiny eyes bulge, and there are two rimmed holes for nostrils but no mouth. No ears can be seen either but only plugs of lead that seem to fill two holes where the ears *should* be. Some manner of cured hide covered with plates make up the Demon's armor. Reddish brown muscles throb when it regards the car.

"What the HELL is that?"

Howard answers. "The Keeper of the Turnstile, Mr. Hudson—an Imperial Truncator, of the genus *Bellicosus Silere*. It can't hear or speak; it can only observe and *act*. The Imperial Conditioning is self-evident; note the spread jaws of a Ghor-Hound which suffice for the helm."

You notice it, all right, but don't like the way it approaches the car.

"Should the Truncator entertain even a single anti-Luciferic thought? Those jaws slam shut and bite off the top of its head."

Hard-core, you think. "And its his job is to—"

"Anyone or thing who enters the Turnstile without authority," Howard says, "will be diced into bits, tittles, and orts."

Just as the sentinel's cleaverlike hands raise, the Golemess lithely leaves the car and shows it a sheet of yellowed parchment.

The guard nods, steps back, yet oddly beckons the Golemess with one of its hooks. In the torchlight, you wince at the stark beauty of the clay-made creature, the flawless curves, the high, tumescent breasts and jutting gray-plug nipples. The Golemess follows the Demon to a cozy corner, and drops to its knees.

"What's that all about?"

"It's customary for authorized guests to give succor to the sentinel," Howard says with some relief. "Another toll, so to speak. I can only thank the Fates that this particular Truncator is of the *heterosexual* variety."

You get the gist as you watch the Golemess unbutton a front flap on the Demon's armor, revealing its penis, if it could be called that.

"You gotta be kidding me!" you exclaim. "That's it's-it's-it's—"

Howard sees fit to not respond.

The limp shaft of the Truncator's penis looks like six red arteries grouped together, perhaps as thin as six-foot-long lengths of aquarium tube. You wince worse at the scrotum, which looks more like a cluster of Concord grapes, but even more appalling is the Demon's glans: a pink, lopsided sphere of shining flesh at the end of the corded shaft, tennis ball–size, with not one but half a dozen urethral ducts.

You look away when the Golemess begins to . . . render oral "succor."

Howard grabs the stick on which your head is affixed and climbs out of the car.

"So . . . what now?"

"Time to charge the Turnstile," Howard says. "It's quite a fascinating apparatus which harnesses cabalistic energy lines that exist in the Hex-Flux—Hell's version of electromagnetics—and effects what we refer to as Spatial Displacement—one of Lucifer's favorite cosmological sciences." And with that—which you understand none of—Howard approaches a black-plane wall. There, you see a circle of engraved notches; at each notch there's a small geometric etching.

"So this is a revolving door through space and time?"

"Just space," Howard corrects. "There is no time in Hell. The use of this facility will give you the opportunity to see a variety of the Mephistopolis's landmarks, which we hope will impress you."

Impress me, you ponder, *enough to stay? Is that what he's talking about?*

Howard touches one of the etchings, then—

A great, nearly electronic hum fills the black room.

How do you like that jazz? you think.

The configuration increases in size until it's as large as a typical doorway. Yet a sheet of black static is all you see beyond the threshold. That's all you see, but what you hear is something else altogether:

Screams.

"Shall we go, Mr. Hudson?" Howard asks, holding your head-stick like an umbrella.

You feel stunned, half by curiosity and half by dread. "What about the Golemess? Shouldn't she go with us?"

Howard veers the stick aside, to show you the corner. "As you can observe, Mr. Hudson. The Golemess is . . . detained."

"Oh."

Howard smiles and adjusts his spectacles. He steps through the uneven doorway of black static and takes you through . . .

Even though you don't have a stomach, a nauseating sensation rises up. Stepping through the egress feels like stepping off a high window ledge; you expect a deadly impact but none arrives. Instead you hear a crackling that sounds more organic than electric. Fear seals your eyes and you scream, plummeting . . .

"We haven't fallen even a millimeter, Mr. Hudson," Howard chuckles. "It's merely the nature of the concentrated Flux we've just traversed."

Your head feels overly buoyant when you open your eyes. You leave them open only long enough to see that you are on a cacophonic street clogged with monsters, steam-cars, and carriages drawn by horned horses that look leprous.

Flies the size of finches buzz around sundry corpse-piles on corners, a sign stuck in each pile: RECYCLE BY FEDERAL ORDER. You notice the sidewalk as well as the walls of most buildings are made of roughly crushed bones and teeth hardened within pale mortar. One storefront window boasts TORSOS: HUMAN & HELLBORN—ON SALE, and another window has been streaked on the inside with blood: OUT OF BUSINESS.

The sheer noise prevents you from ordering your thoughts: the clang of metal, the sound of hammer to stone, shouts—"Come back with my ears, you Imp fuck!"—vehicular horns that sound more like the brays of tortured animals.

"Pandemonium in sound and vision," Howard says, wending down the stained sidewalk with your head-stick in his hand. "Take the opportunity to look around."

This is the mistake.

As far as "looking around" goes, there's nothing to see save for horror and revulsion. In no time, you find that when you dare look at something, your psyche is arrested by some adrenaline-packed inner scream—perhaps the sound of your soul rebelling at the wrongness of this place.

A *city, a city,* you keep thinking in a panic. *Hell is a city . . .*

You can only look for a second at a time, in grueling snatches that demand an alternating surcease. Each "snatch" shows you something either horrific or impossible:

—blood-streaked skyscrapers rising higher than any building on Earth, each leaning this way or that. When one collapses in the distance, before the churning bloodred sky, hundreds leap off corroded balconies with wizened shrieks—

—street gutters gushing with lumpy muck over which dilapidated Demons and Humans—obviously homeless—hunt for tidbits, while packs of cackling Broodren—Hell's children—stalk through the sidewalk horde hunting for the elderly or the defenseless to quickly eviscerate so to make off with their organs—

—Arachni-Watchers, like spiders the size of box turtles, crawling up walls and across high ledges. A cluster of eyeballs form the body, ever watching from all directions for citizen behavior in violation of current Luciferic Laws. Psychic nerve sacs at the body's core immediately transmit real-time hectographs of infractions to the nearest Constabulary Stations—

—streets, gutters, and alleyways aswarm with indigenous vermin such as Bapho-Rats, Caco-Roaches, Brick-Mites, and Corpusculars, all hunting for the unsuspecting to infect, to ensile with larva, or to eat—

—shapely She-Demons—some brown, some black, some spotted—chatting inanely behind a salon window as trained Trolls paint their horns and administer pedicures with their teeth—

—sewer grates belching flame, while beneath the iron grills faces strain, screaming, charred fingers wriggling in the gaps. Over some grates more Broodren roast severed feet on sticks—

—hot-air balloons floating in and out of soot-colored clouds overhead, each suspending iron-bolted baskets from which dog-faced Conscripts dump buckets of infectious waste, molten gold, or Gargoylic Acid onto the masses below. The skin of the warped balloons reads SATANIC NOBLE GAS FLEET—

—more storefront windows passing by. LIVE SEX WITH THE DEAD SHOW! LIVE PULPING SHOW! LIVE EYE-SUCKING SHOW! LIVE HALVING SHOW! When you peer into this latter window, you glimpse destitute Demons and half-breeds being drawn slowly across tables fitted with band saws, while spectators applaud from rows of theaterlike chairs—

—and Broodren, Broodren, and more Broodren—the hooligans of the Abyss—shifting stealthily through the throng with eyes bright and fangs sharp, absconding with whatever they can tear away from passersby: purses, wallets, skin, pudenda. One Broodren runs off with half of a Troll's face, only to be palmed flat into the sidewalk by a vigilant Golem—

—and a final dizzying scan of the noxious city's skyline: a sea of smoke, sinking rooftops, and screams; endless rot-encrusted buildings atilt; mile after mile of crackling power lines dipping from rusted towers decorated by corpses hanging from gibbets; evil winged things gliding through the mephitic air, forever and ever—

—and ever and ever . . .

. . . and then the "snatches" end.

"Of course, acclimation takes a while," Howard mentions. "But you'll scarcely take in anything with your eyes closed most of the time."

You're too afraid to take in another glimpse; it's all too tumultuous because you know that every impossibility here is utterly real. You open your eyes, then, to slits, careful . . .

"Here's something you'll find interesting . . ." Howard approaches a business establishment with a saloon-style swing-door as an entrance. The sign reads: LOODY'S MAMMIFERON TAPROOM.

"Taproom!" you exclaim. "Beer?"

"Regrettably not, Mr. Hudson. Kegs of lager aren't on the offering, just kegs—so to speak—of milk."

"Milk?"

"Mammiferons . . ."

You enter the narrow bar. Various Demons and Humans sit about slate tables sipping from crude metal cups.

Howard points to the craggy brick wall behind the bar top. There is, indeed, a row of "taps" as one would expect in a beer hall but . . .

Are those . . . BREASTS? you ask yourself.

"Mammiferons," Howard repeats. "They're Hexegenically manufactured; particularized genes are spliced and then enspelled, for the desired result."

All you can do is stare.

Six carriages of flesh hang along the wall, each sporting two bulbous breasts as large as basketballs. Veins pulse beneath the stretched, translucent skin. At first you think they must be torsos of preposterously endowed Human women but then you recall what Howard said about their "manufacture." Betwixt each pair of breasts there seems to be an organic "chute" of some sort, and each rimmed chute yawns open as if in wait of something.

"It's a wall of boobs!" you have no choice but to yell.

"The Mammiferons exist to produce milk in these more upscale taprooms."

The metal gird that surrounds each enormous nipple reminds you of the connector on a car battery, and affixed to the top of each gird is a tap.

You watch as a shockingly attractive werewolf yanks down on a tap and fills a cup for a demonic customer.

"The barkeeps are Lycanymphs," Howard elucidates. "Erotopathic female werewolves, oh, and look." He points to one of the organic chutes between one of the pairs . . .

The bar's janitor—some manner of ridge-browed Troll—lackadaisically drops a shovelful of sloppy refuse into the chute. The chute closes, pauses, then *gulps*.

"They're brainless," Howard goes on. "You can think of Mammiferons as living beverage dispensers. Miss?" he asks of the furred attendant. "A cup of the vintage, if you will."

The voluptuous She-Wolf holds a metal cup beneath one of the massive teats, works the tap, and fills it up with slimy off-white milk.

"All we need do is feed them garbage and they produce milk for eons . . ." Howard smiles at the cup. "I must have some sustenance, lest exhaustion supervene the necessary ambling to come." Howard drinks the cup of dense milk. "Such a treat!"

Yet all you can do is gawp at the row of preposterous, sodden breasts on the wall.

Hell really is a screwed-up place . . .

The feisty werewolf pours more drafts from the papillic taps.

"Howard?" you ask. "Can we get out of here? This is too much for me."

"As you wish." Howard takes you back out to the hectic street, and turns. "This is the 'artsy' District, though the insinuation, like all else in Hell, is quite false. It's all petulantly commercial, I'm afraid."

You pass some sort of café that reminds you of Starbucks, but the cups of coffee look more like cups of mud. Trendy Hellborns yak pretentiously, batting their eyes. When you pass what appears to be a bookstore, Howard exclaims, "Drat!" and then you spot the window sign that announces BOOK SIGNING TONIGHT! EDGAR ALLAN POE WILL AUTOGRAPH YOUR COPY OF HIS LATEST RELEASE, *THE RISE OF THE HOUSE OF USHER!*

"I can't abide to miss a signing," Howard laments. "But duty does indeed call."

Marquees of lights blink around the next corner, and suddenly your inhuman ears pick up a punchy beat behind a low, crooning voice that sings, "Hardheaded shovel, stone-cold ground, six feet under's where *I'll* be found, so don't you, step on my blue-suede shroud . . ."

"Hey, that voice is *very* familiar!" you insist and when your head-stick passes the little honky-tonk's front door, you glimpse a flaming stage before a packed house. On the stage itself a man in a pompous white suit fringed with silver locomotes about, jerking his pelvis. He's got heavy black sideburns and horns in his head.

No! you think. *It can't be!*

Or . . . can it?

"Six for the money, six for the show, six for Lord Lucifer—go, cat, go!"

No!

"I'm not attuned to that particular genre of music," Howard says, "though the singer seems to be very popular here. However, Mozart plays with regularity, and so does Paganini. In fact, the former's latest opera, *Gloria de Satanus* is marvelous." But then Howard seems to catch himself in an oversight. "Oh, I suspect we'll be rephasing soon; I haven't been counting—"

"Counting *what?*"

"My steps. The Turnstile is programmed to rephase our location every 666 steps—"

"I never would've guessed," you groan.

"Don't scoff, Mr. Hudson. The Imperfect Number is quite a powerful force of Nether-Energy. As God proclaimed seven to be the *perfect* number, he unwittingly empowered the *imperfection* of one digit lower. Lucifer *embraces* it. In fact, when God cast his Once Favorite off the Twelfth Gate of Heaven, Lucifer, the Morning Star, plummeted in the configuration of the number six. Through that number, in one manner or other, all occult science is activated—the *Senarial* Science. You're about to behold more examples."

You suddenly grimace as the crackling black fuzz of the Turnstile shreds the sights before you. You feel the pressure drop, and again that feeling of falling recurs to the point that you wail, when—

PUNITARY FILLING STATION #5096—HUMANS ONLY, the next sign reads. NEXT LEFT.

You shake off the vertigo to find yourself being walked into a compound supervised by figures in policelike garb. Every six of the figures is joined by a hooded monk with an aura of luminous black mist. "The Constabularies are the federal police," Howard says. "They're mostly Human-Demon Hybrids who undergo extensive training and Spirit Manipulation. And the hooded gents are Bio-Wizards, in the event of, shall we say, civil disobedience."

As usual, you're duly confused. "That sign said *filling* station, but I don't see any cars. They have gas here?"

Howard ruefully shakes his head no, and carries you farther . . .

"It's a *Human* filling station, Mr. Hudson. Another demonstration of Lucifer's execration for the Human Damned." Then Howard gestures a prison wagon being drawn in by more unnameable horned beasts. Within the wagon's iron bars, you can't help but see the group of naked Humans. They're either pleading for mercy, or down on their knees in desperate prayer.

"This Cove tends to Humans who have the audacity to continue to pray to God. It should go without saying: Lucifer does not approve of such behavior . . ." Now Howard points upward to a high water tower but when you look at it, you do a double take.

The tower reads, URINE ONLY.

"Every urinal in the District empties into that collection tank. It's 66,666 gallons, by the way."

You're already getting sick in the contemplation; then your eyes follow several pipes leading from the tower's base to six objects that appear almost identical to gasoline pumps in the Living World.

Six at a time, then, Humans from the prison wagon—male and female alike—are strapped to gurneys and rolled before the pumps.

You feel your spirit paling as you watch . . .

Equally identical nozzles are brandished by Imp attendants. "Fill 'em up!" a Constable shouts, and then the Imps part the jaws of the Humans and insert the nozzles down their throats. The handles are depressed, and bells begin to ring for each gallon dispensed.

The Human prisoners are promptly *filled*.

"Next!" shouts the Constable. "Keep 'em moving!"

"Exactly six gallons are pumped into each captive," Howard adds.

The gurneys are moved off, to be replaced by more. Of the Humans already filled, their abdomens *bloat*. More Imps move now, holding objects that look like blowtorches but when the triggers are pulled, mist, not flame, shoots out. The mist is applied across the mouths and anuses and urethras of the captives, and before your own eyes, their lips and excretory orifices are impossibly sealed shut.

Howard explains further, in his piping accent, "You see, Lucifer wants them *filled*. And what they're filled with—the urine of Hell—must remain *contained*; hence, the Flesh Welders. A gasified pontica dust provides the occult mist, which seals them shut. This way, the urine can never be voided."

Gagging, you watch more. The captives, now swollen as if pregnant, are roughed off the gurneys and shooed out of the camp, their mouths and crotches "welded" shut forever.

Then your eyes steal back to the hideous pumps where the next deposition of unfortunates are being filled. Each gallon dings a bell, abdomen's quickly distend; then they're sealed with the welder and moved on. A stolid efficiency.

"Why?" you rail. "This makes no sense! Why are they FILLING PEOPLE WITH PISS!"

Howard shrugs off your alarm. "Because the very notion pleases Lucifer. He quite simply thrills at the idea—he likes for his detractors to be *filled*. Wombs, bellies, bowels. By your abhorrence, I take it that you'd prefer *not* to witness the Excrement Pumps at the next compound?"

"Get me out of here!" you shriek.

"Fill 'em up!" the Constab yells again, and as Howard hastens you out, that steady *ding-ding-ding* of the pumps follows . . .

A mental fog veils your vision as Howard lopes away. You pass several Agonicity Transformers, which each contain a Human dangling from a trestle by his or her wrists. Wires threaded through tiny holes drilled in their skulls coil upward to sizzling capacitors. Constabs heave pitchers of boiling water on each "power element," and the resultant rush of agony fires the pain center of the brain, which is then converted to occult energy and dumped into the local power grid. "Power without surcease," you think you hear Howard comment, "made possible by the immortality of the Human Damned. It's curious to ponder, eh? When God made the Human soul immortal, did he ever even conceive that some of those he condemned to Damnation would be utilized by his Nemesis as inexhaustible generators? Likely not!" More small compounds pass by and you can't help but notice the signs: BONE MELTERS, FACE RIVETERS, BROODREN KILN, PENECTOMIST. The compounds are interestingly arranged throughout the Reservation, each intersected by quaint walkways, and it's along these walkways that you notice chatty groups of well-dressed Demons and Hierarchals traipsing along. They stop by each compound and peer in with dark smiles, some fanning themselves, others looking more closely with objects like opera glasses. Finally your curiosity pushes past your loathing, and you propose: "All these Demons on the walkways . . . They don't work here, do they? They look more like—"

"Spectators?" Howard says. "Indeed. Because they are. Punishment Reservations such as the State Punitaries prioritize not only punishment but also commerce. The societal upper crust is urged to patronize these areas. They pay admittance. In Hell, punishment exists as sport, and such places as this serve equally as amusement parks."

"Oooo's" and "Ahhhh's" resound around the next bend where the sign reads: ROASTERY—BETS TAKEN. Several Coves stretch out in a line, while revolting spectators clamor to buy tickets printed with various numbers from small huts before each exhibit. *Roastery?* you wonder but can already smell something. "Step right up, folks," a ghoulish barker announces before the first Cove. "Let's watch and see which one of these despicable anti-Satanic insurgents can last the longest with a head-cooking." Then you notice three grim-faced Imps lashed to iron chairs facing the audience. Horned attendants busy themselves at a large circular oven in which a considerable pile of small stones are heated till they are red-hot. Chain mail sacks are then filled with the stones and carried over with tongs. Atop the head of each Imp a sack is lain, sitting much like a hot water bottle. Spectators watch in hushed fascination as each Imp's face billows and then they begin to let rip with soul-searing howls. Eventually, of course, their heads cook, but the one who screams the longest is the winner. Bets are taken more excitedly at the next Cove where demonic *mouths* are filled with the scorching stones and held shut by unfeeling Golems. Worse was the last Cove, where three stunningly attractive Succubi have been hung upside down by their ankles, legs widely spread, and vaginas opened with retractors. It was into their vaginal barrels that more of the red-hot stones are deposited. For efficiency's sake, a Golem with something akin to a bore cleaner for a cannon stands by and packs down each allotment of rocks. The first Succubi's eyes immediately pop out from the jolt of pain, and the second heaves so hard her bones are heard snapping. The third merely shudders and screams, smoke jetting from her mouth. When the screams treble in intensity, nearby glass shatters.

"The winner!" revels the attendant.

"This is what rich people in Hell do for fun?" you object. "They bet to see which one lives the longest? Good Lord!"

Howard winces at the name. "I will add, Mr. Hudson, that the art of wagering was invented by *Humans* . . ."

"Then why aren't *Human* beings tortured here, too?"

"These particular Coves function to judicially torture only the Hellborn, Mr. Hudson. All of the victims here have been convicted of terrorist activity or traitorous thoughts via a Psychical Sciences Center. But soon enough it'll be my pleasure to introduce you to a facility for very *select* Humans only."

You finally put the Roastery behind you, the revel of bettors fading in the background. "I don't want to see anymore," you say, drained. "None of it makes sense. Head-cooking? Filling monsters' vaginas with hot rocks? Pumping *piss* into people? It's hideous."

"Well, certainly you understand that this is the intention in the Mephistopolis, Mr. Hudson. Notions expressly *not* hideous are conspicuously bereft." Howard carries you through a gate exit manned by Ushers. Beyond this gatehouse steam-trucks empty hoppers of dead Hellborn onto conveyor belts that carry the piles into a warehouse marked, MUNICIPAL PULPING STATION #95,605.

Your vaporous mind feels like dead meat as the Turnstile's black magic sizzles before your eyes, and next—

"Perhaps you'll be pleased by the present change of scenery," Howard remarks. "Welcome to Shylock Square, a government-accredited Shopping District for Hell's most privileged and monetarily endowed. And the thoroughfare we're traversing now is the most recent addition."

When the black static dissipates you espy a street not unlike those in the Living World—save for the scarlet sky and black moon above—which is lined by fancy shops, cafés, and the like. Well-dressed She-Demons and creatures in business suits window-shop along the crowded lane. The street sign at the corner reads HELMSLEY BLVD.

"It can be likened to the Fifth Avenue of Hell," Howard adds. "Here you will see the city's most posh, most elite, and most upper crust—indeed, demimondes extraordinaire . . ."

Window signs pass by: DEMONSWEAR BY MARQUETTE, FINE HUMAN LEATHER, THE HARRY TRUMAN HAT SHOP—ONLY THE FINEST MERCURY USED, CUSTOM PORTRAITS BY GUSTAV DORE. It takes a moment for your vertigo to drift off; then you peer into a window stenciled HAND-COUCH MASSAGE and see a shapely, greenish-skinned She-Demon stretched nude on a couch made of severed hands. The hands meticulously knead every muscle in her body while a servant Imp stands by with a tray of refreshments. ELITE APPAREL FOR DEMONIC WOMEN reads the next window, and hanging on Human mannequins made of salt are an array of Tongue-Skirts, Lip-Sweaters, and Hand-Bras, and next—MATTRESS RETAILERS—PROCRUSTEAN BEDS—where an unfortunate female Troll, knob-faced and high-breasted, is forced to demonstrate before a group of more chatty She-Demons. Blades slam down to sever the creature's feet the instant she lay down; and next—COSMETIC AND DENTAL TERATOLOGY—where an attractive Human Concubine sits tensed in a chair while a Warlock extracts her teeth and replaces them with baby toes.

"And this is how rich people in Hell live it up?" you ask, revolted.

Howard seems surprised by the tenor of your remark. "Mr. Hudson, the clients on this selfsame street are among the most favored and most advantaged in the city. Barons and Blood Princes, Dukes and Archdukes, Viceroys and Chevaliers, and their superlative concubines—She-Demons and Fellatitrines, Erototesses and Succubi, Sex-Imps and Vulvatagoyles. The men possessed with the most *power* are always followed by women with the most desirability. What they merely *wear,* Mr. Hudson, bespeaks their sheer social status." And that's when you take closer note of just what some of these ritzy monsters are wearing—

Good God!

One curvaceous She-Demon taps down the sidewalk in Bone-Sandals, wearing a bra whose cups are Gryphon faces, while the monstrous woman's hot pants seem to be composed of stitched-together eyeballs. The eyeballs look at you when she prances by. Hand-Bras and Tongue-Skirts are prevalent as well but then a vivacious bluish-skinned Succubus turns the corner dressed in an entire bodysuit of tongues. You groan when you see that each and every tongue is alive. Through another window you steal a glance at a sleek and perfect-bosomed Imp as she tries on a teddy made of shellacked bat wings, while yet another Succubus tries on a negligee made from various scalps. In a Surgical Salon next door, a fussy She-Imp appraises her own round rump in a mirror and complains to an attendant, "My ass is too big. I want hers!" and then points to one of several Human women standing on display. A man in a white smock says, "A fine choice, miss," and promptly slices both buttocks off the Human who is held down on a cutting board by a Golem. The smocked man—presumably the cosmetic surgeon—hefts each buttock in his hands and says, "Come along to the surgery suite, miss. I'll have these transplanted in a jiffy." And if that's not enough, your senses stall when a bell rings and then a crystalline door opens—fancily labeled COSMETIC GRAFTING—and out steps a petitely horned and very lusty She-Demon. Onto every square inch of her skin a nipple has been grafted. She seems delighted with the service and enthuses to Howard, "Oh, my husband, the Grand Duke Desalvo, has such a fetish for nipples, I just *know* he'll love this!"

"Charming," Howard compliments, then back to you,

he continues, "Indeed, Mr. Hudson. Hell's most exclusive are what you are beholding now. No indulgence, no luxury is deprived of this select group. In fact, there is only one class of inhabitant *more* favored, and that would be the members of the Privilato Class."

You offer Howard a funky look. "The Privilat—"

"And, look! There's one now!" Howard says and excitedly points upward.

An odd groaning sound ensues and fifty feet above the street, you notice something that can only be described as a wavering hole in the sky, approximately ten feet in diameter. A bizarre, fluidlike green light rims the hole and within stands a long-haired Human man wearing clothes fashioned entirely from sparkling jewels. His face appears ordinary, yet it is set in the widest grin, and then you see that even his teeth are exorbitant jewels. On his forehead is a fancy Gothic mark: the letter *P. Hmm,* you think. *What's with that guy?* But what you notice even more profoundly are the man's companions, six of the most beautiful naked women you've ever seen.

"No wonder the guy's smiling," you mention, your own lust sparked. "Check out the drop-dead gorgeous women he's with."

"And they'll be with him *in aeternum*, Mr. Hudson, or until he wearies of them in which case they'll be replaced by more. The women are known as Soubrettes—the very pinnacle of sexual servitor. Inhuman Growth Hormones are occultized and injected, to augment their most desirable body parts, and they're trained quite exhaustively in the Sexual Arts. The technology they're flying about town in is called a Nectoport."

You stare incredulous at the spectacle—literally a hole in the sky, or a portal that's *moving.* The oozing green light about the rim throbs. "What the . . . *hell* is it?"

"Hell's answer to flying carpets, you could say," Howard

chuckles. "Did you know that I read *The Thousand and One Nights* when I was but a lad of eight years? Oh . . . of course you wouldn't know that. Nevertheless, a Nectoport is quite obviously a mode of transportation . . . as well as a very exclusive one. With only very rare exceptions, they're only to be operated by either the Constabulary, the Satanic Military, or the highest members of the Governmental Demonocracy."

"Oh, so that guy with all the hot Demon girls is in the government or army?"

"I said, Mr. Hudson, only *very rare* exceptions. Nectoports are able to constrict great distances by reprocessing psychic energy from the Torturian Complexes. Sorcerers trained at the De Rais Labs devised the unique method. It's possible for a Nectoport to travel a thousand miles of Hell's terrain without the occupants ever really leaving their debarkation point. Do you comprehend me?"

"No," you emphatically state.

"It's neither here nor there. But to elucidate, the Privilatos are entitled to unlimited Nectoport usage, due to their staggering rank."

You shake your gourd-head in more confusion. "Okay, so the guy's not in the government, he's not a cop, and he's not in the military but he's superprivileged?"

"Precisely."

"Okay. *Why?*"

Howard beams through his pallored face. "Mr. Hudson, I'm absolutely delighted that you've made the inquiry . . ."

As Howard talks, your eyes flick to the Nectoport. The crush of sexy Soubrettes are cooing in the Privilato's ear, feeling him up with deft hands.

"—the gentleman's name is Dowski Swikaj, formerly a friar from Guzow, Poland—"

But as Howard goes on to answer your question, you

continue to stare upward. The Nectoport hovers closer now, and the razor-sharp vision afforded you by yourOcularus eyes scrutinize each of the jeweled man's nude consorts. Several are Human, and their sexual enhancements are obvious, as though every aspect of what men find desirable in women has been accelerated tenfold, while the others, however demonic, are just as outrageously desirous in spite of genes that make them technically monsters. One, an auburn-haired Fellatitrine, has four full breasts on each side of her supple physique, yet each nipple is a puckered mouth, while the mouth on her orb-eyed face is a hairless and perfectly cloven vagina. Next to her stands a sultry Vulvatagoyle, with skin the hue of chalk but shining to a gleam as if lacquered. Wide hips and a flawless flat belly entice further staring, and then you notice the veritable *cluster* of vaginas packed between her coltish legs. Each vagina seems to be that of another life form, and they all *throb* in excitement. Her navel, too, is a vulva—more petite—while another vagina exists in each armpit, and yet another where her anus should be. Lastly, a lissome Lycanymph—even more stunning than the barkeep at the Taproom—coddles the Privilato. She's covered with the finest red hair beneath which a perfect Human physique can be seen. Gorged teats the size of baby pacifiers stick out from marvelously sloped breasts, and she grins fang-mouthed as her furred hands slip beneath her master's sparkling trousers.

An uproar rises from the street as the Nectoport lowers to the bone-hewn pavement. *It's landing,* you think. The Privilato stands hands on hips within the Port's green-glowing oval, looking upon the ritzy crowd of uptown Demons in a way that reminds you of an old picture of Mussolini looking down into the town square from a stone balcony. The crowd in the street hoots and hollers, the females in particular nearly apoplectic with enthusiasm. "Privilato!" a corroded chorus rises. "Privilato!"

"Oh, dear." Howard frowns. "He and his entourage are coming out." And then he takes you back to an alley. "I'm just not attuned to boisterous crowds, never have been. Indeed, New York was stifling enough but this—this *elephantiasis* of nonhumanity exceeds my demarcation of tolerance."

You barely hear him, squinting at the loud rabble. For some reason you can't figure, this jeweled man—this *Privilato*—intrigues you. The glowing rim of the Nectoport's aperture dilates, and before the Privilato can step out—

"Holy smokes," you mutter.

"All Privilatos, too, enjoy a full-time detachment of bodyguards. Note the Conscripts from the lauded Diocletian Brigade."

From the Nectoport, two formations of said Conscripts dispatch. Some wield swords, others brandish mallets whose heads are the size of fifty-five-gallon drums. Plated suits of Hexed armor adorn each troop, while their shell-like helms possess only slits to look through. The crowd's uproar turns chaotic; then a horn blares, and one of the Conscripts raises a large, hollowed-out horn to his mouth like a loudspeaker. "Attention, all elite of Hell. A Privilato wishes to debark. Do not encroach upon the exclusion perimeter." And then more Conscripts run lengths of barbed chain from the Nectoport's mouth to the door of one of the shops on the street.

"The Privilato is about to step into your midst! Bow down and pay reverence to our esteemed favorite of Lucifer!" blasts the horn.

Most of the crowd falls to its knees, though many females in the audience can't control themselves when the Privilato finally emerges onto the street. One shapely She-

Demon in a gown of bone-needle mesh leans over the barbed cordon, reaching out with a manicured hand. "Privilato! I'm honored by your presence! Please! Let me touch you!" But once she inclines herself over the chain—

SWOOSH!

—a great curved sword flashes and cuts her in half at the waist.

But the crowd continues to surge forward. You actually groan to yourself when two more Conscripts unroll a red carpet before the Privilato's jeweled feet.

Talk about the high life . . .

"Back! Back!" warns the loudspeaker. "Disperse now and let the Privilato enjoy a refreshment in peace!"

The Privilato comes forth, his robust concubines trailing behind. The crowd roars louder, which only doubles your perplexion. You look at the jeweled man and notice that, save for the jewels, there is nothing extraordinary about him. His long hair sifts around a bland, unenlivened face. His eyes look dull. Nevertheless he offers the crowd a smile and when he waves at them the uproar rises further.

Finally you object: "This guy's acting like Kid Rock. What's the big deal?"

Howard doesn't answer but instead shoulders through the crowd toward the storefront. "You'll be interested in seeing this, Mr. Hudson. One of Hell's greatest delicacies. We'll have to settle for watching through the window, of course."

Hell's greatest delicacy?

"Behold the ultimate indulgence, Mr. Hudson. One snifter carries a monetary value of one million Hellnotes," Howard sputters. "And to think I fed myself for thirty cents a day on Heinz beans and old cheese from the Mayflower Store."

The sign on the window reads: FETAL APERTIFS.

Now the crowd watches in awe as the Privilato approaches, his busty consorts in tow.

"Let me blow you!" comes the crude plea from a vampiric admirer.

The Soubrettes grimace at her, then one—the Vulvatagoyle—expectorates yeast onto the haughty fanged woman.

When one surgically enhanced Imp jumps the cordon and begs to put her hands on the jeweled man—

WHAM!

—a Conscript brings down his mallet and squashes her against the street.

"Back! Back!"

Even Howard seems awed when the glittering Privilato and his entourage pass by and enter the classy shop.

"The guy looks like a long-haired Liberace," you complain. "Why is he so important? And what the hell is a Fetal Aperitif?"

"Something I've never partaken in—I'm not *privileged* enough, though I did have cotton candy once at Coney Island." Then Howard smiles at you in the oddest manner. "Mongrel fetuses exist as quite a resource in Hell, Mr. Hudson. Akin to ore, akin to cash crops."

The notion—the mere way he said it—makes you queasy.

"Economic diversification, by any other classification."

"Baby farms?" you practically gag.

"Yes! Well put, sir, well put. Like choice grapes selected for the finest wineries, choice *fetuses* are harvested for this four-star aperitif bar." Howard's finger directs your gaze to the rearmost anteroom of the establishment, where you see a great tub made from wooden slats.

No no no no no, you think.

Worker Demons empty bushel baskets full of fetuses into the tub . . .

"I was always amused by the French cliché," Howard goes on. "The idea that our shifty enemies in the Indian Wars would pile grapes into tubs and crush them barefoot . . ."

When the tub has been filled with squirming newborn Demons, a nine-foot-tall Golem steps in and begins to ponderously walk on them. Eventually the contents of the tub are crushed, and a tap drains the precious liquid into kegs that are then rolled aside to ferment.

Howard looks forlorn. "It's supposedly delectable, not that I'll ever receive the opportunity to sample it, not on my pitiful stipend. Lucifer has seen to it that the poverty which mocked me in life will continue to do so in death . . ."

Inside, the Privilato eyes trays of bizarre food placed before him by licentious servers. Wicked versions of shrimp and lobster (lobsters, of course, with horns), braised roasts of shimmering meat, steaming vegetables in arcane sauces. In spite of its alienness, it all looks delicious.

"You see, Mr. Hudson, the *elite* in Hell gorge on delicacies the likes of which would sink the banquets of Lucullus to tameness, and the wine? Splendid enough to green Bacchus with envy."

You watch now as the Privilato raises a tiny glass of the evil wine and shoots it back neat. The occult rush sets a wide smile on his face, and he looks past the table, right through the window . . .

At you.

The Privilato nods.

You're sure that if you actually had hands you would grab Howard by the collar and shake him. "Why are you showing me this stuff? And what's the big deal with that guy in there? He's got the best-looking girls in Hell for groupies, he flies around in a *Nectoport,* and he gets to drink wine that costs a million bucks a glass. Why?"

"Because," Howard answers, "and I'll iterate, the gentleman's name is Dowski Swikaj, formerly a friar from Guzow, Poland."

"Yeah?" you yell. "So what!"

"In the frightful year of 1342 AD, Mr. Swikaj won the Senary . . ."

Chapter Five

(I)

The great, even gouge in the Hellscape that was the Vandermast Reservoir gave rise to the most abominable stenches, though one well-accustomed to the most evil odors—as Conscript Favius—grew used to them. Stomach-prolapsing smells were as commonplace here as screams. Yet fastidious and well-trained infernal soldiers such as Favius learned to use the sense of smell to their advantage. For instance, when something smelled suddenly *different* . . .

Something could be wrong.

Favius called the rampart under his command to its highest alert state, which entailed observation teams of lower-ranked Conscripts readying weapons, while the Golem Squads went from static to marching patrols. The thuds of the unliving things' clay feet resounded like thunder; and, meanwhile, Favius's nostrils flared as the cryptic new odor heightened in potency. *What in Satan's name is happening?* he thought, his halberd ready in one massive hand, the sword ready in the other. Within minutes, he could see all the nearest ramparts of the reservation coming to alert as well.

It was a vicious stench that suddenly whelmed the place. *An insurgent gas attack?* he wondered. This would not kill Human Damned Conscripts such as himself, nor Golems, of course, but everything else? Yes.

However . . .

No insurgent sightings had been reported, and this far out in the Hellscape? *Their supply lines would become exhausted before they'd even traversed one one-hundredths of the distance from the city to the Reservoir . . .*

What, then?

When the hectophone at the sentry post began to glow, Favius knew who it was.

"Conscript First Class Favius reporting, Grand Sergeant, at your command!" he answered the severed Gargoyle head that had been modified for this purpose. The thing's frozen-open maw sufficed for the earpiece; its ear was what Favius spoke into. Occultized Electrocity signals served as the frequency through which such long-distance communication was achieved.

When the dead Gargoyle's mouth moved, it was the voice of Grand Sergeant Buyoux that Favius, in turn, heard.

"Conscript Favius. Why is the entire reservation on emergency alert? Answer quickly."

"An anomaly, your Wretched Eminence—a stench, uncharacteristic and quite sudden. I took it unto myself to call my rampart to alert."

"Yes, you have. And it seems that every rampart in the enter site has done so as well."

Favius began to sweat. Buyoux's voice was unreadable. "I did not want to take a chance, my Despicable Commander. If I am in error, I will report for punishment at once."

A long pause, then a laugh. "Vigilance is everything, Conscript—it's what wins wars and conquers nations. I commend you for your quick thinking."

"Thank you, Grand Sergeant!" Favius shouted in relief.

"But you'll be gratified to know that the anomaly you detected is in no manner a threat."

"Thank Great Satan, sir!"

"Yes . . . Call off your alert and have your troops stand down, but first . . . prepare to rejoice and don your Abyss-Glasses. Train them on the great portals of the recently installed Y-connectors of your Main Sub-Inlet."

Mystified, Favius did so, focusing the supernatural viewers on the closest of the dual, sixty-six-foot-wide connector portals.

His massive, sculpted muscles froze.

There, exuding however traceably at the bottom of the pipe, was a trickle of befouled scarlet liquid. It didn't take Favius long to calculate what the inbound effluent was:

Bloodwater, his thoughts whispered. *Just the slightest trickle, yes, but it can only mean . . .*

"There, faithful Conscript, is the cause of the strange odor you noticed." Buyoux's enthusiasm could be decrypted by his own conscious silence. "And we've just received confirmation. They're priming the pumps in the Rot-Port Harbor, and that stench? It's the stench of the Gulf itself, channeled all the way out here . . ."

"Praise Lucifer," Favius's eons-roughened voice rattled in disbelief.

"It's happening even sooner than we'd prayed for, friend Favius," his commander rejoiced. "And in short order . . . that paltry trickle of Bloodwater will *gush*."

Tears nearly came to Favius's soiled eyes. "All glory be to Satan," he hitched.

"Stand your troops down, Conscript, and yourself, too. You all deserve a short recess. Good work."

"I am honored by your praise, Grand Sergeant!"

"No, Favius. It is *I* who am honored to command you." And then the hectophone's vicious mouth went limp.

Favius set the hideous phone back in its cradle, then called off the alert. He smiled—something he rarely did—when he gazed out over the empty Vandermast Reservoir, and then envisioned it full to the brim with six billion gallons of the detestable Gulf of Cagliostro . . .

(II)

Archlock Curwen, the Supreme Master Builder, felt a nearly sexual exhilaration as he watched sixty-six Mongrels drop simultaneously into the Central Cauldron. The sulphur-fire beneath the great iron vessel roared; its contents—liver oil from a single Dentata-Serpent—crackled and boiled at a thousand degrees. All those filthy Mongrels dying at the same time, and at temperatures so high, caused the things to scream in unison, and for many of them the pain was so heinous that chunks of their lungs flew out of their mouths with the screams. The rush in the Hell-Flux trebled then, bringing to the air a heady, gaseous brew that enlivened all who inhaled it. Furthermore, it amped up the power in the constantly running Electrocity Generators, whose storage cells were crucial to giving the Demonculus otherworldly life.

Curwen sighed at the tingle of pleasure.

He was on rounds now, on the field itself, as the various Occult Engineering crews busied themselves in the gas balloons above. Those Curwen could see from down here were but floating specks, while most couldn't be seen at all for their sheer altitude.

Sweet, he thought in his shimmering surplice. *This is MY project, entrusted to ME by the Morning Star himself. I will not fail.*

Fanged and leprous-skinned Metastabeasts—a team of six, of course—hauled Curwen's Hex-Armored carriage about the field. The foul sky's eternal bloodred light coruscated high above; its dread illumination covered half the entire field in the shadow of the spiring Demonculus. But when *another* shadow approached, the Conscripts and Ushers of Curwen's bodyguard regiment parted.

It was a shadow shaped like a man—but a man with horns—that strode down the divide created by the bodyguards. The field fell silent.

Aldehzor, Curwen knew at once, *Lucifer's Grand Messenger.* It was this shadow-shape's duty to deliver all-important ciphers from the Morning Star himself. Only a precious few of Hell's Hierarchals were on the list to receive Aldehzor.

The carriage door was opened; the semisolid figure came in and sat down. When the door was closed again, the ranks of bodyguards stepped backward, turned, and readied their weapons, forming a wall of monsters to protect the two occupants.

"Exalted Aldehzor," Curwen greeted.

The shadow nodded. "Supreme Master Builder." The eyeless black face peered upward through a window. "Your progress is exceptional. I'm impressed, and I'm sure our lord will be, too, once I've reported back to him." Aldehzor's voice existed much as his physical being: indeterminate. He came from a pre-Adamic line known as Incorporeals—he was a living shadow who disguised his movements by slipping into the bodies of passersby, wearing them as camouflage. He was simply a silhouette with no discernible details save for his basic outline—a horned, wedge-shaped head atop a Human*like* body. No eyes could be seen within the wedge. If anything his voice bubbled like the ichors of Hell's deepest trenches. "And as you might suspect, I have a message for you."

Archlock Curwen struggled not to betray his unease. With Aldehzor, messages were either good or bad. Was a terrorist attack imminent? Had a flaw been discovered in the Demonculus's cabalistic programming?

Am I being usurped? the Master Builder wondered in restrained dread.

"I am ready for your message, Aldehzor."

"It has been calculated that there exists a minor chance of a power shortage here."

Curwen sat stiff. "We've always known that. A *minor* chance."

"Any chance is unacceptable," the hideous voice intoned. "However, in his genius, Lucifer has devised a solution."

"Pray tell . . ."

"Much is astir in the Mephistopolis, Archlock." The wretched voice burbled on. "Plans and projects that even one as exalted as yourself have no clue . . ."

Curwen stared. Was the Grand Messenger trying to insult him? To belittle his status? Aldehzor's jealousy of the exalted Human Damned was well-known. *He WISHES he could be me,* he felt sure, but wasn't comfortable voicing it.

The ink-blot face looked back at him. "Your own constant sacrifices in the Cauldrons won't be enough. I'm alarmed that your own engineers weren't able to verify that." A protracted pause. "However, my own alarm was apparently *not* perceived by our lord. For some reason he holds you in the *highest* favor, higher than *any* of the Human Damned."

"Are you trying to intimidate me, Aldehzor?"

A wet, slopping chuckle. "Certainly not, Supreme Master Builder. I honor you. Surely you've heard of a crucial endeavor at the Vandermast Reservoir?"

"I've heard bits and pieces. Some mode of transposition, perhaps even a Spatial Merge, it's been guessed."

"Yes, but a permanent one."

Astonishment caused Curwen's guard to fall. "*Permanent,* you say? But that is . . . impossible."

"Once upon a time, yes—if time existed. The Bio-Wizards at the De Rais Laboratories cracked the code."

"But a permanent transposition would require multiple millions of Hellspawn and Humans to die *simultaneously*."

The black shadow nodded. "Sixty-six million, to be exact. And a solution has been devised. It's quite simple, actually. Those millions *will* die, all in the same instant. This shall bring the amperage of the Hell-Flux to immeasurably high levels. That much occult energy will be more than enough to effect the Merge. And the reserves will be transferred to you and your . . . Demonculus."

Curwen felt light-headed. True, the possibility of insufficient power had already been cited, but with *this?*

It's more power than has ever been generated in Hell, in all of its history . . .

"How," the Master Builder demanded next. "How can this be, that multiple millions shall die simultaneously?"

Did the warped shadow actually shrug? "The Municipal Mutilation Squads throughout the entire Mephistopolis will do it—"

"But that's not feasible at all! How could they all be calibrated to strike at the same *moment?*"

"By psychic command."

Curwen stalled.

"The De Rais Labs have recently invented the process," the shadow added. "So, in spite of *your own* miscalculation, you needn't worry yourself. Indeed, we are in the hands of a great lord, are we not?"

"We are," Curwen croaked.

"You're a brave one, Supreme Master Builder, and I must say"—Aldehzor's invisible gaze strayed upward again, at the immense Demonculus—"that you have my utmost admiration."

"Why?" Curwen nearly spat.

"To sacrifice forever your Hell-given Spirit Body in order to become . . . that *thing?*"

"You refer to the Demonculus with vehemence, dear Messenger. It is the greatest entity to ever be manufactured here, and it is the *Demonculus* you'd do better to admire, not I. I am blessed like no other in this opportunity to serve Great Satan. Be he forever praised." Curwen's silver teeth flashed bladelike with his smile. "It almost sounds as though you're afraid of the Demonculus's success; for when, through me, it rids the Mephistopolis of all opposition . . . whatever shall *you* do to stay in our lord's good graces?"

Aldehzor seemed to *hiss.*

Yes. What use will there be for a messenger with no messages to deliver?

The veiled joust was over—Curwen had won.

"Be prepared," came Aldehzor's whisper like the smoke off a ball of pitch. "What you long for will come soon."

Curwen stared the Incorporeal down.

"In the name of all things unutterable, hail the Prince of Lies," the Grand Messenger said and got out of the carriage.

Curse ye, and be gone with you, Curwen thought, and then when he saw another sixty-six Mongrels dropped at once into the Cauldron he nearly swooned as if opiated. Their screams were like the sweetest of songs to his ears.

(III)

The hollow sound in your head follows you as the Turnstile's evil formulae are triggered and you and your guide are pressed yet again through the gauze of distance-collapsing sorcery. When the vertigo passes, you jerk your gaze to Howard.

"So that's it? The winners of the Senary get to become Privilatos?"

"Ah, I see your observations have at last heightened the acuity of your powers of deductive reckoning. I gratefully affirm."

You frown.

"However, our chancing upon Mr. Swikaj and his comely harem came quite by happenstance. We're on our way to behold further facets of the abyss that should deliver a more formidable impact."

Shylock Square is long behind you now, though curious occult graft work is still visible among passersby. One stunning woman in hot pants and a bra of the finest leaden fabric has no face at all but only smooth white skin and a belly button where her nose would be. Her face has been transplanted upon her abdomen, and when that fact finally registers, you notice that she is smiling at you. A buff man, Human save for elaborate horns, walks confidently into an enterprise called CRIPPENDALE'S; he's wearing a vest of penises, and onto his earlobes have been sewn scrotums. Lastly, a slyly smiling She-Imp passes, her majora replaced by what appears to be a baby's buttocks.

"I can perceive that you're finally acclimating," Howard remarks. "Your revulsion appears to be growing staid—quite a good sign."

Finally you're able to blurt, "You want me to accept the Senary, which means I'll become a Privilato after I fucking die. Is that it?"

"Yes," Howard says, his already long face lengthening further; his distaste obvious. "However, if I may conjecture, profanity does not suit you at all. It's quite inappropriate and wholly uncharacteristic of a studious and devout man such as yourself."

You fix on what Howard just said. *Profanity? Yes, I cussed, didn't I? I said "fucking die," instead of die.* The speculation unwinds like a coil of string. "I never swear," you tell your guide. "Sure, a *damn* or a *hell* or an *ass* on occasion, but *never* . . . the F-word or the S-word."

Howard is frowning. "It's *uncomplimentary*, sir. It bespeaks ruffianism and roysterishness. Better to maintain an air of the dignified, even in so *un*dignified a habitat as this."

Trivial as the matter seems, it bothers you. *I must hang out with Randal too much . . .*

"But, yes, you've unveiled the intrigue at last," Howard goes on. "It is indeed the motive of the master of this domain that you accept the Senary and rise to Privilato status upon your earthly demise." Howard scrutinizes your impossible face. "And now you are weighing that possibility against the possibility of an eternity in Heaven, are you not?"

You stare. *Am I? Yeah . . . of course I am . . .*

"But you needn't choose just yet. Let's take in more sights before we arrive at the clincher."

"The *clincher?* I can't imagine."

Does Howard smile? "No, I'm certain beyond all cogitation that you cannot. No one can . . ."

Your senses reel as you cross a footbridge over a mucus-filled creek. Several destitute Trolls nod as they stand on the rail, fishing. One Troll has eyeballs in his bait can, the other, tongues yanked from their seats.

But your hideous eyes go wide when you notice several twitchy Human women crossing the footbridge . . .

"More addicts," Howard notes, "regrettable, but no more so than the seemingly illimitable *Human* capacity to 'chase the dragon,' as they say. Clearly beyond the bridge there's a public Flenser's in business."

But you simply continue staring, for these women seem to have had all of the flesh cut from their arms and legs, while their heads and naked torsos remain intact. It is horrendous to behold, yet also, somehow, perversely fascinating.

"Street parlance refers to such types as 'Bone-Limbers.'"

The implication collides with your psyche. "Like those people selling their skin for dope. Those two sold the *meat* on their arms and legs?"

Howard nods. "Every scrap, and mind you, a skilled Flenser can finish the task in moments—they're quite *deft of knife*. And believe me, the potency of the narcotics of Hell are more than formidable. Human males tend to sell nearly every fiber of flesh from head to toe; women, however, are far less likely to follow suit as that instance could make the prospect of prostitution pitiably moot . . ."

With skeleton arms and skeleton legs, then, the pair of addicts cross the bridge, oblivion in their eyes and ruined smiles.

Yes, sir, you think. *This is one big-time fucked-up place.* But there you go again, so errantly thinking in terms adorned with profanity. You wince in your confusion.

In the distance, hulking Conscripts stand guard around a narrow black building that must be a mile long. MATERNITY BARRACKS, a high sign reads. Even from the distance you can hear the wails of infants . . .

You open your demonic mouth to speak but pause and don't bother. You agreed to come here and *see.*

And now you will be shown.

Macabre, cancerous horses whinny as a prison wagon (identical to those you saw at the Punitary) stops before a guarded entrance. Now you stare hard.

"It's loaded up with . . . really good-looking women," you mutter.

"The acme of Human female stock, Mr. Hudson," Howard augments. "The best in all of Hell—indeed—the proverbial cream of the crop. They're hunted down with the zeal of children at an Easter egg hunt."

Naturally, you don't understand. So far you've seen unbelievable life forms, most hideous but some attractive, and Human women have comprised a fare share of the latter. This wagon, however, beggars superlative description. It is full to bursting with Human women who are among the most attractive you've ever seen anywhere.

"They could be runway models," you utter.

"It's part of the new Luciferic Initiative, and Lucifer—however plodding he can sometimes be—has grown fond of efficiency. Two birds with one stone, so to speak. You see, the inhabitants of these queer barracks make up the very finest, most attractive Human women in all of Hell. And in their stay, they will serve dual purposes."

"I don't know what you're talking about," you drone as you approach, and now you watch the sinisterly helmed Conscripts haul the women out of the wagon. They're all gagged, shackled, and stark naked. In single file, then, they're led at trident-point into the barracks.

"There must be forty or fifty women packed into that wagon," you exclaim.

"Sixty-six, to be precise," Howard redresses. "And there are exactly sixty-six Impoundment Wings in this Maternity Barrack."

The number staggers you, but then you ask, "What do you mean, dual purposes?"

"Pardon me while I get us in-processed," Howard says aside.

The two gate guards—a pair of pugnacious, phlegm-eyed creatures in scaled armor—stand at a spiked iron gate.

"I'm with the Office of the Senary," Howard relays and holds up his palm. It's the first time that you've noticed it: a luminous six branded into his palm.

The sentries bow and step back; then the spiked gate rises. But before Howard escorts you in, the chain gang of sixty-six outrageously beautiful woman are led in first. Hopeless eyes stare back at you as they're hauled onward.

"Ah, and here comes the most recent Impoundment Block to expire," Howard points out.

Another chain gang of women are being led in the opposite direction, preparing to exit. This consignment, however, differs from the first group in two ways.

One, they're emaciated, haggard, and bone-thin, and—

Two, they're headless.

"Out with the old in with the new as they say," Howard explains. "The production cycle of these unfortunates has expired, while it's only about to begin for the group we just saw entering . . ."

"Production cycle," you say more than ask. The headless women are *worn out* (as if having one's head removed wouldn't wear one out enough), and then you suddenly have an idea why. Their bellies hang like limp sacks streaked with stretch marks, their breasts but emptied flaps of skin.

"This particular barrack, by the way, is the major supplier of fetuses to the aperitif bar we visited upon earlier." Howard leads on down the reeking corridor of sheet iron. "The women, once beheaded, are taken to a Decapitant Camp. You'll recall the Luciferic Initiative I referred to earlier? It's officially titled the Beheadment Initiative—the law of the land now. Human women deemed attractive enough for Preeminent classification must *all* be beheaded, and the process functions twofold. It's a constituent of their punishment, and while the wares of their wombs supply the lucrative gourmand market, their heads provide an exclusive construction component."

Again, you scarcely hear Howard, your attentions fixed instead on the troop of headless women shuffling out of the complex. Moments later, several hunched Imps in laborers' garb exit the complex as well, each pushing wheelbarrows *full* of Human female heads. As the barrows pass, the eyes on the heads all hold wide on you.

"Why, why, why?" you plead.

"It's elementary, Mr. Hudson. Lucifer *loathes* the Human Damned, but this unadulterated hatred burns exponentially hotter for the Human *Female* Damned." Howard pauses at a trapdoorlike window in the iron wall. "This may afford you an acceptable view . . ."

He raises the square metal viewing port and holds your gourd-head up to look.

Beyond the Barracks stretches a region of barren land that must encompass several square miles. The parcel is circumscribed completely by a high fence laced with barbs and within they trod aimlessly in a vast circle: tens of thousands of headless women.

"The idea enthralls Lucifer, that they walk headless for eternity, while their heads live on elsewhere and with equal permanence."

You're too appalled to even react now, but you have the creeping impression that there are worse things waiting to be seen . . .

"The *Beheadment* Initiative?" you question, dazed from the sight. "A *law* that all beautiful women come here to be decapitated and . . ."

"All beautiful *Human* women, Mr. Hudson. Lucifer is quite nonchalant about *Hellborn* females. His utter hatred for Human women in particular is plainly explicated. You see, it was a *Human* female who destroyed his original abode, the 666-story Mephisto Building. This cunning female—whose name it is forbidden to speak or even think—undermined Lucifer's most powerful defenses and turned his monumental edifice of evil into a pile of rubble, and she did so with *white* magic, not black."

You gulp. "So now he takes it out on every drop-dead gorgeous woman in Hell?"

"Yes, and to quite an effect. Remember when I inferred: two birds with one stone." Howard smiles. "Be patient, Mr. Hudson, and you'll learn more in due time."

Metal pots along the corridor sputter with burning pitch. You watch the shadow of your own hideous head bob as Howard leads you down a labyrinth of squalling hallways and, at last, into—

"This is the initial processing point. The consignment we just saw entering? Here's where they come first," Howard explains.

You peer in through the ragged metal doorway . . .

All sixty-six women have been laid on a wide conveyor belt, with hip and neck girds to keep them in place. Midway along the belt stand two Imps in white lab coats. One wields a pair of scissors the size of hedge clippers and perfunctorily cuts off a woman's head while the other places the severed head between the woman's legs for further transport. At the next work station two more demonic surgeons slip metal tubes into each of the woman's breasts and the breasts—amid a wailing motor noise—quickly deflate.

"As you can see, first the heads are removed and then vacuum-powered cannulae are inserted into the breasts, to draw out the valuable mammary glands, which are sold to Surgical Salons for implanting—"

They chop off their heads and liposuck their tits, the grueling fact sinks in.

"—after which they're conveyored to the next available Impoundment Block," Howard finishes and reembarks down the corridor.

Every so often, as you're taken deeper into this nefarious network, wheelbarrows full of mongrel newborns are rolled briskly past by more Imp and Troll laborers. You don't have to ask where they're going.

"And here," Howard announces after a long spell of walking, "is a typical Block in full swing . . ."

Your now-numb eyes look in to behold the spectacle: a long, low-ceilinged room containing exactly sixty-six gynecological beds, complete with stirrups. Each bed is occupied by a squirming, decapitated woman, legs forced apart and ankles locked in the stirrups. Most of the occupants display varying stages of pregnancy, and the few who don't are being vigorously copulated with by a variety of sexually enhanced Demons, Trolls, and Imps. Many possess genitals like veined batons of meat, while others brandish odd, ridged tubules of flesh with nozzlelike coronas. Several even have penises with *faces* on the end.

"Each Impoundee is subjected to fornication on a fastidious level, until pregnancy shows. Then they merely wait out their term until the process begins again. And as for their *heads,* well, I'm sure by now you've taken proper note . . ."

You have. The severed head of each "Impoundee" is evident, placed atop a pole set back several yards between the subject's spread legs.

"It simply wouldn't do to merely use their bodies as production vessels; it's very important to Lucifer that the conscious head of each woman be forced to *watch* the entire process; in fact, our Master *delights* in that particular effect. Not only is each woman forced to watch herself be raped by monsters, she is forced to watch herself *give birth* to monsters. Over and over and over again."

"How long . . . do they have . . . to stay here?"

"For sixty-six full terms," Howard enlightens.

One woman, bloated as if to pop, shudders on her table, while her accommodating head screams in agony. The belly quakes, then collapses; a basket on the floor catches the squalling newborn and afterbirth. Not a minute passes before the viscid monster-fathered infant is tossed into a wheelbarrow, and not another minute before a heavily genitaled Sex-Demon steps up to begin the fornication period anew. Meanwhile, the head of a woman several beds down is shrieking like a machine with bad bearings, the medicine ball–size belly tremoring. When a lab-coated Imp with goggles comes to inspect, he calls out, "Womb-Press, rack forty-nine," and then instantly a great piston-backed droning is heard. Overhead, on a geared rail, the oddest device clatters along: like an inverted metal salad bowl stemmed by a greased screw. Eventually the "bowl" positions itself directly over the squirming woman's great, bloated belly. *Oh, my God,* you think when its function finally occurs to you. The screw begins to turn, lowering the bowl until it presses tight against the monster-filled belly.

Lower. Lower. Lower.

You close your eyes for you cannot watch the entire process, but you do hear the escalating shrieks and then the finality of the great *SPLAT!*

When your eyes reopen, the dizzy, headless woman is no longer pregnant, and already the demonic newborn is being spirited away in a barrow.

"Take me the fuck out of here!" you yell.

Howard rolls his eyes, scratching at some tiny red pocks on his face that appear to be ingrown hairs. "Really, Mr. Hudson—was the profanity necessary? And, truly, I regret your distress, but it's necessary that you recognize the systematics that exist here. You must *perceive* Lucifer's ultimate ideal of pursuing an order of faith antithetical to God."

"Fuck that shit," you cuss again, and now even you are shocked by the sudden use of the vulgar. "This sucks. None of this makes any sense—"

"Excellent! You're beginning to comprehend!" Howard enthuses, taking you out.

"It doesn't make any sense at all for Lucifer to go to all this effort to do all this evil stuff!"

Howard continues to beam. "Exactly! Because, antithetically speaking, the absence of logic is the *perfect* logic in a domain that must exist contrary to God!"

Your confoundment dizzies you when Howard finally wends you back outside into the creeping scarlet daylight, and as you move away from the Barracks, the wails of newborn Demons and the shrieks of women in labor follow you like an atrocious banner.

Still, details bother you, and now that the shock of your witness is past, you slowly observe, "They use their babies for the 'gourmand market,' and they use their mammary glands for demonic implants, and once they've had sixty-six babies, their headless bodies are sentenced to eternity in the Decapitant Camp. Have I got it right so far?"

"Quite," Howard confirms.

"So . . . what happens to their heads? Earlier, didn't you say something about—"

"An exclusive construction component!" Howard continues to be pleased by your attentiveness, but then—

The black static veil crackles and surges and—

Here we go again . . .

—you psychically plummet into the next stop on the tour . . .

"This, Mr. Hudson, is the second bird from the stone," Howard intones.

You stare out, mortified, mystified, and transfixed all at once . . .

Part Three

Manse Lucifier

Chapter Six

(I)

Krilid rubbed fatigue from his oblong eyes. He waited, sitting on the luminous rim of the Nectoport's mouth within the sooty cloud he'd found at the prearranged coordinates. He still felt himself psychically recovering from the sheer vision of the Vandermast Reservoir. *Just a great big empty black hole in the ground,* he tried to convince himself. Why should the sight of the place fill him with such dread?

They haven't told me everything. When will they? This isn't fair . . .

He was serving God now, after all, but could God hear prayers from Hell? No salvation would be in store for him upon his Hellbound death, so . . .

Do I really need this?

But when he wiped his brow, which the Head-Bending had transformed into a warped cone, he remembered his true motives.

One way or another, I'll make them pay for what they did to me, and if I die trying? So what?

When one was unfortunate enough to be *born* in Hell, there was not another Hell to follow in afterlife. Only the sweetness of nonexistence . . .

Krilid made a mental note not to forget that. His mood improved at once.

BAM!

More reflex than the awareness of danger flung his runneled hand up to fire the sulphur pistol. Blackish glop and curls of tentacles flew all about, some of the glop slapping him in the face. Frowning, he wiped it off on his sleeve. *Great . . .*

He'd almost sensed rather than seen the repulsive Levatopus that had crawled out of the clouds. Had he been a second late, the gravity-defying encephalopod might have wrapped about his head and driven its beak through his skull, to suck his brain.

Like a candle, he'd blown out his Hand of Glory—it would be needed later, and evidently there was a shortage of them. "Frugality of resources," Ezoriel had phrased it. "Not one of God's gifts to us may ever be used unwisely. Gifts taken for granted offend the Lord." Krilid figured that was the Fallen Angel's way of saying the Contumacy itself as well as all the other Anti-Luciferic Units were sucking wind and shit out of supplies.

His Troll's belly squirmed; he was famished, and worse, thirsty. He smirked to himself for not retrieving the pieces of the Levatopus before they'd floated away. He could've squeezed the juices out of them, which were better than nothing. But then a bleak joy kindled in his nine-chambered heart at the familiar humming and then the verifying sound—

Sssssssssssssssss-ONK!

—and then a terrifying CLAP! cracked in the air along with several blindingly bright flashes like a camera flash, only the light was a gooey green.

The open mouth of another Nectoport now hovered just before Krilid's.

The grand figure moved forward, and the lightlike voice: "Grace be unto you, Krilid."

"And you, too, Ezoriel."

Try as he might, the more Krilid stared at the Fallen Angel's face, the more impossible it was to actually see. He could see the tall, chiseled body and its toned muscles, plus the straps of armor, and even the burned stubs of Ezoriel's long-gone wings sticking out over his shoulders. Just never the face.

The perfect Human hand reached over into Krilid's Observation Port, proffering a small vial. "Fresh, distilled water for you, Krilid. I regret the paltry volume, but . . ."

Krilid's eyes nearly popped out of his warped head from the delight. "Aw, wow, Ezoriel! Thanks!" He took the vial and gulped it down.

"Only seven ounces," the Angel's voice sparkled, "but just as Lucifer finds such nefarious function in the number of his name—six—*blessed* fortune is found in the *perfect* number, seven."

Guess that means it's good luck. Krilid nearly felt drunk from the immaculate water. "God, that's good."

"God—oh, yes. His gifts are great." A pause in the aura-like voice, then a sniffing sound. "You expended a round?"

"Yeah. Levatopus. The clouds are crawling with the things."

"I believe it's their egg-laying season. But have no fear. God protects those who serve him." Next, the Angel's unseen eyes seemed to veer toward the Hand of Glory. "Ah, you haven't forgotten the necessity to be austere with your implements. God smiles upon such disciplines."

Does he? Krilid wondered. *Does he really? Does God even give a shit about me?* "Sure, Ezoriel, but you know, I could use some more rounds for the pistol and rifles."

Again, the Angel's hand crossed the Port and handed Krilid exactly one gold bullet.

Krilid laughed. "Oh, don't empty out the entire arsenal just for me!"

"I'm sorry I can't provide more, my brave Troll. But we

mustn't be selfish, correct? We have many operations ongoing."

Jeez. One lousy bullet to replace the one I just popped.

Ezoriel seemed suddenly concerned. "And . . . how many rounds have you expended from your rifle?"

"Oh, the seventy-seven calibers? None."

"Blessing to you!" Ezoriel exclaimed. "You're as conscientious as you are sure of eye!"

"But you haven't even told me yet who you want me to snipe," Krilid began his next complaint.

"That's because you don't yet have a need to know—"

"And you haven't told me anything about this extraction target I'm supposed to pick up, or when it will happen."

"Again, your need to know is not yet at hand. Krilid, Christ knew well in advance that he would be betrayed, apprehended, and crucified, yet he *never told the Apostles.* Why? Because they did not have a need to know. Had they been forewarned, God's plan might've been tainted. Trust me, my brave friend. All will be made known when the time has come."

Krilid frowned. "And who told you that? No, let me guess! Your *unimpeachable authority?*"

"You sound cynical, Krilid. Remember, cynicism is spiritual death—"

"But I'm a *Troll.* I don't even *have* a spirit."

"That's hardly the point."

"I don't know anything about your information source. Sorry, but that gives me the heebie-jeebies."

A humming pause. "Surely you don't think I'm lying to you—"

"No," Krilid blurted. "But maybe *they're* lying to *you.* Come on, I hear stories every day about Lucifer's counterintel systems. He's got *whole complexes* of Wizards and Channelers filling the Hell-Flux with phony transmissions. How do you know—"

"How do I know I haven't been duped myself by such a trick?" the Fallen Angel challenged. "Hear me. I know because *God* told me."

Krilid was hard-pressed not to laugh. "Oh, God did, huh? God—what?—he called you up on a hectophone personally and *told you* the intel was on the level?"

"He did it *spiritually*, Krilid. Calm your worries—believe me, I understand them—"

"You want to know the truth, Ezoriel? Half the time I feel like I'm on a suicide mission. Otherwise there'd be a hundred more insurgents in the Nectoport with me. For a mission like this? But, no, just little old me and no one else. Almost like someone said, 'Well, if the intel turns out to be bad, then it's better to lose just one guy than a whole company.'"

When Ezoriel laughed, there came a sensation like one's reaction to sudden lightning.

"It's not that funny—"

"Krilid, please. You *worry* too much. Best to think only of God's glory and the entails of your mission. You're in God's hands; therefore . . . you'll do fine."

Yeah . . .

"So your reconnaissance at the Reservoir went well," the higher being said rather than asked.

"Sure. I mean, I found the landmark and the pickup point. But the Reservoir's still empty. Once it's filled, it'll be harder to relocate the extraction point—"

"Just use your sextant, and you'll have no trouble—"

More gripes came to the Troll. "And I don't know *when* they're going to fill it, or with *what*. I feel like I'm standing at home plate in a headball game but I'm blindfolded . . ."

More illuminating chuckles issued from the Fallen Angel. "I'm happy to impart to you, Krilid, that I have been permitted to answer those questions now, as your particular need to know has been sparked."

Krilid sat up stiff, keenly and suddenly attentive.

Ezoriel's voice seemed to lower to a glittering whisper. "The time will be *very soon.* And just exactly *what* the massive Reservoir will be filled with . . . is this: six billion gallons of the Gulf of Cagliostro . . ."

"What!"

"It's true," Ezoriel said. "That Pipeway is impressive—hundreds of miles long and quite a feat for Lucifer's Engineers. Oh, we might've been able to bomb it but then . . ." The refulgent Angel seemed to smile. "Powers far more lofty than I insisted that that not happen . . ."

Krilid refrained from sarcastic comment.

"All things for a purpose, yes? It's all part of God's plan, and we are tiny yet essential *pieces* of that plan. Expendable? Yes. But loved by God as well, even in our Damnation."

Oh, that makes me feel MUCH better, Krilid's thoughts sputtered.

"Have *faith,* in this place of the faithless."

"Fine, fine," Krilid interjected, "but . . . *why* does Lucifer want to fill that ridiculous Reservoir with six billion gallons of disgusting Bloodwater from the Gulf?"

Ezoriel's undetectable gaze fixed on Krilid.

"All right, I get it," Krilid droned. "I don't have a need to know yet. You're afraid if I get captured, I'll spill the beans."

The illumined presence seemed to nod. "God's work calls me to depart. The coordinates for your next reconnaissance will be delivered telepathically very soon." The Angel raised a finger. "Rest assured that, just as Daniel had no fear of the lion's pit, you need not have fear of what awaits you." Ezoriel passed Krilid a small cloth sack. "Until we meet again . . . go with God." And then—

Sssssssssssssssss-ONK!

—the Fallen Angel's Nectoport was gone.

Krilid opened the sack and withdrew—

"Oh, wow! What a great guy!"

—a big chunk of Ghor-Hound sausage.

(II)

What an ass I am, Gerold thought. A male intern who looked like he hadn't slept in days wheeled him through the hospital lobby and out into blazing sun. Once outside, the stubbled assistant lit a cigarette and frowned right at Gerold.

"What?" Gerold asked.

"I'm supposed to be off now, that's what," the guy said. "I've been up thirty-six hours but now I've got to do *this*."

"Sorry." Gerold felt sheepish. "So . . . *where* am I going?"

"VA." The guy rubbed his sandpapery chin. "You're what we call a 'punt.' "

"A . . . what?"

"A punt. We're punting you. It's tax dollars paying for this stunt of yours—"

Gerold's well-developed arms tensed. "It's wasn't a *stunt*—"

"Yeah, it was. We get 'em all the time. Look, I'm sorry you can't walk but—shit. My brother can't walk either—he got hit by a drunk. And you know what? He's never pulled a stunt like this. Clogging up a busy hospital with bullshit is no way to vent your need for attention."

Gerold winced. "You're worse than that lady upstairs! I wasn't trying to get attention! I was just trying to kill myself, but I fucked up!" His tempered sizzled. "And I wish to God I hadn't."

"You and me both . . ."

Gerold rolled his eyes.

"Anyway, we're punting you." The guy tapped ashes disgustedly. "See, we gotta file for the damn money we burned on you last night. We have to send in a bill, and then wait months for the provider to pay—"

"I didn't *burn* any money," Gerold spat.

"Sure, you did. Every square inch of this place costs money, pal. And us having to give you a bed in the precaution ward last night is a big ticket, probably a couple of grand—"

"Bullshit."

"Yeah, see, you don't even give a shit. Typical. You think everything should be free while guys like me gotta work our asses off catering to you. The fact is, caregivers—like me—love to help people in need. It's our duty. But what we *hate* is having to help people who pretend to be fucked up in the head."

"This is some real compassionate care, man . . ."

"Fuck off. Let VA have your ass. You can burn *their* tax dollars."

"I was fuckin' fighting for my country!" Gerold bellowed.

The guy expectorated loudly. "You were fighting for a bunch of political *war pigs,* man. If you want to be a patriot, you *protest* the war, you don't *fight* in it."

Gerold groaned. "Your political views are your business, but I sure as shit—"

"What?" snapped the intern. "You don't want to hear it, G.I. Joe? Well, tough."

Gerold dared to laugh. "I'd love to see you on a bivouac. You wouldn't last a day, you'd be cryin' like a baby, cryin' for your mother with your thumb in your mouth."

The intern lurched forward, gnashed his teeth, then pulled back.

"Yeah, go ahead, tough guy," Gerold said. "Punch a guy in a wheelchair. Shit, I'd *still* kick your ass."

"In your dreams."

The hits just keep on comin', Gerold thought. "We're sitting out here in the hot sun for *what* reason?"

"Waiting for your transport, and *I* have to go with you," the intern seethed. "I have to check you in."

"Tell you what," Gerold posed. "Go on home for your much-needed beauty sleep, and I'll check myself in."

"Right. You'd just go somewhere and pretend you're trying to kill yourself again, to get more attention."

Gerold would've paid any price just to be able to stand up for one second and clean this guy's clock.

"Aw, shit!" the guy spat, and looked at his watch.

"What? That time of the month again?"

"Fuck off. I forgot your out-pross papers." He pointed right in Gerold's face. "Listen, dick, I have to go back inside and get your papers. I'll only be five minutes, and when I'm back you *better* still be here. Don't even *think* about eloping."

"Eloping?" Gerold stretched the word. "*That's* what they call it?"

"Yeah, you're an *elopement* risk. Says so right in your records. Elopement is when a *pseudo–mental patient* tries to escape from the people trying to help his sorry ass."

"Where am I gonna go in five minutes, man!" Gerold yelled.

The finger kept pointing. "Just know this. If you *do* try to flee, I'll find you, and you'll be *real* sorry."

"What, you're threatening me?"

The stubbled face grinned. "Yeah. So what're you gonna do about it, Hot Wheels?"

Gerold laughed hard now. "That's what I like about interns. It puts the good ones into the system."

The intern gave him the finger, then turned and headed back toward the building.

Gerold could only shake his head, chuckling morosely. *This has been the worst twenty-four hours of my life. Wouldn't it be nice if just once the Fates would let something* GOOD *happen to me?*

A second after the automatic doors closed behind the intern, a city bus pulled up at the shelter not ten yards from where Gerold sat. "Yo, yo! Hold up!" Gerold launched himself forward with such force his wheels nearly left the pavement. Immediately the wheelchair lift began to beep, the ramp lowering.

"Come on in," the uncharacteristically friendly driver invited. In no time, Gerold was on the ramp, going up. *Come on! Come on!* he fretted. "Is this a time point?" he asked. "I got a connection."

"It is but I'm running late," the driver said and belted Gerold's chair into the cubby. "We gotta leave right now."

All right! Gerold sat hunched, peeking with half an eye out the window. He just *knew* that before the bus pulled away, that intern would be running after them.

The bus pulled away.

No sign of the intern.

Go! Go! his thoughts pleaded, and he rocked back and forth with his fingers crossed.

The bus made the turn, roared onto the main road, and was on its way.

Gerold stared desperately behind until the hospital disappeared. He went slack in his chair. *Thank you, Fates.*

The bus was empty and deliciously cool.

"So what's your connection?" the driver said.

"Uh, the 52." Gerold picked the first bus route that came to mind.

"Oh, hell, we'll be at the terminal at least ten minutes before that one leaves."

"Great. Thanks."

Gerold smiled, rocking over the gentle bumps in the road. But a glance down showed him a crumpled newspaper. He snatched it up.

It was the *Tampa Bay Times*, the local popified daily. His eyes idled over the "hip" articles and blaring ads for lingerie and singles clubs. It was a girl in a bikini holding a long fish that snagged more of his attention.

Gerold read the half-page ad—its headline: FUN & SUN AT BEAUTIFUL LAKE MISQUAMICUS!—to learn of a quaint, out-of-the-way camping and fishing resort several counties north of here. Jet Skis, parasailing, freshwater fishing, and, of special note, "Catch your own crawdads! Lake Misquamicus crawdads are the biggest in the state! We have delicious freshwater clams too!" Gerold really liked crawdads . . .

"Excuse me, driver? Now that I think of it, I won't need to go to the terminal. Just drop me off on Ninth Avenue."

"Sure. You taking a Greyhound somewhere?"

"Yeah," Gerold said, still eyeing the ad and its accompanying bikini-clad model. "I'm heading up to . . . Lake Misquamicus."

The driver nodded. "Good choice. They've got great fishing there and crawdadding. They stock the lake every year, and the place isn't all full of tourists."

"Cool," Gerold said. Suddenly he felt wonderful, and he was genuinely looking forward to some fresh-cooked crawdads. They seemed a *perfect* last meal.

(III)

. . . and you're not sure what you're looking at, but when your supernatural vision sharpens—

"It's like a mansion, except it's *got* to be over five hundred feet on each side . . ."

"Sixty hundred and sixty-six," Howard redresses, "*if* you're interested in exactitude, and six floors each precisely sixty-six feet in height. Six belfries and six towers per side, six spires and crockets per tower. Six windows per dormer section, sixty-six chimneys, sixty-six occuli, and six hundred and sixty-six crest spikes along each of sixty-six cornices, not to belabor the evidence of sixty-six—"

"Enough of the fucking sixes! Please!" you wail. "I'm SICK of the fucking sixes!"

Howard waits for you to settle down, a bemused smile subtly set into his sallow face. "It's curious to observe the extent of your acclimation, Mr. Hudson."

"What's that?"

"Your slowly increasing tendency to use profanity—"

I did it again, you realize. *This place is a bad influence on me, and it's no surprise.*

After all, it's Hell.

You look back up at the bizarre edifice you've been escorted to, just as Howard announces:

"Mr. Hudson, it is my doubtless pleasure and unreserved honor to introduce to you the new personal abode of the Prince of Darkness . . . Manse Lucifer."

By now, you've already noticed the most distinguishing characteristic of the colossal manse. Its walls are not constructed of brick, block, cement slab, nor wood, nor stucco.

They're built with female Human heads.

The heads face outward and—to no surprise—they're all still very much alive. They've been laid like mason work, with mortar meticulously packed around each. Millions of heads, no doubt, have been used to construct the mansion's outer walls and immense mansard-style roof.

"The walls are double layered," Howard points out, "so that living female faces form the walls inside, as well—God *knows* what they're forced to witness. All the interior floors, too, are made from the heads, including buttresses and load-bearing walls."

A house of heads inside and out, you can only think. *A* MANSION *of living female heads . . .*

You sense yourself lowering, then perceive that Howard has set your "stick" into a slab of sidewalk filled with bone and tooth fragments. He's slipping something from his pocket. "As you can imagine, an equally spectacular interior exists." Howard, next, holds a small stack of dim photographs before your face.

"Good old-fashioned photographs," you remark. "I'm surprised you have stuff like that in Hell."

"Not photographs, *hecto*graphs. Hell's version of the tintypes of my early days. A process of gold nitrate merged with tin salt. Hectographs are, again, only a luxury for the very wealthy here . . ."

Your eyes hold wide on each macabre snapshot.

"The Atrium," Howard defines.

You are shown an impossible room walled with heads. Columns that ought to be Doric or Corinthian stand at each side of the arched entrance; these, too, are constructed of heads. On one wall hangs a painting of Demons peering in on the Last Supper while platters of chopped infants and goblets of blood wait on the long table to be consumed; on another hangs the Messiah being crucified upside down in Hell.

Next, "Lucifer's master bed chamber . . ."

Not only are the walls made from heads but so is the high poster bed, yet each head of the mattress has its tongue permanently protruded via studs through the lips. Mirrors shaped like inverted crosses ring the room.

Next, "Lucifer's Great Hall . . ."

Columned peristyles stretch down the long, vault-ceilinged room fitted with scroll-backed couches and chairs upholstered in Human skin. The banquet table—which you assume must be sixty-six feet long—occupies the center, with higher-backed skeletal chairs around it. The faces in the floor, ceiling, and walls, here, appear more appalled than in other rooms, and you can only suspect the reason has something to do with what they are forced to watch the Prince of Darkness and his guests dine on.

Next, "And Lucifer's Grand Courtyard . . ."

Nauseating topiary has been meticulously clipped into the configuration of the number six. Noxious rosebushes bear heads of not petals but vaginas, while an ivy of severed penises crawls up a glimmering silver lattice. Human heads only comprise the outer walls and curtilage, but then you see their evidence in one more place: the circular swimming pool that exists at the center of the "six." The entire pool is lined with them, and the pool appears to be filled with urine ever so faintly tinted with blood.

Next, "Ah, and Lucifer's throne in the Central Nave . . ."

Not only is the room floored and walled with heads but the great throne itself is composed of them as well. The throne bears a similarity to a Victorian bishop's chair, with even side-stiles, head backs, and armrests made of heads. The heads forming the center of the seat seem understandably more weary than the rest. To the right sits an ornate grandfather clock, whose pendulum chains are no doubt arteries of more unfortunates; its face has no hands. To the left hangs a painting of a glorious conqueror in a shining breastplate engraved with sixes. He wields a sweep-bladed cutlass while he stands over the headless corpse of, apparently, Christ. The sword-wielder's face seems to glow to the point that detail cannot be discerned.

"And lastly, Lucifer's commode-chamber, which you in your modern parlance would call a bathroom . . ."

The head-formed walls here are circular, presumably so that all may watch the Morning Star's elimination. A beautifully cut mosaic of amethysts make up the actual toilet bowl but the rim of the seat is made of more Human heads. The oddest adornment here, though, is a gilded, flat-topped stand, and on top of it sits a lone Human head on its side. The head is not connected or mortared to anything; it's just sitting there. You squint at it. It's that of a blonde woman, slightly chubby-faced, with an expression of utter revulsion.

"What's with the single head on the stand?" you ask.

"Surely you've noticed a disheartening *absence* of toilet paper, Mr. Hudson," Howard says. "The unfortunate blonde belle's *face* serves the purpose . . ."

Your facsimile for a stomach sinks, then sinks further when you suspect you've seen the face before in some entertainment magazine but you can't quite recall her name.

Howard puts the hectographs away and rehoists your head-stick. "The main house has obviously been completed, but constant additions are in perpetual progress." He points down an empty street—Mephisto Avenue—as a queue of clattering steam-trucks and monster-drawn wagons approach, all manned by various demonic workmen. Several wagons are heaped high with heads while others haul sacks of occult cement. At a certain point near the house, two hooded Bio-Wizards depart from the mansion's entrance. They touch a pair of crooked wands together, then draw them apart to a distance wide enough to permit passage of the construction crew. After said passage, the Wizards reverse the odd procedure, and return to the entrance.

"What was that all about?"

"They were opening and closing the mansion's impenetrable defense perimeter. Nothing may gain entrance without proper clearance."

"Perimeter? I don't see any *perimeter*."

"It's a Hex, Mr. Hudson. It's called an Exsanguination Bridle. Ah, and how convenient! Watch what befalls this gaggle of very *un*wise insurgent ruffians and ne'er-do-wells . . ."

You look up and see a spectacular white Gryphon flying

urgently toward one of the mansion's towers. Saddled to its back are several very determined-looking Imps and Humans, each hefting a keg of explosives. But when the Gryphon's swift wings take it past a certain point—

FFFFFFFFFFWAP!

—white feathers fly as the beast and its riders are immediately stricken by an energy that causes their blood to fire out of their bodies through every orifice. Then the bodies, and a rain of blood, hit the street. The kegs burst harmlessly, poofing billows of something akin to gunpowder.

"Wow," you say, impressed. "That's some security system."

"The very latest Senarial Science. And anyone who *is* granted entrance is thoroughly screened by Prism Veils operated by Warlocks with the Psychical Detection Regiments. They're able to read any and all negative or anti-Luciferic thoughts."

Then you look back at the obscene house; even in the utter evil of its design, you have to be impressed. But your confusion couldn't be more intense. "So this is the clincher? This is the final sight that's supposed to make me accept the Senary—a house of *heads?*"

Howard unreels a high, nasally laugh. "Goodness *no,* Mr. Hudson. This is the final sight that's intended to fully evolve your awareness of the totality of Lucifer's power and forethought. The clincher shall arrive later . . ." Howard pauses, then adds, "But the tour *is* nearly at an end. I dare say a minor respite is in order . . . before our *final* debarkation."

You're taking a final glance at the ghastly manse, at the innumerable living heads facing you, all those lips mouthing silent horrors, and all those eyes shock-wide by the excruciating particulars of their Damnation; and the millions more heads that comprise this entire incalculable place when the black static sizzles yet again and then—

Coolness.

Quiet.

Your gourd-head clears, and you find yourself back in the bedimmed Turnstile. It's uneven, flat black walls emit the faintest indescribable luminescence.

"Ah," Howard utters. He sits down on a squat, companulated protrusion made of the same material of the Turnstile itself. He loosens his frayed gray tie and smiles at you.

"Just as sleep is nature's balm, I daresay *quietude* is its sedative."

Your stick has been leaned against a corner whose angles are precisely sixty-six degrees. Within the polygon's inner vault, you're finally able to relax. The only sound you're aware of arrives as the most distant hum, which is somehow organic, not electronic. That and an occasional *tick* of the steam-car's cooling engine.

Howard unwraps a napkin and removes a cookie of some sort. "I'd offer you a Uneeda biscuit but, lo, your Auric Carrier doesn't allow you to consume food."

"Thanks just the same . . ." You try to collect your thoughts but aren't sure how to; you're not even sure what to think. But you know that Howard is merely giving you time to either consider or recover from all the detestable things you've seen.

You jerk your gaze at a sudden sound: a grunt, a shuffle. Torchlight sputters from a farther corner, and then a shadow lengthens.

The Imperial Truncator—the watchman of this place—shuffles nonchalantly across the black floor, his cleaver-hands swinging, the Ghor-Hound helmet high on his head.

"I forgot all about him," you remark, but then: "Hey! What happened to the—"

"Ah, yes. Our lithe chauffeur, the Golemess . . ." Howard squints; then his shoulders slump. "Ostensibly not so lithe any longer."

Now another, less lively shuffle, and from the same corner

the Golemess appears. She seems winded, wearied now, and when she trudges into more torchlight, you see why.

She's pregnant.

"The dude with the meat cleavers for hands got her pregnant!" you exclaim. The gray clay belly looks *stuffed,* the breasts doubled in volume, presumably full of Golem milk now.

"I was unaware that our Golemess came equipped with fertility features. No doubt before her clay was Hexegenated, the Master Sculptors at the Edward Kelly Institute of Inanimate Enchantment implanted her with a reproductive tract and ovarian process. This is another Luciferic Law that's gradually activating: the Public Gravidity Initiative. Lucifer desires that anything female—even things *un*alive—be fertile. More progeny, more fodder for the machinations of the Mephistopolis. God invented reproduction via Human passion, to bring forth more Children of God to one day enjoy the Firmament of Heaven. Lucifer, therefore, *perverts* God's endeavor, to reduce femalekind to repositories of lust, and bring forth more meat and building material."

You stare at the huge stomach as the fatigued Golemess lumbers to the steam-car. "But what . . . what's going to come out?"

"Immaterial," Howard answers. "It's purpose is served, and the Initiative is duly discharged."

Meat, you recite Howard's information. *Building material.*

"And now, Mr. Hudson," Howard intones. "You've had this moment of respite. I'm curious as to the constitution of your thoughts."

Your hideous head swivels to meet his gaze. "I'm thinking that everything here is illogical—"

"Which serves as the perfect logic within the confines of an antithetical demesne."

"—including my being here." You blink. "What, I win

this *Senary* because I've tipped some scale of sin, some *fulcrum*. It makes more sense to go after some guy who's a hundred percent. A cardinal, a bishop . . ."

"Perhaps in your *own* purview of logic. Just as popes don't question God, we don't question Satan."

You smirk. "Okay, fine. But in that case, your methods are *terrible*."

"Really?" Howard seems intrigued. "Be kind enough to articulate your impression."

You recite them thus far. "I'm a good enough person that if I died right now, I'd go to Heaven, right?"

"Beyond doubt."

"But Lucifer wants me to give that up so that when I die, I come here instead. He wants me to *make that choice*, right?"

"Precisely."

"He wants me to give up Heaven, in favor of Hell, right?"

"Indubitably."

Your eyes lock open. "WELL THEN WHY WOULD I DO THAT? HELL SUCKS!"

Your outburst bounces off the vault's obsidian walls like bullets ricocheting. The Golemess flinches. Even the Imperial Truncator jolts from the start.

"My, Mr. Hudson," Howard says after his own shock. "That's . . . quite an ejaculation . . ."

"You guys must be *out of your minds!*" you continue to rail at the senselessness of it all. "This place is the biggest pile of shit I've ever seen! Bridges made of *people?* Taverns where the kegs are *bare boobs* with beer taps on the nipples, and bars that serve wine made from fermented babies? Towns made of guts and towns made of skin? And the guy who runs the whole shebang lives in a mansion made of *heads!* Who the FUCK would want to live here?"

"Please, Mr. Hudson," Howard urges. "At least *try* to mind your cursing." A long, crackly pause. "But certainly, sir, you can comprehend the unending bliss of one who enjoys Privilato status?"

"The Privilato? That asshole in the jewelly jacket?" You roll your demonic eyes. "He's a putz with a posse of hot chicks who wouldn't give a *shit* about him if he wasn't a Privilato in the first place. Big deal. He drives around town in a flying hole in the sky and gets a red carpet wherever he goes. You gotta do better than *that*, man."

"Ah, well, I see that you are underestimating the *entireness* of the Mephistopolis for those few granted privilege." Howard raises a finger. "Allow me to query. Seeing that the lion's share of your sins—however meager that may be—fall primarily into the *lust* category . . . if you could revel in the carnal pleasures of any woman in the world, who would that be?"

The question, absurd as it is, percolates in your mind. Angelina Jolie? Paris Hilton? Jessica Alba? Just as you think you've been stumped, the answers appears. "Well, I'm kind of old-school, but I'd still have to say Pamela Anderson."

Howard nods. "Bear in mind, of course, that since Mademoiselle Anderson is still a member of the Living World, it defies possibility for me to be familiar with her. However, I can assure you beyond all dubiety that the women awaiting you as a Privilato will be possessed of a desirability no less than sixty-six times that of your coveted Ms. Anderson."

You try to picture that in your mind. *Women . . . sixty-six times HOTTER than Pam Anderson . . .*

Wow.

But still . . . the proposition is folly and you know it. "Doesn't matter if they're sixty-six *thousand* times hotter, Howard. This place is still Hell, and Hell sucks. Not to mention, I'm *celibate*. Next week I'm going to the seminary to become a *priest*."

"Then what could possibly explain your recent intent with those slatternettes?"

"Slattern—*what?*"

"The prostitutes the other night. You fully intended to proposition them, for a *sex act.* You trumpeting the piety of celibacy and the pursuit of the priesthood seems . . . hypocritical."

If you had a finger, you would point in his face. "Hey, I *almost* propositioned them. Part of me . . . wanted to know what sex was like before I officially gave it up for a life of godly servitude."

Did Howard frown as if unconvinced?

"Sex out of wedlock is a sin, and priests—as well as priests-to-be—regard sin as an enemy of the soul. I don't consider agreeing to take this tour to be a sin, and I don't think God does either. It will strengthen me in my purpose; it will verify my faith and make me a better priest."

"Oh, please extrapolate, Mr. Hudson! How can one being temporarily in the midst of Hell make one a better priest?"

"Simple," you explain. "It's an *opportunity* that no other priest but Christ himself has received. By seeing Hell firsthand? I'll be able to prepare Christians more effectively. This will make me work even harder to save souls, and the more souls I save, the fewer Lucifer will get his hands on. It's a victory for God." You grin at Howard. "Glory be to *God.*"

Howard seems disappointedly quelled. "Your mind appears to be made up in quite an *intractable* fashion."

"It is."

"Then explain your seeming turn toward profanity. Is it not true that to profane is to offend God?"

"Oh, God doesn't give a shit about that," you feel sure. "I *never* cuss on Earth. The only reason I've started to here is just due to the environment, I guess."

"Hmmm . . ."

"And my mind *is* made up," you reiterate without hesitation. "So get me out of this fucked-up pumpkin so I can go back to my life like you promised."

"As you wish, if you're sure."

"Sure I'm sure, and this little tour of yours is the *reason* I'm sure. It proved to me that Lucifer's a grade-A *moron*. He's a *nitwit*. All that power and all these resources and technologies, and look what he does with it. He could turn Hell into a great place, and you want to know why he doesn't?"

"I know why, Mr. Hudson," Howard admits. "Because of his pride."

"Right. He's obsessed with being evil and disgusting and cruel because God's the opposite of that, and Lucifer's pissed off at God for throwing him out of Heaven. He's like a little kid having a tantrum because mommy spanked him. I don't want anything to do with this place, *or* him. Lucifer's a *dick*."

Howard's brow rises in a defeated surprise. "Why not let me at least encourage you to take the final leg of the tour."

"No reason to. My mind's made up."

"Then what harm can there be?"

You huff. "Well, what's the final leg? Believe me, I don't need to see any more piss pumps, baby factories, or Decapitant Camps."

"The final leg is the Privilato Chateau that you would occupy if you accept the Senary. At least go and behold all the pleasures you'll be missing."

You pause. *Well* . . . Suddenly it begins to sound interesting again. But, "No. Why tempt myself to do the wrong thing when I've already decided to do the right thing?"

"Right and wrong are relative, Mr. Hudson, and in Hell they're interchangeable. Consider the obvious imperative: in Hell there *is* no sin. You find trepidation in the prospect of temptation? So did Jesus during his forty days in the wilderness. Why not test your resolve as he did? You may *think* that you're doing that now, but isn't your faith only proven after you've witnessed the *entire* tour? Need I remind you that Christ took a similar tour after he died on Calvary?"

"I know that," you say.

"Lucifer offered Jesus Privilato status, by the way, and he obviously turned it down. See all that Christ saw; face the *same* temptations he faced, in which case, if you still decide to turn the Senary down, you will have done what *Christ* did as well."

"My thoughts exactly," you tell him. *I'll become an even better Christian by seeing every temptation and STILL turning them all down . . .*

You think a moment more, then say, "All right."

Howard stands up. He seems relieved.

"Still think you can get me to change my mind?" you ask, a bit prideful yourself now.

"Irrelative time will tell," Howard says. He pats sweat off his brow with a handkerchief embroidered, HPL. *This guy's really sweating bullets,* you think.

Howard picks up your head-stick and approaches the circle of geometric etchings in the black wall. "And the tour goes on," he murmurs.

For a reason you can't define—and just before the Turnstile powers up—you look behind you and see the Golemess lying back on the floor, her knees pulled back to her sleek shoulders. Her back arches. Evil water breaks and gushes; then the enormous belly tremors, hitches, and collapses as it disgorges a slick Mongrel fetus with an accordioned face and arms where its legs should be. Puff-eyed, the demonic thing bawls as nublike horns appear on its bald head. It's almost cute.

Almost.

The Golemess labors to her feet. Her elegant clay hands scoop the fetus up. The last thing you see before the Turnstile's black static shifts you into another phase is the new mother calmly sliding her newborn into the fuel hatch of the steam-car's boiler housing. Just as calmly she pushes the hatch shut . . .

. . . and you fall through that now-familiar combustion of morbid energy amid the crackling vertigo of scintillescent black static, and just as the Mongrel baby was pushed forth from the Golemess's womb, you and Howard are pushed through space and some wicked substitute for time until . . .

Chapter Seven

(I)

The pallid censer smoke thinned from a rising, abyssal breeze, but even this far out in the Quarter Favius thought he could hear drifts of screams from the immeasurable city too far away to see. It brought delight to his horrid heart: the relief of the visual monotony, because for decades or centuries, the Great Emptiness Quarter and the Reservoir pit itself existed only in foul, glittery *blackness*.

But now?

So beautiful . . .

A new color to the terrain had been introduced: bloodred.

The bottom of the Reservoir was almost covered—not very deep yet—but covered all the same by the great scarlet gush from the sixty-six-foot-wide Main Sub-Inlets. Favius crudely thought the inflow into the Reservoir could be likened to a toilet slowly filling, only the toilet was the Reservoir itself and its tank was the Gulf of Cagliostro untold miles away. The Pipeway was running at full capacity now, the enormous pumping stations back in the Mephistopolis—at the harbor of Rot-Port—running at full tilt. Favius looked out across the impossible red vista, which churned and foamed from the force of the inflow. This close to the southern Main Sub-Inlet, the violent gush was almost deafening.

It's finally happening, he thought. Had he been capable of the act, he might've cried in sheer joy.

The Conscripts under his command watched the outer perimeters, high and low, with great vigilance, always on guard for signs of an anti-Luciferic attack. Platoons of Golems marched along the ramparts, their horrid clay faces blank, the sounds of their massive feet thundering on the basalt causeway. And all the while, the sub-inlet gushed and gushed.

Exactly how long it would take to fill the pit to its six-billion-gallon prerequisite, the Legionnaire could not reckon, as time itself was unreckonable. Instead of counting seconds, minutes, and hours, then, he reasoned he could count depth. By the looks of the progress now, most of the pit had been filled to a depth of at least one foot . . .

Only sixty-five more to go.

Next, he stared directly at the sub-inlet's great Y-connector, and in the waterfall-like expulsion of noxious fluid he knew he could see solid objects as well: detritus from the sea, scraps of old boats long since sunken by nauseating nautical creatures or artillery from vessels of the Satanic Navy. Corpses, too, were rife amid the inflow, but closer scrutiny showed him *living* creatures as well, siphoned all the way from the Gulf to here, via the Pipeway. Next, a school of Slime-Sharks burst through, followed by several twenty-foot-wide Gulf Nettles, their milky orb-heads oscillating above even longer barbed tentacles. An excited breath caught in the sentry's chest when, in an instant, an immature Gorge-Worm was siphoned through—nearly a quarter of a mile long. Thousands of Conscripts surrounding the pit cheered at this astonishing evidence. The massive, gilled parasite churned in the shallow Bloodwater, sidewinding like a snake in a shallow pool.

It was spectacular to behold.

The inflow continued to roar. Above, Dentata-Vultures

and Caco-Bats flew mad circles over the Reservoir, inflamed by the Bloodwater's meaty stench. Every so often, they shot straight down into the stew to snatch a buoyant delicacy on which to feed. When one of Favius's Squad Leader's—a Conscript Third Class named Terrod—approached, his armored hand extended to point into the rising gush.

"Commander! Praise Satan for this blessing!"

"Glory be to he who was cast out," Favius replied.

"My heart sings for this great success, Commander, but we are all mystified—"

"As to what?" Favius's voice grated.

"As to the purpose of this wondrous undertaking."

"Keep your spirit on your duty, Terrod. Compared to Lucifer and his Hierarchals, we are unworthy to even contemplate such things."

"Yes, Commander!"

"We exist to receive our orders, which we obey to the death. Just as Judas betrayed Christ, I'm certain that we are but sheep against the greatness of the Morning Star, and therefore incapable of understanding his most unholy plans. It is not for us to muse upon, but only to know that lowly as we are, we are a small part of great black wonders."

"I sing praises to his wretched name, Commander." The lower Conscript looked back out of the scarlet churning. "It's just such a glorious sight that I am beside myself!"

"As am I as well as all of us, good soldier."

"And—look!" Terrod pointed with urgency. "What might those be, Commander?"

Favius peered through his visor. "Hmmm . . ."

"They appear to be kegs or casks of some kind—"

"Ah, yes," Favius said, smiling when he recognized what the half dozen floating objects were. They bobbed like corks in the roiling mire. "Jail-Kegs, Terrod. Clearly much flotsam from the Gulf is finding its way here via the Pipeway. A delightful sight, indeed."

"Jail-Kegs, Commander?"

"For sure. Lucifer's Department of Injustice has recently embarked on cost-cutting measures. Rather than go to the expense incarcerating Human convicts in prisons, it is now deemed more preferable and efficient to confine them to the Kegs. Surely a Jail-Keg costs less than a physical prison cell."

"Of course, Commander!"

Favius nodded, still eyeing the adrift casks. "They merely seal the convicts in the Kegs and dump them into the sea, where they can float sightless and immobile forever."

"An ingenious punishment, sir!"

"Oh, yes—the very idea of it enthralls me." But when the scream-tinged breeze suddenly picked up, Favius raised a concerned glance to the sky. The black clouds seemed aswirl—and seemed to be turning a pallid green—moving in involutionary patterns; in other words, in sixlike configurations.

"Those cloud movements bother me, Commander," Terrod said.

"Yes. We must take no chances. Return to your post. A storm may be coming. Bring the rampart to the ready and brace for emergency conditions."

"Yes, Commander!" Terrod exclaimed and jogged back to his command point, his armor clattering.

The next gust of fetid wind gave Favius a hard shove. He stared up. *Yes, a storm is coming, all right—a formidable one . . .*

But even when confronted with the threat, he gazed out yet again over the detestable churning inflow of Bloodwater and noticed, now, that the level had risen to at least *two* feet.

Only sixty-four to go, Favius thought.

(II)

This high in the Regimental Balloon Skiff—over 600 feet—not Curwen nor any of his crew could hear the steady sacrifices below on the field. It was the massive putrid wall of the Demonculus's chest they faced. So close to the creature's body, the Master Builder could spy details of the miraculous pseudoflesh that composed the thing: like of tar, wet fungus, and putrefactive grave waste all enmeshed together. Curwen could even detect finger ends and teeth in the dread claylike composite, and remnant cartilage from ears long gone to rot, even gallstones and toenails. *A dead colossus,* Curwen thought, *awaiting a glorious Unlife . . .*

Indeed. Awaiting a heart.

Smaller ancillary noble-gas balloons had been rigged to the eyehooks of the titan's chest plate, which had been previously unscrewed and detached by horned Journeymen. Then the plate was allowed to rise high enough to clear the Occultized area of space it had covered.

"We're ready, Master Builder," guttered the sloplike voice of the Project Teratologist. He—or *it*—was a part-Human, part-Ghoul Crossbreed whose brain volume had been doubled with Hexegenically cultured stem cells. This supplement of gray matter was contained by a clear silicon bolus nailed into the Crossbreed's skull. Another physical addendum existed in the servant's hands, which were transplants taken quite abruptly from unwitting Human surgeons who'd recently been Condemned.

"Proceed," Curwen permitted.

"Bring the Auger to bear!"

A pair of goggled Imps advanced, carrying upon their shoulders the aforementioned implement, a Hexed and Incantated manual Auger, which looked like a giant corkscrew.

The laborers carefully aligned the tool's sharpened tip to the X inscribed in the massive thing's chest. Amid grunts and great exertion, the Imps turned the Auger slowly counterclockwise, each turn sinking the screw deeper into the Demonculus's chest. As the screw bore in, loops of reeking pseudoflesh shimmied out.

"Take care," cautioned the Ghoul. "Steady . . . You mustn't miscalculate even by half an inch."

Sweating the most minute error, the Imps continued with their task. Three complete turns, then four.

Five. Then—

"Six!" shouted the Teratologist. "Stop! Right there on that mark! Perfect!"

"Yes," Curwen's voice creaked. The psychic patina of his Wizard's vision told him beyond doubt. *It is. Perfect.* "You and your Journeymen have done fine work."

"Thank you, Master Builder."

"Extract the Auger."

Chains were hooked into each end of the Auger's handle, then rung through pullies fixed to the Skiff's mast. The Imps grabbed the chain ends and planted their webbed feet.

"On the count of six!" ordered the Teratologist, and when he counted down—

"Pull!"

The Imps' corded muscles tightened, and they gritted their fangs when in unison they pulled back on the chains.

"Yes!"

The Auger was smoothly extracted from the monster's chest. It clanked against the Skiff deck.

Curwen rushed to the newly formed cavity.

"Great Lucifer! The Hexes are working pristinely!"

Indeed. The Auger's removal left a roughly six-inch tunnel in the Demonculus's chest. The tunnel's walls as well as the all-important mounting seat at its terminus glittered with Anti-Light, a sign that the Animation Spells were regenerating.

A great day in Hell, Curwen thought, stepping back with steepled fingers as he appraised the work. His leaden surplice sparkled. "These newest Occult Sciences truly boggle the mind," he muttered more to himself.

The Ghoul nodded, grinning with black teeth. "And I needn't remind you, Master Builder, that these wondrous sciences were theorized and then executed by *you*."

"Yes, indeed, but all by the grace of the Morning Star . . ."

"Bring the chest plate back down," ordered the Teratologist, "and re-cover the cavity. The Diviners have predicted inclement weather in multiple Districts. We can't risk damaging the cavity . . ."

Curwen watched as the great iron plate was pulled back down and rebolted to the Demonculus's chest.

"All I can muse upon, Master Builder," remarked the Ghoul, "is *when? When* might this miracle occur?"

The gravity-defying Skiff began to lower. Curwen's black and yellow eyes strayed out over the smoking District trademarked by a million severed heads on pikes.

"Soon," Curwen whispered. "Sooner than you or any of us may think . . ."

(III)

—you are there.

Your head spins like a proverbial top as your senses first alight and you think you hear . . .

A deep, incessant *throb*, like crickets in a vast field only much more intense. Before you can even contemplate the nature of the sound, it brings an immediate smile to your face.

It's then that your vision turns crisp; you find that you

are indeed standing in a vast, sweeping field of verdant grass a yard high.

It's beautiful.

And the sounds throb on.

"Cicadas," you dreamily mutter. "The seventeen-year kind. It's one of my earliest childhood memories—that sound. It's always been my favorite sound . . ."

"The powers that be are aware of that," Howard tells you, your head-stick in hand as he walks along through the gorgeous, blight-free grass. The scent of the grass is intoxicating. "As a Privilato, everything you are endeared to, everything that brings you jubilancy and exultation will be heaped upon you to the very best of our abilities. And, mind you, *forever.*"

Then Howard turns and you see the castle.

"Noticing a familiarity?" Howard asked.

The castle's great buff-colored blocks gleam atop the grass-swept hill, with five massive bastions rimmed with turrets, merlons, and arrow slits, a moat surrounding all. And come to think of it:

It DOES look familiar, you recall.

"You were quite an aficionado of the Middle Ages when you were in middle school—"

Then the memory sweeps into your head. "Château-Gaillard . . ."

"Correct, the famed bastion of Richard the Lionheart, in Les Andelys, France. Of course, the real one is a ruin now, but Lucifer's Architects have constructed this duplicate, down to every excruciating detail. It appears as it did, in every conceivable way, in 1192 AD. In your early teens, castles, knights, and the like had a tendency to fascinate you."

And he's right; you remember now.

"While the interior has been modified to a scheme you're sure to be delighted in," Howard added.

Incredible, you think. As Howard approaches the drawbridge you notice eleven other magnificent castles on eleven other hills in the dim distance. "Who lives in those?"

"Your neighbors. The other men—er, I should say, ten men and one woman who've won the Senary since it began in 4652 BC."

"Ten men but just one woman?" you question.

"Yes. Women seem to be more concrete about their notions of sin versus redemption. Our only female winner is a quite attractive Judean named Arcela, a concubine of a Roman governor. You're certain to make her acquaintance, along with all the winners." But then Howard clears his throat. "That is, *if* you decide to accept your winnings."

"But I've already decided not to," you remind your guide. "This castle looks like really cool digs . . . but it's not worth my soul."

"Of course, of course, but . . . wait till you view the interior."

Your gourd-head sways along on the stick as Howard carries it across the magnificent drawbridge and through a barbican and iron portcullis. Next, up a stone spiral staircase, and suddenly the air feels cool as if climate-controlled. Through a spectacular archway, you're startled by a brilliant shine, then—

"Oh, wow," you utter.

"This is the Hall of Gold."

You're standing in a long room completely walled in pure gold.

"Stunning, eh? The decorative effect seems to awe Humans. Six hundred and sixty-six tons of gold have been used to wall this room," Howard tells you as he walks on, through another arch, "while six hundred and sixty-six tons of diamonds wall this one—the foyer."

The sight is dizzying. You're now in the middle of another chamber walled similarly with diamonds. The effect is impossible to describe. "This really is beautiful," you admit.

"I should say so!"

"But it's still not worth my soul. Come on, be serious. I get to spend eternity in a neat castle full of gold and diamonds? Big deal. I'm still in Hell."

"Um-hmm," Howard consents. "But you haven't met your house staff—sixty-six of them, by the way." Howard snaps his fingers, and then a diamond panel raises, and through it saunter dozens of beautiful women—Humans and Demons alike.

The drove of smiling women don't make a sound as they enter, stand in rank, and bow.

Yes, the most gorgeous Human women you've ever seen, but now you must confess that some of the Hybrids and Demons are even *more* gorgeous. Fellatitrines, Vulvatagoyles, Succubi. Lycanymphs and Mammaresses, and even a Golemess that puts your sultry chauffeur to shame.

"The sins of the flesh, Mr. Hudson, but not a bad thing in a domain where sin does not exist," Howard's voice echoes in the glittering hall.

You gulp. "Yeah, but I couldn't get it on with all these women in a hundred years."

"But of course you could, and a hundred after that and a hundred after that. Forever. And when you weary of these, *more* will be afforded you."

Now you stare at them. *That's an awful lot of . . . sex . . .*

"But now, we're off to your bedchamber, where your very *personal* harem awaits." And then Howard takes you up more steps, down a torch-studded corridor, and into a long room adorned with all manner of jewels and precious metals.

"Holy shit!" you yell.

Howard frowns.

You're staring at the bed. "I'll bet you didn't get *that* at Mattress Discounters."

The bed is circular, twenty feet in diameter, but the mattress itself is somehow a mass of Human breasts.

"The Breast-Beds are Hexegenically manufactured, for Privilatos only," Howard informs. "I was never possessed of much of a sexual drive—much to my wife's ire, and I'd bet my precious Remington she was committing infidelities in Cleveland." Howard paused amid the digression. "Er, anyway, even I must admit, I wouldn't mind stretching out on such a Breast-Bed."

A bed made of tits, you tell yourself. *And not just any tits—GREAT tits.*

"But didn't you also say something about—"

"Your *personal* harem," Howard went on. "Oh, yes." Again, Howard snaps his fingers.

A door clicks open and in walks a very perfect and very buck-naked—

"It's Pam Anderson!" you wail.

And so it is. The woman curtsies for you, then stands in a displaying pose.

"She's even better-looking than she was in *Barb Wire,*" you observe, but then your eyes bulge when *five more* identical Pam Andersons enter the bedroom and stand in formation.

Your gaze snaps to Howard. "Six Pam Andersons? All for me?"

"All for you, Mr. Hudson, should of course you accept the Senary."

You stare at the impossible line of spectacular women. "But how did you . . ."

"They're products of quite an impressive occult invention, called Hex-Cloning," Howard explains. "They look—and feel—exactly like the genuine woman in the Living World you so desire, but they'll do anything you tell them. Anytime you want."

You gulp again, looking at those six pairs of legendary breasts . . .

"And I suspect you'll enjoy the next prospect: the Bath," Howard says and takes you into what you guess is the bathroom.

Solid gold toilet. Solid gold sink. A claw-foot tub made of still more gold sits on the immaculate floor.

"Pretty nice bathroom," you say.

"You're welcome to partake in baths with pure water, or, if you prefer . . ." Howard snaps his fingers one more time.

Several large-bosomed and sultry She-Demons enter next, their bodies nearly as provocative as the half dozen counterfeit Pam Andersons in the bedroom, only these women have petite horns and various colored skin.

"What's the big deal with these chicks?"

"They're your Bath Girls, in the event that you don't want to take a normal bath."

You blink at Howard. "Huh?"

"Girls?" Howard addresses them. "Be so good as to show Mr. Hudson your surgical augmentation."

All at once, then, the She-Demons open their mouths and stick out their tongues.

"Woe-boy!" you exclaim.

Each woman extrudes a tongue the size of a beef liver.

"Their tongues are *huge!*"

"Of course, they need to be. They're Bath Girls. Only Privilatos, Exalted Dukes, and District Emirs are afforded this very expensive luxury—along with Satan himself, of course. Their sole purpose is to administer to you what's known as a tongue-bath."

You stare at the women's tongues as much as you stare at the consideration. *Tongue-baths . . .*

"Anytime you so desire," Howard says. "For eternity. It's my understanding that the sensation is *most* stimulating."

I'll bet it is . . . I've got all these hot chicks here, that I can get it on with anytime I want . . . IF I accept the Senary . . . But then the reality sets in. "Look, I've never even *had* sex before but I've been told that a guy can only do it so many times before he gets worn out."

"Ah, yes, refraction, the bane of all masculinity, but let us convene now on the north bulwark, and I will show you yet one more otherworldly benefit of Privilato status."

The Bath Girls all wriggle their giant wet tongues as Howard moves you out of the chamber and onto a lofty balcony. From here you see the entire castle grounds, the inner wards, various stone buildings, intermediate towers. Birds that appear to be normal—falcons, doves, sparrows—sweep across the sky; while the sky is normal, too. Blue, with wisps of white clouds.

"How can . . ." you begin.

"Hallucinosis Transformers at the fringe of each Privilato estate provide the preferred environment," Howard answers. "Should you so desire, Mr. Hudson, your sky will always look exactly like the sky in the Living World."

"Incredible," you mutter, but then you think of something. "There's an awful lot of—what?—supernatural technology here—"

"The proper term is Occult Science or Systematic Magic."

"Fine, but it's still the opposite of science in the Living World, right?"

"Quite right. It's antithetical. As I explained previously. The subjective on Earth is *ob*jective here. The blacks and whites of the Living World is the all-crucial gray area in Hell. The hard science of God's green earth is magic in Lucifer's kingdom."

"All right!" you exclaim, "but that's my point. If Lucifer can do all of this with Occult Science, then what has God done in Heaven with Godly Science?"

Howard seems taken by your observation. "I am quite regrettably unqualified to render an answer but I must speculate . . . It must be rather dull when compared to all of this."

Really? You stew on the words. *I'll have no way of knowing, will I?*

"But to return to our former topic—there,"—Howard points over the parapet—"the Satanic Chapel. You *will* have to attend Black Mass on occasion, but I would think that little to ask in view of what you'll be receiving, hmm?"

The black church sits in the corner, past the courtyard proper, almost quaintly were it not for the high upside-down cross erected on its steeple. Several bosomy nuns busy themselves about the small building.

"I mean your previous question regarding, um, sexual refraction," Howard goes on, "and your potential concern about the prospect of being 'worn out' by the bevy of sexually available women at your disposal."

"Huh?"

"Privilato status entitles you to your very own personal aphrodisial farm. Note the garden, Mr. Hudson."

You see the area of space, a great square of flower beds tended to by sultry women in white cloaks and hoods. Only their breasts can be seen through apertures in the cloaks.

"The women are Bio-Sorceresses, and they will suffice for your groundskeeping staff. Every Privilato gets his own rod of Orgia Extremus Root. The Bio-Sorceresses are occult chemists who pick the root at harvest time, extract the Inhuman Growth Hormones from it, and then further process a priceless Gonadotropic Elixir that not only abolishes sexual refraction between climaxes, but allows for massive orgasms that last for not seconds but the equivalent of a full hour."

Your demonic mouth hangs open at the information.

"It should go without discourse that Privilatos spend most of their time engaged in one manner or other of licentious congress."

Hour-long orgasms, you think.

"And for such occasions when you *do* long for diversity of a nonsexual mode . . . there, in the corner opposite."

You follow Howard's finger to said corner, and see a troop of well-weaponed Conscripts surrounding one of those glowing green holes you saw the Privilato disembarking before he took his entourage into the Fetal Aperitifs bar.

"The Conscripts of the famed Diocletian Brigade will serve as your bodyguards when you wish to travel, and for traveling, you have at your constant disposal your very own Nectoport," Howard says.

For when I want to go out on the town, you think.

You must admit now . . . the possibility is sounding better and better.

"But wouldn't I need money?"

"Ah. The filthy lucre!" Howard takes you back inside, through one stunning hall after another, and down myriad jeweled corridors. Eventually, he turns into another room.

Jesus!

The room's ceiling causes you to look involuntarily up.

"The Unholy Coffer-Vault," Howard says.

The room must be a hundred feet high and hundreds deep. It is filled with pallet after pallet of banded paper money.

"There must be a billion dollars here!"

"*Six* billion, Mr. Hudson, though not dollars. Hellnotes." Howard's focus drifts off. "I once wrote a longish tale entitled 'Dreams in the Witch-House.' I thought it was most abysmal, but a friend submitted it and got for me the unheard sum of $140. I've often wondered what that would be worth in Hellnotes."

As usual, you don't hear Howard; your attention, instead, has been highjacked by the airplane-hangar-size vault of cash.

That's A LOT of MONEY!

"You also need to be apprized, sir, that once you've expended the entirety of this vault, Satan's Treasurers will simply fill it up again."

Now you're getting dizzy looking at all of it . . .

"In spite of all of Hell's horrors, there's quite a bit for a *wealthy* man to do," Howard goads on. "Especially one who will know wealth for *eternity* . . ."

"Take me out of here," you say suddenly. "I've got to think . . ."

Howard smiles.

Chapter Eight

(I)

When Krilid received the coordinates for his next familiarization surveillance, he squinted hard through the accommodating headache. He had headaches all the time simply as an aftereffect from the Head-Bending job the Satanic police had treated him to; the telepathic orders from Ezoriel's mental antennae array only felt worse. As the illegal Nectoport soared high and fast through clouds like coal dust, the Troll rested his head in his clawed hands and felt it literally throb.

There was no aspirin in Hell.

But he had to hand it to the Contumacy's skill in stealing and then replicating Lucifer's leading-edge Sorceries. Krilid need only receive the coordinates and then *think* once very hard, and he was on his way.

A nebulous intelligence memo had slammed into his head along with the coordinates. When the headache passed, he thought, *This might be very interesting . . .*

If the intelligence wasn't counterfeit.

Krilid had revivified the Hand of Glory only when he finally began to descend toward the next assignment. He liked the idea of nobody being able to see him while he could see entire Districts of Hell with any given glance. Now, miles below, he could see the staggering Pol Pot District and its smoking crematories, its killing fields, and its almost endless landscaping of heads on pikes. *Didn't know this burg was so big,* he thought, but then his gaze fixed on a break in the District's layout, an irregularly shaped construction site of some kind. At this altitude, it was tiny of course, but as the cloaked Nectoport slipped lower . . .

I don't believe what I'm seeing. They really did it.

The thing stood immobile in the middle of the fortified site, a *thing* taller than any skyscraper in the District. The wedged, neck-less head sat propped upon dark shoulders straining with inanimate muscles. The monster's arms—which had to be 200 feet long—hung just as muscularly at its sides; and the corded legs shined blackly in the sky's scarlet light. Krilid took the Nectoport lower, to encroach upon the Demonculus's face and—

Aw, shit . . .

He nearly vomited at the sight at the pitted muck that had been sculpted to comprise the most revolting and indescribable visage.

Krilid retook to the clouds, his stomach in queasy turmoil. *That face'll take a LOT of getting used to,* he reminded himself.

But only *if* he succeeded, and the odds of *that* seemed to be shrinking very quickly. But he knew this full well: *If the Master Builder brings that thing to life, there'll be a world of hurt coming down the pike for Ezoriel and the Contumacy . . .*

Krilid hovered next, to focus his Monocular, actually laughing to himself now that he was considering his odds of success. *I don't stand a chance in Hell—pun intended.* There were Noble Gas Skiffs floating all over the place, full of Conscripts and Warlocks armed to the hilt with every weapon in the Satanic Arsenal. *All I have is this Nectoport, a pistol, and a couple of muzzle-loading long rifles,* and then he laughed again.

He thought: *I'm a pawn in a chess game that Ezoriel KNOWS can't be won . . .*

The field, hundreds of feet below, was impenetrably walled with Hexed Blood-Bricks and full of ranks of more soldiers, not to mention marching formations of Ushers, Golems, and Flamma-Troopers.

All that . . . against little old me . . .

He homed the Monocular in on the Demonculus's chest, noticing the protective plate bolted into it. Two more Security Balloons floated to either side, to discourage a sneak attack. Krilid just laughed and laughed, knowing that Ezoriel's plan meant certain death.

Oh, well. What else do I have to do?

A third balloon seemed to be disengaging from the others about the chest plate. Krilid's eyes narrowed—from that particular Skiff an Imperial Flag was flying from the balloon net. Krilid quickly checked his folder of vellum sheets containing target identification diagrams . . .

The flag's insignia showed an emblem of a bat with a fanged skull-head, while the bat's dripping talons grasped hammers, ladders, and shovels.

The Master Builder's regimental colors! Krilid knew. He focused the Monocular further and saw the crowned, withered-faced Human in the rearmost seat. The shimmering surplice of spun lead told all. It was the Supreme Master Builder himself, the acclaimed Warlock Joseph Curwen . . .

I can't have this pressure! Krilid's thoughts exploded. His gnarled hands snapped up his rifle, fixed the Monocular on the barrel; and then he dumped his powder cartridge and rammed a ball. *If Ezoriel's Clairvoyants are so great, how come they didn't know Curwen would be in the Skiff?*

Krilid brought his rifle to bear, cocked the hammer, and lined up his sights right on the Master Builder's head . . .

He took in one full breath, let half of it out, and began to depress the trigger—

The sudden headache hit him like a ball bat. *Holy shit!* Krilid dropped the musket and landed flat on his back on the Nectoport deck, cringing from the pain like a dentist's drill boring straight into unanesthetized nerve pulp, only the pulp wasn't a tooth, it was his entire brain.

NOT NOW, KRILID, Ezoriel's static-ridden voice slammed into his head. *THE TIME IS NOT YET AT HAND . . .*

"But I had him right in my sights!" the Troll bellowed, hands clamping his warped skull.

THE PLAN WILL MOST CERTAINLY FAIL UNLESS IT IS EXECUTED ON PRECISE SCHEDULE—

"The evil scumbag was right there! I had a perfect head-shot!"

The Fallen Angel chuckled through more corroded static. *YOU'RE A ZEALOUS GODLY SOLDIER, BUT FAR TOO IMPATIENT. YOU MUST WAIT UNTIL YOU ARE GIVEN A DIRECT FIRING ORDER.*

"Nobody ever told me that!"

THAT IS BECAUSE WE MUST DISCIPLINE ALL OUR INTELLIGENCE. REVEALING TOO MUCH AT ONCE MIGHT ONLY INCREASE THE CHANCES OF INTERCEPTION. KILLING CURWEN PREMATURELY WOULD RUIN EVERYTHING.

"*Now* you tell me!" Krilid griped and sat back up when the headache receded.

PATIENCE, KRILID. NOW RETREAT TO SAFE DISTANCE AND EXTINGUISH YOUR HAND OF GLORY. CONSERVE ALL RESOURCES UNTIL THE FINAL MOMENT.

"All right," Krilid sputtered. "But when *is* the final moment, Ezoriel?"

No reply was made, as the Fallen Angel's telepathic signal had already crackled out.

(II)

"You must be a veteran," said the short, overly tan woman behind the counter. Her voice was as craggy as her face.

Gerold sighed. "Why? Just 'cos I'm in the chair? I could've been driving drunk, or fallen off a balcony or something."

The woman—whose '70s-styled hair was blazing white—tittered almost like a witch. Her redneck accent replied, "Well, son, first off, you're young. Second, I can tell by your face you ain't *dumb* enough to drive drunk or fall off a dang balcony—"

Wow. I guess that's a compliment.

"—and third, your buttons are all buttoned up." She pointed a sun-withered finger. "That tells me you was in the army or marines."

"You got me," Gerold admitted. "Army. Got out a year or so ago and put in physical therapy."

When Gerold had gotten off the Greyhound, he'd taken a cab to Lake Misquamicus, having flipped himself into the cab seat while the cabbie stowed his wheelchair in the trunk. Upon arrival, he wheeled toward the dock, marveling at the sight of the silverish lake. *This'll kick ass!* Over the great reflective expanse of water, not one other boat could be seen. *Privacy* . . . So the Fates had granted his wish after all. He'd be able to kill himself here and no one could interfere.

The bait shop proprietor was probably in her late fifties but looked ten years older from being in the sun for—more than likely—her entire life. She was very slim, tattoo-dotted, and still bore some vestige of bygone good looks even with the wrinkles, sun blemishes, and veininess. A far cry from the young and spritely bikini girl in the ad; however, this woman *was* wearing a bikini—a raving, metallic candy-apple red—that was absolutely minuscule. *She's almost too old to be wearing it, but . . . more power to her for doing it anyway*, Gerold reasoned. Her perfectly straight hair shined perfectly white to the small of her back; the bikini top satcheled a sizable bosom, obviously implants dating back to the '70s.

"And you'll be pleased to hear this, hon," she said, grinning behind the counter. "Here, there's no charge to veterans for bait!"

"I appreciate it," Gerold said, managing not to laugh. *Now THERE'S a gesture for servicemen. Free worms, chum, and dead shrimp.*

"And rod rentals and Jet Skis are half off," she added. "But I don't suppose you'd be able to Jet Ski by yourself." Then her eyes glittered. "But I'd be happy to take you out myself and you can hold on to me."

"Thanks, but I came here to rent a rowboat and drop a crayfish trap, that's all."

"Oh, dandy!" She slapped a frozen bag of shrimp on the counter, then rang up Gerold's other purchases: a small wire crayfish trap, a Sterno cooker and stand, and a metal pot. "Crawdads in Lake Misquamicus are the best in the state, some of 'em almost big as lobsters."

"That's what I'm looking for."

"How long you wanna rent the boat till, sweetie?"

"Um, well, probably till late if that's all right."

"Sure is. Some folks rent a boat and fish all night and through to sunup."

"Ring me up for that, please," Gerold said.

"Oh, you don't gotta pay for the rental till ya come back in."

Gerold felt a twinge of deceit. He wanted to pay in advance, now, so he wouldn't be gypping her. After all, he *wouldn't* be coming back, would he? Not in the rental boat at any rate.

It would probably be the county sheriff's department that brought his body back in . . . *if* they ever found it.

"Aw, just let me pay it all up front, keeps things easier. Oh, and some bottled water and a cooler."

The woman winked. "Comin' right up, handsome." She hitched up her overly burgeoned top and retrieved the items; then he paid up and wheeled himself outside.

A long wooden dock reached out into the silver ripples. At the end, several rowboats rocked in the water; the white-haired woman jumped down into the last one and snapped in a special seat with a back on it.

"What's that?" Gerold asked.

"A seat for folks so afflicted. Ya can't row if ya can't sit up straight, and you can strap yourself in. Makes it safer."

"Cool," Gerold approved, not that safety was an issue now.

"Now lemme help ya get in, hon—"

"I got it," he said and expertly flipped himself out of the chair. His arm muscles bulged when he lunged forward once on his hands, then shimmied himself into the handicapped chair.

"You're one strong fella!" the lady exclaimed.

Yeah, but only from the waist up.

The woman stowed his cooler and other items, her zero-body-fat physique exemplified each time she bent over. When one of her implants slid up, Gerold marveled at the briefly betrayed tan line: a patch of lambent white blocked off against the iced-tea-colored tan. Within the white patch, the tiniest pink sliver of nipple could be seen. *Wow,* Gerold mused. Suddenly he found the vision of the lissome older woman densely erotic, and it occurred to him that such a sight—one of his last among the living—was a wonderful thing.

Had she caught him looking? At once her grin seemed sultry, and when she noticed that a wedge of breast had slipped out from the bra, she seemed to take her time correcting it.

"I guess I'm all set," Gerold said.

"Not *just* yet," she corrected, then startled him when she walked right over to him and leaned over. Suddenly her top-straining implants were nearly in his face. "Just lean forward a bit, sweetie."

Now her barely covered *crotch* was nearly in his face, but he understood when she put his arms through a life vest and tightened the straps. "Misquamicus ain't a very *big* lake, hon, but a good wind can cause a mighty rough chop."

The ironic fact amused Gerold: *She's putting a life vest on a guy who's going to commit suicide.*

She placed a small object in a side bin. "And here's an emergency radio just in case. I'll check in with ya so often, okay?"

"Sure. Thanks."

"You'll find the best crawdaddin' right dead center of the lake. It's deeper and there's lots of crannies down there where they like to hide."

"Dead center. Gotcha."

Her tanned legs flexed when she climbed back on the dock. She put on sunglasses, grinning up to the sky, her perfectly flat stomach beginning to shine with sweat. "Nice slow, sunny day like this? I think I'll lay out here a while and catch some rays—"

Gerold gulped.

—and then she took off her top, just like that.

Holy moly . . .

She stretched out in a lounge chair facing Gerold's position in the seat. All at once, the flawless snow-white breasts centered by dark nipples blared at him within the demarcation of tanned skin.

She grinned, Gerold's own astonished face reflecting in her glasses.

"Uh, oh, sorry," he murmured after another moment of staring.

"Hon? A gal my age's got *no problem* bein' looked at by a nice fella . . ."

Gerold raised his oars, tried not to continue staring, then just thought, *To hell with it,* and kept looking. "Um, I have a question, though—"

She giggled. "Yes. They're implants, I gotta admit."

Gerold laughed. "That wasn't the question but . . ." He tried to focus his thought. "A minute ago, you said Lake Misquamicus wasn't a big lake." He shrugged and glanced behind. "Looks big to me. *Real* big."

"Aw, there's at least a dozen lakes in Florida bigger'n this. The biggest, a'course, is Lake Okeechobee, second biggest in the whole country. You never been there?"

It was impossible not to keep stealing glances. "No, but I've heard of it."

"Over a trillion gallons of water in Okeechobee—"

The statement snapped Gerold's stare. "A *trillion?* That's . . . unimaginable."

"Lotta water, sure. Hard to even reckon that much water."

I better start rowing, Gerold told himself. *This woman's hooters are wringing me out.* But the sudden question snapped to mind. "Any idea how many gallons in *this* lake?"

In painstaking slowness, the woman began to rub suntan oil over her belly. "Oh, yeah. Department'a Natural Resources says that Lake Misquamicus contains just about six billion gallons . . ."

(III)

Howard walks you back onto the parapet facing the inner wards and courtyard. Soft, fragrant breezes blow. You take in the scape of the fortress and beyond, more and more awed. *This place makes Bill Gates's house look like an outhouse . . . and it could all be mine . . .*

But—

"Wait a minute. What good's all this money and luxury when I don't have friends to share it with?"

"Ah, there goes your good side shining through once more," Howard replies. "But I'll remind you that you had no abundance of friends in the Living World, and were quite content with that."

You think about that. You've always been a friendly person but you never really *needed* a lot of friends. Your *faith* was your ultimate friend, and the opportunity to serve God. "Well, that's true but looking at this whole thing now, I'd need *some* friends . . ."

Howard shrugs. "I'd like to think that *I'm* your friend, Mr. Hudson. I've *delighted* in your company, and I truly admire your earthy resoluteness and magnificently refined goodwill."

The comment makes you look at him. "You're right, Howard. You are my friend. You're actually a pretty cool guy."

"I'm grateful and touched." And then Howard leans closer. "And not to portray myself too *terribly* mercenary . . . were you to accept the Senary, you'd easily have the power to relieve me of my laborious onuses at the Hall of Automatic Writers and have me reassigned as, say, your personal archivist and biographer? And during any free time you saw fit to afford me . . ." Howard sighed dreamily. "I could forge on with my *serious* work."

"If I accept the Senary, Howard, then I'd do that—"

"Great Pegana!"

"But," you add with an odd stammer. Something abstract seems to tilt in your psyche. *If I accept the Senary*, you repeat to yourself in thought.

Would you really do that?

"I-I-I . . . I don't think I'm going to accept . . ." Yet even as the words leave your lips, you can't stop thinking about all this luxury, all this money, and of course all these *women* at your disposal.

"Alas, our time is nearly done," Howard tells you. He turns his pallid face back to the courtyards. "But I seem to have digressed yet again, with regard to your previous concerns. Besides myself, you *would* have some direct friends and acquaintances."

"What?"

"Behold, sir."

Suddenly you smell a simple, yet delectable aroma:

Burgers on the grill?

And once again your unnatural eyes follow Howard's gesture where a small congregation mingles. Several men and women chat happily about a barbecue, and sure enough, they are cooking hamburgers and hot dogs.

"Wait a minute," you object. "How can there be hamburgers and hot dogs in Hell? They must be fucked up, like *dick*-burgers or some shit, right?"

Howard puts his face in his hands. "Mr. Hudson, *please*. The profanity. I regret this peculiar acclimation you're experiencing. Hell's influences can indeed be quite negative. But ruffian talk bespeaks only ruffians. Men such as ourselves are hardly that."

"Sorry, I can't help it for some reason," you say, still mystified by the instantaneousness with which you cussed.

"But to render an answer, Mr. Hudson, I'll assure you of the contrary. It's true, there are no cattle nor swine in

Hell, at least none that would taste the same as what you're accustomed to, yet through the marvel of Hexegenic Engineering, our Archlocks can produce foodstuffs that taste identical to any food on Earth." Howard's brow rises. "*If* one is so privileged."

"Privileged as in a Privilato, you mean."

"Quite. But, please. Be more attentive."

Next, you take closer note of the actual *people* at the barbecue, and the recognition jolts you.

You *know* everyone there.

"My father and mother!" you rejoice. "My sister, too!" They had all died years ago but now you deduce the direction of their Afterlife. Manning the grill itself is Randal, who glances upward and waves.

"And Randal! My best friend where I live, but . . . wait. He couldn't be here. He's not dead."

"Regrettably, he is, Mr. Hudson," Howard tells you. "As I've been properly informed by the so-called powers that be. He was killed just hours ago by an unstable intruder at his convenience store, apparently a quite obese homeless loafer."

Homeless. Obese. The image pops into your gaseous brain. *The schizo in the stained sweatpants who threw up in the Qwik-Mart!* You consider the situation and nearly chuckle, though there's nothing funny about it. *He must've gotten sick of Randal throwing him out of the store, so he . . .*

"Evidently this inauspicious derelict got hold of a ball bat and, well, introduced it with some vim and vigor to your friend Randal's knees, groin, and skull."

It's ironic at least. Your monstrous eyes squint harder . . .

There's a third man there as well.

No, you think dully.

The man's attire is shocking enough—black shoes, black slacks, and black shirt, and a Roman collar—but when you recognize his face?

"Not Monsignor Halford!" you exclaim.

Howard seems surprised. "Your reaction sounds troubled, Mr. Hudson. I'd think you'd be pleased to find your mentor here."

"What's he doing in Hell?" you yell. "He's a fucking *monsignor!*"

Howard winces at your next implementation of foul language. "It is with great regret that I must inform you of Monsignor Halford's recent demise—some manner of coronary attack. As for being here, I hardly need to explain."

"He's a priest, for shit's sake. Why didn't he go to Heaven?"

Howard's brows rise in a scolding attitude. "I should think the answer would be clear. Priest or not, he didn't *live* his faith as you do. He didn't practice as he preached, so to speak."

That's bullshit, you fume, but then . . . *Well, at least he's here. He's someone I like and know.*

"And the two more . . . provocatively dressed young ladies I'm sure you'll recognize as well. They were killed last night, in an aspect of mishap I'm told is known as a 'drive-by.'"

You blink, and see them.

The two trashily attractive women turn and wave as well. Tight T-shirts cling to impressive bosoms, and they read: DO ME TILL I PUKE and NO GAG REFLEX.

"The hookers from the bar!" you exclaim.

"Indeed, and, look, here comes one more."

Across the yard a beautiful girl-next-door type strides toward the congregation, pushing a wheelbarrow full of iced-down bottles of beer.

"Marcie! My very first girlfriend!" you instantly recognize. "We never had sex but . . ."

"Accept the Senary, Mr. Hudson, and you shall be presented with that opportunity forthwith."

You stare. You'd forgotten all about Marcie. Your first kiss, and in fact the only girl you'd ever made out with. The combination of her beauty, intellect, and demeanor had made her the only person to tempt you not to become a priest.

"We both loved each other but . . . decided we loved God more," you drone, remembering through a fog of heartbreak. "So we parted. I went to college to prepare for the seminary and she went to a convent . . ."

"Well, the lady's convent days were short-lived. Convent *day*, I should rephrase."

"She quit after only *one day?*"

"I'm afraid so, whereupon she immediately pursued avenues of life quite sexual. Whenever she was with another man, however, she always pretended he was you . . ."

First you gulp, but then frown. "You're just saying that, Howard. To get me to accept!"

Howard's pallid finger rises. "I'll remind you, Mr. Hudson, that as the Trustee, I am not allowed to lie or to exaggerate. It must be your *untainted* free will that prompts your ultimate decision."

You shake your gourd-head and sigh. "So . . . how did Marcie die?"

"I'm told she suffered a calamitous misadventure involving a steamroller, but that's neither here nor there. What matters is that she's here, now, in the flesh. She as well as the other Human Damned who mean the most to you." Howard offers you a stern look. "And you'd be doing them all an *immeasurable* service by accepting the Senary, Mr. Hudson."

"How's that?"

"Because there's no purpose in Lucifer keeping them here if you chose not to take up residence in the castle. Your friends and family would be redelegated back into Hell's mainstream, where they wouldn't fare well at all, I'm afraid."

Your gaze at him shifts. "So it's blackmail?"

"Lucifer has no qualms in revealing his motives. He wants something from you very badly, and he will go to great pains to urge you into giving it to him. By offering you the prize of all your dreams and all your fantasies, which you will be able to enjoy forever."

"Sex, money, and luxury . . ."

"Yes, and let us not forget *envy*, for you will be envied, by everyone in Hell. The gift Lucifer wishes to bestow upon you—in exchange for the gift you will give to him—represents the distillation of what all Humans desire most."

Now your eyes drift back to the sky. "I still don't see what Lucifer gets out of the deal. Another soul? From what I can see, he's got plenty of those."

"Plenty, yes, but, lo, not yours. Not the Soul of one who willingly says no to God's promise of Salvation. For someone so entirely on the plus side of the Fulcrum, to cast God aside in favor of Lucifer—*that,* Mr. Hudson, is the only satisfaction Lucifer can ever truly enjoy."

Your vision reels again at the sight of the castle and its spectacular grounds, your friends and family, as well as the sheer carnal pleasures that await.

Carnal pleasure that you've *never* experienced . . .

Like a crack of mental lightning, you know.

You know what you are about to do . . .

Chapter Nine

(I)

Master Builder Curwen watched wide-eyed from his observation minaret. Thus far, the Sputum Storm appeared to be confined beyond the official limits of the Mephistopolis, its sickish green clouds leaving no doubt of its existence. From so far away, it looked like a mere phlegm-colored streak along the bottom of the scarlet horizon, but as Hell's most dangerous type of storm, one could never rest assured. They'd been known to sit still and hang for extended periods, then suddenly move off with no warning at speeds of hundreds of miles per hour. Curwen wasn't certain, but he believed the storm was sliding over the Outer Sectors, probably the Great Emptiness Quarter.

Pray Satan, let it stay there.

For such a storm to move here, over the Pol Pot District, there was no telling what damage might be inflicted upon the Demonculus.

Below on the field, the ancillary sacrifices continued, to keep the Electrocity Generators roaring and the Hell-Flux well charged. The boiled corpses of sacrifants were wheeled away in barrows by slug-skinned Ushers, only to be replaced by more. A wonderful sight, yes, but then Curwen gazed upward at the colossal form of the Demonculus.

Nothing can jeopardize my creation. Nothing.

Footsteps could be heard winding up the minaret's spiral steps, and, next, a figure rose into the small open-windowed chamber: the project's official Psychic Security Minister, a Kathari-grade Diviner.

"Master Builder Curwen," the man-thing's voice etched, and then it bowed. "It is my honor to be in your presence."

Yet not mine to be in yours, Curwen thought. Curwen was Human, and therefore distrustful of all that was not, especially creatures like this, things that could supposedly see the future. Additionally, the Satanic Visionary was *hideous* to behold: it was bald, emaciated, and brazenly naked. The sucked-in skin and stringlike muscles were repulsive enough, but even more repulsive was the Clairvoyant's skin tone, a bruising blue beneath which maroon arteries throbbed. Even more unsettling was the psychic being's eye—not eyes, eye, for it possessed but only one, set hugely in the middle of its gaunt face. An eye the size of an apple. The Diviner's bald head shined, tracked by various suture scars from multiple telethesic surgeries; its ears were holes, and its genitals . . .

. . . were best left undescribed.

"What tidings do you bring me, Seer?"

The Diviner's voice keened like nails across slate. "Great Master Builder, I know that the distant Sputum Storm rests gravely on your mind, but it is with the joy of serving the Morning Star that I tell you to put your fears aside. I foresaw this very storm, and I have foreseen, too, that it shall not venture here."

The aftereffects of hearing the Diviner's awful voice left Curwen's skin crawling, yet it was with relief that he sat down in his jeweled seat. "Praise the Dark Lord."

"Yes."

"But I pity those now in its midst. Is it the Great Emptiness Quarter?"

The visionary's bald head nodded. Scarlet veins *beat* beneath the shining skin.

Curwen began, "I've heard—"

"So have we all—that something of grievous import is taking place there, but what it is, I'm not privy to, via my training and indoctrination." Then the massive eye blinked once, clicking like the snap of a twig.

Curwen squinted out again, in the vicinity of the storm. *What a ghastly thing to happen, even in Hell. A deluge of snot . . .* But he must not worry over projects not his own.

Only the Demonculus and the success of its animation were his personal concern.

I must succeed.

Curwen's gaze turned to his guest. "Diviner—"

The cadaverous figure smiled, showing black teeth. "Is there something you wish for me to divine, Master Builder?"

Of course, it could read his mind. But now that the very Human question had occurred to him . . . he was afraid to ask.

The Diviner's voice screeched as the thing went slowly back down the spiral steps. "The answer to your question . . . is *yes*—"

The Diviner continued to descend.

"—and of this you can be sure, for I have foreseen it . . ."

Curwen sat semiparalyzed for some time—paralyzed by euphoria. He stared at the Demonculus's immobile form through the master window, and the question he'd thought but dared not ask was this: *Will the Demonculus be successfully animated?*

(II)

The wind gusted from multiple directions, each gust resounding like the caterwauls of ravening beasts; and it was a pall of a diseased green that seemed to have lowered in churning layers over the entirety of the Vandermast Reservoir as well as a sizable portion of the Great Emptiness Quarter itself. The Sputum Storm raged, just short of breaking. Since the alert all lower-echelon Conscripts were ordered to tie themselves to the security lugs along the ramparts, while the Golems (much heavier and therefore less likely to be blown over the side) continued their foot patrols, on watch for signs of attack and also physical breeches that the storm might incur upon the black basilisk walls of the perimeter.

Favius watched from his own security barbican along the rampart.

The storm is spectacular but also deadly, he thought. During his entire Damnation, Favius had never seen a genuine Sputum Storm, he'd only *heard* of them. The black clouds would begin to congeal from the force of the wind, and then turn green in a hue like moldy cheese. His training apprised him the potential of a storm like this—whole Prefects had been destroyed by Sputum Storms, it was said, and in low-lying urban areas, the incessant rain of phlegm would bring mucoid floods that rose stories high and drowned residents in an oatmeal-thick, viscid horror. Favius eyed the grotesque clouds that now moiled above the Reservoir: he thought of an upside-down whirlpool of crud-green sludge. *Any minute,* he feared, *the storm will break and those clouds will POUR . . .*

All the while, though, the mammoth Main Sub-Inlets continued to roar as they siphoned still more of the Gulf's horrific Bloodwater into the pit . . .

For as far as Favius could see, there were only the flat layers of storm clouds pressing down. The wind gusts picked up, and one actually caused the rampart wall to nudge . . .

Favius latched onto an astonishing moment of self-awareness. *For the first time in my existence . . . I am afraid . . .*

Perhaps a mile in the distance, over a conjoining rampart, the rain began to fall—the rain of *phlegm.*

Here it comes . . .

The sky, essentially, began to vomit.

The dark green sputum began to fall in sheets. Favius watched the splattering line of phlegm-fall move across the Reservoir's scarlet surface; it was louder even than the sounds of the sub-inlets filling the pit. When it finally reached the Legionnaire's own rampart, the 900-pound Golems wobbled in place in the gale force. Several merlons cracked in the macabre wind and fell into the Reservoir. A rising, whistlelike shriek now encompassed all.

The rampart walls shook again; Favius thought he even heard the very stone crack.

This storm may destroy the entire site . . .

Favius lurched when the barbican door banged open. He reached instinctively for his sword—

"Lucifer in Hell, Favius!" the sudden voice exploded in complaint.

"Grand Sergeant Buyoux!" Favius exclaimed. "It's dangerous for you to have come here, sir!" He bulled against the door to reclose it; then he threw across the bars. "You should've summoned me, and I would've come to you—"

The Grand Sergeant stood dripping residual green muck; his helm and most of his plate-mail smock was enslimed with it. "Help me off with this, Favius," the commander groaned, and then the plates clinked. Favius removed the metallic garment and hung it in the stone corner to dry. Buyoux sat exhausted on the bench, now dressed only in a wool tunic emblazoned with the Seal of Grand Duke Cyamal. The Grand Sergeant brought scarred hands to his scar-badged face. "I've never witnessed a storm like this—ever."

"Nor have I, Grand Sergeant. I have concerns about the physical integrity of the site—"

Buyoux laughed mirthlessly. "A Sputum Storm of this magnitude could knock the ramparts down—it could ruin the entire project." He looked at Favius with his appalling face. "Whatever happened to the luck of the Damned, hmm?"

Favius peered back out across the Reservoir. The rain *poured* over everything, and then a sudden wind gust blew one of his Golems over the side, into the foaming pool.

"Impressive, yes," his superior said. "At least the Golems are expendable. If only we can see to it that no *men* are blown into it as well."

Now the stone barbican itself began to creak in the wind. "The rain seems to be letting up, Grand Sergeant, but the wind—"

"—is *increasing* in velocity, yes." Buyoux rose and looked likewise through the small window. "The Channelers predicted as much; they've even predicted a rapid conclusion to the storm but . . . as you can see . . ."

Favius stared. *Was* it letting up even as they spoke? The sky's green tinge seemed to be lessening . . . but then the wind shook loose several more merlon abutments and blew them into the Reservoir.

Buyoux was smiling. "My good Favius. Aren't you even going to ask why I braved this dismal storm to come here?"

Favius stood at parade rest when addressed. "It is not for me to ask, Grand Sergeant."

Buyoux sat back down, seemingly at ease even as the stone floor was shifting minutely. "I came to see you, Favius—to . . . *tell* you something."

"I *exist* to follow your orders, sir."

Buyoux shrugged. "In the midst of a storm that may well destroy us . . . you needn't be so formal. The truth is, you're the only one I trust on this entire site. I don't even trust my own commanders. I only trust you . . ."

"Grand Sergeant, I am duly honored by your praise, and *un*worthy of it."

The Grand Sergeant picked at one of his self-inflicted facial scars. He seemed to be reflecting inwardly now. "We're the Human Damned, Favius—yes, we're *humans*. Regardless of the extent to which we've been modified, no matter how much amplification surgery we've had, no matter how many demonic transfusions . . . we're still *human*."

Favius stood, trying to comprehend. Was his superior having a breakdown?

"That's why I'm here, friend. It is my human frailty that brings me." Buyoux's voice lowered in a secret excitement. "I *have* to tell someone. I feel as though I'll burst if I don't . . ."

"Grand Sergeant, in my utter inferiority, I do not understand."

The barbican rocked from another gust. Outside, someone screamed.

"You're the only one I trust," Buyoux repeated but now was staring off into nothing. He was smiling. "Not too long ago—just before the storm, in fact—I received a coded cipher, as did every Grand Sergeant on this reservation—"

Favius tensed up. He yearned to ask . . . but knew that he couldn't.

"It was a cipher from the Ministry of Satanic Secrets, Favius, and they finally disclosed the true nature of this project—the reason for the Reservoir's construction, and everything else . . ."

Favius cringed. Why would Buyoux brave a deadly storm to come here and say this? *Unless it is to tell* ME, *because he cannot contain his excitement . . .*

The drone of Buyoux's voice seemed to gleam. "It's for a Spatial Merge, Favius," came the whisper. "Do you know what that is?"

"Yes, Grand Sergeant. I learned about the process in one of my Clandestine Sorcery classes." Favius had to stress his ancient memory. "It's a secret technology whose goal is to substitute a finite perimeter in Hell with an equal perimeter in the Living World. Objects and even living beings in Hell are then able to occupy space on Earth, but it requires a massive Power Exchange, and the Merge is only temporary."

The scar-tissue mask that was Buyoux's face continued to beam as he shook his head. "They're not temporary anymore, my friend. After eons of research and repeated trials, the De Rais Academy has perfected the process. Theoretically, at least, a permanent Merge *can* be effected—"

Favius froze. "But, but, sir . . . Such a feat would require an unthinkable transfer of Deathforce—"

"Unthinkable no longer," the Grand Sergeant intoned. "The technology *exists*. Exactly what it is . . . I've not been apprized, but what does it matter? All that matters is this: it will work. Every Soothsayer in the City has foreseen it."

The prospect made Favius's head spin. He was just a simple soldier, not a scientist. Nevertheless, the information granted him goaded a simple deduction. "A *permanent* Spatial Merge, Grand Sergeant, and then . . ." His jaded eyes returned to the window.

"Yes," Buyoux croaked.

All this hellish Bloodwater and infernal sewage, not to mention the atrocious creatures within . . . His voice sounded parched when he voiced the observation. "They're going to transfer six billion gallons of *this* to the Living World."

"Indeed, they are, Favius—permanently." The Grand Sergeant tittered. "Like dumping one's garbage into the yard of a neighbor—the very idea is thrilling."

"But a Merge requires a target of equal volume, Grand Sergeant. When the contents of the Reservoir is sent *there*, something from there must then be brought *here*."

"You remember your lessons well, astute killer. It's an interesting swap, to say the least." Buyoux pointed to the churning scarlet slop within the massive Reservoir. "We're exchanging six billion gallons of *that* with six billion gallons of fresh water—"

"Great Satan!" Favius exclaimed.

"What a slight to God and all that's holy, yes? There's never been fresh water in Hell, so Lucifer will simply steal it from God's green Earth, and with it he will make his own oasis . . ."

Favius reeled at the implication.

Buyoux's corrupted voice reduced to the slightest whisper yet. "And we will be the first to see it, my friend. And we will even be allowed to *drink* of it . . ."

This, Favius could not even conceive.

"So be on your guard, warrior. *Nothing* must go wrong now. The Reservoir is nearly filled."

Favius's gaze jerked out. "And, Grand Sergeant! The storm has passed!"

"Just as the Channelers predicted. Good omens abound!" Buyoux returned to the window. During their guarded talk, the Sputum Storm has indeed abated, the green clouds were now black again and dissipating before their eyes. Even the infernal wind had died.

Favius and Buyoux went out on the rampart. The Golems were already at work squeegeeing the noxious rain off the black flooring into the Reservoir. Favius immediately ordered a damage report from his underlings.

"The rampart is secure, Grand Sergeant. We only lost three Golems—"

"And Conscripts?"

"None lost, sir."

"Splendid!"

"But, sir, if I may ask . . ."

The Grand Sergeant gave a modest nod, but his eyes said *quietly*.

"When . . . will the Merge take place?" Favius whispered.

"When the Main Sub-Inlets gush no more and the Reservoir is filled to capacity." And then they both looked out over Hell's first man- and demon-made lake.

The fluid level had risen so high that only the uppermost fringe of the Inlet could be seen and therefore only a fringe of the atrocious inflow.

But they both knew this: the Vandermast Reservoir would be filled very, very soon.

Favius ordered a work detail of Imps to clean the ill-colored muck from the Grand Sergeant's armor; in the meantime, the Grand Sergeant himself strolled closer to the rampart's edge, hands on hips, to marvel at the sight of the pit's filling.

It was Favius, not Buyoux, who noticed several jagged cracks in the basilisk stonework.

Alarmed, Favius rushed forward. "Grand Sergeant! Step back, sir—the storm seems to have caused some stress fractures in the foundation—"

Buyoux glanced down, shrugging. "Oh, I don't think that's anything to worry ab—" But before the dismissal of caution could be finished—

"Grand Sergeant!" Favius bellowed.

—the black stonework beneath Buyoux's feet gave way, and then an entire wedge of the flooring fell out of the rampart and tumbled into the pit's roiling scarlet ooze. Grand Sergeant Buyoux had no time to even cry for help as he fell into the ooze, too.

"Man the wall!" Favius commanded at the top of his lungs. "Ropes and ladders! Now!" And then—

SPLASH!

—he dove unhesitantly into the churning, bubbling, and creature-infested Bloodwater, but even before his feet had left the retaining wall, there'd been no sign of Grand Sergeant Buyoux . . .

Chapter Ten

(I)

Gerold laughed to himself when, after hours on the lake, he realized he was still wearing his life preserver. *With my luck, I'd fall in BEFORE I've had my fill of crayfish.* He was on his fourth pot now—and that lady was right, they were almost the size of lobsters. Gerold's last meal was everything he'd hoped for and more.

By nine, the sun began to sink, a spectacular sight from his vantage point in the middle of the lake. The molten orange light slowly turned pink behind the endless range of westerly trees. Gerold stared.

It seemed strange that he would only notice the world's intense beauty on this final day of his life.

But beauty it was—a delirious, sharp-as-cracked-glass beauty that he'd never been aware of until now. *It's easy to take things for granted until you know you're about to lose them . . .*

The Sterno can was lasting longer than he'd expected. He dropped the trap for another haul—why not?

I'm not exactly in a rush, am I?

He leaned back in his safety chair, half dozing and half staring at dusk's shifting cornucopia of light playing on the lake's mirror-still surface . . .

When will I do it? The question kept popping up in the back of his head. *I really* AM *going to kill myself, right?* But he knew that he was, he was positive. Even now, with the beautiful evening, the gorgeous lake, the delectable food, and the utter peace and quiet—he still *wanted* to do it. He yearned for it.

For some reason, he was suddenly thinking about that guy he talked to at the church. *What did he say his name was? Hudson?* He'd read Gerold like a book—*He KNEW I wanted to kill myself.* What was it like to be a guy like that, Gerold wondered. The center of his life was his faith—he was even going to become a *priest.* That was some sacrifice.

And, shit, I promised the guy I'd be in church Sunday, he recalled. *Looks like I'll be breaking that one.*

But what Hudson didn't understand was that things worked different for different people, and so did the world. Gerold wasn't a bad guy, so would he really go to *Hell* for offing himself? If there really was a God, Gerold felt sure he would understand.

Life just isn't for me. It's that simple. No sour grapes, no regrets. It was great while it lasted but now it's time for it to end. Period.

He lounged back and smiled.

He looked at his watch. Midnight seemed as good a time as any. *I'll fling myself over the side at a couple minutes of, and who knows? Maybe I'll die exactly when the clock strikes twelve . . .*

The idea seemed kind of . . . neat.

Every so often, a fish would break the surface and flip. Schools of smaller fish seemed to spiral into one another and form fascinating shapes. When Gerold stared up at the coming twilight, birds roved silently across the water. Not once today had another boat come near him. Just after the sun sank, crickets began to throb *en masse.*

What a PERFECT day to die . . .

Gerold drifted in and out of sleep.

He dreamed of walking, of being with women, of pursuing

his goals and succeeding. He dreamed of all the things he'd lost . . .

Something like a grating sound in his head dragged him awake. His eyes fluttered open, and what he noticed first was how the pulsing cricket sounds had ceased, leaving the lake completely absent of all noise. It was full dark now . . .

What was that grating sound? he wondered, leaning up, but then it came again—

A hard crackle, like static.

Then a voice: "Hon? You there? Aw, jeez—"

The walkie-talkie, he realized. It was the woman from the dock with the outstanding implants. "Hi, I'm here," he answered into the device, imagining her sitting on the pier just as topless as before.

Her Florida drawl crackled over the line. "Oh, gracious, thank God. I thought . . . well, you didn't answer so's I thought somethin' happened, hon."

"Sorry. I fell asleep. But I've had great luck catching crayfish," Gerold said. "They're delicious—" Something cut off the rest of his words. He sniffed.

"Is everything . . . all right out there? You notice anything . . . out of kilter?" the woman asked next.

Out of kilter . . . Gerold noticed something not right about her voice, even over the static. Did she sound distressed? But then he sniffed again, flinched, and also realized his ears felt funny, like when flying on an airplane while descending.

"Now that you mention it . . . My ears are clogged up, and . . . I smell something." The faintly metallic odor seemed just as faintly familiar.

"Like an electric motor sort'a thing?" she asked.

"Yeah! That's it. Ozone, I think it is. Like before an electrical storm—"

A long pause drew over the line.

"Hey, are you okay?" Gerold asked.

"Well, hon, I feel like a horse's heiny but, well, I'm kind of . . . scared."

"What's wrong?"

"I ain't sure but—and this'll sound nutty—but all my hair's standin' right on end, like it's floatin' up off my head—"

Well. That DOES sound nutty, Gerold reflected but at the same moment he saw that the hairs on his forearm—

What the hell?

—were standing on end. Then he slowly raised his hand and discovered that all the hair on his head was sticking up, too.

"This is weird but the same thing's happening to me," he told her.

"Must be a 'lectrical storm comin'—"

"But that's impossible," he replied. Overhead stretched a cloudless expanse of flickering stars, deep twilight, and a radiant white sickle moon. "The sky's clear."

The woman's voice quavered nervously. "Then it's heat lighting or somethin', hon—I don't know! Somethin' don't feel right in my gut. I'd feel a whole lot better if ya'd come in—"

I can't come in! he could've shouted. *I'm gonna KILL MYSELF in a little while!* But then the woman actually croaked a tiny sob over the line.

Wow, she really is scared, Gerold realized. He sighed. *Fuck.* What difference did it make, though? *I'll kill myself tomorrow.* "Look, don't be afraid, I'll row myself in right now—"

"Oh, thank you, sweetie! Somethin' just don't feel right, and I am beside myself with the jitters."

"Just hang tight, I'll be there in a few minutes," Gerold said. He signed off, then pulled the crayfish trap again and found it empty. *Well that's strange. First empty pull all day.* And nighttime was the best time to trap.

No matter.

Gerold grabbed the oars and began to row. It felt good

being needed, though. Paralysis notwithstanding, the woman was scared and didn't want to be alone. *This can be my last good deed, and who knows? Maybe I'll get to see her boobs again . . .*

He estimated that it would take him about twenty minutes to row back in to the dock, but what he *didn't* estimate—what would've been *impossible* to estimate—was that he would never get there.

(II)

Krilid glided the Nectoport high over the green-black clouds. Watching the immense Sputum Storm had been something. *All that hock raining down on the evil bastards.* He'd seen them over urban areas where the winds had toppled skyscrapers and the mucoid rain had caused flash floods. *Good for them,* Krilid thought.

But the storm's moving off made his own job easier.

A moment of directional thought in his warped head collapsed the distance of over a thousand miles and—

Sssssssssssssssss-ONK!

—in an indivisible sliver of a second, he'd relocated the Nectoport high over the Pol Pot District. This second part of his mission, he knew, would be much more difficult to pull off, if indeed it could even *be* pulled off. *I've got no choice but to trust Ezoriel, and if his intel turns out to be bad?*

Shit happens, he reasoned. But it *had* been a lot of fun whizzing around carte blanche in a Nectoport. *How many Trolls get to do that?*

How many Trolls, Imps, Demons, Humans—whatever!—got to see the Mephistopolis from this high up? *It's a privilege, I guess, and it must be worth SOME brownie points. Down here everything is good against evil, and good almost NEVER wins, but I'm on the side of good.*

Krilid supposed this fact made him either very unselfish or very stupid.

He took no chances of being detected, slipping the Nectoport in and out of clouds. All of the scaffolding around the Demonculus had been taken down, and he spotted very few Balloon Skiffs floating about the unliving thing's colossal body. *That means all the maintenance duties are finished. They only have a few more things to do before they bring that disgusting thing to life . . .*

However, there were a few more things for Krilid to do as well, before he could hope to pull this off.

He pulled the Nectoport off with a simple thought, and then found himself hovering high above one of the Torturaries in the Pogrom Park District. This particular compound specialized in Cage Roasting as its mode of slow torture, and it exclusively housed Human Damned who—like Krilid—had defected to Ezoriel's Contumacy or some other anti-Satanic sect. From this range, the compound looked like a typical prison yard, with towers manned by armed Conscripts, and a nearly impenetrable Blood-Brick fence resistant to not only impact but also Breech Spells. The rolls and rolls of "barbed" wire did not sport barbs but instead invisible needle-teeth from exterminated Bapho-Rats.

Krilid loved coming to the Torturaries—they were perfect places for target practice.

Slug-skinned Ushers stalked the grounds to supervise the Torture Attendants, and as for Cage Roasting? Sulphur beds were kept sizzlingly hot by various Crossbreeds forced to constantly pump foot-operated bellows systems. Above each bed hung a cage, quite like an iron maiden, which contained one very unhappy subject. The cages were lowered very slowly, and when the occupant began to burn, the cage was raised, to protract the unassuagible pain. Agonicity terminals were implanted into each subject's brain, to provide the compound with all the power it needed.

Krilid groaned as he watched the machinelike process below: the systematic raising and lowering of the facility's hundreds of Roasting Cages. Eventually a captive would be roasted down to a crisped twig but since almost all prisoners here were Human Damned, those twigs never died. They'd be thrown into trenches where they would twitch, shudder, and think for eternity.

Krilid figured he was half a mile up when he sighted his matchlock rifle. The sounds that came from below could've been a diabolic song. Screams intensified as cages were lowered, then diminished when they were raised. It was a pipe organ in Hell, with Human throats as the pipes.

BAM!

Gotcha! Krilid rejoiced after the rifle's delayed discharge. The horrific head of an Usher in the center of the field erupted like a large, ripe fruit. Consternation ensued after that first shot, Conscripts coming to alert in the towers, Torture Attendants being called back to barracks—

BAM!

The head of a Captain of the Guard burst next. Krilid chuckled as he reloaded. Now alarm sirens were sounding. When an Air Viceroy took off on a saddled Gryphon—

BAM!

—Krilid waited till the winged beast had ascended to a sufficient height before he shot its beaked head off. Spiny feathers dispersed, and the Viceroy fell straight down and landed in one of the sulphur beds.

Yeah!

Krilid knew his time was short. Now that the Torturary was under attack, an Archlock would be summoned to determine Krilid's position. If detected fast enough, Krilid could be blinded or paralyzed via the Psychic Sorcerer's telepathy, but—

I've never killed an Archlock before, he realized.

It was a foolhardy chance he was taking but Krilid felt lucky today. He squinted from the Nectoport's egress. An Archlock wouldn't expose himself on the open field but he *would* have to make a visual assessment of the scenario . . .

Windows, Krilid thought. No Archlock could psychically scan the sky without at least looking out a window.

And Archlocks all gave off auras . . .

Don't dillydally, Krilid ordered himself, his shooting eye wide open behind the sight.

It was in one of the tiny tower windows that Krilid thought he spotted the tiniest flash of liquid-black light, like a wavering luminous vapor. It was a long shot, but he aimed, squeezed the weapon's rickety trigger, then bucked backward when the sizable projectile rocketed out of the rifle barrel.

Krilid kept his gnarled fingers crossed. Then—

You gotta be kidding me!

—the prison tower exploded as if demolitioned, not from the impact of the bullet, of course, but from the spontaneous release of cabalistic energy caused by the bullet's entrance into the Archlock's skull. Bricks, Conscripts, Ushers, blood, guts, and limbs all flew violently into the air, then rained back down. Bolts of black light like stygian lightning cracked in the wake of the Archlock's assassination.

Krilid chuckled when he zoomed the Nectoport out of the vicinity. *I guess that's what you call a hole in one.*

But his amusement and satisfaction didn't last long. True, he'd done a good job, but it was only target practice. Very soon, he would be faced with the Real McCoy—and have to score a similar head-shot on Master Builder Joseph Curwen . . .

(III)

Howard turns around, with you on the stick. Suddenly you're facing all sixty-six of your personal concubines, standing beautiful and nude, in formation, the six Pamela Andersons right up front.

My *God*, you think. *I can't believe what I'm about to do . . .*

"Well, Mr. Hudson?" Howard asks.

You don't even hesitate now. "I accept the Senary."

Howard's pale face seems to flush with relief. "Great Pegana! For a while I truly feared you would turn it down."

So did I . . . You sigh. "So what happens now?"

"Well, I hope you'll pardon the cliché, keeping in mind, however, that clichés are actually quite powerful Totems of classicism here."

"Cliché?"

Howard nods. "You'll have to sign a formal contract."

"In blood, I suppose."

"Yes. Your own."

Then it strikes you: "I can't sign a contract! I'm a pumpkin! I've got no hands!"

"Not *here,* Mr. Hudson. Remember, right now you are still in fact an inhabitant of the Living World. Once I displace you back to the Larken House, the Senarial Messenger will have your contract prepared."

The deaconess, you remember. "So *then* what? I sign and then kill myself?"

"Goodness no! You still have the rest of your life to enjoy, and you will be able to do so in grand style."

"I don't get it," you tell him.

"Upon putting your commitment into writing, Lucifer will grant a so-called 'signing bonus,' in the sum of six million dollars—"

"Six million! In cash?"

"Cash money, sir, this for you to suitably finance yourself until your physical life does, in fact, end. You will die painlessly in your sleep, Mr. Hudson, six days after your sixty-sixth birthday."

Your demonic eyes bloom. *And I'm still young! I've still got more than HALF MY LIFE left to live! And with six million bucks to boot!*

"There's only one point I need to make, though, Mr. Hudson, and I cannot overemphasize its pertinency." Howard looks at you quite seriously. "Once you've signed the contract, no amount of repentance can reverse its terms. *Once you've signed the contract* . . . you've abandoned God forever."

The words sink deep.

Howard shrugs. "But with all you'll be given here, in a lock-solid guarantee? What real man would ever *want* to repent?"

As you stare once more at all those beautiful women and demons, you can think of nothing—absolutely *nothing*—to counter what he's just said. *I've believed in God my whole life. I've done everything in my power for as long as I can remember to SERVE GOD. My faith was so strong that I was going to become a PRIEST. But-but—*

"You've got a deal, Howard," you say.

"And so do you, Mr. Hudson. You have Lucifer's untold gratitude for the victory you're allowing him to score over God." Howard takes your Snot-Gourd off the stick. "We'll all be waiting for you. And I look forward to an eternity of friendship with you."

"Ditto," you say.

"And now? Until that wondrous time . . ." Howard removes the pulpy plug in the back of the gourd, and the gas of your Ethereal Spirit slips out like air from a popped balloon . . .

Part Four

Machination

Chapter Eleven

(I)

When Favius's muscle-girded body dove into the pit, he felt as though he'd landed in a morass of scarlet sewage. He'd done this, though, with no hesitation. The Grand Sergeant may well have already sunk to the bottom, or been consumed by some atrocious seaborne monstrosity that the Pipeway had transferred to the Reservoir, but—

It is my duty to Lucifer to try to save him.

At once the appallingly thick currents turned him this way and that. The chunky Bloodwater remained turbulent from the winds of the passing storm; alternate currents tugged him farther from the force of still more Bloodwater surging through the sub-inlets. His inhumanly strong arms and legs *stroked* in the hot red slop. Small things nudged at him, scenting his presence and also his fear, but then some larger things nudged him, too, Divell-Eels, probably, and Gut-Fish. Favius thrashed them away, knowing all the while that much *bigger* creatures would be scenting him as well, things that could swallow him whole. He knew he had precious little time to find the Grand Sergeant and drag him out.

Holding his breath, he thrust himself down . . .

At the time of the Grand Sergeant's fall, he'd not yet redonned his plate-mail armor—a good thing, for he'd be easier to drag up. But the bad thing was that Favius still wore his armor, and in spite of his superiority of musculature, he needed twice as much strength to navigate in this living stew. During his desperate motions, he managed to slide off his helmet, and unsnap his breast plate, and this helped minutely. Then his hands groped out as he plunged deeper, feeling for *anything* that might be his commander, but he knew that his energy would dwindle in moments.

Satan, help me, I beg you . . .

It wasn't death he feared—as one of the Human Damned, he, like the Grand Sergeant, could not die—but to be swallowed by a Gorge-Worm, for instance, or to have a Gigapede slip instantly down his throat and begin to feed would be far worse than even the grisliest physical destruction. Blind in the Bloodwater, Favius howled bubbles when a Spirochete-Fluke wrapped about his face. He tore it off with one hand, then shredded it with several maniacal swipes of his sword.

A lost cause, he knew as his energy waned. His hand kept lashing out, hoping to grab something that might be the Grand Sergeant but all he came up with were fistfuls of waste, rotten flesh scraps, or body parts.

One last plunge downward, then—

—and he grabbed an arm still connected to a body. The arm moved . . .

The prospect of hope doubled Favius's strength. Yes, a living arm was now in his grasp, and then his columnlike legs kicked, and he was propelled upward—

splash!

Favius broke the surface, hauling in breaths; and moaning in his grasp was Grand Sergeant Buyoux.

May the Prince of Darkness be praised!

The Grand Sergeant was still conscious. He heaved in vile breaths after hacking up much Bloodwater.

"Grand Sergeant! Hold on to me!" Favius yelled over the churning din. "I'm losing my strength—"

Even in his terrified stupor, Buyoux looked astonished at the man who'd saved him. "In the name of all things unholy, Favius! You hurled yourself into the maw of almost certain destruction only in the tiniest chance of saving me—"

Favius's muscles raged in pain from the exertion of breaststroking through the thick liquid horror. "Try to kick with me, sir! My strength is ebbing from this current . . ."

They managed to splash a sluggish course back to the wall of the rampart, where a rope ladder awaited them.

"We made it!" Buyoux shouted.

Not quite yet, Favius realized. While they remained in the Bloodwater, they were still easy prey; and what might've been worse was the fact that the back current at the wall kept forcing them off. Conscripts above dropped more rope ladders; Flavius lunged—

Got it!

—and grabbed one.

What little strength remained was used to shove Grand Sergeant Buyoux up.

"Grab the rung!"

Buyoux's enfeebled hands barely managed to do so. "It should be you on this ladder, not I—"

"Climb, Grand Sergeant!"

Favius used his own weight at the bottom to steady the ladder. It was the back current along the wall that made it almost impossible. Meanwhile, one rung at a time, Buyoux clawed his way up—

"You're the bravest man in Hell, Favius—"

"Climb!"

Feet from the top, several Conscripts grabbed Buyoux and pulled him safely over the wall. The troops cheered—

Favius's muscles spasmed as he doggedly began to climb the ladder.

"Get him up!" Buyoux bellowed.

Another rung, then another. Then—

snap!

The rung broke. Favius fell back into the Bloodwater.

He began to drift backward in the current.

"No!" Buyoux screamed above.

I'm not going to make it, Favius knew. His strength was gone now—he was helpless to fight his way back against the current, but then—

Silence slammed down over the entire Reservoir. The roar of the Main Sub-Inlets . . . ceased.

And the current died.

"Favius! Swim!"

It must have been by the grace of Satan that Favius was able to find more strength and stroke his way back toward the wall where a dozen rope ladders waited for him.

But even in his terror, he didn't understand. *What's happening?*

"Faster!" Buyoux shouted. "The pumps have been turned off, which can only mean the Reservoir is *filled!*"

Filled? Favius continued de-energized strokes toward the ladder. The silence stifled him, but now he thought he smelled something very sudden and *not* characteristic of the heinous Reservoir and its six billion gallons of Bloodwater; and when, on his next stroke forward, he happened to glance up—

Several unhelmed Conscripts seemed . . . out of sorts.

Their hair was standing on end.

"For Satan's sake, Favius! Swim faster! The Merge is about to take place, and if you're in the water when that happens—"

Favius didn't hear the rest. Just as his hand would grab hold of a ladder rung—

The ladder disappeared, and so did the retaining wall and the ramparts and the bloodred sky and the black sickle moon and everything else in the rest of Hell.

(II)

Dorris felt dizzy; she felt *terrified*. What was happening? When she'd first looked at herself in the bait-house mirror, her blazing white hair—feet long—stood on end and stuck out like an aura. Initially she'd thought she was being electrocuted but her rubber flip-flops stood on a perfectly dry wood-plank floor.

When she'd rushed outside, the dizziness—and her terror—quadrupled. *That smell!* Like an electric motor overrunning, and then the simple *feel* of the lake and its surroundings. Nothing looked wrong, but it all *felt* wrong. It reminded her of a bad trip way back in her acid days.

Oh, my God almighty, she groaned to herself. Her slim legs propelled her quickly to the end of the dock. A crisp, cloudless twilight pressed down, a slice of moon radiating. The immense lake sat still, rippleless—surreal in some distinctly unpleasant way. The sudden silence, too, struck her as unpleasant. Summer evenings on the lake brought an absolute ruckus of cricket choruses and night bird songs, but now?

Nothing but proverbial pin-drop silence.

Impossible, Dorris knew.

The wheelchair sitting at the dock-end reminded her of the day's only rental customer. *That young man who can't walk . . .* So she'd called him on the emergency walkie-talkie—she *had* to know if the lake's abrupt strangeness was only in her mind—something she almost hoped was true—but his own observations confirmed her own.

What is going ON?

It had been over a half hour ago that she'd called him in. Had he had some medical problem? Surely his arms were strong enough to row the boat back in less time than that. She stood tense and straining on the dock, her eyes pressed into the binoculars, but even in the strong moonlight, she couldn't see him.

Please, please, son! Get yer ass back here . . .

Was it the first true premonition of her life? As her stomach twitched, and that stiff, ozonelike smell sharpened, Dorris *knew* that something was going to happen.

When she scanned along the lake's coast, she noticed that the usual folks that always fished at night were packing up and hightailing it out. Clearly, they sensed the same inexplicable thing that Dorris did, yet she couldn't imagine what that *thing* was. Then—

There! she thought. Her implants jounced when she shot to her tiptoes; in the binoculars' hourglass viewing field, she could make out the tiny form of the paralyzed man rowing through a pool of moonlight.

The loudest sound she'd ever heard erupted next, not an explosion, not the earsplitting sound that accompanied a massive lightning bolt, but something more like timber splitting or a colossal tree cracking as it was felled. The sound urged Dorris to scream louder than she ever had in her life but even *that* couldn't be heard over the monstrous *cracking . . .*

Then came a single, concussive *BOOM!*

Had a bomb actually been dropped on the lake? The notión was absurd, but what else could it be? A *terrorist* attack? Here, of all places? Not that Dorris could think deductively at the moment; terror and confusion obfuscated all rational thought. In the vicious boom's wake came some sort of displacement of air that slammed her in the stomach, lifted her out of her flip-flops, and flung her down the dock, screaming all the way. She landed hard on her back. All the wind blurted out of her lungs, and when the back of her head smacked the dock, she blacked out at once.

It must've been a dream—a nightmare—that dropped

into her mind during the brief period of unconsciousness: a nightmare of sounds . . .

The sounds were screams, screams of human slaughter en masse—indeed, screams from another world. A deafening waterfall of relentless human and *un*human agony as though millions of people in a thousand different cities were being butchered in place all at the same time, a sound, a living *blare* that raged and raged and raged through some incomprehensible rent in the sky . . .

Silence, then.

Though it seemed like hours, it was only a minute or two that passed before Dorris regained consciousness. Memories dripped slowly back into her awareness yet her daze kept them from making sense. She rolled over, tried to rise to hands and knees but then collapsed back down, heaving. She reeled as if seasick, and now, as she blinked back more and more consciousness, she noticed not only the dead-calm silence but also a deep earthy odor just short of a stench that now replaced the previous ozone smell. An odor like low, low tide . . .

Several more attempts proved to her that she couldn't yet stand. *But I can crawl,* she thought, determined, and crawl she did, on her palms and knees, back down the dock.

That man, she kept thinking. *The handicapped man.* Was he still out on the lake when that awful sound had struck?

At the end of the dock, the wheelchair still sat, and so did the walkie-talkie. She reached for it, but then her hand fell away limp as she looked outward at the same time.

Dorris's soul seemed to flatten like a ping-pong ball under a hammer blow . . .

She used a mooring post to steady herself as she slowly rose back to her feet. The low-tide odor hung everywhere, dense as steam. But that was not what made her eyes feel stripped of their lids. That was not what wiped her cognizance clean as chalk marks off slate.

It was the lake.

Dorris stood paralyzed, staring.

Lake Misquamicus was *empty*. What stretched all about her now was a shallow crater lined by glistening black silt, limp waterweeds, and scores of remnant fish flapping helpless in mud. Every single one of the lake's six billion gallons was gone.

(III)

Gerold could not conceive of a way to assess what he'd experienced, save to say that it was not like waking up. He wasn't even sure if he'd lost consciousness. *I was in the boat, I was rowing back to the dock* . . . Then—

There'd been an horrendous *cracking* noise, then a *boom*.

And now he was *here*.

Madness, he thought now. He was still in the boat, and when he looked over the side he saw that he was still on the lake, only the lake . . .

Madness, madness, madness . . .

The lake was somewhere else now.

One moment he'd been looking at the glittering twilight over Lake Misquamicus, but now he was looking at a sky the color of deoxygenated blood. And the sickle moon was now radiant black, not radiant white.

Screaming never occurred to him when he squinted out in every direction. The water in which the rowboat floated was surrounded by endless black walls pocked with towers like castle ramparts, and along those ramparts men, or things *like* men, prowled about. Men—soldiers—in strange, horned helmets, wielding pikes and swords. Larger figures could be seen interspersed, plodding, drab things with barely any faces . . .

What the fuck is this?

All at once, the horned soldiers on the ramparts began to cheer. Several more were lowering a boat into the water.

Gerold could do little more than stare out.

A drone invaded his ears; then he saw a line of liquid green light hovering toward him—

Sssssssssssssssss-ONK!

Now Gerold *did* scream.

The line of green light dilated to a wavering circle—a hole in the sky—and from that hole two hands that were clearly *not* human reached out, grabbed his arms, and pulled him in.

He was dropped into something like a black cave; then he sensed that the cave was moving off very quickly, soaring up into the alien air. In moments, all he could see was the bloodred sky.

"Don't panic," said a figure with its back to him. Gerold crawled forward, dragging his dead legs behind. He wasn't sure what his impulse was. To see? To confront the figure that had pulled him out of the boat and into this . . . this *place?*

Or to jump back out?

"I can't believe it," the figure said. "The coordinates were right—we made it!" And then the figure turned to face Gerold.

Gerold screamed again, loud and hard. "You're a monster!"

The figure let out a snide chuckle. "Actually, I'm a Troll, thank you very much." His voice sounded like any normal man's, but everything else?

Gerold screamed a third time.

This . . . *Troll* stood hunched over, shirtless, with greenish brown skin stretched over hillocks of muscles. He wore pants that looked like burlap and boots that were stitched up the middle. Each wide hand possessed only three fingers and a thumb and had nails like a bear's. And his head . . .

"Man, your head's all fucked up!" Gerold bellowed in ceaseless horror. "It looks squashed."

"That's 'cos when I was in jail, they put me in a Head-Bender. Don't worry about it." Now the figure took a candle off the side of the interior wall and touched it to each fingertip of a severed hand. "Hand of Glory," the Troll informed. "Got no time to explain, just that it keeps the outer Observation Egress of the Nectoport invisible."

Gerold shuddered where he sat.

"Yeah"—the Troll glanced out the large circle before him in which the red sky soared—"we're safe now, er, at least for the time being."

"WHAT THE HELL IS HAPPENING!" Gerold shouted.

The Troll sat down on an outcropping in the wall. "Look, man, I know you're confused and scared and a million other things. My name's Krilid, and yours is Gerold, right?"

Gerold nodded, teeth chattering. Suddenly he was aware of stifling heat.

"You're in Hell," Krilid said.

Gerold gaped.

"I don't have time to answer all your questions—we gotta be somewhere else, like, *real* soon. But I'll give you the short version—"

"I'm in *HHHHHHH*—Hell?" Gerold managed.

"Only Hell's probably not what you imagined." Krilid picked Gerold up by his armpits, and held him up to the circular opening so he could look down.

Gerold screamed yet again.

"Hell's a big city, the biggest in history. It's bigger than all the cities in the Living World all put together."

Gerold felt frozen as he looked down out of the opening. There was a city down there, all right—a leaning, shrieking, smoke-gusting city without end—

"It's called the Mephistopolis, and this thing you're in is

called a Nectoport, the most sophisticated mode of transportation in the Abyss. We bootlegged the technology. It can travel great distances in seconds by using occult mathematics to collapse values of space."

"I-I-I-I . . . *WHAT?*" Gerold blabbered.

"I understand. Just listen, though, and make of it what you will, okay? Clairvoyants in Heaven foresaw your coming here; that's how I was able to pick you up. I'm a Troll in Hell but I work for God, and a Fallen Angel named—well, forget all that, no time. I pulled you out of your boat for a reason . . ."

"A reason," Gerold droned.

"I'm on a mission, and I'm hoping you'll go along with it."

Gerold's head spun and spun. This couldn't be happening. It had to be a nightmare but then he somehow knew it *wasn't*. Whatever this thing, this Troll, this . . . *guy* named Krilid meant, Gerold found incontemplatable.

The opening continued to soar through the scarlet sky.

"You were gonna kill yourself, right?" Krilid asked, keeping one eye out the opening. " 'Cos you can't walk?"

"How do you know that?" Gerold snapped.

"Same way I knew you'd be in the Reservoir. It was *foreseen*. And let me tell you, it's a good thing you *didn't* kill yourself 'cos if you had, you'd be here."

Gerold stared agog. "I already AM here!"

"Yeah, but not as a member of the Human Damned. You're still alive, man. You're a member of the Living World, but you're in Hell. Why? Because of a fluke."

Gerold pushed his hair out of his face. "Yeah, I'll say."

"If you had really killed yourself, you'd be damned here for all eternity. Period. No exceptions."

"Then how *did* I get here?" Gerold finally regained enough of his senses to ask.

"I told you, a fluke, an accident, but we foresaw that

accident and used it to our advantage," the Troll said. Now he picked up a long musket-style rifle and began swabbing the barrel out. He chuckled. "You happened to be on that lake at the *same exact moment* that Lucifer's smartest occultists pulled a Spatial Merge—"

Gerold winced. "A *what?*"

"It's pretty cool," Krilid said. "There's no fresh water in Hell, so Satan figured he'd steal some—six billion gallons' worth—from the Living World."

Six billion gallons, came the grim thought. "That's how much water was in Lake Misquamicus . . ."

"Um-hmm. And now all that water is here, in the Vandermast Reservoir. It was built especially for this operation. Satan wants to build an oasis or some shit, so he activated a massive Spatial Merge to bring all that water here—"

"All that water," Gerold croaked, "and *me* with it."

"Yep, and, depending on your frame of mind"—Krilid raised a scarlike brow—"you can look at your situation as a bad thing . . . or a *good* thing."

Even in the midst of all this impossibility and all this horror, Gerold laughed. "How can being in *Hell* be a good thing?"

Krilid raised a Monocular with a bloodshot eyeball where the lens should be. "Just . . . be patient, and you'll see."

Gerold was about to crawl forward again, to look back out, but suddenly, the Nectoport's oval opening flashed blinding white, and inertia shoved him back. Immediately there came the sense of *bending*, of his body somehow elongating; the strange walls of the compartment he sat in elongated as well.

Krilid tremored slightly, like one sitting on a trolley over bad tracks. He said, "We're going to the Pol Pot District now, collapsing space." And, next, the white flash ceased, to be replaced again by more bloodred sky. "Take a look now."

Gerold dragged himself forward and looked out.

They hovered maybe a half a mile up, through wisps of soot-colored clouds. The clouds *stunk*, and when he craned his neck over the Egress's rim, the entire city below stunk as well.

More teetering buildings and gas-gushing smokestacks. Bizarre creatures darted quickly up and down decrepit skyscrapers. Anywhere he might look, some figure was seen jumping out of a high window. Gerold gaped closer at the streets themselves. Sewer grates belched flames; masses of figures—Human and otherwise—clogged trash-strewn and blood-splattered avenues. Long, clattering cars putted about as well as carriages drawn by fanged, malformed creatures that sufficed for horses. Clay men loomed on every corner, sentinel-like as they scanned the masses. Any and all free space between buildings were stakes on which severed heads had been planted. There were thousands of them, *tens* of thousands. Additionally, piles of dead bodies lay everywhere, while squads of forced laborers trudged to the task of flinging the bodies into carts and wheeling them away. Gerold was too nauseated to ask . . .

"We're getting close," Krilid said. He handed Gerold the Monocular. "There's the security perimeter . . ."

Gerold gulped with a dry throat when he elbowed up and looked through the glass. A heavily walled clearing existed amid the center of the District, the size of a football field. In each corner, Mongrel Demons and Human Damned were being tortured on racks or boiled in oil vats, and the resultant screams rose and fell like some mad, dissonant background music.

It was not the walled perimeter itself that stole Gerold's breath and constricted his stomach, it was the perimeter's most salient feature.

The fucking thing is HUGE, Gerold thought.

A hulking statue over 500 feet high spired from the

middle of the perimeter. Muck-black like tar mixed with excrement mixed with mud. Its contours had been meticulously shaped to heighten its overall hideousness; Gerold thought of King Kong dunked with pitch. But the face . . .

The face—

Gerold threw up over the side when he zoomed the Monocular in on its face.

"Yeah, don't look at it too long," said Krilid. "I've heaved a couple times myself, thinking about that face. They put an Unutterability Hex on it—what you see is a cross between the most horrifying faces in Hell all wrapped up in one . . ."

"What *is* it?" Gerold gagged, noting that all those delicious crayfish he'd eaten earlier were now raining down.

"It's called a Demonculus," the Troll told him. "The most powerful weapon to ever be invented here."

Gerold blundered with the word. "A Demonc . . ."

"It's like a 666-foot voodoo doll that they're going to bring to life with their round-the-clock sacrifices and spook-show sorcery."

"Bring . . . to *life?*" Gerold gasped. "That-that . . . *thing?*"

Smirking, Krilid nodded. "See all that mist all over the place down there, that looks like it's glowing?"

"Yuh-yeah . . ." The mist sparkled like sheets of fireflies.

"That's the Hell-Flux. It's air that's charged with occult energy, and those transformer-looking things with the coils sticking up are Electrocity Generators. Those are the things that convert horror, pain, and agony into a tangible *force.* The sacrifices maintain that force, but a little while ago, sixty-six million people were all slaughtered at once all over the city by Mutilation Battalions. A lot of that power was used for the Spatial Merge that brought you and all that lake water to the Reservoir, but the overflow was diverted here, to dump into *that.*" Krilid pointed to the immobile Demonculus.

Gerold stuttered. "Wuh-wuh-when will they bring it to life?"

Krilid raised the antique rifle. "Now."

The rifle was fitted with its own Monocular, in the fashion of a sniper sight. "But one more thing has to happen before they can activate the Demonculus. It needs a *heart*. Only then can it come to life to do Lucifer's bidding." The Troll sighted the rifle. "Look down at the thing's chest now."

Hands trembling, Gerold did so. A strange fenced platform was hovering near the immense creature's chest, a platform held aloft by hot-air balloons of some sort. Gerold noticed that a hole seemed to have been bored into the dead thing's chest. Several unspeakably ugly demons busied themselves on the platform, one unsheathing a knife, another lifting up a pair of bolt cutters. But there was another figure there, a *human*, with bottomless eyes and a beard. He was taking off a jacket that shined like polished chrome.

"That's the mission target. His name is Master Builder Curwen—he's an Archlock of the highest conditioning—Lucifer's smartest Sorcerer, and it's *his* heart that will give the Demonculus life."

Gerold shot the Troll a funky look. "But how can—"

"They're gonna cut out his heart and put it in the chest cavity," Krilid said, sighting the rifle and cocking the hammer, "so I have to head-shot the guy before they can do that. Then . . ."

"Then *what?*"

"I'll tell you in a minute . . ."

BAM!

Krilid bucked back when the rifle went off. A gust of black smoke spewed out of the muzzle. But when they both looked back through their Monoculars . . .

"Oh, shit!" Krilid yelled.

"You missed!"

Hundreds of feet below them, alarms began to sound.

The demons on the platform were frantic now, and so was the bearded man. The bolt cutters were brought to bear . . .

Krilid fumbled to reload, but Gerold saw another rifle leaning against the wall. He grabbed it.

"Let me do it, man. You can't hit an elephant's ass with a bass fiddle."

"There's no scope on that!" the Troll yelled.

Gerold elbowed up. "Hey! They already cut the guy's heart out—"

"Then don't shoot Curwen! Shoot the heart!"

Gerold frowned at the nearly impossible instruction. He lined the V-notch up to the breech post, cocked the hammer, then took a breath. Meanwhile, as Curwen's body convulsed on the platform floor, his opened chest cavity welling blood, a dog-faced demon grabbed the severed heart and began to reach upward. He meant to put the still-beating heart into the hole in the giant thing's chest.

"Hurry!" Krilid yelled, still fumbling with his powder.

Gerold let out half a breath—

BAM!

The rudely large bullet shot the demon's hand off with Curwen's heart still in it. Both hand and heart plunged to the ground.

"Great shot!" Krilid celebrated.

Gerold felt a twinkle of pride. "Yeah, not bad, but . . . now what?"

"Now what?" Krilid smiled. The Nectoport soared down, the force of its movement nudging the balloon platform away. "Now's when you get to decide if you want to be a hero."

"What?"

"Look, we're banking on you saying yes—"

"Saying yes to *what?*" Gerold snapped, annoyed.

The Egress of the Nectoport sucked right up to and over the ragged hole in the Demonculus's chest. "What do you want more than anything, Gerold?"

Gerold needed no time to reflect. "I want to walk."

"Well, look, there's no way we can send you back to the Living World, but you were going to kill yourself there anyway."

"What are you *talking* about?"

"But we *can* make it so you can walk again . . . or I should say *you* can."

Gerold was about to blurt out another objection but then—

He stared at the chest hole, then looked back to Krilid.

Krilid nodded. "I offered to do it right off the bat but it wouldn't work. See, it has to be a *Human* heart."

Gerold's mind revved like gears in a machine. He took off his life preserver, then took off his shirt.

"Good man," Krilid said, having already picked up a tool that looked like a branch cutter. "But . . . it's gonna hurt."

"I would never have guessed," Gerold mocked. He lay down flat, hands fisted. He squeezed his eyes shut. "Just do it. I don't care how much it hurts."

"You got balls, Gerold." The branch cutters keened when Krilid opened them . . .

First: *crack!* as the curved blade slunked into Gerold's solar plexus and then the sternum was separated.

Gerold bellowed.

Then: *click, click, click, click, click,* as all the ribs on the left side were snapped.

Pain? Gerold could never have *conceived* of such pain, but, *What did I expect? He's cutting my heart out!* he somehow was able to think even over the insurmountable agony. But just as that same agony reached a terrifying peak . . .

It ebbed away, to numbness, and then Gerold's spirit felt like vapor spinning round in a blender on the highest speed.

Meanwhile, Krilid severed all the necessary arteries and removed Gerold's heart.

And he put it, still beating, into the hole in the Demonculus's chest . . .

Chapter Twelve

(I)

Hudson's eyes snapped open like someone who'd just wakened from a nightmare of falling. He remained sweat-drenched in the attic chair, stewing in the insufferable heat. The hole in the wall met his direct line of sight, and through it all he could see was the straggly backyard tinted by moonlight.

The candles guttered all around him.

"You're back," whispered the deaconess, "from a journey only eleven people in history have taken . . ."

Hudson nodded and drew in a long breath. "It wasn't a dream, was it?"

"No. It was the greatest of all privileges." She stepped from the dark corner, her nude body shellacked in sweat itself. The macabre crucible of the baby's skullcap remained below the hole in the wall, but the Sterno had long gone out.

"I can tell by your aura," said the deaconess. "You've accepted the Senary."

"Yes."

"Praise Lucifer," she sighed. "You will one day be a Privilato, the greatest thing to be in Hell save for Lucifer himself."

"After I die, at age sixty-six. That's what I was told."

The robust woman handed Hudson a towel. He felt

winded yet also content when he dried the sweat off his body and put his clothes back on. "I was also told something about six million dollars in cash . . ."

The deaconess grinned. "Such greed! How wonderful! But . . . first things first." She handed him a piece of paper . . . and an ice pick.

"I guess this is self-explanatory," Hudson commented. He didn't like pain but considering . . .

MEMORANDUM OF AGREEMENT, read the contract, along with a simplification of everything he'd been promised. *And all I have to trade for it is my soul . . .*

He winced as he punctured his forearm with the awl, saw blood well up; then he ran the point along the blood.

Signing his name was harder than he thought.

"There."

The deaconess looked awed at the sheet of paper. "You're so, so privileged . . ." Suddenly she fell to her knees, hugging Hudson's hips. "Please, I beg you. In my own Damnation, recruit *me* into your harem! I would be so honored to serve a Privilato! Please!"

"Sure," Hudson agreed, "but . . . where's that six million?"

Her smile seemed drunken now from what he'd just granted her. She kissed his crotch, and pointed behind him.

Two Samsonite suitcases sat on the other side of the room. *This can't be possible,* he thought, but when he opened them, all he could do was stare for full minutes. Each hefty suitcase had been *filled* with banded one-hundred-dollar bills.

"There are six hundred bands, ten thousand dollars per band," the deaconess told him.

Hudson grunted when he hefted each case. "It's a good thing these suitcases have wheels." But then another thought came to him. "Wait a minute. I can't roll two big-ass suitcases to a bus stop in a ghetto, at *night.* I'd get mugged in two seconds."

The deaconess's bare skin glittered in the candlelight. "Lucifer guarantees your safety, not just in Hell but here also. From this point on, nothing can ever hurt you."

"Really," Hudson replied, not terribly confident.

"Oh, yes. In fact, you'll be protected by not one but two Warding Incantations, which are quite similar to the occult bridle which protects Manse Lucifer from any anti-Satanic endeavor."

"That's hard-core . . ."

"I'll demonstrate." The deaconess wielded the ice pick.

Hudson's heart skipped a beat.

"Any object turned on you as a weapon will be repulsed—" The deaconess threw the ice pick hard as she could right at Hudson—

"Shit!"

—but as it flew directly for his face, it veered harmlessly off and stuck in the bare-wood wall.

"Wow!"

"And any *person* who might attempt to assault you with his bare hands"—the nude woman smiled more mischievously—"will instantly have his blood removed from his body."

Hudson recalled the bold but luckless insurgents' attempt to bomb the Manse, and how their blood had been magically sucked out of every orifice.

He looked at her, at the contract in her hand, then at the suitcases. "I guess . . . all there is for me to do now is—"

"Go home, and enjoy the rest of your life here with your riches, knowing that many more riches await when you die and rise to the glory of Lucifer."

So. That's it, I guess. Hudson scratched his head. "What are your plans?"

"I will rise to that glory now, Mr. Hudson," she said. "As

your Senarial Messenger, I have but one more duty to perform: the execution of your contract."

Contract in hand, the deaconess walked demurely to the chair, then stood on it.

"Hey! You're not going to—"

"But I must, Mr. Hudson." From a rafter she pulled down a previously prepared noose and calmly put it around her neck. "I'll see you at your castle in the future."

Hudson froze.

The deaconess rolled the contract into a ball, put it in her mouth, and stepped off the chair

THUNK . . .

Jesus, Hudson thought. He watched her hang there, the nude body agleam, swaying ever so gently. The rope creaked several times, then tightened to silence.

(II)

"The lake," Dorris muttered, "is empty." How sane she was at this time could hardly be estimated. She'd been standing there on the pier for several minutes—six minutes, to be precise—when, sane or not, some modicum of reason began to wriggle back into her consciousness . . .

What happened to my beautiful lake?

Overhead, the white moon sliver beamed. Stars sparkled in gorgeous, deep twilight, and the cricket sounds that had abated so abruptly earlier began to resume. All that she perceived would've been normal again, save for one irrevocable fact:

The lake was empty.

She remained there, cockeyed, limp armed, and slump shouldered, her eyes holding fast to the vast black depression that had once held six billion gallons of water.

It's gone. It's . . . all gone . . .

A fleeting thought returned again to the young man. Still, his wheelchair remained at the end of the pier, and when Dorris was cognizant enough to look back out with her binoculars, there was no sign of him or the boat.

A crisp static sound made her flinch, like a radio with bad reception. Then: *The walkie-talkie!*

It, too, remained at the end of the pier. Her lithe legs took her desperately to the small device. She snapped it up—

"Hon?" she shrieked when she jammed in the talk button. "That you? Where *are* ya?"

The walkie-talkie crackled back, and within the burst of static she felt sure she heard someone speaking.

"The lake!" she blurted. "Somethin'-somethin' *happened,* and the lake ain't *here* no more." She didn't know what she was trying to say. "But wherever it went . . . I guess you must'a went with it!"

More static after she released the button to listen. But—yes!—a voice *was* responding, however weakly, through the shifting white noise. It said this:

"All hail Lucifer the Morning Star. We bow down and sing praises to his unholy name—"

Dorris stared at the walkie-talkie. There could be no mistake; she *had* heard the voice, and the voice had *not* been that of the young handicapped man. The voice sounded deep, wet, and rotten.

It continued, "It worked! In the name off all things offensive to God—it *worked!*" And there followed a guttering round of the blackest laughter.

Dorris dropped the walkie-talkie, not only from the shock of the hellish voice but from a sudden return of the massive *crackling* sound she'd heard earlier. Again, her shiny white hair began to stand on end, and then—

BOOM!

Just like before, Dorris was thrown all the way back to

the dock entrance, to land hard on her back. It was that same bomb-blast sound, and the concussion that followed in its wake. Half-unconscious, she tossed and turned on the old wood planks, and after many feeble moments of this, she managed to crawl up another mooring post. She took one deep breath—

OH MY GOD!

—and fell back to her knees to violently vomit.

It was not the earthy, low-tide smell that so effectively sickened her, it was something else, an odor so obscene it nearly shut down her senses. Her stomach kept heaving, and when it was emptied, it heaved more. Her eyes stung and her head pounded from what was not only the worst stench she could ever imagine but actually the worst stench to ever exist on the planet Earth.

Bile hanging in strings off her lips, she then dared to look back out . . .

With that second incomprehensible boom, Lake Misquamicus had been *refilled,* but not with lake water.

With blood.

With blood, and body parts, and debris, and sewage, and nameless and unnameable creatures, and myriad else not of this earth.

Dorris's screams flew out of her mouth like tossed ribbons. Fish with vaguely human faces broke the bloody surface to snap at her with doglike teeth. Skeletons, severed limbs, and even some severed heads floated by, some of which moved with impossible life. A shadow beneath the red water wove under the dock, sidewinding and clearly a hundred yards long. Dorris staggered backward, unable to close her eyes, fearing—and even *hoping*—that the evil stench would kill her in her tracks. Several dented kegs floated by, like oversize beer kegs. From within one of them, she heard a rapid beating sound as of frantic fists, and a shrill female shriek: "Would somebody PLEASE let me out!"

The lake *teemed* with sounds now, sounds Dorris had never heard and would never be able to describe. When she managed to backtrack off the pier, another trickle of reason returned in spite of the madness she'd born witness to, and from a tiny pocket in her shorts, she unconsciously withdrew her car keys—

Got to get to the car! Got to get out of here!

But just as she would turn to do so, she froze at another sound.

Footsteps?

Yes, a procession of wet, slopping footsteps, like someone in hip waders marching out of a shallow tidal pool.

And then, in the silverish moonlight, she *saw* that someone with her own eyes, the figure of a man—a very *large* man—marching out of the noxious water and onto the shore.

First one, then two, then three such men.

Doris continued to stare dizzily at the spectacle. Most of her sanity, by now, of course, had been corrupted by what she was beholding. As the shlucking footfalls drew closer, she saw that they weren't really *men* at all but hideous facsimiles: great glistening slablike figures almost ten feet tall. Details of the physical bodies seemed half formed as though they were but massive clay dolls bestowed with only the merest humanity. Their faces barely existed, just slits for eyes, slits for mouths . . .

Dorris couldn't move as the three things approached. Her heart was trip-hammering; she could only pray that it would stop beating before they got to her.

But it didn't.

A wide shadow cast by the tinseled moonlight crossed Dorris's face. She stared and drooled. The things seemed to be staring, too, at her, but not with eyes for they had none, but with gashes where their eyes *should* be.

They looked at her a while, then turned, then moved hulkingly away to eventually stand up near the bait house. They stood perfectly still, in a perfectly straight line, almost as if . . . they were waiting for something.

SomeTHING? Dorris's faltering brain managed. *Or someONE?*

Perhaps the horror had ravaged her consciousness so intricately that she'd been tainted with some psychic inclination, because when she looked dazedly back at the blood-filled and blight-infested lake, she did indeed see someone else coming out—but not another of these looming clay monstrosities.

It was a *man*.

(III)

Oh, wow, I don't like this, Krilid thought after he'd debarked from the Nectoport and sent it back to Ezoriel's headquarters. Suddenly his fear of heights returned, with no more Nectoport to shelter him. *It's just me and the Great Outdoors . . .*

When he dared look down, his belly flip-flopped. Six hundred and sixty-six feet was a long way down . . .

It was on the left shoulder of the Demonculus that Krilid now sat, in a convenient little observation cupola.

When he'd slammed Gerold's raw heart into the monster's cardiac cavity, the Hell-Flux had audibly groaned down below, and its pallid luminescence had momentarily trebled. Meanwhile, the Anti-Light at the end of the cavity had sparked, signaling that the Animation Spells were properly engaged and conduction had been achieved. All the while, the Electrocity Generators down below kicked up into high rev from an occult detection sensor, to drain off all available Deathforce power . . .

These things meant that everything was working right. *All systems go,* Krilid had thought, a bit incredulous that nothing yet had gone wrong.

On the field at the Demonculus's massive feet, throngs of Conscripts rallied, firing up curse-tipped arrows and sulphur guns, but the creature's sheer *size* reduced their efforts to futility. Krilid chuckled. *Like throwing pebbles . . .* But Krilid's chuckle ground down when he spotted several more Balloon Skiffs beginning to rise from their launch platforms. *Not good,* the Troll realized. *We need to be far away by the time those balloons can reach this altitude.* Archlocks and Bio-Wizards would undoubtedly be on the Skiffs, and would try all guises of Hexes and Cabalistic Viruses in hopes of disabling the Demonculus before it became ambulatory.

But . . . when would *that* be?

"Hey, Gerold!" Krilid yelled up from the cupola's little side window. He was shouting toward the crude hole where the Demonculus's ear should be. "Can you hear me yet?"

The giant muck-made head remained motionless.

Krilid began to feel sick.

Why wasn't it working? He'd done *everything* as instructed. Had Lucifer's Sorcerers planted countermeasure devices within the Demonculus? *So much for Ezoriel's fortune tellers,* the Troll lamented.

A mile up ahead, an attack formation of Gryphons were beginning to swoop down . . .

Krilid got out of the cupola and ran to the base of the Demonculus's neck. "Gerold! Come on! Make this thing work!"

No response. The Demonculus didn't budge, nor could any sign of unlife be detected about the creature's appalling face.

"Damn it!" Krilid kicked at a muscle strand in the Demonculus's neck. "The friggin' thing's busted!"

Several flaming arrows zinged by. Below, the Balloon Skiffs had ascended several hundred feet already, and the Gryphon formation . . .

More arrows began to sail toward the monster.

Krilid ducked just in time to miss being hit in the head. His guts sunk when he noticed Conscripts riding the first waves of Gryphons, bearing buckets of pitch. The second wave was manned by Flamma-Troopers. These horned, armless Terrademons were Hexegenically bred to vomit fire . . .

The Conscripts will paste the Demonculus with pitch, and then the Flamma-Troopers will set it on fire . . .

Along with me.

Then—

zzzzzzip!

—another arrow sailed by, this one nicking Krilid's ear. Off balance he flinched, tried to stabilize his footing, but then tripped on a stray bone jutting up from the dead meat and filth that composed the Demonculus's shoulder—

Oh my God, I'm gonna—

Krilid fell.

He fell fast. He didn't scream, and he barely panicked. What he did mostly was frown at his clumsiness as he tumbled head over heels toward the hellish field below.

All that work, all that risk, all that planning . . . all for nothing . . .

Fifty feet. A hundred. He caught glimpses of the Demonculus's nightmarish body as he continued to fall, picking up speed.

A hundred and fifty feet.

Two hundred.

What a way to go, Krilid thought, spinning.

WHAP!

With an unexpected jolt, Krilid landed in muck. The ground? But, no, he couldn't have fallen *that* fast, could he? And if he'd hit the ground and somehow lived, Conscripts and Ushers would be dicing him to pieces. When his dizziness passed, he realized that he felt encased in more of the stinking muck.

Then he felt himself elevating, and whatever steam shovel–like thing it was that encased him . . . opened.

Hot wind blew into his face; Krilid was looking at the scarlet sky.

"Krilid, are you all right?" a voice seemed to crunch and echo at the same time. Not a human voice at all, yet there was something . . . *familiar* about its pitch.

Krilid realized then that he was standing in the opened palm of the Demonculus's left hand, a *fifty-foot-long* hand.

"Gerold!" he shrieked when he got the gist.

The immense hand lifted Krilid until he was face level with the Demonculus.

"Thought I lost you there," the monster's voice crumbled out from impossible lips.

"Thanks for catching me," Krilid said, but then a surge in his heart reminded him that they still weren't out of the woods. "Gerold, listen, we're under attack right now—"

"Under attack by who?"

Krilid pointed like a shot. "Those Gryphon formations—"

The corroded, grotesque-beyond-words face seemed to smirk. "I'm real scared, see?" And then like a crane, the abomination's 200-foot-long arm swept out in an arch and swatted all of the winged things out of the sky. Several of the Flamma-Troopers exploded, which ignited sundry pitch upended from a dozen buckets. Fire rained down on the heavily populated field.

"Great move!" Krilid yelled. He pointed down. "Now step on all those guys down there sticking swords in your feet."

"Oh—" The Demonculus looked down at the field. "I thought I felt some itching." And then—

THUD! THUD! THUD!

The entire District shook while Gerold stomped his feet on the droves of demonic soldiers below; in fact, several buildings actually collapsed. Screams rose upward like steam from boiling pots.

"And see those Balloon Skiffs?" Krilid asked. "They're serious business so do us both a favor and make 'em go away."

The Demonculus's chest expanded as it inhaled an inconceivably large breath, then exhaled it downward at storm-force velocity. The Balloon Skiffs twirled end over end in midair, ejected demonic crew members, then slammed into the ground to explode.

"So much for them," Gerold's new voice remarked.

"And it couldn't hurt to step on those Electrocity Generators while you're at it," Krilid added. "They're *real* expensive and took eons to build. Lucifer'll dump in his pants if you trashed those things."

The Demonculus shrugged, and it was more than likely the most *massive* shrug ever made by anything. Horrendous, tractor-trailer-size feet easily flattened said generators. The presiding explosions threw nuke-style mushroom clouds on either side of the unalive occult creature. The clouds crackled in hues like fresh lava; in only moments, the mushroom clouds had risen thousands of feet.

"Jeez, I didn't figure *that* would happen," Krilid said. "Pretty impressive . . ."

The Demonculus's head turned down to Krilid. "You know something? Destroying stuff's a lot of fun!"

"As long as it's *evil* stuff, Gerold," the Troll accentuated. "And there's plenty of that here."

The creature's inexplicable face suddenly seemed morose. "But-but—" It looked at its horrific hands, then down the line of its corrupt physical body. "But-but . . . Shit, Krilid. I'm a *monster.*"

"You're not a monster, Gerold. You're the most powerful weapon ever made! And if you hadn't come here, what would you be then?"

Nightmarish, fathomless eyes blinked. "I'd be dead. I'd be nothing."

"Yeah!" Krilid yelled. "So stop feeling sorry for yourself just because you . . . *look* different. And you're forgetting the best part!"

A titan pause. "What's that?"

Krilid winced. "You can *walk*, moron! What you wanted more than anything you just got—in spades!"

"I can . . . *walk* . . ." The voice, however inhuman, seemed suspicious. Very slowly, one leg lifted and—

THUD!

—stepped forward. Then the other—

THUD!

The District tremored like a seismic shift.

"See?" Krilid said from the Demonculus's hand. "It might take a little getting used to but, hell, what's the big deal?"

The Demonculus took three more steps in succession. The third step begat a giant crack in the ground. "I can walk!" Gerold celebrated.

Krilid pointed a finger. "Yeah, and look what you get to walk *with*. The biggest legs to ever exist."

Suddenly, the Demonculus began to hitch. Its abyssal mouth hung open, and the two ragged back holes that were its nose actually sniffled. Tears like raw crude oil squeezed from the impossible eyes.

"Aw, come on, Gerold," Krilid implored. "Demonculuses don't *cry*."

"I can't help it," the thing sobbed. "I'm happy. And I owe it all to you. Thank you!"

"Don't thank me, thank your Celestial Destiny—"

"What?"

"Never mind," Krilid decided. His eyes glittered with enthusiasm as sirens and alarms began to blare from every District, Prefecture, and Municipal Zone for miles. "This is gonna be really cool, Gerold. We're gonna kick ass and not take names. We're gonna go on an anti-Luciferic tear-ass like Hell has never seen!"

"Right on!" The ground rumbled when Gerold yelled.

"We're gonna destroy every Pulping Station, Power Plant, Tortuary, Prison, Police Station, every Grand Duke palace and every Sorcerial College in Hell! We're gonna be Satan's worst nightmare and *nothing* can stop us!"

"All right!"

"And who knows? One day we might even stumble upon Manse Lucifer itself—"

"And tear the shit out of it!"

"You got that right, my friend! So let's do it!"

Staring, the Demonculus paused, as if bracing itself for a prospect too good to be true. Then it took a step—

THUD!

And another step—

THUD!

And then another and another and another, each stride consuming the length of half a city block, and that's when Gerold started walking, and he would walk and walk and walk, for time immemorial, each step destroying something vile, each thud of its monstrous feet laying rents in Satan's domain, each stride celebrating the gift that Gerold had taken for granted but had received yet again.

Indeed, Gerold—the first Demonculus of Hell—could walk, and from that point on, he would never stop—

THUD!

—never stop—

THUD!

He would never stop walking.

(IV)

The suitcases thunked as he clumsily got them down the stairs. For some reason he was not the least bit at odds with the prospect of walking out of an abandoned house with two suitcases full of cash. He bumped the front door open with his rump, then wheeled the suitcases out into the teaming night. Moonlight coolly painted his face; crickets throbbed dense as electronic music. Hudson felt enlivened even after this ultimate sin: his complete betrayal of God on High. Nor was he afraid of the fact that he was standing in a crackburg with six million dollars in cash.

A tiny light glowed above the bus stop just down the street. Hudson looked at his watch, then chuckled and shook his head when he saw that the bus would be coming by six minutes from now.

"Yo!" shot the subtle voice. Dollar-store sandals slapped the cement. Then another darker voice—a man's.

"Shee-it . . ."

Bags in hand, Hudson turned to face them, unworried.

"This the fuck askin' 'bout the Larken House," said the prostitute whom Hudson recognized at once: the woman who'd shown him where the house was, in the zebra-striped tube top. Her white teeth gleamed when she smiled.

Two more figures stood on either side, a slouchy black male with his hair stuffed in a stocking that looked like Jiffy Pop, and a chubby, high-chinned white guy in jeans cut off at midcalf, a ten-sizes-too-large T-shirt, and a whitewall. He had snakes tattooed on the sides of his neck.

The black guy took one step. "What's in the suitcases, my man?"

Hudson stalled, then laughed. "You wouldn't believe me if I told you."

The white guy bulled forward: "What's in the suitcases, white boy!" his voice boomed, and from nowhere he'd produced a very large Buck knife.

"Six million dollars. If you want it, you'll have to take it."

The black guy nodded to the white one. "Just another poo-putt white muv-fuck."

"Shee-it," chuckled the white guy, and then he lunged with the knife.

"Cut dat boy!" the girl cheered on. "Cut him!" But it was only a second later when she shrieked. Plumes of blood launched from the attacker's eyes, mouth, nose, and ears. His crotch, too, expelled a copious volume, which saturated the ludicrous pants. Then the knife clattered to the sidewalk and he collapsed.

"Ambrose!" shrieked the girl, fingertips to face. "What he do?"

"Don't know," crackled the voice of the black guy. There was a *click!* when he cocked a small pistol. "But he got somethin' in them cases, so's I'll just bust a cap in his face."

Here was the proof of Hudson's newfound faith. "Go ahead," he said. "Bust all the 'caps' you want."

The tiny pistol's report sounded more like a loud handclap. A muzzle flash bloomed in a way that Hudson found spectacular. More spectacular, though, was the way the bullet was instantly repelled by the otherworldly ward surrounding him, and bounced immediately back into the black man's Adam's apple.

The man gargled, pop-eyed, and actually hopped about in the nearest weedy yard, hand clamped to his throat. He thrashed into some bushes and collapsed.

Hudson looked at the girl. "I'm protected by Lucifer, the Morning Star. That's what I did in the Larken House tonight. I *sold my soul* . . . to Lucifer."

The girl ran away.

"Hmm."

Hudson moved on. The ruckus of helicopters snapped his gaze up to the twilit sky. His ears thumped; several large helicopters—clearly military—roared overhead. They were flying strangely low. Then:

Wow!

Several jet fighters screamed past in the same direction: north.

I wonder what that's all about, Hudson thought. Maneuvers, probably; there were several big air bases nearby. He wheeled the suitcases down the sidewalk and across the street. Exactly sixty-six steps later, he arrived at the glass-shattered bus shelter where he detected the ember of a cigarette brighten, then lessen.

"Oh, you," a ragged voice greeted. "How's it goin'?"

It was the homeless guy from the deaconess's church. "Hi, Forbes. I'm fine."

The bum sucked the cigarette down to the filter, then flicked it away with begrimed fingers. His body odor seemed thick as heavy fog. "You goin' on a trip?" he asked, noticing the suitcases. "Shit, man, the Greyhound station's the other way."

Am I . . . going on a trip? Hudson could've laughed. "No, I'm just going home."

Both men jerked their gazes up when several more jet fighters screamed by overhead.

"Been goin' on for a while now," Forbes said, then burped. "I was with a john 'bout a half hour ago, and while I'm doin' my thing he's got music on the radio but then the music cut off and then an emergency broadcast comes on."

"Really?"

"Yeah, man. Somethin' happened couple counties north of here, some big lake."

"Something happened?" Hudson couldn't imagine why military aircraft would be sent for some mishap on a *lake*. "What was it, Forbes?"

"Don't know. The john turned it off—said it was fucking up his karma or something."

Hudson's perplexion sparkled, but then he sighed with a smile. *What do I care? I'm a Privilato.*

Forbes showed a nearly toothless grin. "Hey, how 'bout I do a mouth-job on yer johnson for twenty bucks."

"Oh, no thanks," Hudson said.

"You can blow right in my mouth. Lotta guys like to do that for some reason, and I can always use the extra calories."

"Uh, no. No thanks." Hudson pulled some twenties out of his pocket and passed them to the bum. "But here's some food money for you."

Even in the dark, the bum's face beamed. "Hey, man! Thanks! God bless ya!"

Not God. Not anymore . . .

Now was the first time he contemplated exactly what he had done. It was a *deep* contemplation. *After a lifetime of SERVING God with my whole heart, I've now ABANDONED him . . .*

He felt a state of exuberance well up from the core of his being with such *power* that he thought his eyes must surely be alight.

"Yeah, I'm takin' the bus to the John's Pass Bridge to sleep," Forbes jabbered some more. He reached into his horrific mouth with two fingers and pulled out a rotten tooth.

"What's that, Forbes? The bridge?"

"Yeah, it ain't bad, ya just gotta be careful of the fire ants.

But there's no way I'm sleepin' in the deaconess's church no more."

"Yes, I remember you telling me. Bad dreams."

"But I sure miss her." His flinty brow furrowed. "Somethin' happened to her, somethin' fucked her up." Now Forbes looked beseeching. "You seen her tonight?"

Hudson stared down at him. "Do you really want to know, Forbes?"

"Well . . . sure. You seen her?"

"Yes. About ten minutes ago—or, more than likely, *six* minutes ago—I saw her commit suicide in a house across the street—the Larken House."

Forbes's pose stiffened. "No way, man!"

"I'm afraid so. She killed herself as a means of executing a contract I had just signed."

"Fuck! A contract?"

"I sold my soul to the Devil tonight, Forbes. Sounds crazy, doesn't it?"

"Shit yeah, man! The Devil? Really?"

"Yes," Hudson calmly stated. "The Devil. I'm protected by the Devil. I am now a *disciple* of the Devil."

"Aw, you're full'a shit," Then—

SCHULP

Hudson never saw the knife in Forbes's mangy hand, until that same hand was already pulling it out of Hudson's lower abdomen.

Holy—You gotta be—

Shock—and also *outrage*—made Hudson's face feel twice its size. Blood like hot soup poured through his fingers; he also smelled his own waste as the knife had clearly punctured intestines. He began to convulse as he slumped to the other corner of the shelter.

"Fuckin' people always tellin' me bullshit 'cos they just think I'm a retarded bum, man," Forbes complained. "Well, fuck them and fuck you."

"Forbes," Hudson croaked. "Call an ambu—"

"Here's your fuckin' protection, fucker." The bum stuck the knife in again, several more times.

What Hudson felt more than the pain was simply outrage.

"I could use some new clothes, ya shit," Forbes said, but he just stared and stared when he opened one of the suitcases. He scratched his beard, begetting dandruff. Then:

"What a fuckin' great day!" He slapped the case closed. "Thank you, God!"

Hudson watched through hemorrhaged eyes as Forbes grabbed the suitcases and ambled away in the dark.

What a rip-off . . .

Each time Hudson coughed, blood sprayed into the air and more innards uncoiled in his hands. He died exactly six minutes later.

(V)

What stepped out of the lake next was a man in a leather strap-skirt studded with brass plates. He wore shin guards, a fat buckled belt, and one arm was covered with metal bands that reminded Dorris however obliquely of a Roman gladiator. He even held a sword, and as he strode up to her, dripping, muscles tensing, she noticed first that the skin of his chest existed as *faces* stitched together, while his own face . . .

God Almighty . . .

Dorris saw that the severed faces of *babies* had been grafted onto the man's own face as effectively as patches stitched onto a shirt.

Dorris stared at the impossible man.

The tip of the sword touched her throat. His voice sounded sonorous and grating like rocks clacking together.

"What place is this? Answer me and you may be allowed to live . . ."

Tremoring, Dorris replied, "It's-it's . . . Lake Misquamicus . . ."

"This is . . . the Living World, then?"

"It's-it's—Fluff-Fluff-Florida . . ." The man must be an alien. "Florida, on the planet Earth."

"God's *green* Earth, then?"

Dorris drooled as she nodded. Her eyes had yet to blink.

"State your name, your function, and your origin."

"My name is Dorris Markle. I ruh-ruh-run the bait shop and boat rentals, and I'm from Ocala, Florida . . ."

The grafted face surveyed her. This man—or this *semi*man—had muscles bugling over more muscles, and when they moved, the severed faces stitched over them seemed to sigh.

The sword point lowered, and the stony voice gurgled, "My name is Conscript First Class Favius, formerly of the Third Augustan Legion and currently of Grand Duke Cyamal's Exalted Security Brigade. I am from Hell."

He turned to the three nine-foot-tall clay men, pointed his sword, and barked, "Golems of Rampart South! Single file, follow me." And then they walked away and disappeared into the woods.

Dorris, in a trance of revulsion and disbelief, stared after them for several minutes. When things began to howl from the atrocious scarlet water, Dorris snapped, and ran and ran and ran.

Epilogue

Was it a dream?

You hear a *THUNK!* as in the sound of a cleaver striking a cutting board, and then comes the impression of rising—up a circular staircase?—and you hear footsteps. Then—open air.

Finally your eyelids prize apart.

" 'Let not thy hand be stretched out to receive, and shut when thou shouldest pay,' " comes a high-pitched, New England accent.

Your vision re-forms and then you know that—

This is no dream.

You are back at the Privilato castle, and the first thing you see is the grand courtyard and inner wards.

It's Howard who looks back at you; he seems elated, but there's also a tinge of scorn in his eyes. "It's a line from the Bible," his voice piped, "which I foolhardily never believed in. The Book of Ecclesiasticus, parablizing the sin of greed. I'd have been wiser to have heeded that book, rather than in obsessing over the creation of my own."

"You promised me I'd die when I'm sixty-six! You promised me supernatural protection!" you wail at him.

"I, personally, forged no such promise, Mr. Hudson. It was, instead—as you're well aware—*Lucifer's* promise."

"I sold my soul for a price!" you scream.

"Consider the author of the terms," Howard lamented. "It's so very regrettable: that resonant and universal power known as avarice. You were a very, very easy victim, Mr. Hudson. But, honestly! Why do you think they call him the Lord of Lies, the Great Deceiver?"

"This is bullshit!" But then only now do you realize something crucial, because when you try to look around, your head will not obey the commands of your brain. "What-what—"

"—happened to you?" Howard finishes. "It's elementary. You died, you went to Hell, and immediately upon the commencement of your eternal Damnation, you were decapitated." Howard, then, holds up a mirror that reflects back your severed head, which has been neatly propped upright within a stone sconce. "And, as you have hopefully cogitated, we are back at the Chatêau-Gaillard—"

"My castle!" you spit in outrage, "where I'm supposed to spend eternity living in luxury as a Privilato! But I can't be a Privilato with my fuckin' HEAD cut off!"

Howard's voice, in spite of its elevated pitch, seems to turn foreboding. "Not your castle, Mr. Hudson. Mine."

Only now do your eyes lower to scan the rest of Howard's form. He's no longer dressed in the shabby 1920s-style shirt and slacks . . .

He's wearing a surplice of multifaceted jewels of every color conceivable and inconceivable. An ornate *P* has been mysteriously imbued on his forehead. More jewels glitter when Howard smiles: the most illustrious dental implants. "You haven't won the Senary, Mr. Hudson. I have. Lucifer is not only notoriously dishonest, he's also *industriously* dishonest. And I'd say your current circumstance demonstrates the extent of his machinations. By effectively causing you to believe that you won the Senary, you disavowed your Salvation, and since I was principal in stimulating your decision, the Senary has been awarded to *me*."

"This is a pile of shit!" you bellow. "You screwed me!"

"Indeed—"

"I could've gone to Heaven!"

"Quite right, but here you are instead." And then Howard picks your head up by the hair and carries you along, holding it over the ramparts. "Enjoy the view while you can. You'll not see my beautiful castle again."

"It's supposed to be *my* beautiful castle!" You're sobbing now. "That was the deal!"

"That was the deal that your greed allowed you to perceive. So intoxicated were you, Mr. Hudson, by the prospect of having all of this, that you never once considered the unreliability of the monarch here. Love is blind, they say, which is true, but it's truer still that greed is so much *more* blind." Howard looks forlorn for a moment. "The *genuine* deal is that I won the Senary and its sequent Privilato status by convincing you of the opposite, for enticing you to give your Salvation to Lucifer of your own free will. It really is quite a prize for my master and I might add, my master rewards those who do him service."

"I won, damn it! Not you! *I* won!"

"You've won nothing but what your greed and betrayal of faith have earned you."

The sound of a breeze stretches over the vast landscape.

"Where's my body?" you moan now, tears running.

"There." Howard holds your head between two merlons where you see the revelers in the courtyard: your mother, father, and sister; Randal, Monsignor Halford, and the two rowdy prostitutes; Marcie, your first girlfriend; and the six Pamela Andersons. They're all chatting happily as they busy themselves around the barbeque. Racks of ribs have already been laid across the grill, while Randal and Marcie are systematically sawing or cleaving steaks off of the headless body stretched across a long butcher block table. *Your* body.

You begin to cry like a baby.

"There, there," Howard consoles, and after a few more steps that familiar black static crackles, you scream, and—

WHAM!

—you're someplace else, and it only takes you a moment to realize that you've seen this place before as well, not in reality but in the hectographs Howard showed you earlier. Thousands and thousands of heads look at *your* head as Howard walks you through Lucifer's Atrium, Great Hall, Dining Room, and, lastly, the Bedchamber.

Wall after wall after wall of living female heads.

Many of them smile when you pass by.

"So behold now, Mr. Hudson, the *true* seat of your destiny. You will remain here forever, and though I can fathom your disappointment in now acknowledging the ruse played on you, you may at least take some solace in knowing that you have inherited a unique privilege . . ."

Oh no, your thoughts croak when Howard takes you into Lucifer's circular-walled commode-chamber, where more, *more* female heads look at you with the most satisfied smiles. The head smiling the most, however, is that of the lone chubby-faced blonde lying cheek-down on the gilded toilet-stand.

"Oh please!" she exclaims in a trashy Southern accent. "Please let it be true!"

"And so it is, my dear," Howard tells the head as he lifts it off the stand and flings it to the floor.

And what he puts in its place on the stand is *your* head.

"You are now the first male head to become a permanent fixture at Manse Lucifer," Howard says.

"Howard!" you scream. "I'm begging you, man! Don't do this to me!"

"Ah, but really, you've done it to yourself, haven't you?" And then Howard turns to make his exit.

"Don't leave me here! This isn't fair! You tricked me! I don't deserve to be the Devil's toilet paper for eternity, do I? My sins weren't *that* bad!"

"Sin is relative, Mr. Hudson," pipes Howard's voice a final

time. "And with those words I'm afraid I must take my leave and enjoy the privileges I've duly inherited." Howard sighs dreamily, and smiles with his jewels for teeth. "At last, I'll finally be able to write *The Lurker at the Threshold*! And thank you, Mr. Hudson, very much. I could never have won the Senary without you . . ."

"NOOOOOOOOOOO!"

Howard leaves the commode-chamber and closes the head-paneled door behind him.

All the heads that form the walls, floor, and ceiling begin to laugh.

And all you can do now is sit there in dread, wondering how often the master of this house moves his bowels . . .

INTERACT WITH DORCHESTER ONLINE!

Want to learn more about your favorite books and authors?
Want to talk with other readers that like to read the same books as you?
Want to see up-to-the-minute Dorchester news?

VISIT DORCHESTER AT:
DorchesterPub.com
Twitter.com/DorchesterPub
Facebook.com (Search Pages)

DISCUSS DORCHESTER'S NOVELS AT:
Dorchester Forums at DorchesterPub.com
GoodReads.com
LibraryThing.com
Myspace.com/books
Shelfari.com
WeRead.com

CPSIA information can be obtained at www.ICGtesting.com
265528BV00001B/3/P

9 781428 511262